ALTANIA
RUNEHEIM
THE REALM OF
MIDREL ISTAN

DRAKE MANOR
FELDOR BAY
SEA OF GLASS
DUNEBAR
FOG MARKET
DRY LAKE
SWAMP
LASTORUM
MOSISLE DUR
ADURAK

REY WICKS

CITY OF THIEVES

The Legend of Chaos

2

TRIGGER WARNINGS: Includes acts of violence, bloodshed, sexual assault, and death

CHAPTER 1
A King's Revenge

Midrel Istan in the ancient tongue means, The Motherland. Before kings and kingdoms, there lived the gods that reigned over the land. On a starry night, men from afar sailed to the western shore, bringing a new magic the gods' had never seen. Axius Bolin, a sorcerer from the great city of Altania was crowned "King of Men". Axius worked to build a world for people to dwell in that was beyond the grasp of the gods' power.

As time passed, the bloodline of Bolin royals held the throne. King Ansel, the great-great-grandson of Axius, grew anger in his heart. Plagued by the desperate desire for power, he gathered an army of non-magic humans and led them to war against the gods. On the 113th night of gruesome violence, King Ansel stood before Baze, God of Fire. Iron rang through the air, as men battled for the leadership of Midrel Istan. In his victory, the gods accepted their punishment and sailed to a land far across the sea and to the north.

As time passed, in another country that would become Erras, the god, Dragon, son of Baze, would take siege over all the lands. Wars tore through the streets of the kingdoms. Kings were slain in their castles. The gods gathered the queens and princesses and walked the earth with magnanimous presence. This was a time of witches, black magic, and the crowns of those who divided the world.

Crows flew from east to west and north to south. Each carrying a message meant for the gods eyes. Witches intercepted the birds, cursing them before sending them home to their masters. These curses introduced new magic that no one knew. Even Dragon was unsure of this power. He stood on the war room terrace and called out for the cursed to come to NorthBrekka. "Blackbirds, fly," he chanted. War arrived at his keep led by a Bolin king. Dragon and his Blackbirds fought until only one remained.

Sebastian stood behind the wheel of the Hetta Horizon. The ship cut through thick, drizzling clouds that rested on the ocean's surface. It was bone-chilling cold on The Midnight Sea. Cyrus stretched his back and yawned. He narrowed his eyes each time he would face Sebastian. The water was dark and ice crunched as the ship cut through.

Jace watched out over the portside and the cold became more bitter. "You really wish to go north, Your Majesty?"

Sebastian clenched his jaw. "I said, we go north. And what I say goes."

Jace shook his head. "No, we are searching for a teacher. You will not find him north."

Sebastian groaned. "I have... unfinished business."

Jace scowled and shook his head. He shouted at the crew. "Drop the foremast's sails, Kastor. His Majesty has requested that we travel north. Thus, we will. I need you to keep an eye on things up top, Peter. Cristian, assist Kastor right away." Jace paused and turned his attention to Sebastian. "Everyone else, brace yourself for what craziness lies ahead."

Sebastian reached out for Cyrus's hand.

Cyrus reached out to meet him but pulled back. "You do not need to do this. The war is over. You won. Let it go."

In the weeks that followed, Cyrus and Sebastian had little conversation between the two of them. Many nights Sebastian fell asleep laying on the deck while gazing at the stars. Early one morning, he woke to the sound of boots tramping across the deck. He sat up to see a shroud of cloud drifting quickly by as the Hetta broke through the fog. Peter shouted from the crow's nest above. "Land, straight ahead!"

A smirk crossed Sebastian's lip. "Ready the cannons."

The crew stared at their king.

Sebastian felt his cheeks burn. "Did you hear what I said? Ready the cannons now! Archers, take the line." The sound of boots thundered across the deck. The crew leaders shouted orders. Sebastian gripped the wheel tight. "Cyrus, go!"

Cyrus straightened his back and curled his lip. "I will join the archers on the starboard side."

Sebastian's palms grew sweaty as his heart raced and his chest burned watching Cyrus disobey him. The passion, the touching, and the adoration he once got from him were gone. To break the curse and cure him, Sebastian would have to find someone gifted in special dark magic. Although, he wanted nothing more than just to see his Cyrus smile, laugh, or even wake up happy to see him. Sebastian's heart threatened to shatter knowing his beloved was gone. It would take a scholar gifted in the darkest of magicks to break Cyrus' curse. But his mission could not be sacrificed for his own selfish wants. He had to find a teacher, not a cure for Cyrus.

He shook his head and looked at the shore. Some of the men of the island nation of Khan Khar shouted and waved flags while others ran back and forth hastily, seemingly in a panic. Sebastian closed his eyes and took a deep breath, remembering Barron betraying their family and bringing war among NorthBrekka with the aid of the armies of Khan Khar. He looked up to see Trebuchets lining up along the sandy beach. The large wheels crunched against the shale as they edged up to the water. The sound of wood cracking made Sebastian flinch. Every snap stung into the scars on his back from the whip of a Kuhar soldier.

Cyrus counted aloud before turning to Sebastian. "Ten trebuchets, at least forty men on the beach, and more on the wall above. Sebastian, if they fire on us, we will not hold against them."

Sebastian let out a huff of frustration while mumbling and watching the men. "One man to load the sling, another to release the counterweight, and one to fire."

The trebuchets shifted into position with a loud thud that boomed across the shore.

"Sebastian," Cyrus said.

"Cannons ready at my command. Archers, prepare to fire." Sebastian's voice was calm. "Watch for them to reach for the release handle."

"Your Majesty, if they hit those levers, it is all over," Kastor said.

"Steady. Stay calm, men. Trust me." Sebastian took a deep breath. He stretched his arms out and felt a familiar hot, tingling sensation in his eyes.

"Sebastian, what are you waiting for?" Cyrus shouted.

The islanders shifted around again, and the soldier on the catapult stretched out his hand.

"Sebastian."

"Shut your mouth, Cyrus!" Sebastian's head twitched, causing his shoulders to jerk back, and his spine to arch. His eyes seared and watered as he locked his focus on the men of the island. "You will feel my rage." His voice was heavy and cracked and his belly churned with fiery pain.

The men on the shoreline stamped their feet in the sand.

Jace came to the top of the steps. "What are you doing, Your Majesty?"

Sebastian stepped to the railing and stomped his foot hard into the deck. The sea let out a booming echo that swelled from the Hetta. A wave lurched from the sea, and rushed toward the island, followed by a gust of wind. The men's arms slammed forward in unison, and the trebuchets burst to life. "Fire!" His throat seared, and his voice sounded deeper than usual.

"Fire the cannons!" Jace shouted.

The Hetta Horizon jerked back. The ocean rippled as the loud boom of twelve aligned cannons came to life from black powder and fire.

"Archers, fire!"

The trebuchets thundered as the sling rolled over once more. A sea of arrows appeared through the thick clouds. There was an explosion, followed by a bright flash of green light. Sebastian raised his palm to the sky as lightning flashed from his fingertips. The silhouette of a storm dancing within the clouds turned hazy in the mist.

Sebastian murmured, "Catalysts." These were weapons designed by the Kuhar to blind their opponents and destroy anything they encountered.

The Midnight Sea flashed in veils of emerald and gray, as the enemy's weapons succumbed to the fury of the storm. Massive waves surged for the beach. Wood exploded in shards as the trebuchets paid homage to the sea. Arrows pierced into the mast of the Hetta, while others ran from the raging water. Sebastian caught a shimmer in the corner of his eye. It was high within the clouds, but the final catalyst's green color was still closing in on the ship. Sebastian strung an arrow and aimed, following the ball as it fell below the storm. His fingers released their grip and an arrow sailed into the sky. The sky erupted into a vivacious show of flashing blue light and a bone-shaking rumble made Sebastian's eyes widen and his stomach tighten. A strike of lightning left its cloud and then, the mast cracked in two.

"Peter!" Kastor rushed to the falling crow's nest.

The intense emerald light made it hard for Sebastian to see. Peter crashed down into a pile of broken wood and sails as the glow from the catalysts disappeared. Sebastian stepped back to the ship's wheel and threw his hand into the air. The wind snapped the sails. They moved north once more.

Jace hurried over. "Your Majesty, you have done enough damage."

"Prepare the cannons on the port side!" Sebastian said while staring at Jace.

Cyrus ran upon him and jerked the wheel from his grip. "We will sail away from this."

"Go to our quarters, Cyrus."

"No, you go. You have caused enough damage. Look at Peter!"

Sebastian grabbed Cyrus by his neck but did not squeeze, instead, he stared him in the eyes and kissed his lips. "Do not stand in my way, my love." He pushed Cyrus away. "If you want me to stop, you will have to fight me."

Cyrus backed away, narrowed his eyes, and shook his head.

"Prepare the cannons," Sebastian shouted. "Now, Jace!"

Jace shouted to the men below deck to prepare to fire. Sebastian guided the ship around the island. He saw smoke rising in the distance as the mist began to clear.

Jace shouted, "Watch out for the rocks ahead."

Sebastian turned the wheel. Cyrus fell, crashing into crates of apples as the Hetta lunged away from the boulders.

"Don't you have waterpower somewhere inside of you? Because that would have been the time to use it." Cyrus climbed to his feet and stomped to the railing.

"I only know how to manipulate the water with a storm. Tomas is the one who has power over the sea," Sebastian said.

"And it still couldn't save him from you, could it?" Cyrus's face glowed red under all the sweat.

Sebastian's stomach felt as if it were being stabbed over and over. He blamed himself for Tomas' misfortune but hearing it from Cyrus sent him into a fury. His anger turned into a cold but soft voice. "Are you doing this on purpose, Cyrus? Are you trying to hurt me or make me do something stupid?"

Cyrus sighed and stepped toward Sebastian. "You don't need me to do something stupid. You have proven that over and over. You've had little training. Tomas has had less. When you use your power to do damage, someone you care about gets hurt. You need to stop. Sail away from this place."

Jace interrupted by stepping between Cyrus and Sebastian. "Gentlemen. Keep your lover's quarrel confined to a time when we are not approaching the enemy's city. Your Majesty, what is your plan?"

Sebastian looked at Cyrus and rolled his eyes. "We will head out to sea. Take the wheel, Jace. I need to have a word with the man I love in private." He waited to ensure they were out of the reach of Khan Khar, then grabbed Cyrus by the arm and led him to his quarters. Cyrus hurried to the opposite side of the bed.

"Do you think I am going to hurt you?" Sebastian said.

"You are either going to kiss me or hit me. You are Chaos. That means I cannot expect one or the other. You could stare at me like you want to kill me, throw me down and make love to me, scream at me, or lock me in here alone. Which one will you choose?"

"What if I did all those things to you?" Sebastian's voice was silky, and he wore a smirk on his mouth.

Cyrus's lips twitched into a nervous smile, and he bit his lip.

Sebastian glared at him, feeling a burning sensation in his eyes. He walked over, grabbed Cyrus's arm, and gripped his neck harder than before. He kissed Cyrus, expecting rejection, or a slap, but he felt a hand run down his chest. Cyrus's fingertips tickled Sebastian's ribs. He craved Cyrus more than anything. His heart raced, he began to sweat, and his lust turned to obsession. He pinned Cyrus to the bed and tied his wrist to the post with a leather strap.

"You are mine to do as I please," Sebastian said. "Don't fight me."

"I won't," Cyrus whispered.

After they made love, Sebastian dressed. Cyrus's eyes followed his every move. Sebastian stopped as his hand reached for the doorknob.

"You didn't say no when I said I would do all those things you listed. Don't be mad at me."

"You didn't do everything. You haven't screamed at me, and you haven't locked the door."

Sebastian smiled and opened the door far enough so he could leave. "Cyrus, do not ever undermine me in front of my men." He began to push the door closed, then stopped and looked at the men behind him before a smirk crossed his lip. "I won't tell you again, Cyrus. Stay in our room!" He slammed the door and locked it.

He walked below deck to find Kastor stitching some deep cuts on Peter's face and chest. The crew got quiet and stared at him as if they expected orders.

"Easy men. Rest. You all deserve it." Sabastian sat down.

"Your Majesty, are you alright?" Kastor nodded at him.

"I may be a fool, but I am an honest fool. I led us into that turmoil for selfish reasons. Unfortunately, some sustained injuries and for that, I apologize." He reached his arm out to Peter.

Peter gripped Sebastian's forearm, and they shook. "I fight for my king. We all knew what we signed up for. The Sinook will always follow you."

Kastor put his hand out as if he wanted Sebastian's attention. "What inspired this attack?"

Sebastian sighed and looked around at his crew. "Revenge."

CHAPTER 2
The Siege of Sea

Sebastian walked out to the wheel that evening and breathed in the warm salty air.

"Why didn't you hire a captain?" Jace asked. "You are a king. You don't have to do anything."

"I wanted to learn to captain a ship. It is the sense of freedom I crave."

"Even over the open sea, you are the king."

Sebastian shrugged. "All I know is, I won't return home until I have learned all that there is to know. I wish to rule Erras in the shadows and sit Tomas on the throne in NorthBrekka. I wish for somewhere quiet, beautiful, and peaceful."

"I cannot see you as someone who can sit and be silent for too long," Jace replied.

Sebastian avoided Jace's comments. "How do you know this teacher?"

"My Father knows of him. He told me all about this man when we found out about you. From what I know, he is a sorcerer, but nothing more is known of him. Not a name or even a city to look for. He said the old kings buried his legacy long ago, and it has been gone since."

"How would your father know him if this man is not from Erras?"

Jace moved closer to Sebastian. "My Father is not from Erras either," Jace said. "My father is from Midrel Istan. He moved to Erras long before I was born. It is far, the journey is dangerous, and you will not find a welcome there." He gently punched Sebastian's shoulder. "So be aware and learn to control that temper before we arrive."

"What about you, Jace?" Sebastian let his eyes meet Jace's. "What is a good man like you doing out here? Surely you have a girl at home who's waiting impatiently."

Jace laughed. "Umm, no, not really. I had a girl, but my father didn't think she was good enough to fit into our family." He paused as his cheeks flushed. "So, I brought home a boy I cared for…" His face paled and he took a deep breath. "But my father said things. Horrible things. Then he hit me. And that is when I came to NorthBrekka. I wanted to follow the true king and run away from my homeland for good."

"I'm lucky to have you." Sebastian leaned against Jace. "I would be lost out here without your guidance."

Jace met his gaze. His lips were rosy, and the light cast a soft glow across his skin.

Sebastian stepped back. "I am going to speak to Cyrus, then go to sleep." He started to leave, then turned back to Jace. "You need to rest as well. I need you to be awake when I am awake. Have Cristian take the wheel."

"Or you could forget Cyrus and stay here with me." Jace brushed his hand against Sebastian's forearm.

Sebastian pulled his arm away and tilted his head. "What are you doing?"

Jace's cheeks turned red. "Nothing. I just was…" He turned his face away and stared at the sea.

Sebastian grinned. "Do you like me?"

"What? No. You and I would be horrible together." Jace smiled and stood to meet Sebastian face to face.

"Don't get feelings for me, Jace." Sebastian stepped back. "Anyone who gets close to me gets hurt. If I were you, I would run away."

Jace brushed his lips against Sebastian's mouth. Sebastian felt his lips tingle but saw movement in the corner of his eye. He jumped back and pushed Jace away.

Cyrus was holding a bent knife and walked toward Sebastian and Jace. "After I was a prisoner in NorthBrekka, I learned to pick locks so it would never happen to me again. What is going on here?"

"Nothing." Sebastian backed away from Jace.

"Then why were you about to kiss me?" Jace said.

Cyrus walked over. "Why were you going to kiss him, Sebastian?"

"I wasn't," he snapped at Cyrus. "I love you and only you."

Cyrus's face flushed with sweat. "Why did you bring me with you?"

Sebastian grabbed his shoulders. "Because I want to help you so we can be together. I want you to be the Cyrus I remembered before."

Cyrus's face turned red, and he puffed his chest. "You were about to kiss Jace. Why should I trust you?"

Sebastian shook his head and started to walk away. "I don't need this, Cyrus. I spend every waking minute trying to prove myself to you, but you refuse to see that. What more do you want from me?" His heart pounded as he paced back and forth.

"I want to leave," Cyrus said.

"Where are you going to go, Cyrus? We are on a fucking ship!"

"You keep saying you want me to see the good in you, but I can't. You are bitter and angry. Everything I have learned about you from Sacha is true."

Sebastian squeezed his shoulder tight but let go. He pointed his finger at Cyrus's face and scowled. "Never mention his name in front of me again."

Cyrus broke free and limped away while rubbing his shoulder. Sebastian moved to reach for him again, but Jace caught his attention.

"Gentlemen. This should be a conversation kept private."

Sebastian swung around. "Jace, not now!"

"Sebastian," Cyrus said.

He kept his focus on Jace. "Cyrus, I am done talking—"

"Your Majesty, you should see what Cyrus is trying to show you." Jace patted Sebastian's chest.

"Seriously, what is wrong with the two of you?" Sebastian turned and stepped to the rail. "Holy hell." He paused, feeling his stomach sink. "Jace, what is that?"

"Hurricane." Jace stepped back. "Your Majesty, let me take the wheel."

Sebastian slipped away from Cyrus. "Secure the ship! Tie down the cannons, secure the cargo, and stow the sails. All men to your stations, now!" He grabbed Jace's arm. "This is my ship and my crew." The Hetta Horizon came to life with the crew running about. Sebastian took the wheel again. "Cyrus, go—"

"That's not going to happen. I am going to stow sails." He walked to the forward mast to help the crew.

Sebastian felt a pain in his chest as he turned his attention toward the storm. "Jace, tell me what I need to do."

"Take on the waves steadily. Do not let the ship turn, or it will swallow us. Sebastian, do not fight the storm."

Sebastian eyed him, then looked back at the sky. "Let's begin, shall we?"

Rain coated the deck, making it slick as the wind rushed over the sails that the men fought to pull down. Cyrus got tangled among a mass of black fabric and rope and took cover as another gust rushed by. Over the port side, a wall of deep blue water climbed, towering over the Hetta.

Lightning spiderwebbed in the clouds above. The Hetta met the incline of a wave. Sebastian felt a rush in his belly as they glided back down, as a monsoon of tidal power pounded onto the deck. The crew held onto anything they could grab. Sebastian felt his arms rip free from the wheel and his back stung as it slammed against the boards. The Hetta leaned hard to one side as they ascended the monstrous, angry sea.

"Sebastian, the wheel!" Jace screamed.

Sebastian coughed. "Don't fight the storm, he says. Just let it crush you. Everything will be fine!" He slung himself against the wheel.

"You have to turn the ship around," Jace said. "When I say go, you must turn the wheel hard to the left."

Sebastian's knuckles turned white as he waited for Jace's call.

"Get ready. Go," Jace said.

Sebastian threw his arms to the left, letting the wheel spin furiously on its own. The deck cracked and split. Creaking and popping sounds erupted all around his feet. The Hetta turned around until Sebastian only saw a tower of water in front of him.

"Now you are in trouble," Jace said. "What did you do that for?"

"Don't worry, Jace. I've got it all under control." Sebastian waved his arm. "Kastor, I need your help at the helm."

"What are you doing?" Cyrus asked. "You are not going to do what I think you are."

Sebastian smirked at Cyrus before once again focusing his attention on the storm. He let go of the wheel. It spun with fury. The ship jerked hard and crackled from the rough seas. Everyone threw themselves at the most secure thing they could grasp.

"Ready, Kastor?"

"For what, Your Majesty?" Kastor shouted against the wind and rain.

"On three, we stop the wheel." Sebastian looked at Kastor, hoping he wouldn't ask questions. The ship tipped onto its side, the foremast nearly touching the water. "Hold on!" He crouched down. "One, two..." Sebastian looked at Kastor and nodded. "Three!"

They dove into the wheel. Sebastian growled and pulled with every fiber of his muscles. Waves crashed into themselves next to the Hetta, wedging it between two mountains of the sea. The ship slammed down onto its bottom and faced forward again. The rush of water swept Kastor away. He plummeted into Cristian and they tied each other to the railing and waited for the next wave. Jace and Cyrus ran to stow away cargo that broke free of its net before they stood together on the ship's bow and watched the raging waters ahead. Sebastian's attention focused on them. Jace touched Cyrus's back, then held onto him. He saw Cyrus smile, and suddenly felt the hot, boiling jolt of jealousy hit him.

Yet, Cyrus turned and stared at Sebastian, walking toward him with teary eyes and rosy cheeks.

Sebastian waited for him to get close. "Cyrus. You remember something about us, don't you?"

"We were just kids back then." He started to say Sebastian's name, but a crack boomed above them.

The hair on Sebastian's arms stood. His skin felt like needles were burrowing their way inside. He watched the lightning in the sky web it's way to a meeting point above his head. There was a flash and a rumble. Sebastian saw Cyrus stop to lean against the mast while holding onto a rope.

Sebastian's body tingled and his heart raced. The sky over the ship spun and shook. "Cyrus," he screamed.

Lightning surged from the clouds, crashing into the mast. Sebastian felt like he couldn't breathe, speak, or move. He held his hands up toward the sky as the ship sailed into calming water, leaving the hurricane behind.

Sebastian put his hand up to silence the crew from talking as he walked toward Cyrus. He thought briefly of Peter, before seeing Cyrus appear on the edge of the rubble, getting lifted away by Jace. Sebastian knelt in front of them and reached out. Cyrus slapped Sebastian's hand away.

"This is your fault."

CHAPTER 3
The Island

"Broken masts, torn sails, fresh water is gone, the food washed away, and half my crew got injured. How much further are we from Midrel Istan, Jace?"

Jace ran to Sebastian's quarters and returned with a few scrolls in his arms. Several maps tumbled onto the deck as he dropped everything onto the table. He sat on the steps, grabbing one that fell and began to mumble as his finger shot across the parchment. "We are somewhere around here," Jace pointed. "It does not look like we will make it to Midrel Istan in this condition if we do not stop and get a supply of food and water. We can use what is left of the sails, but without food, we will all die."

Sebastian rubbed his face as he looked over the maps. Cyrus huffed as he paced and began mumbling, "Jace told you not to use your power against the storm."

Sebastian slammed his hand on the table. "I didn't use my power." He looked up at Cyrus. "I felt the storm like it was a part of me, and then I saw your face. It was the same look you used to give me before."

Cyrus stared at him with a blank expression, and returned to pacing.

"You will never love me again, will you?" Sebastian said.

"No. I don't think I will." Cyrus walked away, disappearing downstairs.

Sebastian clenched his jaw and listened to each footstep grow more distant. He waited for Cyrus to return, growing more and more upset as the silence settled. Jace walked over to his side.

"Your eyes are red again. Do not let him get to you, Your Majesty. He doesn't understand why he is here. To him, you are the enemy, and he is the hostage."

Sebastian slung the maps off the table. "He is mine." He turned away quickly and stared at the sea. "I'm not giving up on him."

"You are obsessed," Jace said. "Please do not tell me that you dragged all of us out here to rekindle your relationship. When are you going to grow up?!" Jace started toward the stairway but stopped before heading below deck. "Apologies, Your Majesty."

That night, Sebastian slept little and wandered the ship early into the morning hours. Downstairs, Jace had his own private space where Sebastian went looking for Cyrus. As he snuck past sleeping sailors and found the tiny back room that held nothing more than a bed, he saw his beloved. Cyrus slept soundly with Jace's arms wrapped tight around his chest. For a quick moment, Sebastian was relieved, but it was replaced with the fear that Cyrus had left him for Jace.

As the week passed with each grueling day slowly dragging by, the mood aboard the Hetta grew stale. Men moved about without sharing words. There were no smiles, no cheerful songs, and no eye contact. Many walked slowly or with a limp. Towards the end of the week, Sebastian asked Cristian about their food supply. He'd grown to trust this former soldier from NorthBrekka. Cristian was only a few years older than Sebastian and had been trained under Barron.

"We are out of fresh water," Cristian said. "The men are sick. We have already lost several to either dehydration or hunger. We are not going to make it much farther without food."

"Take my rations. It isn't much but give it to whoever needs it the most," Sebastian said.

"Your Majesty. Not one man on this ship would take your food. We need you more than anything. This crew will sacrifice their lives to make sure you survive."

Sebastian had never felt so guilty as he did right then. He noticed Jace look off into the distance before running to the bow.

"Land," Jace said with a cracking voice. "Land! Over there, look!" The men turned.

Sebastian ran to meet him. "Is this Midrel Istan?"

"No, Your Majesty. It is an island."

"Food and water." Sebastian stopped and looked at the island with a clenched jaw. "That is all we are here for, then we sail. Do you understand?" As they approached, the crew took row boats to shore. Sebastian stayed on the ship and watched the beach.

Cyrus stayed behind with him. "Can we talk?"

Sebastian did not make a sound.

"Please, Sebastian."

Still nothing.

"Talk to me," Cyrus whispered.

Nothing.

Cyrus walked to the rail and leaned over.

"I have nothing to say to you," Sebastian said.

Cyrus turned around. "Then I will talk."

"You have already told me you are going home. You told me you didn't love me and never will. There is no reason for us to communicate other than orders." Sebastian refused to look at Cyrus.

Cyrus walked over, cusped Sebastian's cheek, and kissed him. Sebastian's legs shook.

"You're blushing," Cyrus said. He paused for a moment. "I remember my men shouting about a storm in the early hours of the evening. We rode as quickly as we could to the wall between Torrdale and NorthBrekka. I didn't believe it to be true, so I went to see for myself. That is when I saw you. You were peeking over the wall."

"Well, to be fair, the wall is only as tall as you. It wasn't hard." Sebastian smiled at Cyrus. "So, you do remember me."

"I remember seeing you, then you disappeared," Cyrus continued. "I saw the storm swirling over the lake and suddenly stop. A flash of lightning and a loud crack of thunder shook so hard the ground moved. The lightning came from you. Your Father tried to cover it up for two years, but I knew. I told my brother. That is when I read the prophecy. I remember your face when you looked at me as your Father discussed meeting with Roman. I couldn't stop thinking about how beautiful you were."

Sebastian took a glimpse of Cyrus's face before looking away. "I will never not be madly in love with you, Cyrus. I have loved you since that moment."

"There is something deep down telling me that we belong together. But every time I chase that feeling, it seems like light flashes in my head, and I instantly want to kill you. When I said I would never love you again, it is because this curse will never let me have you."

Sebastian took Cyrus's hand. "I thought the tea Lorna gave you erased all memories of me. Why did you get to keep that one?"

"Maybe it is because it is about you becoming Chaos. Lorna's magic isn't as powerful as yours."

"Cyrus, you must understand something. I am not being selfish, and I am not trying to take over the world. I want to be a better man and a better king. I don't want my people to fear me."

Cyrus looked at the ground. "Did I know you were like this before the tea?"

"When we were together, I didn't want to be king. I was angry, hurt, and lonely. I just wanted to feel something. When you and your brother came to Castle Drake, I saw you, and all the anger I had for being this person disappeared. You make me feel human. I love you for that. You bring out the good in me."

Cyrus turned and looked at the beach, but Sebastian gently cupped his cheek.

"Give me one more chance, Cyrus. Let me prove how good I can be with you by my side."

Cyrus glanced at Sebastian and returned to watching the island for signs of the men. "I... don't..." He stuttered. "I can't."

Sebastian felt like his insides were set on fire. He shoved Cyrus away. "Fine. I am going ashore to help my men. Why don't you dog besides stand there and break me down?" His heart raced as he walked away before Cyrus could finish talking. Sebastian threw his coat on the deck and stood at the gangway opening.

"Sebastian, come back!" Cyrus stopped when Sebastian dropped his axe and bow onto his jacket. "You're not going to swim to shore, are you?"

"That is my plan. Why?" Sebastian said.

"You are a king. That means someone should be here to take you to shore."

Sebastian laughed. "Are you volunteering to row me to the beach? No offense, but it would be faster for me to swim. Are you coming?" He dove into the crystal-clear lagoon. When he surfaced, he turned to the ship and shouted, "Are you afraid to jump? Can you swim or do you need me to carry you to shore, my darling?"

Cyrus jumped from the ship and swam to Sebastian. He pecked a kiss on Sebastian's lips. "For now, while we are stuck together, I will give you your one chance. When we arrive in Midrel Istan, I will decide."

Sebastian felt his cheeks burn. "Thank you," he whispered. He swam to the beach, walked past the men fishing, and kept going without a word.

"Where are you taking me?" Cyrus said.

"I do not know any more about this island than you. We are bound to find someone soon enough."

They walked late into the sunset before Sebastian finally heard a rushing sound in the distance. "Water. Come on."

Sebastian and Cyrus fell to their knees at the edge of the narrow river that crossed through the field.

"This is good. We need to bottle this. Where are my men?" Sebastian walked over to the edge of the cliff and looked at the crystal blue water at the bottom of a waterfall. A hand slipped around his mouth, then an arm looped around his neck and threw him to the ground. Standing above him was a woman. The woman had piercing black eyes and wore beads and leather in her braided hair. Her bright red skirt whipped in the breeze. Sebastian couldn't help but stare. She was unlike anyone he had ever seen.

"Ombak, feycha, oha," she said.

Sebastian turned his head and raised his eyebrows, then smiled. "I am afraid I do not speak your language."

The women frowned. "So, you are one of them?"

"You speak my language. How? Who is them?"

"Do not lie." The woman grabbed Sebastian by the neck. "Men like you come here and take. They destroy and kill my people to steal food, blankets, and water."

"We have never been here before," Cyrus said. "Our ship got damaged in a storm. We barely made it to this island."

The woman let go of Sebastian and went over to Cyrus. Behind her, Sebastion saw dark shadows emerge. She had six men with her. All were holding spears.

"Can you tell me where we are?" Cyrus said.

The woman pulled his face close to hers. She touched his cheek and stroked his hair, then took a short breath. "You are troubled. Your eyes never lie." She stood and turned to Sebastian. "We do not welcome heretics here. Leave now, or we will kill you."

"Heretics? We are not heretics. We need a little food and water to make it to Midrel Istan. I will pay for everything. I have gold on my ship," Sebastian said.

"Your eyes are red. There is something about you that I do not understand, but you have my people terrified. And your friend is empty inside. Something dark has happened to him. There is evil among you both," the woman said.

"What is your name?"

The woman paused for a long moment. "Meecah."

"Meecah. That is a lovely name. My name is Sebastian Drake. I am from NorthBrekka in the land of Erras. My people are starving and dying. I promise there will be no trouble."

"I said leave." Meecah's voice was low and quiet. "My men found yours in the woods. They are being taken to our village. Those who do not have evil will stay and work to repay us for ravishing our land. The rest will leave Padora. We don't want gold. It is all cursed. In Midrel Istan, they will kill you for gold."

"You cannot have my men."

Meecah stared at him for a long moment. "It takes nine days to sail from here to Midrel Istan. Can your people survive that long in the hot sun?"

Sebastian jumped to his feet and towered over Meecah. The sun dissipated and there was a hint of thunderclaps in the distance. The sky darkened with storm clouds. They stared into each other's eyes.

"If you will not take gold, I will fight for it. If I win, we get water and food, and my men leave with me," Sebastian said.

Meecah looked at the sky, then back at Sebastian with wide eyes. She turned her head toward her men.

"Moh way, ben toku sih." She looked back at Sebastian.

"What did you say?" Sebastian said.

Meecah smiled. Three of her men stepped over, grabbed Cyrus by his arms, and tied them together.

"Cyrus!" Sebastian said. "Let go of him." Lightning flashed from his fists. He put his hand on the hilt of his sword but felt a sharp pain. He became woozy and everything tingled.

Sebastian fell to his knees. Before everything went black, he heard someone shout, "Sebastian." He felt his body become weightless as he fell into a deep sleep.

CHAPTER 4
Rebellion

The rumble of footsteps pounding on the ground woke Sebastian. He sat up, put his hand on his head, and coughed as he tried to see clearly. The forest was dense, with a village of palm brush homes built along the river. Fires burned in pits with young women flipping fish over on a spit. A shadow cast over him.

"Oh good, you are still alive." The blurry vision of a beautiful woman pacing before him became clear.

"Meecah?"

"Do not speak as if we are friends." She pointed a spear at his throat.

Sebastian looked around and saw Cyrus tied up with his arms behind his back before spying Jace laying on the ground, blood covering his leg. Before he could react, Meecah squatted down and put her hand on his shoulder. "Don't overreact, or I will have to kill you," she whispered. "Like your blond friend who got a little mouthy with one of my people."

Sebastian shook his head, confused until a group of men marched over, spears in hand, along with swords and bows he recognized as those made in NorthBrekka and The Far North. He clenched his fists as spurts of fire flickered between his knuckles. The men he sent ashore were tied up, side by side, along the riverbank, each with arms behind their backs like Cyrus.

Meecah stood and bowed softly. "Father. This one is their captain."

"Oomha tredo."

"No, Father. He isn't one of the men from before. That is what he says."

Meecah's father was tall and had a large belly that poked out from his robe. Jewelry dangled from his neck that bounced from his stomach with every spoken word.

Sebastian stood. "I apologize for our intrusion. We are not here to take anything from you. We just need food and water to make it to Midrel Istan. I am willing to pay."

The man put his hand on Meecah's shoulder and spoke in English. "Daughter, you say he is a coward. If that is so, he will be easy to defeat."

Meecah looked at Sebastian, then back to her father. "You still want me to fight him?"

"If this traveler is searching for food, he will have to earn it, and we don't accept gold for payment." He glared at Sebastian.

"Father—"

"No more words, daughter!"

"What is happening?" Sebastian asked.

Meecah sighed. "You got your wish. We fight... to the death." She walked away.

Sebastian hurried after her. "Can we talk about this? I don't want to fight you."

Meecah stopped suddenly and turned, causing Sebastian to bump into her. "You do not understand."

Sebastian shrugged. "Help me understand."

Meecah sighed. "On Padora, we live simple lives free from the rule of kings and witches." She put her hand on

Sebastian's chest. "Men like you come, sent from kings of the great lands of the world. They want our food, and water, and they take our people to work on their ships. They take everything from us, and it is my duty to stop it at any cost."

Sebastian nodded. "I am here asking for food and water, but I don't mean to harm you to get it. You must understand—"

"You." She poked his chest. "You must understand. Padora was once peaceful, beautiful, and our people were happy and kind. Then the great kings sent their soldiers here and now we fight back." She shook her head and turned away.

"We do not have to fight." Sebastian searched for her eyes to meet his again.

"It has already been decided." Meecah snapped her focus to him. "First, we fight. Then I am to be married to the man my father has chosen. And then I take leadership of my people and raise a rebellion against your kind."

Sebastian's mouth dropped, then closed. He replayed Meecah's words over and over in his head until he raised an eyebrow. "Your father is forcing you to marry?"

"So?" Meecah said.

"And you don't love him?" Sebastian let out a little laugh. "My father did the same to me. Tried to force me to marry this girl."

"What did you do?" Meecah's head turned slightly toward him again.

Sebastian grinned. "I rebelled." He reached his hand out for hers. "I promise you that if you let my men and I go, I will stop those men from ever setting foot on this island ever again. It is my destiny to end the darkness that clouds our world."

Meecah furrowed her eyebrows. "Who are you?"

A booming voice interrupted their conversation with words Sebastian could not understand.

Meecah pulled her hand away. "Coming Father." She turned back to Sebastian. "We will fight. It is best you go say your goodbyes to your loved ones." She stormed away and followed the chief into a hut.

Sebastian ran over to Cyrus and pulled the gag from his mouth. "Are you alright, my love?"

"Are you?" Cyrus coughed. "You're bleeding bad."

"I'm fine." He hurried over to help Jace but was stopped by two men with spears.

"Go," one of them said.

The tribesmen formed a circle in the center of the village. Meecah paced while spinning a pair of daggers in each hand. Sebastian saw his men through the crowd. Cyrus tilted his head then looked at Jace. The sound of Meecah's footsteps crunching on the sand rang in his ears. He slowly approached a tribesman. "Do I get a weapon?"

The man shoved him away.

"I guess not." Sebastian marched forward. He stepped before Meecah and watched her hands. He balled his fists, and fire ignited.

Meecah stopped pacing and looked at his hands, then into his eyes with her mouth slightly dropped. She didn't speak, only started twirling her blades again.

Sebastian looked over at Jace, who was holding his leg. His face was red, and he was sweating. But it was Cyrus's expression that made his stomach flip and heart skip a beat. Cyrus's lower lip twitched into a frown, and a tear was in his eye andSebastian thought that maybe Cyrus did love him after all. He turned his sights to Meecah. A burn filled his chest, and his body shivered. He focused on her spinning daggers once more. "We don't have to do this."

Meecah's shining skin glistened in the sun. She tightened her grip around the hilts of the blades she carried and pointed herself into a fighting stance with her knees bent low and arms held high. "Fight me, man-child."

Sebastian laughed. "It's your funeral, madam."

Meecah shouted and swiped her blade toward him. He pushed her arm away, pulled his hands into his chest, and with a gust of wind, threw her backward. She jumped to her feet but was knocked over by another gust. She punched her fist into the sand, grabbed her knife, and lunged.

Sebastian shrieked in pain and fell to one knee. He ran his hand down to his gut, feeling only the handle of a blade. He gripped it and pulled as his head started spinning. The hot spurting blood and the intense pain sent him into a swearing fit. Sebastian dropped the knife and glanced at Meecah. She was poised and ready with her other dagger in hand. He let out a hoarse scream. The island shook, the tribesmen braced themselves, and Meecah backed away.

Lightning erupted in the sky and flickered from Sebastian's fingertips. He stepped forward, his eyes locked on hers. One of the tribesmen yanked Meecah aside and took her place in Sebastian's path. He was taller than Sebastian, more muscular, and dashingly handsome. He kissed her cheek and then ran at Sebastian with her knife clenched in his fist.

Sebastian let out a scream and jerked his body toward the tribesman. The sky rumbled and flashed before coming still. He stood, panting, with his foot placed firmly on the man's chest. Sebastian looked down to see a man laying lifeless with webbed burns across his chest and face.

The chief stomped into the circle, shoving his daughter away, and bent over the man. He looked at Sebastian. "What are you?"

Sebastian shook his head.

"Take what you need and leave before my men tear you apart, monster."

Sebastian held his stomach and backed away painfully. His men collected water and the animals they caught and ran for the beach. Kastor and Cyrus helped Jace while Peter and Cristian escorted Sebastian down the steep hill that led to the boats. They started to push away from the shore when a noise came from over the cliff.

"Wait!"

"Keep going," Sebastian said.

"Wait, please!"

Sebastian caughtat the shadow of a woman in the corner of his eyes, before seeing her red dress flip in the wind.

"Stop, I am begging you!"

Sebastian stood as Meecah's feet hit the water. "Back away!"

"Take me with you." She fell to her knees.

"No."

"Please, I can't stay here. I am a healer. I can help you." Meecah pointed at his stomach. "I can save your life." She held her hands like she was praying.

Sebastian saw tribesmen filing over the hillside. "Get in the damn boat. Let's go!"

They rowed away as the villagers reached the water. Most stopped while a few started to swim after them.

"They won't make it far," Meecah said. "They have no ships to chase us. Thank you."

"Tell me why I shouldn't throw you overboard once you've healed me?"

"You killed the man my father chose for me to marry."

"I'm sorry, but he tried to kill me first," Sebastian said.

"Don't be. You were right. I did not love him. I hated him." Meecah tilted her head down. "My father is a bad man. He wanted my people to destroy you and steal your ship so that he could send the last of our men to the mainland to fight the king. Imagine fifty men against an army of thousands. The man my father wanted me to marry is exactly like him. I was to marry him so that he could be chief and lead our people into revolution. But you freed me from those chains.I swear my fealty to you, my lord."

"Just focus on healing Jace and me. Then we will discuss loyalty."

CHAPTER 5
The Motherland

Jace healed well but walked with a minor limp that he swore did not bother him. For Sebastian, the mending took longer. His wound went quite deep. He walked around his quarters for the first few days, slowly. The rough seas made it difficult for him to get the exercise he needed. Cyrus brought him food and catered to him day and night. At night he held Sebastian tight in his arms and refused to let him move without assistance.

"You're smothering me."

Cyrus smiled but looked sad. "I thought this is what you would want. Am I wrong?"

"Do not fret over me. I will be well soon enough." Sebastian smiled and held Cyrus tight in his arms. He loved having him back and secretly loved that Cyrus was attentive to his every need.

The days passed and Sebastian began walking around without help. One morning, he was out at the wheel when he realized the air was much warmer than anticipated.

"Jace. Where are we?"

Jace brought over a map. "Here is the island we left a while ago. We headed west from there. We should be somewhere near here." He said, pointing to an empty section of the map.

"How are we doing on supplies?"

"We have plenty of fish and crab and have been collecting rainwater. We are moving slowly without having the foremast, though. We can only hope Midrel Istan comes over the horizon soon."

"One can only hope. How are you feeling?"

"As good as new, Your Majesty." Jace stroked Sebastian's arm.

"Jace, I want you to stay with us when we find a place there. You mean a lot to me. I care for you." He glanced up at Cyrus, hoping he did not hear him say that. Cyrus was helping Kastor and Peter stretch the sails as the winds picked up.

Jace's face brightened. He smiled and blushed as he looked over the map some more. "Well, back to work then. Thank you, Your Majesty."

Sebastian counted four moon cycles before the weather turned from rough to warm open seas and never-ending sunlight. Cyrus started talking to him without anger in his voice. One morning they awoke together and watched the sunrise. Sebastian's mood was better, Cyrus seemed content, and Jace kept his distance giving subtle looks of wanting when Sebastian caught his gaze. Sebastian once again took his place at the wheel, feeling peaceful. Cyrus wrapped his arms around him and rested his head on Sebastian's shoulder.

"I love you."

"Does this mean you will stay with me in Midrel Istan?"

"That depends." Cyrus grinned. "Are you going to stop flirting with Jace?"

Sebastian frowned, but Cyrus laughed. "Forget it. Everything that happened before, forget it. Let's start anew.

Clean slate. I keep reading the passages in your book about how you and I first met and the feelings you have for me. It's beautiful. I want to fall in love with you again."

"You are the only man I want. I love you and only you."

"There it is!" Jace shouted. "Midrel Istan!"

Sebastian steered the ship to where the land was spotted. As they came closer to the shore, they saw a harbor filled with boats and people working.

"This is a sign," Meecah said happily. "We need the ship repaired. Maybe they can help us."

"Or they will kill us."

Meecah slapped her hand against Sebastian's chest. "Do not be so dark. We need positivity right now."

"You are right. Maybe they will not kill us. There, is that better?" Sebastian laughed.

"You are hopeless." Meecah joked. "I do not know how many more we will lose," She whispered. "They are dying down there. I ask you to be kind to these people. Like it or not, we need their help."

"I promise to be polite. But if they try anything, I will have no choice but to attack."

"You have so much anger in your heart. Maybe you will find happiness out there. At least try, Your Majesty."

As they entered the harbor, they noticed the people stopping to stare. The Hetta was easily the most significant ship docking there. The broken masts and ripped sails were a sight. A red-haired squat man walked down a dock, shouting at them. Sebastian left the wheel to Cyrus and approached the port side to speak with him.

"Who is the captain of this vessel?" The man said with an annoyed tone.

"I am the captain. We are in desperate need of repair, and my crew is starving. May we dock here?"

The man groaned, then nodded and waved toward the long pier near the end of the harbor. As the Hetta was anchored, the man walked quickly with a forceful expression to meet Sebastian.

"Sebastian, please be careful. These people do not look friendly," Cyrus said.

He was right. The people of the harbor town were observing them. They did not wave or smile. Instead, they sat frozen, glaring at the men aboard the ship with distrust on their faces.

"Who are you and where are you from?" The man said as he stood next to the Hetta, looking up at the crew.

"My name is Sebastian Drake. I am the captain of the Hetta Horizon, and we have sailed from Erras."

The man interrupted. "Did you say, Erras?"

"Yes, that is our homeland. It is far across the sea to the north. We were in search of new lands when we encountered a massive hurricane. As you can see, we are in desperate need of repair, my men are hungry, and some have become ill."

"It will be expensive." The man had a smug look. "Repairs of this magnitude will take quite some time and a lot of labor, plus room and board for the crew and yourself. How do you propose to pay for this?"

"My crew can assist with the repairs once they are rested and fed. I have gold and gems as well. Do you take gold for payment?"

The man's eyes shot wide open. He straightened his composure, and his annoying smirk vanished. "Gold, you say? Any man with enough gold will receive anything he needs here. Welcome to Feldor Bay. My name is Bryson, and I am at your service." He bowed a little overly enthusiastically.

Sebastian nodded in approval and sent Meecah with the sick and injured to the local clinic. The others made their way into the town. Sebastian demanded that Cyrus, Jace, Kastor, Peter, and a few other of his most high-ranking men stay with him at the town's nicer inn.

Over the next few months, crew members were assigned duties around Feldor Bay. Some went to help the lumberjacks cut trees in the forests near the mountains. Others helped at the docks and joined fishing boats. Sebastian and Cyrus met with Jace to discuss where they needed to go from there.

Sebastian sat at a small table next to a bright window in a local pub. "Where do we find this teacher?"

"How would I know?" Jace sat in the chair across from Sebastian. "I have never been here. Give it time, Your Majesty. I will ask around. In the meantime, maybe you should consider finding suitable accommodations."

"I agree," Cyrus said. "We need to find our place. We could very well be here a long time."

"Where do we begin? Do you want to stay here in this town?"

"I don't care." Cyrus slumped back. "But I know I tire of the whispers and stares. If you wish to make this work, we need our place."

Jace stood and walked to the door. "While the two of you work that out, I am going to go ask around. See if anyone knows anything about this teacher."

Cyrus and Sebastian bought horses and went for a ride, making their way down the shoreline. Sebastian suddenly halted upon a spot of land on a beautiful white sand beach and shimmering blue water. He looked over at Cyrus, who was smiling. "It is perfect."

"We need to hire men to build. If we are to stay, I want it to be perfect. Anything you want, my darling. Whatever will make you happy."

"As long as I share this home with you." Cyrus kissed Sebastian softly. "Only with you, I hope."

"Cyrus, I promised Jace a home."

"With us? Why?" Cyrus's voice was rising. "It doesn't matter. He can stay with us until he finds his way."

"Good. Do not worry, Cyrus. It will still just be you and me. Let's go find a builder."

They thundered down the beach, sand kicking from behind the hooves of tired horses, until they arrived back in Feldor Bay, finding Bryson at the harbor. Bryson's face fell at the sight of them and walked over in a pant. "What can I do for you, Lord Sebastian?"

"I need someone who can build a home for Cyrus and me. We found a plot of land down the shore, west of here. I would like to buy it and begin on the manor immediately."

Bryson took a deep breath and whistled while waving his arm. A large man walked over. He towered over Sebastian with a sharp glare, and his mouth curved into a snarl. Crumbs trickled from his scraggly red beard, and his eyes were bloodshot.

"This is my brother, Balir. He and his men have built much of this town. Tell him what you require, and he will give you a price."

Sebastian grimaced at the sight of a messy, dirty giant standing before him. He described their needs briefly while Cyrus went into elaborate detail. Balir nodded in understanding and then explained what he would build, which was completely different than what either of them had said. He insisted on stone and heavy wood for the exterior with large windows for view with thick shutters for when storms rolled in. Sebastian agreed and paid the men to begin work. The winter passed into spring and summer was quickly approaching. The trees from the mountains had just dried from the snow melt and the stone was no longer frozen into the ground. Workers labored hard through the mild, chilly nights cutting glass and shaping rock into walls and windows.

The beachside palace glistened against the sand, complimenting the teal water that it overlooked. Sebastian rode into Feldor Bay to find Jace and bring him home. They had spent the long months waiting for their home to be complete searching for answers on how to find the teacher. They remained empty-handed.. Sebastian went to the town's library and hall of records in hopes of any written scrolls notating a person gifted in magic, but the documents had little information about Midrel Istan. Sebastian settled on the idea that this teacher no longer existed. Feldor Bay was home, and he was happy that he had Cyrus, although having Jace by his side all the time made his heart flutter more and more.

Sebastian and Jace sat in a café one afternoon before heading home. "Tell me, Jace." His cheeks burned. "What do you want out of life?"

Jace smiled and flashed his bright eyes at Sebastian. "To be happy and be loved."

Sebastian cleared his throat. "Look, I don't know what the future holds for any of us. I fear if I don't find this teacher that all of this will be for nothing. Everything we have been through. And Cyrus is only one wrong move away from snapping at me again. I have to fix everything, and I need help." He reached out and touched his fingertips to Jace's hand. "I need you, Jace."

Jace raised his eyebrows. "Are you saying you like me?"

Sebastian felt his face get hot. "We would be terrible together." He bit his lip. "But I do need you. You seem like the only one who understands me."

"I thought Cyrus was your one and only." Jace's face turned down toward the table. "You love him."

"I do. Very much. He is everything that is good in the world. But that doesn't mean I cannot feel something for another." Sebastian's heart began to race. "Besides, I see how he looks at you. It's the same way he used to look at me."

"Your Majesty, I would never touch Cyrus. It would hurt you too much and I don't want to hurt you."

"You can't hurt me, Jace."

The months were warm, and the summer solstice was nearing. Sebastian lay in bed with Cyrus on his chest. Cyrus reached up and brushed Sebastian's hair behind his ear. "Are you happy, Cyrus?" Sebastian whispered.

"I am trying to be. But there are demons fighting within me, tearing me in two directions." Cyrus sat up. "I don't know if I can continue to fight them."

"Cyrus, please let me help you."

"We have been away from Erras for all this time and you have yet to try to help me." Cyrus's voice grew louder. He closed his eyes and sat back. "I have been thinking about this for days now and I believe it is time for me to return home. It is better for you and me. Perhaps I can find Lorna and force her to reverse this hex."

"I need you, Cyrus."

"No, you need to focus. If it is my job to kill you, then you must be as dangerous as they say. This is the only way I can show my love for you. By saving your life, from me."

The pain in Sebastian's stomach was unbearable. There was nothing more he wanted except one thing, to marry Cyrus. "Please, just stay through my birthday. Give me until then to try and change your heart."

"We will celebrate the solstice together and then I will make my choice." Cyrus climbed out of bed and left the room.

Word spread across the town that anyone could come to celebrate under the blood moon on the night of the great harvest. In Feldor Bay, harvest was on a rare night when the tides brought loads of crab that migrated near the shores to mate. The innkeepers tapped into their finest meads and wine, and all traveled to the Drake manor for festivities.

As the evening commenced, many were quickly drunk, singing, and dancing on the beach. Men chased women, stripping them of their dresses and carrying them into the water to have their way with any drunken lady who was willing. Music filled the woods, carrying far into the distance as bonfires lit the night sky. The townspeople gathered into a circle and danced what they called "The Sailor's Lore". Everyone crossed their arms and took the hands of the person next to them. They would spin quickly, kicking after every third step. If you fell, you had to step away and drink a pint. When one fell, the circle turned faster.

Sebastian held onto Jace and Cyrus with all his strength. After only a few minutes, they were down to only six in the circle and were spinning so fast they could barely keep from tripping in the sand. Sebastian slipped, wrapped his arms around Cyrus and Jace, and pulled the whole circle down at once. Four men and two women smashed into one another.

Sebastian looked toward the trees as he stood and noticed a boy watching him. Cyrus handed Sebastian a mug. He drank the pint, sat down, and checked over at the trees again, seeing the young face coming out a little more. Cyrus climbed onto his lap and started tearing at his clothes. The other three in the group started doing the same. The women pulled each other's dresses off while the man, a dock worker, kissed their necks. Cyrus nearly had Sebastian naked on the ground. Jace started to move away, but Sebastian grabbed his arm and pulled him down, kissing him lustfully. Jace's face turned bright red as Cyrus began kissing him too.

The party went on around them. Drunk men sang and played music, eating and drinking while slapping women on their backsides as they danced around. Sebastian threw himself on top of Jace and made a man of him before all who wanted to see. Jace moaned loudly, his eyes rolled back, and his mouth trembled with ecstasy. Cyrus crept his way in, pulled Sebastian to him, and endured the aggression of his lover as he used his body for his personal pleasure.

When they finished, the party still echoed loudly. They brushed the sand off and dressed. Sebastian walked toward the beach house but stopped suddenly at the sight of a black-haired young man cautiously approaching the festival. Sebastian's heart pounded in his throat and his vision went blurry.

"Who are you? You are not from Feldor Bay." He walked over to the boy.

The intruder's eyes grew as wide as the moon above. He started to speak, but his voice cracked. Sebastian spoke over him. "Don't be afraid. All are welcome here. I just want your name."

"Dani." The boy squeaked out.

"Dani. Where are you from?"

"There is a farm not far down the shoreline to the south. Word spread from travelers that there was a party for a wealthy traveler from afar, so I was sent to...investigate."

Sebastian smiled. "Come and enjoy the celebration with me. My name is Sebastian, and I own this manor. Please feel free to have some food and drink. Perhaps a woman or two." Sebastian laughed as he noticed the same two women now on top of another man.

Dani stared at the ground with a smile across his lips. "That is kind of you. Perhaps I could enjoy your company as well, Lord Sebastian."

The corner of Sebastian's mouth twitched into a smile. "Perhaps so."

Sebastian led Dani to the house after noticing Cyrus and Jace watching them. Cyrus stood to follow.

"Forgive me, but I lied." Dani stopped suddenly. "I was sent to work, not for my pleasure, but for yours if you would like."

Sebastian, still drunk, hesitated for a moment before realizing Dani was offering himself as a whore. "You were sent to work? By whom?"

"My adoptive father. We are poor and need the money for food."

"I have never paid for sex, but I would pay a fortune for you. You are incredibly beautiful." Sebastian stumbled a little, then fell into a chair.

Dani's face turned red. His dark hair hung over his crystal blue eyes as he grinned at Sebastian, then looked away quickly. Sebastian fumbled with a trunk in the corner and returned with a pouch he placed into Dani's hand. Dani quickly shoved it in his coat and took Sebastian's hand.

"Anything you wish, my Lord. I am yours for the night."

Sebastian, drunk from not just the ale but from his position of power, reached in to kiss Dani. Dani shivered and wrapped his arms around Sebastian's neck, pulling his body tight against his own. Sebastian saw Cyrus standing at the door. His face was red.

"What is going on here?" Cyrus said.

"Cyrus, my love. I must be really drunk. I'm sorry." Sebastian stumbled and fell. "Besides, you weren't complaining when I was ravishing Jace moments ago."

"That's different!" Cyrus's voice got loud. "You said you were mine. And I allowed you to be with Jace, not him." He pointed at Dani.

The crowd began cheering and clapping. "Gentlemen! I think it is time for a little game. Let's see who can endure in a tournament of champions," Kastor shouted from outside.

"Not right now, Kastor," Cyrus said. "My darling lover was about to take another man into his bed. I think we have had enough fun for tonight."

"Leave him be. He is probably all tuckered out and doesn't know what he is doing. I challenge you, Lord Cyrus." Kastor held a sword and pointed.

Cyrus tightened his jaw, his eyes grew red, and he frowned. He walked outside and snatched the sword from Kastor's hands. "May the best man win. Jace, you have my side."

"But Cyrus, Sebastian—"

Sebastian followed them outside.

"I do not care." Cyrus raised his voice.

Jace's eyes widened as he glanced at Sebastian, but he turned and followed Cyrus.

The men circled the swordsman. Iron crashed against iron as men strutted around, showing off their finest maneuvers. Men fell in defeat, scurrying away so they wouldn't get hurt by the next challenger who faced off. Kastor fell out quickly, but Peter proved to be competitive. Eventually he fell to Jace, who surprised everyone with how talented he was with a sword. After a short time, the music began playing again in the background, but Jace and Cyrus stood in the circle, still holding their swords.

Sebastian walked toward the circle to witness the fight, noticing the angry, sweaty face of Cyrus and the cocky smile on Jace's. He assumed neither of them had noticed he joined the crowd.

Cyrus whirled his sword and then gripped it tight. "I suggest you back down, Jace."

"Not a chance."

"I have been training to wield a sword since I could walk. You will get hurt if you don't step away." Cyrus smiled.

"How do you know I haven't been training my whole life either? I am every bit as good as you."

Cyrus swung and was blocked by Jace. Their swords rang loud. "Jace, back away. I need to speak to Sebastian."

"Why? What concern do you have for him? You sneak off all the time, disappearing all day. What are you doing? Do you even love him?"

"How dare you question me. My drunken, idiot boyfriend, the King of NorthBrekka, is standing there with some pretty little thing while you and I are fighting. Do you think he loves either one of us?"

The circle of men quieted. The people from Feldor Bay were stunned with confusion. "King? Did he say, king?" Bryson said.

Cyrus swung. Jace spun around, ducking below the blade, then punched Cyrus in the chest and knocked him down. Cyrus growled and lunged at Jace. "I will kill you!"

"Oh no you don't!" Peter shouted, grabbing Cyrus. "Calm down. I think you need to sleep."

"Let me go!" Cyrus thrashed and jerked. "Get your hands off me. I will kill him."

Kastor clonked Cyrus on his head with the hilt of his sword. "Someone had too much to drink. Set him down over there. Let us settle down now."

Sebastian laughed and returned to the house while the men challenged one another to a dual. Sebastian looked at Dani and was overtaken by his beauty, but his love and passion for Cyrus guilted him.

"Dani, I am sorry. I can't do this. Keep the money so your time is not wasted. I am helplessly attracted to you; trust me, you are incredible, but I am madly in love with my Cyrus. I cannot break my bond with him."

"I understand. Let me get you into bed, My Lord. You have had too much to drink. I will stay with you until you get to sleep, then I will send your Cyrus to you."

They stumbled to the bedroom. Sebastian laid down and pulled Dani onto his chest. Sebastian held onto him as he drifted off. Early the next morning, he felt Dani slip away. When Sebastian got out of bed and walked outside, Dani was gone.

CHAPTER 6
The Summer Solstice

"Happy birthday, my king." Jace caught up to Sebastian.

"I do not celebrate my birthday, so that is unnecessary."

"That is ridiculous." Jace grabbed him by the shoulders. "You still deserve a gift, whether you like birthdays or not."

Jace leaned over, cupped Sebastian's cheek, and kissed his lips. Sebastian wanted to pull away but instead, he jerked Jace against him, kissing him intimately. Jace wrapped his arms around his neck, holding Sebastian so he could not get away and Sebastian did not struggle. He wanted attention. He wanted a lover.

"What is it you crave, my king?"

"What I desire would be meaningless for us. I love him, Jace. I love Cyrus more than anything in the entire world."

"But he does not feel the same about you." Jace turned his back away. "Take me instead. I would give you so much affection that you would send me away so that you could rest. You cannot keep denying your feelings for me."

"My feelings for you are only lust." Sebastian walked back toward the house and went inside.

Jace followed Sebastian while tearing his clothes off. He threw him onto the bed and climbed on top. Sebastian felt a sensation intensify through his body like lightning shocking his every sense. His eyes flickered as he gasped for a breath between thrusts. Pure bliss shot through his veins until he found the strength to grasp Jace by the hips and flip him onto the bed, climbing on top of his waiting body. Sebastian pinned his arms together in one hand while gripping his throat in the other. He bit hard on Jace's neck, making him wince with a smile twitching across his face.

"I knew you couldn't resist this." Jace gasped with a winded breath.

"Shut up, Jace. You are being used. This is not love. I want nothing more from you."

"You lie. I can feel it. You are falling for me."

Sebastian gripped tighter on Jace's throat and continued to have his way with him until he could no longer catch his breath. Jace laughed, still lying on his back on the bed. He ran his hand across Sebastian's sweaty torso, feeling his muscles contract.

"I knew you would enjoy my gift to you." Jace kissed his chest. "Do you still hate birthdays now?"

Sebastian glared at him, pushed his hand away, and marched outside to the water to clean off. Jace followed. "You will say nothing of this around Cyrus. Do you understand me, Jace?"

"Yes, of course. I get it. Pretend I don't exist."

Sebastian swam out into the warm sea and dunked his head under. When he emerged, the smells of burnt wood filled the air. Men and women were scattered here and there. He shook off the water and ran over to the tree as Cyrus started to wake up. The guilt burned through his entire body. He looked at Jace, then back at Cyrus.

"My love, good morning." He held Cyrus's face in his palm. "Are you alright? That is a nasty bump on your head."

"Why do you look flushed? Did that man you were with last night cause that?" Cyrus said.

"No, nothing happened with Dani. I just went for a swim."

"We need to talk… about last night."

"Yes, we do. There is something I want to ask you, Cyrus."

"Sebastian, look, I have been beating my brain trying to unlock whatever feelings I once had for you, but I—"

Sebastian held up his hands. "Cyrus, before you say anything else—"

"Let me finish. I don't think this is going to—"

"Cyrus, please." Sebastian grabbed his hands and held them tight. "I am begging you to listen for a moment."

"Stop interrupting me. I know what there was once was real, but—"

"My darling, I need you." Sebastian pulled him close. "That day, on the lake, when I saw you for the first time when our eyes met, and we got lost staring into each other's souls, I knew you were the only man I would ever love. I never felt like that about Will or Dom. That is why I tried so hard to get you back from Sacha. I have to have you, Cyrus. I can't live in this world without you."

"Sebastian, please stop talking. I need to tell you that I have decided to go—"

"Cyrus, you are the love of my life." Sebastian fell to one knee. "I know I can help you find your way back to me. Please. Marry me, my love."

Cyrus paused and stared at Sebastian in shock. He tried to speak, but only a stutter escaped him.

Sebastian's heart started pounding. He squeezed Cyrus's hand. "Will you marry me?"

"No." Cyrus ripped his hand away. "No, Sebastian. What I was trying to say is that I am leaving. I have tried to love you, but every ounce of blood in my body boils with the desire to cut your throat as you sleep. I know I should be saying yes to your proposal, and I should be madly in love with you, but I can't, so I am departing tonight."

Sebastian felt a sharp pain shoot from his throat to his stomach. His eyes burned, and he felt like everything inside of him was broken. "Why did you let me have your body last night?" Sebastian's body intensified with burning and tingling pain. "You told me that you wanted to start over. You lied!"

"I never lied. How can anyone love you?" Cyrus bent over to meet Sebastian at eye level. His face was red and sweaty. "You are a monster... no, a—"

"Don't you dare say it."

"Dragon." Cyrus's eyes were bloodshot, and his teeth were clenched.

Sebastian silenced and let Cyrus walk away but followed him into the manor and stood in the corner. Sebastian heard Jace shouting as Cyrus walked past him.

"How could you hurt him? All he did was love you." Jace stuttered but still blurted out angrily.

"Do not speak to me about him!" Cyrus screamed. "He is an abomination, and his presence in the world will bring doom to mankind. You are aware that Sebastian is the Dragon, right? He is an evil curse, and I warn you to run for your life." Cyrus grabbed him by the throat, inspecting the bruises and bite marks on Jace's neck and chest. "He used his fake vulnerable, sweet little puppy eyes on you, and you fell for it. He will be your end as well unless you do as I say. Run away, Jace. Go before his rage consumes you. If you value living, you will disappear!" Cyrus slammed his fist into the wall next to Jace's head.

"Cyrus, get away from him!" Sebastian shouted.

Thunder cracked as the peak of sunrise turned to clouds and stormy skies. Cyrus released Jace, reached for his sword slowly, and stared at Sebastian. He screamed and swung, aiming for the throat. Sebastian ducked out of the way and pummeled Cyrus to the ground. A fist met his jaw, then the other hit his lip, splitting it open. Cyrus reached into his boot, but Sebastian threw him down and held his arms against the hard floor. A ruby-encrusted dagger slid from his hand.

Sebastian stared at it for a moment, then turned to Cyrus. "I do not want to fight you. I love you."

Cyrus's eyes had dark circles forming under them and the creases in the corners showed more than usual. "Then you will die." Cyrus shoved Sebastian away. He shook his head and crawled to his sword by the fireplace. He climbed to his feet and turned to Jace. "Are you still here? Oh well. Guess I will have to kill you too."

Sebastian kicked him in the hip, knocking him over the chair. Cyrus leaped to his feet and threw a punch but was thrown against the wall and pinned. He shoved his weight against Sebastian but slipped and fell to his knees. Sebastian glanced at the floor at the same time as Cyrus, noticing the familiar dagger within reach.

It was the same one Barron had used to kill Fiona and stab Sebastian in his thigh. He watched Cyrus take it in his grasp. Sebastian fell to his knees. "Cyrus, before you kill me, you must know that I am okay with dying." He inched closer and touched Cyrus's hand. "I told you I can't live without you." Sebastian stared into Cyrus's eyes. "I love you," he whispered, watching the love of his life push the bejeweled dagger into his chest.

Jace came from near the door and wrapped his arms around Cyrus, throwing him to the side. He leaned over to Sebastian and put his hand on his forehead. "My King." His eyes filled with tears.

Sebastian felt empty. He didn't feel the dagger, but he felt the blood running out, taking the warmth of his body with it. He felt it begin to fill his throat. Sebastian smiled as flicks of lightning cracked across his skin. Jace jerked his hand back. He reached over to touch his chest, but Sebastian screamed out a ghastly shriek, and a bright blast of lightning, wind, and fire shot from his body. The room filled with dust as the stone walls collapsed, letting in the sun and the ocean breeze.

"I told you, Jace," Cyrus shouted. "He is a monster. He will kill you if you do not run! Go and never come back!"

"I can't leave him," Jace said.

"Go!" Cyrus screamed. Jace looked at Sebastian, terrified, and took off in a sprint into the forest.

Cyrus laughed. "They were right about you. You are the Dragon. I hope you enjoyed your last birthday. Now do the world a favor and die." Cyrus sheathed his sword, let out a prideful grunt, and walked away.

Sebastian sat with a dagger in his chest as the fire surrounded him. "Take my life. I don't want it anymore." He stared at the sky as everything went dark.

CHAPTER 7
Waking Up to Blue Eyes

Sebastian awoke to someone's hand on his chest. His voice was soft and high-pitched, and his eyes twinkled in the sun. He mumbled something that sounded distorted as the warm sensation returned to his body. He sat up, choking on his own blood and felt a sharp pinch shoot through his chest. His blurred vision slowly became clear. Dani sat on his knees holding the dagger. Sebastian stared at him as his vision returned.

There were still small fires burning and smoke filled the sky, along with dust and ash. The crowd from the party formed around the once white sandy beach now scorched black.

"What are you doing? Get away from him!" Kastor said to Dani.

"Where is Cyrus?" Sebastian looked into the most stunning bright, blue eyes he had ever seen peeking out through the messy black hair that hung over his face.

"I do not know where he went."

Sebastian stared at him in wonder. Even the soot on his face and messy clothes couldn't soil Dani's beauty.

"Your wound should heal well. It did not pierce your heart," Dani said.

Sebastian checked his chest, and then looked around at the crowd.

"Jace? Where is Jace?"

"Your Majesty, I have not seen Jace all morning," Peter said.

"Your Majesty?" Dani's face scrunched up. "You are a king?"

"Yes. I am. Has no one seen Cyrus?"

"We saw him riding fast to the west. I tried to speak to him, but he kept riding. I thought it was odd, but he was always a tad bit off. Is everything alright?" Kastor said.

"No. It is not alright. Cyrus tried to kill me. When he stuck this knife in my chest, I lost control of my power. I think I may have hurt Jace. He ran away. I have to find him. I have to go after Cyrus." He sat up fast but became dizzy and fell back down.

"Easy. You still have a hole in your body." Dani held him down.

Kastor and Peter came to Sebastian's side. "Come now, Your Majesty. Let us help you to town. Meecah will fix you up right."

"Dani, will I see you again?"

"I believe you will." Dani smiled and walked away into the trees and disappeared.

"He is a strange lad," Kastor remarked.

CHAPTER 8
Reaching Tomas

Sebastian woke suddenly with a cold chill filling his limbs. It was raining in Feldor Bay. The cool breeze and smell of the sea were normally refreshing on mornings that he sat on the windowsill and watched the dock workers scurry about. He thought about the mornings he sat in his bedroom with Tomas when storms kept him inside, watching the people who worked along the castle grounds running about. Now, depression kept him in bed and all he had was his thoughts to keep him company.

"Having nightmares again?" A woman's voice interrupted his thoughts.

"Excuse me?"

"You were thrashing in your sleep, and you are all sweaty."

"Who are you?"

"Astrid, my Lord." She blushed. "I am a nursemaid. Can I get you anything? Water? A bath maybe?"

"I am fine."

Meecah popped around the corner. "Bath. He needs a bath. He smells."

Sebastian looked at Meecah with a grin.

"I said to go take a bath. It has been a week. Go on, Astrid. Take him to the tub and wash him."

Sebastian started his rebuttal but decided it was not worth the effort. Astrid giggled as she put out her hand for him to take. "Come on, Lord Sebastian. I will take care of you."

He sunk into the steaming water, letting the scent of lavender soothe his mind. Astrid washed his back and hair gently and nervously.

"You are shaking. Why?" Sebastian said.

"I apologize, my Lord." Astrid shook harder.

"No need for that. Do I make you nervous?"

"A little." She giggled. "Your skin is soft. I like it. Most men have tough skin."

"Umm, thanks."

"What were you dreaming about?"

"Cyrus. I wish I knew why he came all this way with me only to leave so suddenly."

"I know nothing of you or Cyrus. Who was he to you?" Astrid stopped washing.

Sebastian choked out a little strain of words. "The man I love."

"Oh." Astrid gasped. "I, I, did not know you were, umm." She stopped talking and began washing his arms and chest faster than before. "Your eyes are red. I've never seen red eyes before."

"They are? Oh. That's odd. They usually only turn red when I am angry."

Astrid dropped the washcloth and soap in the water and stared at him.

"Don't worry. I am not angry with you," Sebastian said.

"Oh." She laughed and reached into the water for the soap, accidentally touching him in a place that made him jump. Her face turned bright red and her eyes grew large. Sebastian smiled.

"Sorry. I did not mean to, although you are unbelievably handsome... The men here are not quite as attractive as you." She started to mumble, "Shut up Astrid." She backed away from the bath. Sebastian continued to smile, watching her struggle to get on her feet. "I will let you finish." She ran out of the room.

He hopped out of the bath and dressed, then went to his bed where a plate was shoved into his hands. "Meecah, have you seen Cyrus?" He shoved a piece of crab in his mouth and took a seat.

"He rode through about a week ago. I was sitting on the porch when he passed by here. He slowed to look at me, then kicked his horse and galloped away to the west."

"A week? I have been here for a week."

"Yes, you were very ill from your wound." Meecah sat down next to Sebastian.

Sebastian set down his plate. "What is west of here?"

"Balir said there is a city called Altania. The City of Men. Apparently, an awful place according to the people here. Why he went there, I do not know."

"Cyrus said he was departing for Erras. Do they have ships?"

"Yes, big ones. Like the Hetta. Warships from what I have heard."

Sebastian finished eating and went outside to ask Balir and Bryson about Altania, and if their ships journeyed to Erras. Both shrugged their shoulders in unison but spoke of the old days, seeing Altanian ships attacking Adurakian ships during times of war.

"Adurak?"

"Yes, Adurak, The City of Thieves. It was once the greatest city in the east until King Maxen and his daughter, Empress Petra of Runeheim destroyed it and imprisoned their leader, who happened to be Maxen's brother. He was a sorcerer, a powerful one, more powerful even than them. That is why they were at war. They feared he would rise against them. The east has the manpower and numbers to overcome the west, but without a strong leader, we fear King Maxen and Empress Petra. They have power unlike anyone we have seen in the world. Dark magic."

"Where is the sorcerer now?"

"Locked away in some mountain. If you want answers, you should find Samir Kinjesto. He resides in Dunebar, the last outpost before the dry lake that separates the east from the west."

"Thank you."

Sebastian left to find Kastor and Peter working on the dock loading supplies into a fishing boat. He looked out at the Hetta bobbing on its dock, still tattered and torn. He wanted to take the Hetta and chase Cyrus but knew it would never make it far in its condition.

"Kastor, how far do you sail on your outings?"

"A few days out, why, Your Majesty?"

"Do you think you can make it to the Eastbay Pass Harbor? I need a letter taken to my brother."

"In a small ship like this? You are mad. If we run into a storm—"

"I need you to try. For your king."

"Aye, Your Majesty. Whatever you need of us."

"You have no need to return here. This is your chance to go home." Sebastian patted him on the shoulder.

Sebastian felt Kastor squeeze him tight in his thick arms.

"Are you going to be alright, Your Majesty?"

"I will find my way. Thank you for being there through my madness."

"I fear the madness has yet to begin. Good luck, my king."

"To you as well. I will bring a letter to your ship before you leave. Place it in Tomas's hand yourself."

Sebastian hurried back to the clinic to get parchment and ink to write home, but as soon as he sat down to start, he stared at the page, struggling with how to warn them or what to say.

Sebastian sealed the letter and passed it to Kastor and wished him and Peter well on their sailing. He watched the men who once worked on the Hetta board the fishing vessel, and set off to sea to return to Erras. He feared he had sent them to their death, but he turned to take his horse and head into the mountains to the south.

As he made it to the edge of the town, he heard a familiar voice shout behind him.

"Wait!"

"Not this time, Meecah. Go back."

"You should know by now that I do not listen to you. I am coming along."

"No."

"It is too late. I already told Astrid she is in charge. She was still embarrassed when I mentioned your name. I think she likes you."

Sebastian sighed. "Go away."

"Come on, your highness. We have a long road ahead." She kicked her horse and headed into the mountains. Sebastian knew nothing he said would make her go back to Feldor Bay, so he chased after them.

CHAPTER 9
A Road to the Unknown Land

They pushed hard through Feldor Bay's mountains, past the mining towns, and off into the land beyond. The mountains ended in a broad valley full of trees, grassy plains, and a river flowing into a large lake. It was filled with all sorts of life but was devoid of the noise and chaos of human beings. Even the fresh, crisp air and sparkling water could not raise Sebastian's spirits. From ocean to mountain to grassy plains, now into the hills where he could see sharp jagged tips of tall mountains far off on the horizon, the terrain of Midrel Istan was constantly changing.

Sebastian killed rabbits to eat and Meecah found berries in the thorny bushes along the edge of a river. As the horses chomped on some lush grass in the marsh, Sebastian sat with his bare feet in the cool water, sharpening his sword on a rock. There was a rustle in some nearby thickets that caught his attention. Thinking it to be an animal, Sebastion returned to his work.

The sun began to set behind the hills as storm clouds threatened his position. Sebastian pulled on his boots and approached his horse preparing to depart when the rustling sound caught his attention again. Animal or not, he wanted to know for sure so he hopped onto his horse and guided it across the shallow part of the river. Meecah stayed on the other side and waited.

Sebastian strung an arrow in his bow and aimed. The rustling halted, but the sight of a tuft of thick yellow hair stuck up from atop the bush. He had never seen an animal with yellow hair. Sebastian jumped off his horse and got closer. He pulled back on his bowstring. Lightning crashed and thunder shook around him as a storm approached. He released the arrow, but it pierced nothing. He saw the streak of yellow disappear around a rocky mound. He nodded and followed in the same direction. Meecah joined him and they rode away, onto the next stretch of land.

The next evening, Sebastian sat with his back against a rock and tried to sleep. When he nearly dozed off, he heard his horse give a pant and stomp. His vision was blurry but saw something slip from behind a tree. Sebastian rubbed his eyes quickly, jumped to his feet, and saw a cloaked figure disappear. He jumped up and ran after it, but nothing was there once more. Sebastian stumbled back to the tree, noticing something pinned to the trunk. On the tree was a slip of parchment unrolled revealing a road between the hills. It was a map and the map led to a town in the direction of some mountains he had been watching for days.

"What if this is a trap?" Meecah said.

"What if it is an answer to my problems?"

"It could be dangerous."

"Did you think this was going to be easy?" Sebastian smiled.

Meecah grinned and went to get some rest.

They stumbled on, following the mark on the map that showed a small town lay straight ahead. It was dark, the sun slipped below the horizon leaving a deep blue haze. The moon lit the dirt and rocks that formed a road to what looked like shadows ahead. The city was old and rundown, and the homes had no windows. Tattered curtains covered the doors.

"It's still too early for everyone to be asleep." Meecah peeked through a window.

"Perhaps it is abandoned."

What sounded like laughter came down from the far side of the town. A firepit in the middle of the road lit up a wooden door with a sign hanging overhead from rusted nails. Noise filled the air and light could be seen from oil lamps hanging in windows.

They hopped down from the horses and walked up to the door. Sebastian looked up at the sign that read The Broken Glass. He smirked and pushed the door, walked inside, and was met with a blast of noise aspeople rushed around the room with drinks, shouting at one another, and stumbling from table to table. The people were strong but weathered. Everything from their dry and dirty hair to their sunburnt skin and blistered knuckles, showed these townsfolk lived a hard life.

Sebastian and Meecah did not look like everyone else in the town. A glance in a partially broken mirror showed a handsome and well-maintained man. Even in his depressed and road-worn state, he still looked poised. Meecah was an islander with her brightly colored clothes and twine jewelry a stark contrast to the people of the city who looked tired. He caught the attention of the woman behind the bar and asked, "Where am I?"

"You are in Dunebar." She clenched her jaw and nodded as she wiped her curly blonde hair out of her sweaty face. "Where are you from, dear?"

"Feldor Bay."

"You do not look like a man from the bay." Her voice trailed at the end of every sentence. Sebastian had a hard time trying to understand if she was asking him a question or making a statement.

"I was not born there. I am from a land far away called Erras. I have been living in Feldor Bay for some time now."

Everyone in the saloon quieted down. "So, you aren't from Midrel Istan at all?" The barmaid asked, confused.

"No. Not at all."

"And what about your friend?"

Meecah stepped up to the bar and replied to the barmaid. "I am from Padora. My people are called the Maydrial."

The barmaid nodded in understanding. "So, what brings you to my fine establishment, dear?"

"We need a place to rest, and food and water for us and our horses?"

"Can you pay?" She pointed at her palm.

"Of course, I can pay. I have gold."

The Inn broke out into an uproar asthe word gold was mentioned repeatedly. The barmaid's eyes lit up, and she smiled, revealing a broken front tooth.

"Anyone with gold is surely welcome here at The Broken Glass." She said. "My name is Issa, and I am at your service, my lord."

Issa whispered to a boy who sat behind the bar, andturned back to Sebastian. "I sent my son to go take your horses to the stable and give them a feeding and some fresh hay to lay on. Let me make you something to eat, then I will show you to your rooms." She hurried to the kitchen.

"So, you must be highborn carrying gold around these parts." A gruff-sounding man approached Sebastian.

Sebastian had to look up to stare into his eyes. Chest hairs showed through the top of his tunic, and each muscular arm pinned Sebastian against the bar. The smell of dirt and sweat mixed with ale and mead seemed to seep from the man's body. Sebastian's stomach burned as he pushed back, trying to show the people he was not afraid. Meecah stood next to him, ready to fight if need be. Sebastian clenched his jaw and said, "You couldsay that."

"Where is this, Erras, you speak of? Is everyone there well off?"

"Of course not," Sebastian said. "Erras is far across the open sea."

The man glared at Meecah. "I have heard of Padora, and about how the people are savages that rip men's hearts out and eat them."

"Maybe we do. Do you want to find out?" Meecah said, stepping forward. Sebastian grabbed her arm and pulled her back.

The man laughed and continued to speak to Sebastian. "How did you get here?"

"I have a ship."

The room once again broke out into mumbles.

"A ship? Only kings own ships large enough to travel across the seas. Are you a king?" The man grunted.

"That is not your concern," Sebastian stated as he watched the town folk start to gravitate toward him, their faces serious and nostrils flared.

"Yes. Yes, this man is a king. Do not let him lie to you. His name is King Sebastian Drake, and he is the King of Erras." This voice made Sebastian roll his eyes and throw his head back. The handsome face, wavy blond hair, and cocky grin came face to face with him.

"Jace." Sebastian's heart skipped a beat. "What are you doing here? Where is Cyrus?"

"Looking for someplace to go in this godforsaken land. I have no idea where Cyrus is. I have not seen him since the summer passed." Jace straightened his back up and pointed his chin. "Why are you here?"

"Doing what I came to this dreadful country for in the first place. Why did you leave me alone on the beach?"

"I thought you would kill me, or Cyrus would if I did not follow his orders."

"I fear Cyrus may be gone. No one seems to know what happened to him."

"Are you alright?" Jace reached towards Sebastian's chest. "How did you survive being stabbed in the heart?"

"Dani." Sebastian stared blankly at the wall. "I mean, he helped me until they took me to Meecah."

"I had to deal with him." Meecah pointed at Sebastian. "And you ran away like a coward. I thought you were loyal, Jace?"

"Don't blame me. I only got to know him when we left Erras. I had no idea what he iwascapable of, but I wasn't about to die before I had the chance to find out. I left, but I also brought the both of you to me." Jace wore his cocky smirk.

Sebastian stepped forcefully forward and came nose-to-nose with Jace.

"That is enough, both of you." A voice came from the back of the room. "Come here and sit."

Jace blushed as he ran his hand across Sebastian's cheek. "That would be Samir Kinjesto. He is the leader here. You must show respect, or they will rip you apart."

At a table in front of a large fireplace sat a handsome older gentleman that wore a kind smile and welcoming voice. "Sit, please. Jace has told me much about you, Sebastian Drake. Who is your beautiful friend?" Samir gestured to Meecah.

Sebastian tilted his head and then glanced at Jace. "Then surely you have only heard bad things."

"No, no, on the contrary, Jace speaks highly of you. Almost admirably. It is a pleasure to put a face behind the story of a man with such power. May I look at your hands?" Samir said, holding his hands out toward Sebastian.

Sebastian raised his eyebrows and stared at Jace. He stretched his hands forward for Samir to take. Samir looked at his palms, then pushed back his sleeves to look at his tattoos. He laughed as he touched his fingertips to Sebastian's.

"What is funny?" Sebastian was confused. "Did I do something odd?'

"You are not burnt. When young Jace informed me you can make fire from your own hands, I could only imagine a man with charred skin, but your hands are normal."

"What else did you tell them about me?" Sebastian growled.

Jace laughed. "Everything. They know everything about you." He winked at Sebastian while Samir finished examining him.

"I hear you are in search of a man who understands what you can do. I am familiar with this man. Of course, I was just a boy when I last saw him. You have to understand, if you release him, you will disrupt the balance of the nations of Midrel Istan. However, Mandrel Istan is in desperate need of said disruption."

"He is in prison, correct?"

"Yes. He is locked in a cell deep within the caverns of Mosisle Dur. It is a mountain in the forbidden lands of Adurak. They say the entrance to the caverns is enchanted and only he who is blessed with magic can enter."

"What happens if you are not blessed with magic?"

"Well, it is not just any magic. You must be possessed with dark magic. It was made that way so that no one would be able to get inside. There is no person in this land skilled with dark magic except those who put him there. Those who have tried were cursed and died painfully, drowning in their blood and bile before they reached the bottom of the caverns."

"Delightful." Sebastian sounded amused. "So why would you think I could do this?"

"Jace said the people of Erras called you evil because of your powers. Of course, there is only one way to be certain."

"I would rather not suffer a painful death. Well, thank you very much. I think I will be on my way to Altania now. I have to go find Cyrus."

Sebastian stood. Meecah started to walk away, but Samir stopped them.

"You will never make it out of Altania alive. You have no idea how important this man is to you and all of Midrel Istan."

Sebastian stopped and turned. Samir continued. "This man is the only hope we have for destroying the greed of the men of the west. The King of Altania is a violent and dangerous man. Many people in the east were killed or enslaved by either King Maxen or Empress Petra of Runeheim. The Empress is the person who created the enchantments on Mosisle Dur. We here in the east have lived a life of starvation and suffering. If the sorcerer within the mountain is liberated, there will be real changes for us. We can begin to live again."

"If I do this, you must understand that I am only doing this because I need that man to help me understand who I am so I can save my husband and go home. I am not some kind of leader for your resistance. I want nothing to do with your war."

"I believe you are home, and when you learn who you are, you will feel like this land is where you are meant to be."

Sebastian began to rebuttal, but Samir interrupted. "That is enough conversation for tonight. Please, join me at my home tomorrow for tea. You are both invited. We can discuss this more then. However, I have business to attend to right now. Good night, my new friends."

Samir quickly left The Broken Glass, leaving Sebastian, Meecah, and Jace at the table. Issa came and set down three bowls of stew. "Eat up, then I will take you to your rooms."

Jace immediately grabbed his bowl and began eating. Meecah was a little hesitant but ate slowly with her eyes watching Jace. Sebastian locked his eyes on Jace as well, not giving any thought to eating.

"Jace. What are you actually doing here?"

"I found a place where I can be useful. It is nice to be wanted by someone."

"How are you being useful?" Sebastian snapped.

"By finding something that can help save these people from their decaying lives."

"And how did you do that?"

"By finding you and making sure you came here."

"I found this place all by myself. You had nothing to do with that."

"Oh?" Jace interrupted. "Do you recall something watching you from the bushes? And the parchment you found pinned to the tree with a map? You are welcome. Good night, Sebastian." Jace hurried up the stairs before Sebastian could stop him.

Sebastian sighed and dug into his stew. Once they were finished, Issa walked over and invited Sebastian and Meecah to follow her upstairs. "I have two rooms. My dear, you may stay here. It is quiet and comfortable." Issa opened the door and gestured for Meecah to enter.

Sebastian stopped her before she closed the door. "Do not answer the door for anyone but me. I do not trust Jace. Rest well."

Meecah nodded and closed her bedroom door.

"You can sleep here. It is one of the nicer rooms. If you think of anything you need, come downstairs and tell me. Anything at all."

"Where can I wash up?" Sebastian asked.

"The bath is at the end of the hall," Issa said, pointing to the door. "Let me heat some water for the bath, and I will knock on your door when it is ready."

Sebastian thanked her, then went into his room and shut the door. He looked around at the old furniture and the half-burned candles that melted wax all over the tables. He lay back on the bed, closed his eyes, and quickly fell asleep.

He was awoken by a sharp knock at his door. He jumped out of bed, startled, and hurried to the door. Issa waited with towels in her hand, then smiled and walked away. He walked to the bath, stripped off his worn clothes, and slipped into the hot water, groaning as it engulfed his body. Sebastian laid back after washing the dirt from his skin until his head and body were completely submerged. He scrubbed his hair and face, rinsed the soap away, then laid back to enjoy the hot water more before it cooled.

He slept restlessly through the night. He kept thinking about Cyrus and tried to imagine him lying next to him but would tear up at the thought that his love had tried to kill him. When the sun started peaking over the horizon, he was caught between being awake and asleep until he heard his bedroom door handle click. Someone entered, and closed the door behind them. He laid on his side with his back to the door, thinking it might be Meecah until he felt someone slip into bed andwrap their arms around him.

"Jace! What do you think you are doing?"

"I was just making sure there was not anything I could do to make you feel better," Jace said as he ran his fingers down Sebastian's bare chest, then reached and kissed him.

Sebastian was stunned by his audacity. "No, get out of my bed!"

Jace laughed and stood. "You have a meeting with Samir. Get up."

"What is this meeting about? What does he want from me?"

"You will find out when you get up and come with me."

"Are you going to leave so I can get dressed?"

"Not a chance," Jace said, smiling while looking at Sebastian from head to toe.

Sebastian rolled his eyes, then stood up, revealing his body to Jace. Jace stared lustfully and studied every part of his body. He walked over as Sebastian was about to put his pants on. He threw the clothes back on the chair, grabbed Sebastian's arms, and pushed him back onto the bed.

"Samir can wait a little longer." He said as he held Sebastian's arms down and began kissing him. "I still want you."

Sebastian freed his arms, threw Jace down on the bed, climbed on top of him, and pinned him down. "You will never have me again." He said, then shoved off him and started dressing again. Jace watched him, enjoying every movement.

"Stop staring at me!" Sebastian demanded.

"I can't take my eyes off you. You are so perfect." Jace said, then he laughed and got up to wait by the door. "Hurry up. Samir is waiting."

After Meecah joined their party, three of them walked through the streets of Dunebar. The little town was waking up to another day of hard labor as they started their ten-mile walk to the salt mines to the east. They walked down the street, Jace leading. Sebastian was behind, watching Jace closely, distrusting his intentions. Jace walked along with a proud stride in his step, checking behind him often to ensure Sebastian and Meecah were still following. They approached a large manor at the far side of Dunebar. Jace turned fast and got close to Sebastian's face.

"When we go inside, you will be courteous. You will listen to what Samir has to say and not act like...well, you."

Sebastian smirked, then returned his face to its usual irritated expression. They walked into a large open room filled with paintings and sculptures. Sebastian looked around, confused as to why the town was so poor, and the town leader was so well off. They walked into the parlor and saw Samir sitting behind a beautifully crafted desk in an oversized chair.

"Tea?" Samir offered.

"Yes, please," Sebastian said in his most courteous tone.

He sipped his tea, watching Jace from the corner of his eye. Samir smiled at both of them as he observed both Jace and Sebastian. Jace would subtly run his fingers across Sebastian's hand, trying to keep his attention, which only made Sebastian more irritable. Meecah sat in the corner, watching out the window that overlooked the mountain range in the south.

"What did you want to speak about?" Sebastian finally said, breaking the tension in the lounge.

"Right the business, of course. So, this sorcerer was imprisoned many years ago."

"Why was he imprisoned?" Sebastian interrupted.

"Because he is a warlord, like you."

"I am not a warlord," Sebastian said defensively.

Jace laughed and grasped Sebastian's arm. "Be polite, and yes, you are. You led your army against your land, destroyed an entire city, and incited a war among a civilization of tribesmen." Jace nodded at Meecah.

Samir smiled and stared at Sebastian. He started to speak but was interrupted as Samir continued.

"This man is imprisoned in the high mountains of Adurak. It is a cursed city on the southern edge of Midrel Istan. The prison entrance is high near the tallest mountain peak. Take caution traveling there. These lands are not forgiving. The east houses refugees, thieves, criminals, and mercenaries. They do not know you, and if they see you, they will try to kill you."

"Sounds lovely." Sebastian moaned. "You realize I am doing this only because I need a teacher for my power. I am not doing this for you or your people."

"What do you need to complete this journey?"

Sebastian took a deep breath. "I will need food and water, warm clothes, boots, weapons, and him."

"Me?" Jace said, sounding exasperated.

"Yes, you. You are the reason I came to Midrel Istan, to begin with. You are the reason I came to Dunebar. You are the reason I lost Cyrus. You will be my companion on this quest, or I will cut your throat."

Samir drummed his fingers on the desk. "You may take Jace, but you will leave her behind with me in return."

Meecah jumped from her chair. "Absolutely not! I am here to serve Lord Sebastian, not sit behind and wait."

"It is alright, Meecah. You have done enough. I will not risk your life on the road to Adurak."

Meecah looked perturbed and left the lounge in a huff. Samir smiled. "She will be safe here. She is just insurance, so you bring Jace back alive. He has become particularly useful to me over the short time I have known him."

Sebastian let out a little laugh but agreed.

CHAPTER 10
The Market in the Fog

The following morning, Sebastian woke early and found his requested items waiting in his room. He dressed and stuffed food into a bag, donned his sword and bow, then marched to Jace's door and knocked loudly. "Get up! We are leaving."

Jace whipped the door open fast and was met with Sebastian smiling overly enthusiastically. He straightened up and smiled back. "Ready when you are my king."

They hopped on their horses and rode south into the desert. Sebastian did not look at Jace nor speak until Jace began humming a song. As they reached a cliff, Sebastian climbed down from his horse to look over the edge.

"Will you stop that annoying noise and help me find a way to get down?"

"Oh, are we speaking again? Let me check the map."

"You have a map?"

"It is not my fault you came unprepared."

Sebastian balled his fists and gritted his teeth. "Fine. Tell me where we are."

"Apologize to me."

"What?"

"I said, apologize to me. Say, 'I am sorry I was mean to you, Jace. It is not your fault Cyrus left me. Cyrus left because I am a selfish, needy jerk.'" Jace demanded.

"I am not going to say that." Sebastian snapped.

Jace hopped down from his horse and rummaged through his bag. Sebastian climbed down to join him.

"Then I guess only I get to see this wonderfully drawn map. I bet you are wondering where we need to go. If only you had thought about asking for a map. I guess I am just smarter than you."

"Jace, I do not have time for this!" Sebastian snatched at the map, but Jace pulled away.

"No. The only way you get to read the map is if you apologize. I am in no hurry."

"Apologize for what? You are the one who ran away and left me to die."

Jace stopped and stared at Sebastian. "Apologize for choosing him over me. I told you I was the one who loved you. Yet, you still chose him and it almost cost you your life."

"I love Cyrus, Jace. I still love him. I wanted nothing more than to save him. I thought he was better. He seemed like he wanted to make it work between us. I had no idea how hard he was fighting a demon inside himself."

Jace sighed and returned to looking at the map. "Why are you afraid of him?"

"I am not afraid of anyone."

"Lies. You are weak when it comes to Cyrus."

Sebastian grabbed Jace by the throat and pulled him close. "Why do you care?"

"Let me go."

"No! Give me the map, Jace."

"Why are you afraid of fighting Cyrus?"

Sebastian let him go. "I am not afraid of the fight. Give me the map."

"Answer me!"

"Why?"

"Because I asked! Why are you such an ass?"

Sebastian shoved Jace away, knocking him to the ground. Jace stared at him angrily as Sebastian took the map, set it aside, then knelt. "I am afraid of finding him dead. The thought of it makes me sick because it will be my fault. Not yours. None of this was your fault, Jace."

Jace put his hand on Sebastian's knee and sat up. "I only have you left in this world. Being by your side is my only future. I need you to understand that you can trust me. I can't go home, Sebastian."

"Your father is the leader of Oyster Cove. Why can't you return home?"

"My father despises me. He says I am a disgrace. Therefore, I forfeit any rights to my father's estate, money, or title. I am not even allowed to carry his last name."

Sebastian breathed hard, looking at Jace painfully. He stood and held out his hand for Jace to take. "When we leave this wretched land, we will return home, and you will be by my side. You will not be left to fight alone."

Jace smiled and handed Sebastian the map. They looked it over, trying to find a way down the cliffside. It was a dry waterfall that fell into a dry lake. Ahead lay the mountains of Lastorum, with Adurak towering behind, but it was foggy in the dry lake. They had no idea how far they had to go, so they climbed back onto the horses and carefully guided them down.

As they reached the bottom, the haze instantly washed over them. They continued slowly on foot. There were eerie dead trees and a foul smell, but with the heavy fog surrounding them, they could not determine where the smell was coming from. They found an arrangement of large boulders where Sebastian demanded they stop for food and rest for the night.

"I can't go with you, Sebastian. To Adurak. The curse on that mountain will end me. But I promise I will be waiting in

Dunebar for your return. Know that I truly hope you find this man. I know you are destined for great things."

They ate in silence and when they finished, Sebastian laid his head back to get some sleep.

When Sebastian awoke, the fog still blanketed the dry lake. He yawned and stretched looking around to gather his direction.

"Jace?"

Silence.

"Jace, where are you?"

Silence. He walked around, looking for Jace, then noticed the horses were gone too.

"Jace?" He shouted.

Sebastian paced back and forth, turning his head in every direction. He sighed and shook his head. "You bastard, Jace," he snarled, then picked up his bag and continued.

As the day droned on, he grew tired and started murmuring to himself until he heard noises ahead. Through the thick haze, faces began appearing, and he saw carts filled with wares. Sebastian pulled his hood over his head and stepped into a bustling market. The people hurried back and forth to each merchant. Carts were filled with unusual weapons, strange herbs, and liquor bottles. As he kept his head down and continued moving forward, he heard the noise of business suddenly grow silent. He turned around and saw the faces staring at him, looking irritated and curious.

"Who are you, and what are you doing in the Moors?" The voice was deep and echoed across the market.

"I do not know anything about the Moors. I am just passing through on my way to Adurak," Sebastian said.

"Just passing through he says." The man laughed. "To Adurak, he says. Boy, no one goes into Adurak uninvited."

"Who says I was not invited?" Sebastian snarled.

The man next to the cart filled with axes and hammers stepped toward him. Sebastian stood firm before a young, black-haired man came and stood by his side. "He was invited by me."

Sebastian's eyes darted to Dani.

"Leave him alone, Cassius." Dani stepped between them. "He is my friend. We got separated by the fog."

"Keep an eye on him, Dani. He has a smart mouth that will get him killed around here."

Dani nodded, then grabbed Sebastian's arm. "Come with me."

Dani stared down the merchants as he passed by, clutching Sebastian's arm. "You shouldn't have come here alone. You are a stranger in these lands, and this place is dangerous."

"What is this place?" Sebastian said.

"The Moors. It is also called the fog market, but people say "The Moors" in passing because it is a swamp. No one wants to visit a swamp. So here we are."

Dani led Sebastian into a shabby-looking tent occupied by men lying naked with women. Others bustled about, serving the men drinks, food, and pleasure.

Sebastian's stomach tightened and his heartbeat fast. "Why did you bring me in here?"

"You are welcome." Dani held his hand and led him over to a couch. "Why are you in The Moors? Don't you know this place is hidden in the fog for a reason?"

"I did not know it was here." Sebastian Looked around quickly. "I need to move on. How do I get out?"

"You should wait until the fog lifts. It is just another day or two. Don't worry. I will keep an eye on you." Dani put his hand on Sebastian's chest. "Just sit down and relax. I won't tell anyone who you are. You will be safer that way."

Dani expected him to argue, but Sebastian sat on the couch while keeping his eyes locked on his face. He noticed that the other workers kept glancing over at him.

"Dani, you are being requested," the bartender said.

"Stay right here,' Dani said. "You cannot go until the fog lifts. If you continue, you will walk into the swamp. If you slip up in the swamp, you die."

"Where are you going?" Sebastian asked.

Dani stared at Sebastian, then smiled. "It will just be a moment. I promise."

He walked over to the bar. The bartender pointed to a corner where a sheet hung open. A man who resembled an Altanian soldier sat on the cot watching him. Dani stepped over, looked back at Sebastian, then closed the curtain.

Sebastian peeked through the slightly open door. He saw a man who appeared to be a soldier talking to Dani.

"You are a beautiful little boy," the man said. "Come over here and give me a kiss."

Dani smiled and crawled onto the bed and kissed him. Big hands gripped his upper arms, throwing him on his back. He banged his head on the edge of the post next to the bed and winced/ The soldier pinned Dani's hands with one fist n while tearing at Dani's clothes with the other.

The soldier stopped and lifted him onto his knees by his hair. "It would be a lot easier if you didn't fight."

"Let go of my arm, and I will help you. You hurt me." Dani reached for his head again.

"Get over it, pretty. Now be a good boy and do what I paid you to do." The man pulled down his pants.

Dani tightened his jaw but allowed the man to do whatever he wanted with him. The soldier moaned loudly and bit the back of Dani's neck while finishing. He shoved Dani away as he rolled off the cot to dress. Sebastian hurried over to the couch and waited.

Dani appeared through the curtain. His eyes were wet, and he was sweating.

Dani hurried toward Sebastian but was stopped when a man grabbed ahold of his arm. "You. Now."

"Easy. Let me go, you big, hairy beast of a man." Dani pulled away.

The man wrapped his meaty fist around Dani's throat and threw him against a table.

"Stop fighting me, boy or I will strangle you after I fuck you," the man said.

Sebastian took his axe in hand and swung it back, prepared to intervene. The man let out a loud growl as Dani laid back with his hand gripped on the man's crotch. The man let out a wheeze and crouched over.

"You need to learn that when I say no, I mean no," Dani said. His voice was calm, and his eyes remained fixed on the man. "I will not tolerate being hit, pushed, or threatened. Now take your ugly backside out of this tent and do not come back in, or I will rip your balls off and send you home with them in a box. Do you understand?"

"Yes." The man trembled.

"Now apologize."

The man stuttered and started to back away. Dani's hand clasped into a fist as the man squealed. "I said apologize. Now."

"I am sorry."

"Say, I am sorry I am a disgusting pig with no manners." Dani's face was bright red.

"I'm a disgusting pig with no manners. I am sorry. Please don't crush my goods. My wife would have my head."

Dani pulled his arm back. "Get out."

The man dashed away, tripping at the door as he passed Sebastian.

"Stop staring," Dani yelled at the people in the tent.

Sebastian reached out to take his hand. "Are you alright?"

"I am fine." Dani jumped off the table and pushed Sebastian onto the couch. "Play along, okay?"

"What?"

Dani sat on Sebastian's lap. "Put your arms around my back. Make it look like you want me."

"Maybe I do want you." Sebastian wrapped his arms around Dani and pulled him close. "But not like this. I could never—"

"You could never be with a whore." Dani blushed. "I am not asking you to have sex with me. I am just exhausted. Although, if you wanted me, you could have me. This is my life."

"It doesn't have to be," Sebastian said. "I don't know what has come over me, but I cannot take my eyes off you."

Dani leaned inward with his mouth close to Sebastian's. "If you want to be with me tonight, I will be everything you will ever desire again. No one ever said a man like you can't have whores in his bed." Dani quivered as Sebastian kissed his neck. Then Sebastian pulled back.

"Dani, I can't do this. I have to go." Sebastian sat Dani on the couch and stood. He started backing toward the entrance.

"Your Majesty, wait." Dani quickly covered his mouth. His eyes grew wide. The entire room stopped and stared at Sebastian. "I'm sorry. It just slipped out."

"I have to go," Sebastian said.

"Will I see you again?"

"Yes. I promise you will." Sebastian kissed Dani's cheek and backed out of the tent.

Sebastian stopped in the middle of the market and turned back to the tent. He felt guilty for leaving Dani in there. "I will come back for you," he whispered and continued on his journey.

CHAPTER 11
Mosisle Dur

It was dark, and the fog was thin. The putrid scent of the swamp was overwhelming. Sebastian watched his every step as he passed bubbling pools of liquid that sprayed yellow foam. He glanced down to see bones sticking up and what seemed to be melted flesh floating on the surface. As he wondered, he started feeling tired and dizzy. The fumes from the orange water were stifling. He found himself stumbling off the path several times, going in the wrong direction of the mapped pathway, and trying to figure out which way was correct. "It all looks the same." He gasped.

A bird flew down before him and landed softly in his path. He stopped and watched it as it stared at the liquid. The bird didn't move or make a sound. Sebastian knelt, waiting for it to break its gaze. As he shifted his position, the bird leaped and flew over the moors toward a haze softly hidden by fog. The bird crowed as it passed over him once more. He halted suddenly on the edge of a pool he almost stepped into.

Sebastian looked down and shouted when he saw a face looking back at him. He fell back, and crawled to his knees to see if it really was a person. It was only a rock tucked just below the surface. He felt the ground spin as he stood, and he colors of the water began to change. Sebastian felt his head swim, realizing he was crawling on his hands and knees.

He saw the edge of the moors and dragged himself toward it until he found rocky ground again. Ahead he spied the sharp pointing mountains hidden by the orange glow of sunset. Sebastian sat and stared until he drifted into a deep sleep. Cyrus entered his dreams, lying in Sebastian's arms on the beach as they told each other stories of their past and reminisced about the day they first met.

His dreams changed to him ruling on the throne of Alta Prime with Cyrus by his side. Erras appeared as a dark land where the sun never shined. The people were in chains, starving and bleeding, while his family was outcast to Khan Khar as traitors. He was the evil the prophecy spoke of and ruled heavy-handed as a ruthless tyrant. The people rebelled and invaded the palace, where he watched them rip Cyrus apart. Sebastian snapped awake, sweating and shaking.

Late the following day, Sebastian came to the foot of a vast mountain range. He checked the map where a mark lay brighter than the other mountains. It showed a peak with two points, one higher than the other. The name Mosisle Dur was written in bright red ink, and under it had a small note scrawled that read It's on the other side.

Sebastian tilted his head to the side, read the map again, and looked up at the massive mountain that waited. "What is on the other side?" He shook his head and climbed.

Mosisle Dur was steep and jagged. The dry, sandy rocks became slick as snow mixed into the mud. He sloshed his feet through the paste until the ground turned cold. He rested on a tall boulder that dangled gracefully over the mountain's edge. The icy winds froze his face and made his hands ache.

He came to the face of the mountain where the path ended, and there was a jagged rock towering above. The summit was close, but the snow was thick, and the cold was bitter. Any sign of an entrance did not show. The rocks against the split peaks were solid. No caves, no doorways, just the steely gray of stone. Sebastian checked the map again, feeling a twisting pain in his stomach upon reading the inscription again.

"It is on the other side. Wait, the entrance is on the other side?" He said aloud. Sebastian craned his neck and wandered around the peak where a narrow trail lay against the side of the slope. He flattened his body and hugged the mountain as he shimmied his feet side to side. It was dry but bone-chilling, with gusty air swirling around. When the summit turned to the back side, a thrashing thunderstorm appeared to be rolling in fast from the black sea that sat below the peak.

Sebastian faced Mosisle Dur again and looked up. A dark opening showed clear on the next landing, only a few feet above his head. He turned back to the sea in time for the rushing storm to slam into The Creed. Rain and snow streamed angrily from the clouds. "Of course," Sebastian said and turned to the mountain again. He dug his nails into the rocks and pulled himself up, careful with each move as the storm slammed against his back. Every time he took his hand away from the mountain, the rain and ice nipped at his fingertips. He ignited a fire in his hand and slammed his grip into the next step until he reached the flat ground where the opening sat empty.

The door looked threatening with the skeletons of birds, goats, and men scattered on the ground. A musty smell breathed from the mountain. He slowly reached his hand toward the archway, remembering being told how people were incinerated as they attempted to enter through the enchantments. With bated breath, he closed his eyes and pushed his arm through. He felt a hot tingling sensation on his skin, then pulled back, noticing his arm remained unharmed.

"I really am cursed, aren't I?" He said aloud, then stepped forward, allowing his entire body to slip through the spell.

Everything inside him lit up, prickling uncomfortably, but then a loud crackle erupted, and a pop made it clear the magic had been broken. Along the dark hall there were old torches that had never been lit. Sebastian ignited a fire in his fist, took a torch, and set the fabric on fire. The light brought a dismal picture of charred bones from those who died trying to enter or escape.

Sebastian walked into the room where there sat a deep crevasse in the center. He dropped the torch to see how far it fell, but the light disappeared into blackness. With another torch in hand, Sebastian descended the stairway around the ravine's edge. He passed by cell doors, looking into each one, wondering if anyone else was still locked inside. There were bones of deceased inmates in some. A few doors were open, and some broke open. He saw claw marks along the walls like something had tried to claw its way out.

The descent was exhausting, but he reached solid ground and faced one solitary cell door. He approached it slowly, peering into the space, but the darkness made it difficult to see if anyone was alive inside.

"Are you there?" He asked.

No one answered.

"Sorcerer, are you alive?"

No answer.

Sebastian was irritated. He came all this way for a dead man. He balled his fist as flashes of lightning cracked from his hands, then punched the wall. "Answer me! I know you are there."

"Ahh. There is the voice of a man who is vile enough to enter Mosisle Dur and live to tell the tale."

Sebastian's head snapped toward the voice. "So you are alive. I am here to bust you out. Let's go."

"How do you think you will manage to get my cell open? I do not have a key."

"I thought you were the sorcerer," Sebastian said.

"My brother would not have me locked in a cell that I can escape from. Sorcery will not open these doors."

"What makes you think I know how to break out of prison? I was a king in my former land, not a criminal." Sebastian gripped the bars in his fists. "I came to find you. I need your help."

There were footsteps on the cell floor. "You must be Chaos. I've heard of you."

"How would you know about me? You have been here."

"I learned of your story nineteen years ago. Just before I was locked in here. Stories like yours travel far. Twins born to bear the gift of the gods. Everyone in Midrel Istan knows who Chaos is, but now they have a face to put with a name."

Sebastian backed away. "I don't want anyone to know."

"Your Highness, they must know. I will tell you everything you need to know in good time, but first you have to break me free."

"I don't know how to do that."

"Where is the map?" The sorcerer's hand showed through the bars.

"How did you know I have a map?" Sebastian reached for his pack.

"You must have a map to get here and there was only one map to Mosisle Dur ever made. It was kept in the archives in Altania since this prison was designed for me and my following. There used to be ten of us."

"One of my men had this map in his possession. He never went to Altania..." Sebastian suddenly paused. "Cyrus," he whispered.

The sorcerer turned his head sharply and came close to Sebastian through the bars. "You need to get me out of here, now." He reached for Sebastian's shoulders. "On the map is a spell. Only a god can read it. There are only two gods in the whole world and it's my lucky day that one appeared before me with a map."

Sebastian grinned and looked over the map. "Is it this here?" He pointed to the corner of the page.

"I cannot see it," the sorcerer said. "Only a god can read it. Just try it, boy!"

"Fine, calm down." Sebastian straightened his back. "It says twenty knots and thirty-three clicks." There was a loud pop and dust filled the air. Sebastian laughed. "Wow. What the hell?"

"Continue," the sorcerer said. His weathered face seemed to brighten in the dark cave.

"From the wings of birds as dark as night, a curse will break, and the birds take flight."

Sebastian felt a pain in his gut so powerful, it drove him to his knee. He gasped for a breath and screamed. It felt as if his body was on fire. He couldn't catch his breath. The dizziness made him fall over. He clutched his chest, and his head spun. The bars of the cell turned to vapor and the smoke vanished as quickly as it came. The sorcerer stepped from the cell for the first time in nineteen years, stood over Sebastian, scooped him up over his shoulder and began their ascent Sebastian drifted into a deep sleep.

CHAPTER 12
When Love Still Burns Deep Inside

Before the summer solstice, Cyrus took trips into the far western corners of Feldor Bay, meeting with Altanian merchants in old, dusty taverns on the forest edge. As he sat at the bar on a cold, rainy night, a short and fat man flopped down in a chair next to him.

"What do you want to know about the Altanian king?" The man's voice was shrouded by phlegm and bits of coughing.

"I hear he is not a kind man," Cyrus said. "I need an audience with him. I hear you know him personally."

"Yes," the man said. "Let's just say he and I go back years."

"Tell me how to get into Altania unscathed."

"Arrive in the bazaar and find a small shop at the foot of the palace. It has a tiny symbol carved above the door that looks like a sun. If the soldiers ask, tell them Fenton Paark sent you."

When he left the beach, Cyrus rode through Feldor Bay
without a thought in his head even as Meecah attempted to
wave him down. He continued west in search of the city of
Altania. He stopped at the bridge over the bay to wash the
blood from his hands. Cyrus stared at his reflection as the
water turned from clear to red. The look in Sebastian's eyes,
the innocence and beauty Cyrus saw replayed in his mind
over and over. He splashed water on his face and continued
on his mission to speak to the king.

He released his horse among the crowds of the early
morning bazaar as onlookers stared at him curiously. The
smell of spices and perfumes stung his nostrils, and the
bright colors of clothing and wares held his curiosity about
the strange place he found himself in. His mission was simple
enough. Find a ship to sail to Erras and a crew he could buy.
Cyrus entered a small establishment on the end of the
winding road where a woman with long blue hair waited.

She smiled at him with adoration. "Young Prince Cyrus.
You sure have grown up to be quite handsome."

Cyrus shook his head. "Have we met?"

"You don't remember your cousin Petra? I am offended."
She laughed.

"Petra?" He grabbed her shoulder. "I don't even
remember my parents. They died when I was three."

"I see. Shall we go see the king?" Petra walked through a
door in the back of the building.

Cyrus followed without question into the passageway
and down the hall. They walked through an oak door and
entered a narrow hall with high ceilings. Petra shooed away
nervous maidens that came to greet them as they passed.

"Keep up," she sang, walking faster.

Cyrus tried taking everything in as he hurried to catch
up. He stumbled upon entering a giant hall that had ceilings
higher than any castle he had been in, including his brother's
palace in Alta Prime. The stained glass showed pictures of sea
creatures in battle with merpeople. The archways depicted

men with various weapons fighting a war against a Kraken. Cyrus halted at a painting hanging above a set of oak doors. It showed the house sigils from all the rulers of Erras.

The griffin, for House Bolin of Torrdale. The lion, for House Bolin of Alta Prime, which was burned. The owl, for House Astra of Oyster Cove. The horse, for House LaBeaux of Safareen, and finally, the dragon, for House Drake of NorthBrekka. Cyrus heard a whistle which snapped his attention to the large set of doors that were opened by soldiers. He entered the throne room and saw an old man wearing a gold crown waiting.

"Welcome, Cyrus. Come forward and let me look at my nephew."

"You are—"

"Your father's brother. Your Uncle Maxen."

"My uncle? I didn't know I had any family left anywhere." Cyrus stared at the ground. "I thought I was alone."

"You have no idea who you are, do you, Cyrus?" Maxen sat up straight. "I guess your father would be to blame for abandoning you all, but yes, you have family in Midrel Istan."

"Is that why you have the sigils of Erras in the hall? You are from there." Cyrus kneeled.

"Correct. I came to Midrel Istan long before your father and mother."

Cyrus stared at Maxen oddly. "Are my parents alive?"

"Your mother died at sea. Your father was…lost a long time ago."

"Why did they leave Erras? They left us, my brothers and me. Why?" Cyrus felt his face get hot.

Maxen looked at Petra, who was pacing in front of a window. "They wanted to return for you, but they didn't quite make it, did they?"

Cyrus shook his head. "I need a ship and a crew to return to Erras."

"Running away from Chaos, are we?" Petra snarled. "You are better off on his good side than the other way around."

Cyrus walked toward her. "If Sebastian becomes the Dragon, we are all in danger. There will be terrible wars everywhere. We all know the stories. But I don't think he deserves to die. He just needs to be stopped."

"Leave Chaos to me," Maxen said. "I know how to break down a god. Our ancestors have destroyed the line of the Dragon for centuries. That time has come for us Bolins to rise once more."

"Sebastian should be my responsibility. I know his weaknesses." Cyrus wandered over to a wall of scrolls.

"Lovers." Maxen smiled. "You failed to run a dagger through his heart. It is clear you can only be used for one thing. To torture the boy, which makes me question why you are leaving when you are so useful against him?"

"How did you know I stabbed him?"

"I have eyes everywhere."

Cyrus sighed. "I don't want any part of this anymore. I want to find out more about who I am and maybe build my empire from the ground up. I just want peace." Cyrus looked up to see soldiers on the rafters, pacing, just as soldiers paroled the streets, guarding doorways, and lined the halls within the palace. Maxen's men were everywhere. His hand glided across a row of dusty old parchment before landing on one that was labeled Valirus Bolin. Out of the corner of his eye, he saw Petra pestering a bird that sat on the windowsill while Maxen drank wine from a golden cup. Cyrus slipped the scroll into his shirt. "So, about a ship."

"Give it a day, nephew. In the meantime, why don't you go for a walk? Enjoy the feel of grass before returning to sea." Maxen gestured toward the doors.

That afternoon, Cyrus walked outside of the town toward a tree line where a narrow bridge crossed the bay into the eastern territory. He stared into the fast-flowing water and watched the fish swim in and out of the cattails. He walked down to the shore, kicked his boots off, and soaked his feet in the warm saltwater.

"So, you've been hiding from Sebastian in Altania."

Cyrus jumped to his feet and looked around fast until he saw a movement under the bridge trusses. "Jace?"

Jace moved along a wooden walkway that snapped and popped, sending shards of debris into the bay. He climbed down to the same shoreline Cyrus waited upon.

"Have you seen him since… it happened?" Cyrus rubbed his chest.

"No. When you screamed at me to run, I found my way here. I had no idea it was Altania until a group of guards nearly caught me. I have been sleeping under the bridge since." Jace tousled his hair and straightened his clothes. "Why are you in an enemy country?"

"That enemy is my uncle," Cyrus said. "I am leaving, Jace. I am going home." He reached into his shirt and pulled out the scroll. "I saw this in Maxen's castle. I think this might be the map Sebastian needs to find the teacher. If he is alive, please ensure it reaches his hand."

"Why are you giving me this?" Jace looked at the parchment.

"I have to go, Jace. Take that to Sebastian." Cyrus backed away and left in a rush, ignoring Jace's questions and shouts.

The following morning, Cyrus boarded a ship and departed for Erras. On the night of the last day of autumn, he watched a speck on the horizon become too familiar. The city of Safareen lay in the desert of southern Erras.

The castle sat directly in the center of a massive township that was filled with bazaars of all kinds. Some for food, some for jewelry and clothing, and others for whores and gambling. The people dressed in as little as possible in the hot southern desert. The women wore dresses that barely concealed their breasts, and the men wore just a thin wrap around their waists. Cyrus smiled as he took in the sight of muscular guards lining the interior of the castle. He spotted

Lorna, former Queen of Alta Prime poking out from a doorway. "I need to speak to your brother."

"You don't give orders here, Prince Cyrus," Lorna said.

"I am well aware of my position here, but King Lucian would be angry if I fail to relay information from Midrel Istan." Cyrus walked past Lorna and straight into the throne room.

"Prince Cyrus, it has been years," King Lucian said.

Lucian was the youngest of the LeBeaux siblings but was chosen to rule due to his kill records. Of all his brothers, he had killed the most men. He was only sixteen years old, yet his demeanor was cold. The Safar groomed boys to be emotionless, so they do not fight with their hearts in battle. Lucian was no exception. A girl stood nervously in the corner, watching Cyrus from the corner of her eyes.

"That is Elessi. She is my wife," Lucian said.

Cyrus sighed. "Do you understand what we are facing if King Sebastian returns from Midrel Istan?"

"The Dragon, God of Fire, Chaos, king, heathen. He means nothing," Lucian said.

"You say that when he is on another continent. Once he stands before you, your heart will change." Cyrus sat down at a table. "If he comes, he will sail to NorthBrekka, gather his army, and rip Safareen to pieces. Your best hope is for my uncle, Maxen, to kill him before he leaves Midrel Istan."

Lorna sat down next to Cyrus. "Sebastian is up against one of the most dangerous men in the world along with his daughter, the empress."

Cyrus shook his head and laughed. "If he found the teacher, it would be over for all of us. No one can defeat the Dragon."

"That isn't true," Lorna said. "Have you ever heard of the Blackbirds?"

"No."

Lorna held up a kettle. "Would you like some tea?"

Cyrus's face turned hot. "I do not want tea."

CHAPTER 13
The Fortress of Lastorum

Sebastian woke up with the chill of winter in the air. Smoke drifted whimsically across his nose from an incense on the bedside table in his small, dark room. There was a lantern lit that hung from a hook on a door. He had no recollection of taking himself back to Dunebar or anywhere outside the prison. In the fireplace, embers began to wear down to ash. Sebastian sat up and tossed the blanket aside. He was drenched in sweat, and his skin was molten.

The sound of a chair creaking came from the corner. "I put clothes on the table for you in case you decided to wake up."

Sebastian fell back onto the bed, then noticed he was completely naked. He snatched the blanket over himself.

"Relax. I undressed you before. It is not like I have never seen a naked man. I have three sons, after all."

Sebastian sat up. "Who are you?"

The man was older but well-kept. Handsome with a striking facial structure and neatly cut gray hair. His brown eyes were familiar, but Sebastian stared at him oddly.

"My dear boy. You don't recognize the man you rescued? I suppose after a few weeks, one would forget. That was quite a show you put on in that mountain."

"Sorcerer?" Sebastian squinted. "Did you say a few weeks?"

"Valirus. My name is Valirus. You have been asleep for many days and nights. I would awaken you to feed you and bathe you, but you probably don't remember."

"What happened?"

"Fire and wind burst from your body with fury," Valirus said. "It was magnificent. You are truly special, Sebastian. Extraordinary."

"Can you help me control it?"

"All in good time. Rest. Once you are feeling up to it, get dressed and meet me on my terrace."

Valirus left the room. Sebastian laid back on the bed, thinking about going back to sleep. He shot up again and slowly shook as he climbed out of bed and dressed. As he looped his belt around him, he saw the sword he was gifted by Aspen back in The Far North. A grin crossed his lips as he thought about being yelled at to make a fire in the fireplace.

In the corridor, the walls were lined with torches. The stonework was intricate and led Sebastian to an open room that went deep into a cavern. Only a few young men and ladies bustled about. Guards surveyed the halls in pairs. The walkway was slightly damp from the drip of the rocks in the ceiling. The fortress was built inside a cave which had Sebastian intrigued. A light came from across the room that invited Sebastian into the bright sunlight onto a balcony where Valirus patiently sat on a stone bench, nibbling on some berries.

"Good. You decided to get up."

"Where am I?" Sebastian said.

"This is Lastorum. This is my home. It is between Dunebar and Adurak on the eastern coast, near the Sea of Glass." Valirus paused for a moment and chewed on a blueberry. "I want to first say how much I appreciate you finding me. Many have tried, but all failed. I worried my sons would come. They are not gifted in magic. They would have died."

Sebastian shrugged. "Where are your sons?"

"I am unsure. It has been a long time since I have seen them. Are you prepared to begin your training?"

"Yes, but first, I want to find out where Cyrus went. He is... I mean, he was my lover. He betrayed me. I need to find him."

Valirus's head shot up and his eyes widened. "Cyrus? You said that name before. Is he from Erras as well?"

Sebastian stared at Valirus for a moment. His mind raced but he nodded. "Yes. From Torrdale." Sebastian paused and paced for a moment. "He had been cursed by a witch. The enemy uses him like a weapon against me."

"Cursed, you say. Shame." Valirus scratched his chin and bit his lip. "Does he have any family in Erras that can protect him?"

Sebastian narrowed his eyes and tilted his head. "No. His parents are dead, and his brothers have also passed. He is alone."

"How awful." Valirus sat back and held his hand against his chest. "For now, you will train. You are Chaos, and you will learn the potential of your powers. Only once you have mastered your skills can you return home. But first, you need a place to call home. This will not be quick."

"Am I not training here?"

"Absolutely not. Do you think I would let you destroy my home? No, I have a place for you nearby, but it is not ready yet." Valirus handed him a book. "Read this front to back. It will open your mind to what is expected of you. Once you are finished, your home will be ready. Now go away."

Sebastian took the book, read the title, and looked at Valirus with a frustrated look. "Demon Gods and Their

Tyranny Over the Years." He snapped his head up fast. "Are you serious?"

"Just read it."

Sebastian squinted at Valirus before walking away to his room. He fell onto his bed, looked at the book, rolled his eyes, and began reading. As he worked through the chapters, his attitude went from annoyed to intrigued. To Sebastian, being considered a demon god was insulting but there it was, clear as day. A chapter titled Chaos, God of Fire.

After days of reading passed, Sebastian closed the book. He went to find Valirus, who was again relaxing on his terrace, sipping tea, and smoking a pipe. He smirked upon seeing Sebastian step into the sun.

"I wondered how long it would take before you would emerge from that room. It was starting to smell, and the maidens began to worry."

"You said to read the book. I read the book. Now what?"

"Did you learn anything?" Valirus stared at him with a smile on his face.

"Only that I am everything they say about me." Sebastian looked over the edge. The fortress sat to the east of the dry lake. He could see a hint of a town far across the desert.

"That was not the lesson, Sebastian." Valirus stood by his side. "Are you dense?"

"My father tried hard to hide me from the world and it took me years to understand why. He was murdered for covering my secret. Now the world wants revenge for a crime my ancestor committed. I am doomed by my prophecy, but I need you to teach me to use my powers so I can be good. I don't want to kill everyone."

The time finally arrived for Sebastian to discover the home Valirus had created for him. He donned the most refined leather money could buy, strapped on his sword, and found the quiver Dom had given him years before. He sat on the edge of the bed and ran his hand over the shaft on the bow, remembering how Dom had loved him even through all the horrible things he was destined to become. He threw the bow over his shoulder and hurried to find Valirus again.

Horses waited outside, and they set off on a new adventure.

CHAPTER 14
City of Thieves

Sebastian followed behind Valirus under a wide-spread stone arch that connected mountains. The road led up a steep hill that looked out over a village at the base of the range. The town was alive with merchants selling their wares while children played in the street. To Sebastian, it was as normal as any city he had seen.

"It is a treat to see this valley full of life again. It is all because of you. You gave them hope," Valirus said.

"What did I do? I have never been here."

Valirus stopped and pulled Sebastian's hood over his head. "Do not let them see you yet."

Sebastian raised his eyebrows, sighed, and followed him into the marketplace. The people stopped to stare and greet Valirus. Past the market was a set of taverns across from each other with men of all kinds passing back and forth. Fights erupted as a man was thrown through the door of a pub called, The Golden Mace. The horses became spooked. Sebastian and Valirus jumped down as the men became violent, with others began joining in on the brawl.

Bottles shattered against walls and men's heads. Knives soared across the alley that stuck into the door of the other tavern, Fat Angry Crow. At least ten rugged and vile-looking men shoved each other and spat curses at one another. The people of the market gathered behind Sebastian and children peeked out from behind grown-ups' legs. A sword sliced through the air, nearly grazing him as he realized he stood too close to the battle. The noise and commotion rang between the buildings as a pair of men slammed into Sebastian.

Valirus stepped into the circle and shouted, "Everyone kneel in the name of your king!"

Suddenly, the entirety of the city screeched to silence, and the people fell to their knees and bowed. Sebastian thought the men knelt before Valirus. Then he saw Valirus take a slight bow.

"No. Absolutely not." Sebastian shook his head.

"Ladies and gentlemen, it warms my heart to see this old city burst at its seams with gallant and strong souls. Once there was no place on these lands for the likes of this crowd to live without persecution. Criminals, thieves, and mercenaries alike, welcome home to Adurak, the City of Thieves." Valirus turned to Sebastian and removed his hood. "And what good is a valiant kingdom without the most powerful king the world has ever known? Dear people of Adurak, I give you King Sebastian Drake. Chaos, God of Fire."

He backed away to let the people take in the image of their new king. All eyes shot to Sebastian. He did not want speeches or attention and turned his watch to Valirus.

"How could you do this to me? I said no." Sebastian walked away in the direction of a large fountain and suddenly halted before an enormous structure soaring into the mountains.

"Your castle, Your Majesty. Moonlight Castle. Named for the majestic shimmer of the moon as it rises over The Creed and casts its fantastic glow over Adurak. You deserve this." Valirus pushed Sebastian into the entrance of his new palace. "Oh, and I have one more gift for you." Valirus clapped twice.

From around a corner came a face that Sebastian knew well.

"Jace. What is he doing here?" Sebastian grabbed Jace by the collar. "Why are you here?"

"Valirus informed me you will need someone to assist you while transitioning to your new position. I am here to serve you once again, Your Highness."

Sebastian gritted his teeth. "You betrayed me. Twice now!"

"I did no such thing. I was told to get you to the lake and go no further. I did my job."

"I needed you."

"For what?" Jace threw his hands in the air. "The great Sebastian Drake needs no one. He is almighty and powerful. Chaos, God of Fire, God of Fury."

"That just proves my point that I do not need your assistance. Now go away."

Valirus let out a chuckle and disappeared to another room, leaving Sebastian and Jace alone. The atrium was bright and warm, and the sun shone from a large gap in the ceiling, all the way up four stories, and to the outside. A thick webbing of roots disappeared into the stone floors, holding a massive, large leafy tree that grew through the opening.

Sebastian felt something tickle his palm. Jace blushed and wore a boyish grin as he ran his fingertips across the back of Sebastian's hand. "Don't." Sebastian continued forward, taking in the wonders of his new castle.

Trees and flowers bloomed from a garden that fed from the stream that flowed through the center of the atrium, from the mountains to the east, and to an edge that drew Sebastian's attention. He followed the creek to the end of a balcony. He took a deep breath, looking out into the vast desert that lay to the west, separated by a wide, rocky gorge. The stream turned into a wispy waterfall that fell into a river at the bottom of a ravine. The castle was open, with walls that stood only where needed to support the high ceilings above.

"This is incredible," Sebastian whispered.

"It is all yours. Everything. This castle, this city, and me. Anything you want will be yours. All you have to do is say the word." Jace wrapped his arms around Sebastian's waist.

Sebastian pulled Jace's arms apart and freed himself from his grip. "Go away," he said sternly before marching up the stairs to find his bedroom.

His room was set above the waterfall with a balcony expanding far over the canyon. The fireplace roared next to a table and a large soft bed that Sebastian fell into. He drifted into a restful sleep.

The sound of coyotes echoed, waking Sebastian from his dreams. He rubbed his face and dragged his feet to the terrace. The sky was a deep shade of gray with a hint of light coming from behind the mountains. Sebastian noticed clothing on the table and a letter.

Jace burst through the door. "Valirus is waiting downstairs." Jace was startled at the sight. "I am sorry, Your Majesty. I did not realize you weren't dressed." He kept staring at Sebastian's body. "Do you need help?"

Sebastian kept his eyes locked on the letter. His voice was deep and gargled. "Get out."

I know I cannot convince you to wear the crown, so dress and come meet me. You have no idea how important you are. We start training as soon as you decide you are willing to learn. -Valirus

Sebastian rolled his eyes, then dressed quickly before heading downstairs. Valirus smiled without turning to notice Sebastian was standing by his side. They wandered through the halls and corridors slowly, taking in the castle's beauty with every step, finally coming across a throne. Sebastian sat for a moment, then quickly stood.

"It is your birthright to sit there," Valirus said. "You will learn it is not so bad in the City of Thieves. These people are mercenaries at your beck and call. The most violent and dangerous men and women on the planet—"

"Enough. When do we start training?"

"Come with me." Valirus sighed and walked quickly outside. Sebastian followed, assuming it was another one of Valirus's attempts to prove that Adurak was everything he desired in a home.

They walked toward the mountains without a word. Sebastian looked back to notice Jace following at a distance. At a path cut between two high peaks, Valirus halted and turned.

"This is the foot of The Creed. These mountains have sheltered the discarded dissidents of this world. Have a look around."

Sebastian saw the jagged, rocky hills that towered over the meadow. He followed the range from the southeast, all the way around to the base of the gateway.

"Do you see what The Creed represents?" Valirus said.

"It looks like Adurak is being embraced."

"Correct. The Creed has been the most feared territory in all of Midrel Istan. Not only is it treacherous, but those who reside in these hills know nothing but pain. The King of Men has taken everything they have. He stripped them of any trace of honor and exiled them to these desolate lands where they had to steal and fight for a meal, hence why Adurak is known as the City of Thieves."

Sebastian looked around again. "What do they want from me?"

"This city has not seen rain in quite some time. It would help the farmers out tremendously if it did. Sebastian, bring in the rain from the sea."

"Excuse me?" Sebastian spun around. "And how do you propose I do that?"

Valirus waved his hands in the air. "I am not an elemental. You are. Figure it out."

"My brother, Tomas, is the god of water. Not me."

Valirus rubbed his forehead, then turned to Jace. "Is he always so argumentative?"

Jace let out a snort of laughter. "Always."

"I said to conjure the rain from the sea."

"I do not know how!" Sebastian felt his face get hot.

"Because you do not try. Conjure the rain!" Valirus snapped.

"I do not even know where the damn sea is!"

"Use your intuition, boy. You have senses others do not. Try harder."

Sebastian stood silent with his eyes closed. He took a deep breath and felt a cool breeze come from behind him. He focused on the smell that passed through his nose and noticed the scent change. He opened his eyes, then jumped back. "Jace! What are you doing?"

Jace was inches from him. "Do you feel anything? You were making some odd faces."

"Anger. Back away, Jace."

Valirus gripped his staff tight, then swatted Jace. "It is not the time. Give him space. Sebastian, try again."

Sebastian closed his eyes again. He wrinkled up his forehead and his stomach began to burn. His heart raced at the familiar scent of salt water that filled his nostrils. "The sea is before me."

"Good. Keep reaching."

Sebastian dropped his arms. "I don't know what I am doing, sorcerer. This is pointless."

"It is not pointless to help your people." Valirus groaned. "Now stop being a child and do what you are meant to do."

"I told you—"

"You were born of fire and lightning. There are secrets buried beneath the dragon scales that burn under your skin. You are more dangerous than you will ever understand, and the blood of your kin protects you. The all-mighty King of Kings, and Chaos, God of Fire." Valirus put his hand on Sebastian's forehead. "You are the only one who can kill Maxen, King of Men. Born human, just like our ancestors, until a new era of magic and witchcraft emerged, my brother and I were the first sorcerers of Erras. Maxen's only mission is to destroy you so that he may rule as King of Kings. If you have even the slightest bit of hope to defeat him, you must unlock all your powers. All of them! This isn't just between you and him. This war is of ancient bounds and will remain until one of you dies. Do not let my brother win. Now, show me water!"

Valirus stepped back, releasing Sebastian, and gasped for air. Sebastian looked at Valirus, then Jace. His hands were trembling, his jaw hinged open, and heavy tears filled his eyes. He focused on the scent again. His arms reached out like wings and a strong gust of wind whipped from the pass, knocking him to the ground. Valirus and Jace had fallen over one another. Sebastian punched the dirt and stormed to the castle.

The next few days were quiet. Sebastian sat upright in his bed, staring out over the canyon. Jace offered him food and water, but Sebastian did not speak or eat. He heard Valirus shout from downstairs, "Are you alright, Your Majesty," every time Sebastian would throw a plate or a glass against the wall.

"Please, Sebastian, you must eat." Jace sat on the edge of the bed. "Talk to me. I am here for you."

"Get out." Sebastian choked out with a raspy voice.

"Seb—"

"Leave me alone, now!" Sebastian stood and screamed louder. "Get away from me. I don't want you in my life. Go far away and never come back."

"I am all you have left, Your Majesty!" Jace grabbed him by the shoulders. "Cyrus is gone. Maybe he still loves you, but for now, he has left Midrel Istan, and I am still here."

Sebastian's eyes narrowed. "How would you know Cyrus left?"

"When I ran away, I ran in one direction for days. I found water and stopped to soak my aching feet. I was asleep under the bridge when Cyrus came to the river. My heart nearly dropped into my stomach when I saw him." Jace paused. "I went to speak with him, and he gave me that map. The one that led you to Mosisle Dur. He stole it from the archives in Altania... for you."

Sebastian tried to catch his breath. He slapped his palm on his face and let out a scream. He marched over to the balcony, doubled over with a fiery pain in his chest, then fell to his knees. As the pain overtook him, it started raining. Valirus took notice, ran upstairs, and looked astonished as he saw Sebastian on the floor, locked in a stoical trance with his hand pointed toward the sky.

"You did it, Jace. You broke through. You released the beast within."

Jace knelt before him and bowed his head. "I did not want to hurt him, but he had to know the truth."

"He truly is the Dragon." Valirus looked around, seeing the lightning that cracked through the clouds.

Sebastian turned his palms up and raised his arms to the side as he sat on his knees, facing the ravine. Fire whipped from his hands and rocks lifted into the air from the canyon below their feet. "Please do not call me Dragon," Sebastian said calmly. "I don't like that."

Jace never left Sebastian's side as days turned to nights, seasons changed, and the world went on. Sebastian barely spoke. He ate enough to sustain himself and remained locked in his trance, but he knew he was never alone. Jace slept in Sebastian's bed every night, holding him tight so if Sebastian got up, Jace woke up.

After spring came and went, summer snuck by and Sebastian threatened Jace not to mention his birthday to anyone. Autumn arrived peacefully as Sebastian wandered Moonlight Castle. He stumbled upon a glimmer coming from the seat of the throne. It was of sharpened steel and gemstones. The voices of many came suddenly along with the clack of Valirus's staff against the stone floor. Sebastian turned and placed the crown upon his head and sat, fidgeting with a goblet on the table beside him. He gracefully flickered his fingers, making the water dance above the cup. He smiled and then noticed the townsfolk bowing to their king.

Once the last citizen sat down, Jace approached and knelt, then put his hands on Sebastian's knee. "Are you alright?"

Sebastian narrowed his eyes. "Why are you still here?"

Jace's chest bounced with his exaggerated laughter. "You can't get rid of me."

"I can do anything I want." Sebastian looked around until he locked his focus on Valirus.

"I need to get away from this place. I can't focus on my training, my purpose, or anything. I need something that can clear my mind." Sebastian stared around the room, looking for answers. His eyes stopped at an old man holding a young boy in his arms. The man wore a ripped jacket, dirty boots, and soot on his face. The boy was small, thin, and had bright blue eyes. Sebastian's mind eased when he thought of Dani.

He smiled and turned to look at Jace. He let out an amused huff and then got up to leave the throne room. Sebastian went to the balcony that overlooked the Creed Mountains. He heard the sound of the click clack coming rapidly.

"Not only do you run away from your people, but you come to my private space."

Sebastian spun around and raised his eyebrows. "This is my castle."

"I come out here every morning to calm myself before I have to deal with you and I have never once seen you standing here," Valirus said.

Sebastian shook his head. "When does the fog set on the Moors?"

Valirus's face scrunched up. "That is not the kind of place a man of your stature should be found lurking."

"I enjoy seeing new weapons, but that was not why I asked. There is a boy there. He is maybe twenty years old. I need to speak to him," Sebastian said.

"You can't go to the Moors alone. It is too dangerous now that—"

"I have been there alone." Sebastian was angry. "I was there alone. When I came to find you, I was alone. Jace abandoned me before the fog. Why do you think I am so angry with him now?"

"Jace did not have a choice." Valirus crossed his arms. "He would have died if he had followed you inside the mountain. That man is loyal to you. He will stand by you until the end if you let him. You will lose yourself if you run off chasing unicorns, Your Grace. You have a mission. Do not let the boy in the Moors distract you."

Sebastian stared at the ground as he shook his head. "I am going with or without your consent. I am the king. I make the decisions here, Valirus. All I asked of you was a question. When is the market open in the Moors?"

"It will open in three days. I know what you are doing. It is not only about the boy, is it? There is something more you seek in the fog," Valirus said.

"That is my business and mine alone. I will be riding north in the morning. I ask you to accompany me."

Valirus nodded. "We ride at dawn."

That night, Sebastian sat in his room sobbing with his face buried in his knees. He glanced up upon hearing footsteps coming into the room. Jace crouched down and placed logs in the fireplace.

"What are you doing in here?" Sebastian said.

"I was just making you a fire."

"I can make my own fire, Jace."

"I know. Let me do something for you, and saying thank you would be a nice change."

"Get out." Sebastian's voice was raspy and deep.

"No!" Jace stood quickly, dropping the rest of the wood onto the floor. "I took care of you for all those nights you fought me and screamed in your sleep. I fed you, bathed you, stayed by your side day and night to ensure you were safe, and all I got in return was being told to go away. I deserve some appreciation, dammit!"

"You want appreciation?" Sebastian grabbed Jace, dragged him over to the chaise, and threw him down. He got within inches of Jace, their lips nearly touching. "Do you want me?"

"Yes," Jace whispered, his lips trembling as he hoped Sebastian would kiss them.

"What is it that makes you want for me?"

"You are the only person who has ever cared about me," Jace said. "It feels so natural to be with you like we belong together. Back home, no one ever paid me any attention. My father always shouted at me if I were seen. But you…" He blushed and sat back against the wall. "Do you ever stop to think that maybe you and Cyrus weren't meant for each other. That maybe it was just lust."

Sebastian squinted his eyes. "You know nothing of love. You have never felt its cold, cruel knife in your heart."

"Every time you reject me, that is what I feel." Jace stroked Sebastian's chest and clawed at his face for a kiss.

Sebastian kissed Jace's neck. "Is this what you want, Jace?'

Jace whispered into his ear, "I want you to be mine."

Sebastian tore Jace's clothes off as he kissed and bit at his neck and shoulder. He jammed his hand around Jace's throat and squeezed. Jace struggled and clawed at Sebastian's hand. He managed to break free, then Sebastian slapped him hard on the cheek.

"Stop! Get off me. What is wrong with you?" Jace shoved him away. "You are being vile."

"This is who I am now. If you do not like it, go away when I tell you to."

Jace wrinkled his face from fear to anger, then broke Sebastian's grip on his neck. "Something poisons your mind. I love you, Sebastian, but I will not be treated like your pet."

Sebastian laughed, "What makes you think you are that important?"

Jace choked. "You are horrible! How could I have been so stupid to love a creature like you? You are not even a man. You are the—"

"Don't you dare say it, Jace."

"Dragon."

Sebastian jerked Jace from the lounge and threw him against the wall. "I will show you dragon." His fist burst into flames before he slammed it against the wall next to Jace's face.

Jace punched him hard in the jaw and broke free of Sebastian's grip. "You deserve to be alone. Cyrus left, not because his mind is messed up, but because of you."

Sebastian's jaw tightened. He took short breaths and tried to calm himself. "That was cruel," He whispered. "Come here, Jace."

Sebastian gripped him tight, and they fell back onto the lounge. Jace wiggled for only a moment, then laid his head back on Sebastian's chest. They stayed there in silence until the fire turned to ash.

"I love you, Sebastian." Jace fell asleep.

Sebastian wrapped himself around Jace and closed his eyes.

CHAPTER 15
The Moors Dark Secrets

Sebastian dressed before the sun peeked over The Creed. He made a fire and wrapped Jace in a blanket before scribbling a note.

Jace, I am leaving you in charge until my return. Forgive me for last night.

Sebastian, Valirus, and an accompaniment of soldiers rode north. The first night, they stayed in Lastorum. Valirus called Sebastian to his balcony, where they had first spoken about beginning training.

"You still have so much to learn. Your training is critical, and you are running out of time. This side quest had better be worth it. Why is this boy so important?"

Sebastian took a deep breath. "Because if anyone in the world deserves to live a free life, it is him. He is forced to work in a brothel. There is something about him that makes me feel clear. It is like I can do anything when he is near me. Plus, he saved my life. I owe this to him."

Valirus shot a look at Sebastian. "Who is this boy? Where is he from?"

"Again, that is my business." Sebastian narrowed his eyes.

"You are going to take him to Adurak? You have a war to fight. If you take him, you will condemn him to death," Valirus said.

"Perhaps not. He isn't weak. I have seen him stand up to a man twice my size."

Valirus nodded his head without a word.

The fog ahead on the dry lake was thick like a pile of blankets. The path through the swamp was as horrible as Sebastian remembered.

"Dead animals, human limbs, and fresh blood on the ground. Bodies lay naked in the acid water that will kill us if we slip or fall into its orange and blue water. This tells me that the Moors used the dense fog to cover up something evil. Killing is not unusual, but this was a massacre," Valirus said.

Sebastian sped up. "We are taking too long. If something terrible has happened, I need to get there and find Dani."

"Dani?" Valirus stopped suddenly. He stared at Sebastian.

"Stop wasting time." Sebastian disappeared into the fog. There were loud noises ahead. He could see flashes of torches coming closer, then faces appeared through the mist. Some passed by him without a look, and some stopped to stare. Sebastian walked faster toward a set of white tents ahead. He heard the people gasp, and the noise stopped. Valirus held his staff in the air and a white glow spread from around him. The fog lifted above the market.

Sebastian watched the way the people interacted with the sorcerer. He smiled as he saw brooding men groveling at Valirus. Then his smile vanished as Valirus gestured toward him.

"Good people of Midrel Istan. What has happened here this evening? The Moors are full of death," Valirus said.

"We were invaded." A young man stepped forward. "By Altanian Kingsmen."

"What are Kingsmen?" Sebastian walked toward Valirus.

"King Maxen's most trusted knights."

"They were searching for something," the young man said. "I saw them going in and out of tents and tossing over carts of wares."

"Dani. Did they take him?" Sebastian said.

"I am here." A voice came from behind Sebastian. He turned and saw Dani smiling at him.

"I told you I would return for you," Sebastian said. "Tell me, what has happened?"

Dani grabbed Sebastian's arm. "They were searching for me."

"You?" Sebastian backed away a little. "What do they want with you?"

"King Maxen is my father. I don't know what he wants from me, but I think it has something to do with you, Sebastian. I mean, Your Majesty."

Valirus stood before Sebastian, then glanced at Dani before addressing the crowd. "Ladies and gentlemen. I give you, our new King of Adurak, Sebastian Drake, or Chaos as some know, God of Fire."

The crowd gasped and whispered. Sebastian stepped into the middle of the market, looking around at the men's and women's faces. The men were large, muscular, and burly. The women appeared tired and afraid.

Sebastian paced within the circle. "You are angry. I can see it in your eyes. I can feel it all around me." He nodded and looked a few people in the eyes. "You think I am just another king here to do harm. I will tell you that I certainly can hurt every last one of you. I can set this sad little town on fire and burn you all alive in your beds tonight, but that is not why I came here." He paused and smiled. "People of the Moors. I am not an ordinary king, and you are not required to follow me. But I am here to offer you something you will not want to refuse. King Maxen ruined your lives, correct? He took away your land, family, and people, and for what?" He looked at the crowd.

Valirus grabbed Sebastian's shoulder. "These people sell weapons that are outlawed in the country by King Maxen. Merchants sell banned liquor and opiates. These people have been deceived and do not trust a crown. I ask you again. Why did you want to come here, Your Majesty?"

Sebastian glanced at Valirus, then turned to the crowd. "What would you say to a place where you can live free and sell your goods in the daylight above the fog? What would you say to a new life? All I ask for in return is loyalty. I have the power to change the fate of Midrel Istan, but I need help. Together, we can take back what is yours. Are you with me?" Sebastian said, feeling proud of himself. The crowd looked at one another. There was quiet mumbling, then they all stopped.

"I will follow you anywhere," Dani said, breaking the silence.

Sebastian smiled and held out his hand for Dani to take. The people of the markets looked around, nodded, and nervously bowed to Sebastian. As the sun peaked high, the people packed their carts and followed Sebastian from The Moors toward the mountains.

CHAPTER 16
Two Hearts Combine

Tomas sat by his father's office window as thick sheets of ice and snow fell from the stormy sky. Castle Drake was quiet. The morning had just brought enough light to blanket the courtyard. Guards and knights struggled to make their way toward the gates. A light knock came on the door. A little boy waited, giggling while holding a piece of parchment in his jelly-covered hand.

"Thank you, Declan." Tomas smiled and curtsied in his chair.

"Sorry, Tomas." Nadya, the oldest of the Drake sisters, ran into the room. "He is too fast for me."

"I still can't believe he is already two years old. He looks just like Jon."

Jon spent most of his days in NorthBrekka since joining Sebastian in Icefall and following him into battle against Barron. But he stayed because he fell in love with Nadya Drake and of course because of his loyalty to the king.

Nadya was pregnant again and struggled to keep up with Declan. Jon traveled back and forth between Icefall and

NorthBrekka with the changing seasons. As winter had set in and he was back with his family in Castle Drake. Viktor, Sebastian's younger brother, spent his days moping around the corridors or finding a dark corner in the library, where only Tomas knew to find him.

Kristoff, the youngest living Drake sibling, had just returned from the sea. He and a crew of Sinook and Northbrekkian men went to explore the world and only returned home once per season for supplies. Tomas was healthy but had trouble walking on his own since the battle in Alta Prime that had left him pinned beneath boulders from a broken palace. He still had nightmares about the fight. The anger of Sacha, his unknown brother and bastard son to King Ivan, and the storm conjured by Tomas and Sebastian that crippled a kingdom and Tomas's body.

He used a cane primarily, but more often, someone assisted him at all times. Tomas took the letter and sat back in his father's chair. His eyes popped wide open when he saw the name scrawled at the bottom. He gasped in excitement and began reading it aloud, with Nadya listening and Jon joining them.

His smile quickly faded when he read about Cyrus attacking him and Sebastian wishing for death. He clasped his hand over his mouth. Nadya rushed over to read over his shoulder so Jon could hear. Tomas shook.

"He is in trouble," Jon said. "Well, that tears it. I am gathering an army and going after him. If war is imminent, he will need us."

Tomas said nothing. His hand rested on the desk, still shaking.

"Tomas, calm down." Nadya backed away as the room got cold and frost formed across the desk. "It has been a long time since he wrote this. Anything could have happened by now."

"I need to go after him. He needs me more than anyone," Tomas said.

Jon stepped forward. "Your Majesty, allow me to go after him. Kristoff has a fast ship and a strong crew. He can take an army to your brother."

Tomas stood with difficulty. "My brother needs me. I will go to him." He stumbled and fell back into his chair.

"Tomas!" Nadya reached out to help him. "We don't know where he is and with your injuries, time on a ship will only make it worse. Let Jon and Kristoff go."

"I'm going too," Viktor said. "I am going whether you like it or not, Nadya. My brother needs as much family as we can spare."

"Bring him home. Please, whatever it takes," Tomas stuttered. "Make sure Sebastian comes home alive."

Loud footsteps filled the hall outside the study. A ruckus of voices shouted, "You cannot go in there."

Nadya shot to the door. "Cyrus," She whispered. "He tried to kill Sebastian. What is he doing here?"

Jon unsheathed his sword, and Tomas stumbled to his feet. Nadya picked up Declan and backed to the window. The door burst open and a once sweet face with kind eyes and wispy brown hair was now emotionless and hardened.

"Tomas Drake," he said. "How's the leg?"

"Why did you come here after what you have done?"

"I missed his heart on purpose." Cyrus stared at the floor.

A dimple appeared on his left cheek as Tomas lightly laughed. "Well, it seems my brother is angry with you, so that means you are my enemy as well."

Cyrus stared at him. "You look just like him. The two of you make the same face. You blush a little, then smile and laugh. Everything is the same."

Dom, the warrior captain of the Sinook, walked in with the alpha wolf that had once imprinted on Sebastian. "Forgive me, Tomas for my intrusion, but I saw Torrdale soldiers outside." He turned. "Prince Cyrus. Welcome home. Is Sebastian with you?"

"We cannot trust him, Dom." Tomas sat back with the letter from Sebastian in his hand. He passed it to Dom, who read it aloud. His eyes widened as his lips moved quickly through the words.

Cyrus held his hands up. "Dom. I am not here for violence. I came to warn you."

"Warn us about what?" Dom stood within inches of Cyrus's face.

"I stole a map from King Maxen of Midrel Istan."

"Who?" Tomas stood with difficulty.

"Maxen. He is my uncle and the king of Altania in Midrel Istan. I stole the map for Sebastian." Cyrus explained the story of the King of Men rising against Dragon centuries ago. "Now, history will repeat itself. While Sebastian and Maxen battle for the world, others will rise against us… I mean, you."

"No one is coming for us, Cyrus." Tomas paced.

"Others will come, and I fear they will use me against Sebastian." Cyrus's voice trailed off. He walked over to the door. "Everything in my mind tells me I should have killed Sebastian, but my heart begs me to think otherwise. I was made to be a weapon and therefore I can never be with him again, but I can at least try to help."

Dom looked at Cyrus. "I beg you to reconsider. He loves you, Cyrus. My mother is a great healer, as well as Amara. Please, let us try to help you."

"It will never work. My time is done. My bloodline is at its end. My only living relatives are my Uncle Maxen and his daughter, Petra, and trust me when I say, you better hope Sebastian kills them. I am returning to Torrdale to rest and prepare for Sebastian's return to Erras. I only came here to tell you that I didn't want to betray him. I am still your ally. Good evening." Cyrus backed out the door.

When summer came again, Dom trekked to Sedda to spend the warm season with his daughter. Nadya was due to give birth any day, and Tomas sat in the garden on the bench where he was born and stared at the pond glistening in the sun.

"Happy birthday." A voice came from behind him.

"Oh, good morning, Amara. Thank you." Tomas invited her to sit.

"I made you a present. I hope it keeps your hands from getting blistered on your cane." She handed him a pair of gloves.

Tomas put them on, smiled, and laughed a little. "These are perfect. Thank you." His heart skipped when she hugged him. "I wonder what Sebastian is doing right now."

"Probably telling everyone not to say happy birthday to him." Amara laughed. "You miss him, don't you?"

"Every day. It's been years. I don't want to talk about this, Amara." Tomas shook his head.

"Then let's talk about what you want for your dinner tonight."

"You don't have to—"

"Tomas Ivan Drake, your birthday is one of the most special days my people celebrate, so don't tell me not to do nice things for you. What is your favorite meal?"

"Lamb. I like lamb and carrots. Potatoes. And maybe a little wine as well. What?"

Amara was smiling wider than he'd ever seen. "I'm just excited. I love cooking."

"We have people for that."

"No! I want to make it for you." Amara paused. "That sounded a little odd, didn't it?"

"You are an amazing woman, Amara." Tomas touched her cheek. "Very beautiful."

Amara's face turned pink. She started to speak, but Tomas stopped her with a kiss.

"Is this okay?" Tomas said.

Amara nodded.

Tomas kissed her again, then stood and invited her to follow him. "I know something better than the food you could give me for my birthday."

"Tomas, you are a terrible boy, but I also hoped you would say that." Amara took his arm and walked with him to his bed.

After they made love, Amara slipped on her dress. "Stay here. I am going to make you that supper I promised."

Tomas smiled and watched her leave. His heart raced; he was sweating and couldn't stop smiling. He got up and stared out the window that looked over the lake. Tomas's smile faded, remembering everything wasn't as perfect as what had just happened. There was going to be a lot of bloodshed in the world. He hoped Sebastian would return home and teach him to use his power, but then worried about what would happen if Sebastian never came back. He put his hand against the wall and closed his eyes. A few moments later, the bedroom door opened. He could tell by the footsteps who had come to see him.

Nadya's voice was soft. "Tomas—"

"I can't stop thinking that Sebastian is dead." His hand was shaking as it rested against the wall. Ice formed across his fingertips.

"Why would you think that? Are you alright?"

The sound of her steps got closer. "I'm fine. I just want him to come home."

"Tomas, your eyes have turned blue—"

"I said I was fine. Look, things are going to get worse before they get better. Perhaps you, the children, and Amara should head to Icefall for winter. You'll be safe there."

"I am not leaving my home," Nadya said. "I will be here for when my husband comes back to his children, and I will be here when my brother steps foot in NorthBrekka. You will not take that from me, Tomas. You may be in charge now, but—"

Tomas jerked his head up. A loud crack and shattering of ice fell from the wall as he broke his hand free and turned to face Nadya. Water dripped from his fingertips from the melting ice that spread from his hands to his elbows. "But, what, Nadya?"

Nadya shook her head. "You are just like him. Angry."

"I have a right to be."

"Yes, you do, but don't forget the good in you. It is what makes you our beacon of hope. We feel safe with you, Tomas. Amara loves you more than life, and the men listen to you. Remember that you are just as great as Sebastian in every way. I love you so much, brother."

Tomas smiled. "I just wish I was with him now. I apologize for my outburst." He placed his hand on her pregnant stomach. "I can't wait to have my own someday."

The following morning, Tomas limped across the castle grounds and into the stables. He saw the new blacksmith working in the forge behind the barn. "Good morning, Mikhail."

"Oh, Prince Tomas." The blacksmith bowed. "Good morning to you as well."

"I fear I have not taken the time to get to know the people who work for me." Tomas looked at the swords Mikhail had crafted and left to cool. "My brother, Sebastian, was always better at getting to know the hands."

"What can I do for you, Your Grace?"

"With the looming thought of war becoming probable, I need to know where the loyalties of the men who serve me lie, and I know nothing about you." Tomas tossed a shard of iron into the forge.

"I follow the true King of Kings and therefore, I follow you, Your Grace." Mikhail bowed again. "I know little of my family and where I am from. I know I am from these parts, but I was sent away when I was a child to live among the Sinook."

"What is your father's name?"

Mikhail shrugged. "If my memories serve me, his name was Grimmel."

Chapter 17
The Invitation

The sun glistened over the dew on the grass early in the haze of dawn outside of Lastorum. Sebastian helped Dani into his saddle and wrapped his arms around his waist as the accompaniment set off for The Creed.

"Why do you keep looking at me?" Dani said to Valirus. "You have been watching me since we were in the Moors."

"I cannot believe what your father has done to you. You are a prince." Valirus's knuckles turned white as his grip tightened around the shaft of his staff.

"No, I am not." Dani felt Sebastian squeeze him tight. "I am disgraced."

They climbed through the pass under the archway that led into Adurak. The clattering of carts and goods filled the night air from the noisy market. The season was changing to the cooler months of fall. Sebastian was told winter was only a few weeks in Adurak and it did not snow, except near the summits of the mountains.

"So, where do you want me to stay?" Dani said. "The brothels came as well, so I... I will—"

"You will stay with me, Dani. I promise you will never have to work another day in servitude. I just need you close to me."

"Your Majesty—"

"No. Call me Sebastian."

"Sebastian, when my father finds out I am here, he will come for me. It is not safe for you to be with me. By taking the fog market, you have disrupted the Altanian gold trade. He will seek revenge."

"I promise I will protect you. It is time I did something good in this world." Sebastian placed his fingers against Dani's lips and kissed his forehead.

Dani started to argue but stopped. His face turned red.

"It'll be alright, Dani. You saved my life that morning on the beach. I am giving you a chance to choose your fate."

"I want to be with you, Sebastian." Dani wrapped his arms around him.

Jace hurried down the road between the Inns, stopping suddenly when he saw Sebastian and Dani holding one another. He looked at Dani. "Who are you?" His eyes darted to Sebastian. "Who is he?"

"He is a friend, Jace. You would have met him if you didn't abandon me that night in the dry lake."

"Are you going to start that again? I said I was sorry. You know I couldn't have gone with you," Jace said.

"His name is Dani. He is going to live with us." Sebastian turned to Dani. "Jace has been with me since Erras. He is very dear to me and will help you get comfortable."

Dani smiled at Sebastian, then turned his head toward Jace. "I would like to get to know you, Jace. We could be friends."

"Jace, take Dani to the castle," Sebastian said. "Show him where he can rest, bathe, and get something to eat. I will be there shortly."

Sebastian woke up the following day to loud conversations coming down the corridor. He stepped into the atrium to hear Jace talking to Dani in the kitchen. He peeked through the crack in the half-open door and listened.

"I don't know what I am supposed to be doing," Dani said. "Sebastian hasn't given me any instructions."

"You say his name so informally," Jace said.

"He said he doesn't like being addressed formally."

"He likes you." Jace turned his head away. "The way he looks at you. I have only ever seen him look at Cyrus that way."

"Cyrus, the boy who stabbed him? Is Sebastian still in love with him?" Dani asked.

"Ask him. What do you want? Why are you here? Besides tormenting me."

"I don't know why I am here." Dani shrugged. "Tell me about Sebastian. I don't know much."

"There is a lot to be said about Sebastian's past." Jace set down a plate of pancakes in front of Dani. "Have you ever seen the scars on his back?"

Dani shook his head while shoving a bite in his mouth.

"Ask him to tell you a story about his past. He has a book of his life up through now. He still writes in it as we move forward. I suspect your name is already in there. Maybe you should read that."

Dani looked toward the door. He sat up straight and craned his neck. "Sebastian? Stop being shy." He stretched his arm out with his palm facing up. "Come here."

Sebastian pushed the door open. "I'm not shy. I just wanted to hear what Jace said. Thank you, Jace, for your suggestions."

Dani wrapped his arms around Sebastian and kissed him. "I want to know who you really are?"

"I can't even answer that mystery, Dani." Sebastian kissed him, forgetting Jace was in the room.

"Well, that escalated quickly," Jace said. "Also, you should be thanking me for taking care of matters while you were away fetching a boyfriend."

Sebastian laughed, let go of Dani, and walked over to Jace. He slapped his hand onto Jace's shoulder and squeezed. "Thank you, Jace." Sebastian paused and stared into his eyes. "You are most helpful." His voice was gruff and deep. "I appreciate you." He let go.

Jace rubbed his shoulder. "One of these days, you will realize that you and I work well together. You don't have to be mean."

Sebastian turned his eyes toward Jace, smiled, then licked his lips. "Wasn't it you who once told me that I can do anything I want because I am a king?"

Jace's jaw tightened, and he nodded his head. "Yes, Your Majesty. Is there anything I can do for you?"

"No. You may leave," Sebastian said. He pulled Dani against him. "I want you."

Dani kissed his cheek. "I am yours," he whispered.

Sebastian ran his lips from Dani's mouth to his collarbone. He felt his body warm and his heart fluttered. There was a tingle in his cheeks and his breath felt hot as he took short breaths against Dani's neck.

"Practice, Sebastian, let's go."

Sebastian jumped back. "Valirus, you have impeccable timing."

Dani ran through the door. "Valirus. You are my father's brother. My uncle."

"Yes. I am happy that you are safe and happy but do not interfere with his training. He needs to focus on war."

"But we are family. My father and my sister are horrible. I need you," Dani said.

Sebastian stopped. "So, you are Maxen's brother and Dani's uncle. Did you think I shouldn't know these details?"

"Apologies, Your Majesty. Now, enough of the love and lust. Our little baby dragon needs to grow into a man and a king. War is coming. There is no time for love."

"What good is going to war if not for love?" Sebastian walked with a bounce in his step. "Practice, Valirus. I do not have all day."

Later that morning, Sebastian sat on the cliff's edge and watched the waterfall cascade into a pool far below his feet. He enjoyed the sounds of water. It made him remember Tomas and why his return home was essential.

"Valirus! Come see me outside. It is urgent," Sebastian said.

Valirus appeared next to him. He did not sit but stood close to the edge.

"Careful, old man." Sebastian smirked. "One wrong move and you will…" He pointed down and shook his head. There was a long pause before Sebastian looked up again. "Am I ready for this?"

"No. There is still plenty left to learn."

"I must be all-knowing before I return home. I know nothing of magic. My father never told us anything until my powers emerged. He hid everything that I needed to know to defeat Maxen."

Valirus nodded. "Your father was scared. When you and your twin were born, word spread far and wide across the world. There were riots, fires, looting, hangings, and night after night of bloodshed. It is the darkest night in our history. I believe Ivan was trying to hide the two of you from ever being discovered. If it were up to him, the dragons would have never seen outside of NorthBrekka."

"That explains why he was always so angry when I came home late. Is this story meant to guilt me, old man?"

Valirus raised his eyebrows. "Of course not, Your Majesty. Every king should know his own story. I feel you don't know who you are."

"Help me understand." Sebastian stood and faced Valirus. "Teach me everything. The prophecy—"

"The prophecy," Valirus spat. "You wouldn't let your fate reside on the words of Dragon's evil magic, would you?"

Sebastian shook his head. "The obvious answer is no."

Dani appeared in the doorway with a letter in hand. "This came for you, My King."

"What is it?"

"I did not open it. But it is from Altania. That is my father's seal." Dani gave the letter to Sebastian, then cuffed his arm. "Don't let the old man make you mad. You are all powerful to me." He kissed Sebastian's cheek.

"Stop, Dani," Valirus said. "Read the letter."

Sebastian opened the parchment and mumbled to himself. He stopped and said, "Maxen is inviting us to a jousting tournament in Altania. Dani, why does this sound like it will not be festive?"

Dani took the letter and read over the words. "Jousting tournaments are vicious sports. Nothing that happens in Altania is good."

"I thought he wanted to go to war, not enjoy a show of sportsmanship together," Sebastian said.

"He thinks it will scare you to see how awful he can be without magic," Dani said.

"Back home in Erras, all kingdoms come together near the North and South border every five years for a... celebration. Each kingdom sent men to build a stadium, then each would choose a champion to fight to the death for their country against the four other men. If he thinks a joust will spook me, he does not understand me. He doesn't know I was tortured, beaten, and exiled from my homeland, soaked in blood and scars."

"Then we will attend. No arguing," Dani said. He kissed Sebastian and curtsied to Valirus before heading back inside.

"What about Jace?" Sebastian shouted at Dani.

Dani came back to the opening. "He should be there as well. Jace is protective of you. He is someone I would want to have at my back in battle."

Sebastian turned to Valirus. "I want to practice some more today."

"Then I suggest you get to work. When is this tournament?"

"The day after the harvest. Whenever that is," Sebastian said.

"That is less than a month away," Valirus said. "Be ready to work very hard."

Over the next week, Sebastian did not argue or talk back during training.

"I want you to learn to be devastating without becoming emotional. With this, you can do great damage when you need to, and you won't destroy everything around it in the process," Valirus said.

Sebastian looked around across the valley. "I need to practice somewhere outside the Creed. I need to be able to unleash. I cannot do that here."

"It is not safe for you to leave Adurak, Your Majesty," Valirus said. "Not without your soldiers. And not before we depart for Altania. They won't kill you. They will capture you."

"Then where do you suggest I break everything and not hurt people?"

"Come with me. Dani, you too." Valirus walked across the atrium of the castle to the front steps and stopped. "Don't start disobeying me now."

Sebastian and Dani hurried to catch up to Valirus as he marched into the market.

"For a man his age, he is really fast," Dani said.

"He means to punish me."

"No, he wants you to kill his brother." Dani gripped Sebastian's arm.

Sebastian saw the sun reflect off of Dani's pale skin, making his eyes appear crystal clear. Sebastian's throat tightened and he felt sweat form above his temple. When Dani held him, Sebastian felt invincible. The empowerment was euphoric and seemed to awaken something deep within that was bursting to escape. "Dani, I never bothered to ask, but do you like being here?"

Dani's eyes contracted and his lips were pouty. "I love being here with you."

Sebastian was warm, could smell spice, and heard merchants conversing about everything from the weather to stories of some miraculous adventure they went on to find such wares they were selling. He smirked and glanced at Dani. His infectious smile had Sebastian in a trance. In the fog, he remembered Dani's demeanor was defensive and serious, and he rarely smiled.

Valirus stopped suddenly. Sebastian looked up at Valirus and then at Dani.

"That is the gateway into Adurak," Sebastian said. "I thought I couldn't go out there."

"You're not. You will practice here."

The path was lined with low mountains. There were loose and jagged boulders waiting to fall if provoked. Sebastian walked to the middle of the road, held his hands out in front of him, and closed his eyes. He took a deep breath, turned his head a little, and looked up at the mountains again.

"I wonder if those rocks will fall if I make the mountain move."

He saw Valirus look at him and then at the mountain. He did not speak. Sebastian exhaled and turned his attention to the ground. It began to shake lightly. He heard cracks come from above his head. The rocks moved with the environment. But it did not make them fall.

"Gentle," Valirus said. "That is what you will learn here. If you lose control, you will bring those rocks down onto us, but if you can create a strong force and not disturb the rocks, you will have control of your chaotic power."

"You didn't think that through carefully, did you?" Sebastian said.

"I am confident in you." Valirus looked over his shoulder. "Dani believes you are his savior, so he would follow you off a cliff into a lake of lava if you asked him."

"That is dreadful," Dani said. "Don't ask me to walk into lava, Sebastian."

"I promise I never will." Sebastian smiled. "Let's see how this goes first." He reached his hands out again and stared at the mountains. Sebastian's mind raced. He thought about NorthBrekka, Tomas, and Dom. Then he felt a pain in his chest when Cyrus's face came to mind. The mountains shook. The boulders shifted and slid a few feet.

Sebastian heard Dani gasp. He closed his eyes, took a deep breath, and raised his arms slowly with his palms up. His biceps flexed hard against the fabric of his coat. He felt his shoulders set back and back straighten. There was a burn in the pit of his stomach. Sebastian's eyes rested on Dani. His head tilted and he let out a gust of breath that sent a ripple of wind into The Creed. The boulders shifted and tumbled, then froze in mid-air.

"He is so beautiful," Dani whispered.

Sebastian set the rocks down and stopped. "Did I do that correctly?"

"It was a little rocky." Valirus winked.

Sebastian tried to contain his laughter. "Unbelievable." He walked back toward the castle with Dani and Valirus by his side.

Late that evening, Sebastian sat on his balcony next to the fire, sipped wine, and watched the waterfall disappear into the darkness of the canyon below.

"May I join you?"

Sebastian turned around quickly. "Dani. Of course. Come sit with me and stay warm. It is cold tonight."

"I am not used to cold nights. I do not have the right clothes for it." Dani was wrapped in a light blanket. He sat between Sebastian and the fire. "Tell me a story."

"You can read the book," Sebastian said.

"I want you to tell me."

Sebastian told Dani about how he discovered he was Chaos and how he and Cyrus fell in love but ended before he reached the part about getting whipped. "That is all I want to talk about for tonight. It gets dark from there, and we are finally alone."

Dani loosened up the blanket, revealing that he had no clothes on. Sebastian felt his cheeks get hot and his heart raced. He kissed Dani's lips and pulled his body against his.

Dani gently pushed Sebastian onto his back, kissing his neck and chest as he started to undress him. "Relax, my love. Let me give you what you deserve," Dani said. "You should be able to make love to a man who is madly obsessed with you. One that has the experience to make your every desire come true. I have wanted you for a long time."

"I want you too, Dani. It is all I think about." Sebastian gently brushed his lips across Dani's jawline. "Swear to me that I will be the only man you lay with from now on. I want you to myself."

"I have never wanted anyone. Not ever. Not until I met you," Dani whispered.

Sebastian drifted into a daze of ecstasy, his moans cracking with a hoarse voice after they made love on the floor the third time. He tried to catch his breath as he rested his head back.

"I love you," Dani said softly as he kissed Sebastian's neck. Then he sat up quickly. "Is it too soon for love?"

"No. I love you too."

Dani stared at Sebastian as if he hoped for something. Sebastian wasn't sure what to say. He pulled Dani against him, holding onto his body like he would lose him if he let go. "This is the only place I ever want to be."

"Can I ask you why you fell for me?"

Dani smiled as his cheeks turned red. "You are the first man I have laid with that has ever been nice to me. You came to rescue me" He rested his head against Sebastian's chest. "I have never felt love before, but from all the stories I have heard, I am sure this is it. If not, then I don't want to live anymore."

The next morning Sebastian awoke with Dani lying on his shoulder, fast asleep. He kissed his forehead and squeezed him tight. His mind alluded to remembering Jace sleeping on his chest for days while he was lost in his thoughts. He heard footsteps coming up the stairs.

"Go away, Jace. I am not dressed," Sebastian yelled. "Dani is naked too."

The door opened. Valirus smacked his lips and rolled his eyes as he turned away. "Get up and get dressed. Dani, go find something to do for now. Sebastian needs to train. No arguing, no backtalk. You will work until I break you." Valirus marched out of the room.

Sebastian looked at Dani and laughed. "Why is he always yelling at me?"

"To be fair, he is always yelling at me to stay away from you. I'm not doing a perfect job," Dani said.

"I will find out what is happening in that old man's head."

That afternoon, Valirus pushed Sebastian hard. He would smack him with his staff when Sebastian did not perform to his liking.

"I said to make the water into ice! Are you a god or not? No, you are a pathetic boy who wants to be lazy and lie with Dani all day."

Sebastian screamed in rage. He swung around and reached for the water, lifting it into the air.

"Ice!" Valirus shouted. "Chaos, the god born to destroy the world. Violent, dangerous, evil. Some will call you Dragon. The unloved, the spawn of hellfire and fury. Look what you have done. You have made it rain. Are you going to flood Maxen out of Altania? I think not," Valirus sneered.

Sebastian looked at Valirus, then glanced up the stairs, seeing Dani creeping down from his room.

"Don't look at him! Pay attention." Valirus snapped.

"You have been in prison for nineteen years. What do you know about defeating Maxen?" Sebastian snapped.

"I know of one thing you have that Maxen wants." Valirus walked to the stairs and stared at his nephew. "The last time I saw Dani, he was eight years old. He was a beautiful child. In Altania, he would run from the castle to the beach every morning after breakfast. He would play in the water and dig in the sand. It is tragic what Maxen did to such a vibrant and sweet soul. I didn't know Dani was sold and whored until you released me from that cell. I was told all of this in Lastorum. I looked for Dani but couldn't find him. I went to the farm but was told he was not there. When you described this boy you had to find in the fog, I felt it was Dani."

"Then why did you try to stop me from going?" Sebastian said.

"Because he is Maxen's son, nonetheless. You and he are in danger if you are together. Dani is extraordinary. He already has shown signs."

"Signs?" Sebastian grabbed Valirus's arm. "What do you mean, wizard?"

"Dani is—"

"Uncle, please don't—"

"Dani, you are gifted," Valirus said. "Now, no more distractions or else," Valirus yelled. "Make the water deadly."

The room darkened as fires were extinguished into puffs of smoke. Sebastian held his hands crossed on his chest, closed his eyes, and stretched his neck back and forth. He threw his arms open wide and sniffed the air. The scent of salt meant he wasn't reaching into the freshwater mountain spring that ran through his castle but the sea.

Inside Moonlight Castle, in the illustrious atrium filled with trees and a flowing stream sat the men and women of Adurak. Sebastian cracked lightning in one hand and fire in the other, causing a gust of wind to whirl around him. "I am Chaos. God of Fire. May your lands profit from my gifts."

The display of fire, water, lightning, and air dissipated. Sebastian brought his hands together in a thunderous clap, and the ground trembled. The smell of saltwater came with forceful winds from the south. Sebastian walked to the balcony and looked across the canyon. Others slowly joined him.

"Was that your big finale?" Valirus smirked.

A loud boom shuttered trees in the distance.

"This canyon wasn't created by chance," Sebastian said. Dani took his hand in his. Sebastian stroked Dani's cheek and continued. "There was once a river here that fed a lake. One day it all dried up, and the land died. Then, the people began to starve. That will happen no more."

Birds soared from trees and thunder rumbled in the sky. Snaps and cracks echoed loudly along the canyon wall as the ground shook. Jace arrived by Sebastian's side and his mouth dropped open. A cascade of sea burst into the side of the mountain, crushing rock and plant life until it met the ravine and could snake its way toward Adurak.

Jace's eyes were soft, his lips trembled, and he put his hand on Sebastian's chest. "That is incredible."

Dani pulled Sebastian close and whispered in his ear, "I love you." He pulled away as his face turned red.

Sebastian smiled. "I love you, Dani."

"My King." Dani bowed. Valirus and Jace followed suit, dropping to one knee and bowing. Sebastian heard the sound of others. Townspeople and soldiers alike witnessed his power and turned to their almighty king. Sebastian stepped forward and stood before them as a vision of a great legend.

A young soldier stood before the crowd and faced his king. "We are all outcasts. That is why we hide in the shadows of The Creed. Mercenaries, criminals, thieves, and traitors. We have seen who you are, and we will follow you until the end. Adurak is forever your home. You can rule as King of Kings in the greatest city in the world. The City of Thieves is yours, Your Majesty."

"We all stand with you," Jace said. "I have been by your side for a long time now. Most of that time, you were pissing me off, but I have grown quite fond of you. I believe in you, and I will follow you anywhere."

"Thank you." Sebastian's lip twitched into a smile. He looked around the atrium, at Valirus, then finally at Dani. "These are going to be difficult days ahead. I cannot promise you safety. I do not know what is to come. But if you can put aside your differences between the old kings and me, I assure you that you will see a new Midrel Istan. One where you can live free of fear and dishonor. One where your children won't become orphans before they can walk. And one where you will get to eat, rest, and become strong. A new era is standing before you. With your loyalty, we will prevail."

The people of Adurak cheered. Jace hurried over and grabbed Sebastian's arm. "Can I speak with you?" He looked at Dani. "Alone."

Sebastian nodded and let go of Dani's hand to follow Jace upstairs. They entered a dark room that smelled of mildew and dirt. "I have never been in here. What is this?"

Jace lit the candelabra, revealing a bed, table, and fireplace that never seemed to have been used. "This is my bed quarters, Your Majesty."

"Why did you choose this room? It is depressing here. There are plenty of bedrooms in this castle that are much nicer."

"This was the closest one to you," Jace said. "I don't think you understand that my allegiance is to you and only you. I love you, Seb—"

"Jace—"

"Let me finish." Jace gripped Sebastian's arms. "I know we will never be together. You have proven that by bringing Dani home. So, I ask for two things. One, I want to be your advisor. I want to be the man you trust on your back, to guide you, protect you, and lead."

Sebastian smiled. "I would want no other for the job. What else?"

"Kiss me."

Sebastian stepped back. "Jace, I do love you, but Dani."

"One last kiss, my king. I will never ask you again." Jace brushed his lips against Sebastian's cheek.

Sebastian's body flushed hot and his stomach felt like it was full of butterflies as he took Jace's face in his palm and kissed him. When he stepped back, Jace grabbed his hands.

"We could have been good together," Jace whispered.

"I know. I am sorry for hurting you, Jace. You deserve better than me, do you understand?"

Jace nodded and let him go.

Sebastian walked to the door, then turned back to face Jace. "I am proud to have you leading my men. I promise not to be too overbearing."

"That will be impossible for you, Your Majesty." Jace laughed.

"We ride for Altania in three days. Gather forty men. Make sure you leave soldiers to protect Adurak in our absence," Sebastian said.

"See. You are already being bossy."

"I still wear a crown. Oh, and choose a better room. This one is just awful." Sebastian shivered and left. He ran up the stairs and walked into the warm sunlight that spread across the floor. The smell of the sea filled the air. Sebastian stared thoughtlessly at the shimmering river that now passed by his castle from an ocean he had never seen.

CHAPTER 18
The Road to Altania

The road through the archway into the desert that led to grassy plains before Lastorum was quiet. Only a few merchants and traders made their way in crossing from Dunebar and Adurak. Early the next afternoon, Sebastian jumped from his horse and ran over to a dark blue body of water. "The swamp was once right ahead. Now it's—"

"Gone!" Dani said. "The fog market, the swamp... it's all gone." He hopped down from the horse and fell to his knees at the shoreline.

The lake spread as far as the eye could see. Jace tapped his boot in the water. "So, how do we get to Dunebar now?"

Sebastian's eyes shot wide open. "I suppose we go around."

The journey took an extra day of riding, but late in the evening, the familiar dusty old town was seen from around the bend. There were torches lit along a pathway and shops were open, unlike how it was when Meecah and he first arrived in Dunebar. Sebastian headed straight into The Broken Glass.

A woman shouted from across the bar. "Ah, the handsome lord returns, or should I say, the King of Adurak." Issa smiled.

The tavern got quiet. Sebastian smiled. "Yes, madam, and we are hungry."

Issa rushed off to the kitchen. Sebastian heard clapping and laughing coming from the corner. He knew that laugh from before.

"Samir Kinjesto. It has been a long time." Sebastian reached his hand to Samir.

"I see you, Your Majesty. I also see you have my dear friend, Jace."

Jace stepped forward and shook Samir's hand. "Yes, ever loyal as always."

"We are on our way to Altania. There is a jousting tournament hosted by King Maxen," Sebastian said.

"Oh, a joust! That sounds like my kind of party. I am coming with you," Samir said.

"I am coming as well."

Sebastian rolled his eyes and turned around slowly. "No, Meecah—"

Meecah put her hand over Sebastian's mouth. "We both know what happens when you tell me no. I get my way."

Sebastian laughed and wrapped his arms around her. "Good to see you too."

"You look well. Stronger than before," Meecah said.

"I am not the same man you knew before."

"I know. I think I like this new Sebastian." She pinched his cheek. "At least this one smiles."

"Meecah, this is Dani." Sebastian kissed Dani's hand, then nodded to the man with his hickory staff in hand. "This is Valirus. The teacher I had been looking for."

Meecah bowed to Valirus and Dani. "And how is Jace feeling about all this?"

"Jace is doing fine." Jace strutted over and stood close to Sebastian, lightly stroking his hand with his fingertips.

Meecah looked down and nodded. "I see what is going on here."

"There is nothing going on here," Sebastian said. He nodded to Samir and Meecah. "I see that the two of you are getting along."

"You have brought me such a treasure." Samir reached for Meecah's hand. "We have decided to get married."

Sebastian laughed. "Congratulations. I am glad I could help make that happen."

"Aww, don't you start turning red, Sebastian. For someone so loud, you are shy. It is a good quality." Meecah touched his head. "Your hair is a mess. Go and wash it, then I will braid it."

"She is right," Valirus said. "If you want Maxen to know you are a powerful king, you must look like one."

"He needs a new coat." Dani tugged at Sebastian's old, torn jacket. "Probably boots as well. Meecah is right. You are a mess."

"Thank you, Dani," Sebastian closed his eyes and shook his head. "When we arrive in Feldor Bay, you can groom me however you wish, but we need to rest for now. Dawn comes soon."

The sunrise shone through the thin, ivory curtain and cast an amber glow across Sebastian's face. He yawned, stretched, and started to dress until he felt his arm being pulled. Sebastian wrapped his arms around Dani's hips and kissed his neck. It was a quiet morning at the Inn. Soft fingers traveled along Sebastian's forearm, outlining the tattoo he received so long ago in The Far North.

"It looks like a dragon's tail." Dani studied the tattoo closely.

"I wouldn't put it past the Sinook to chisel that on my skin." He kissed Dani's forehead and pulled him against his chest.

"Are you going to marry me?" Dani said.

Sebastian's eyes widened, and his mouth dropped open, but no words came out.

Dani's face turned red, and he backed away. His eyebrows were furrowed, and his jaw clenched tight.

Sebastian sat up and pulled Dani to him. "Dani, of course, I want to marry you. I just wanted to ask you under happier circumstances. If your father finds out about us..."

"I'm not afraid of my father, Sebastian. He can't hurt me any more than he already has. You don't know what it is like being hated by your father so much that he would give me away to slavery." Dani wouldn't look Sebastian in the eyes.

"Do you feel safe with me?" Sebastian whispered.

"Of course I do." Dani kissed his lips while caressing Sebastian's collarbone.

Sebastian kissed his cheek, then his ear, and bit onto Dani's neck while grasping a fistful of his hair. Hethrew the blanket aside and laid him on his stomach. He wrapped his hands around Dani's hips, making him gasp and moan as Sebastian stroked his body. Footsteps echoed from down the hall, then stopped, and a shadow appeared under the door as the lock clicked.

"Issa should watch where she leaves these." Meecah jingled a ring of keys. "Oh, look at what we have here." She leaned against the door frame and smiled. "Astrid is going to be disappointed. She was hoping you were over Cyrus by now so she could stand a chance."

Dani climbed out of bed and walked naked to the bathroom in the hall. He smiled a little too over-enthusiastically at Meecah as he passed. Sebastian slipped on his pants and stood with his back toward the door. He flinched when he noticed Meecah's reflection in the mirror.

"Are you going to watch me get dressed?"

"I have seen you naked before," Meecah said.

"You sound like my sister, Nadya." Sebastian paused. "That did not sound right… I mean, she always nursed me back to health, and I came home bloody a lot. You should meet her someday. I think you would be friends." He yanked on his pants while hiding his back from Meecah.

Meecah sat on the bed. "Are you inviting me to come back to Erras with you?"

Sebastian slipped his shirt over his head. "Yes. And Samir as well. You both could have a good life in NorthBrekka. It is cold, but it's lovely."

"I don't know if Samir would leave this behind," Meecah said. "But I would like to see your homeland. You are still my king. Therefore, I will follow you." The sun cast across her face, making her dark brown eyes appear amber. "And stop hiding your scars. They show your strength and courage. It proves you are different from other kings. You have suffered. It makes you normal, like the rest of us." She paused and stared at the ground. "You helped me find my place in this world. I want to say that I love you like family, Your Majesty. I will always stand by you."

"You will always be one of my people." Sebastian sat on the bed and put his arm around her. "You are my sister now. I am happy to have you with me on this journey."

They left for Feldor Bay soon after. The road north toward the mountains was bustling with merchants in wagons waiting for travelers to pass on their way to Altania. Up in the steep, high hills was a tiny village that was centralized around a large open mine shaft. The men were broad, strong, and dirty. Sebastian went to introduce himself and learned that they called themselves The Men of the Mountain.

"Have you always lived in these mountains?" Sebastian addressed the man sitting across from him.

"Most of us have been here since we were boys, but we come from all over the map."

Sebastian leaned forward. "What are you mining for?"

"The king's gold," the miner said.

Sebastian sat up straight. His face got hot. "You work for King Maxen."

"Any man would do what was necessary for their family." The man towered over Sebastian. "We work, and our kids get to eat. That does not mean we pledge loyalty to anyone in particular."

"Why is gold so valuable here? Everyone seems to panic when I present gold." Sebastian pulled a coin from his bag and handed it to the man. "This gold is from Erras."

The miner's eyes lit up, and his eyebrows raised. "Now, this is rare here. This is worth something. Tell me you haven't been spreading it around Midrel Istan."

Sebastian felt his heart skip. "It is how I have paid for my needs. Why? What is wrong?"

"King Maxen took all the gold from the people of Midrel Istan." The miner sat back down. "It is only used as currency in Altania where the lands are rich with farms, livestock, jewelry makers, brothels, and anything else you could ever want. If the gold leaves Altania, it is a crime to he who carries it. The only place it can be legally traded is in the fog market, but it all goes back into the hands of King Maxen at the end."

Sebastian took the coin back from the miner. "This is how he found out I was here. I paid for my ship repairs with Erras gold. Anyone in Feldor Bay could have taken the coins to Altania. Are you aware that Maxen is from Erras?"

"Few people know." The miner quickly turned his head from side to side, then leaned over. "Most believe Maxen is some kind of oracle sent from the heavens to build a better world. Anyone in his lands would be fed, bathed, and dressed. It is the price some are willing to pay to have a meal, yet many in the east are loyal to you, Your Majesty."

"You know who I am?"

"Everyone knows there is a new king who lives in the shadows of The Creed." The miner stood. "You should rest. It is getting late."

Sebastian agreed. He found Dani next to the fire, curled up like a cat. Sebastian held him against his chest to keep him warm. He mumbled quietly while staring at the stars. "Ever since I went inside Mosisle Dur, I have been dreaming about dragons. I don't understand why."

"What happens in the dream?" Dani said.

"I am in NorthBrekka. There is a blizzard, and it is lightning. I am walking down from the mountains to the overlook. I see Cyrus standing at the edge, not moving or speaking, and when he turns, his face is white and there is blood pouring from his eyes, nose, and mouth. Then he falls." Sebastian paused to take a breath.

Dani sat up and kissed him. "I know you will always love him, but I want you to understand that I love you more than you can imagine. You won't stand on that cliff alone." Dani paused and kissed Sebastian again. "Now, what does that have to do with dragons?"

Sebastian laughed and shook his head. "Yes, I was getting to that. I walk to the edge to look for Cyrus when a bright light erupts in front of me. It is so powerful it knocks me down. When I clear my eyes, a dragon lands before me. It starts running straight for me, but I cant move. The dragon and I became one. That is when I wake up every time."

Dani nodded his head. "There is a deeper meaning to dreams than many think."

"I think it means I have become this dragon prophecy I was born to be. But now I think I can control it, and I can teach Tomas, and he and I will rule over both Erras and Midrel Istan."

"Does that mean you intend to return to Midrel Istan?" Dani said.

"I'm not sure. But NorthBrekka is my home, where the throne of the King of Kings has sat ever since I destroyed

Alta Prime. But wherever I rule, you must be there with me. Mine and only mine."

"I am yours, my king." Dani cuddled up against Sebastian.

The night turned to day, and the company left the mountains for the familiar road into the small harbor town.

CHAPTER 19
A Brother's Journey

Sebastian kicked up his feet at a table at the Inn in Feldor Bay, where Meecah braided his hair, and clothes were purchased for everyone who would step foot inside of the Altanian walls. Through the window, he could see the Hetta Horizon sitting tied off at the end of the long pier. Repairs were complete, and she was ready to set sail. He spoke to Bryson briefly before a group of men showed up and took a list while Sebastian paid his dues, smiling as he passed the gold to one of the men. Afterwards, he walked over to the clinic. Meecah was on the front porch speaking to Astrid.

"We are leaving soon," Sebastian yelled. "Best make your rounds and meet me at the harbor." He turned to Astrid. "It was good meeting you again, Astrid. Thank you for taking care of me all that time ago."

"Oh, yes, of course, Your Majesty." Astrid's face turned red. "It was lovely to meet you as well."

"The harbor?" A voice came from behind him. "We must ride west into the forest to get to Altania."

Sebastian turned to see Jace and his people. "We are not taking the horses any further. We will sail into Altania. I want Maxen to know I have power, gold, and everything he possesses. Besides, we may need firepower." He walked through the crowd until he bumped into Dani.

Dani stopped at the sight of him. Tiny dimples formed on his cheeks and his mouth spread into a wide smile. His sapphire eyes shimmered against the sun. "You look... beautiful."

Sebastian kissed his hand. "I have never seen you smile like that. You look incredible as well."

"Okay, we all look great!" Jace barged between them. "Are we going?"

The dock workers finished loading the Hetta with supplies as the crew made their way down the long pier. Dani walked up the gangway and onto the deck. He seemed to have frozen in place fixated on crates that passed by.

"Cannonballs. Are you planning to blast Altania to rubble?"

"If it comes to that, I want to be prepared," Sebastian said.

"So do I," Dani said. "I need a weapon."

"What do you know how to use?" Sebastian reached for his sheath. "A sword? Perhaps a bow?"

"I prefer a dagger." Dani smiled and raised one eyebrow. "I prefer to make my attacks intimate."

Sebastian laughed, took two knives from his belt, and passed them to Dani. "Don't get yourself into trouble."

"Don't treat me like a child, my love. I used to steal knives from the men who raped me." Dani paused and took a few steps back and cast his eyes to the deck. "That way if they tried it again without paying, I would be prepared."

Sebastian cusped Dani's cheek and kissed him until he saw someone staring. "What, Jace?"

"The two of you are disgusting to be around." Jace folded his arms.

"Thank you. Would you like to watch, or do you have a word for me?" Sebastian said.

"We are ready to sail."

The Hetta burst to life with sailors running about. They tied down cargo and manned the halyard for each mast until all the black sails were wide open. Jace purchased maps of Midrel Istan and studied them while Sebastian prepared to embark. "We have to go north until we come to this little island here." Jace adjusted the map so Sebastian could see. "Then we travel west where we will see a large rock. It looks like a good place to have a rest before going into Altanian territory."

"Good. We will need the time to prepare for anything they might throw at us. I mean that literally." Sebastian smirked at Jace.

Jace let out a gasp. "Tell me this isn't going to be Khan Khar all over again."

"No. I am intrigued by this joust. I need to learn what kind of man Maxen is. The cannons are cautionary."

"Aren't you concerned about Dani, your new favorite toy?" Jace raised his eyebrows. "It didn't take you long to get over Cyrus."

"I will always love Cyrus, but Dani is everything perfect with the world. I love him, Jace. I am a king that fell in love with a whore. Imagine what my father would say." Sebastian stared at Dani, who was sitting on the railing, looking out at sea. He turned his back and faced Jace. "Are you ready for this?"

Jace laughed. "Just don't make me go through another hurricane, and we will be fine."

Sebastian stepped away and reached one arm back. He felt his body intensify with a hot, burning sensation in his chest that tingled to his fingertips. The weather was calm before a rumble came from the mountains south of Feldor Bay. Sebastian tightened his fists into a ball and threw his hands forward as a gust of wind snapped the sails wideopen, and the

Hetta lurched forward with a crack and pop of the new wood expanding against the gale force.

They sailed following Jace's heading until the evening became hazy and orange. Many of the crew were settling in for a meal when the sea became calm and a deep shade of blue. Seagulls were flying high above, and the smell of earth passed through the air.

Dani looked at Sebastian from the rail. "Come here, my love. Look at this."

Sebastian left the wheel to Jace and walked over. The men remaining on deck stepped up behind him, looking out over the horizon as the sun began to set. Torches stood tall out of the ocean made from tree trunks. The firelight was bright like the sun. As the Hetta got as close as it could reach, Sebastian stepped closer to the rail, his mouth twitched, and his nostril flared. "How do they have that?"

A black and red flag flapped back and forth in the breeze. Once it opened flat, Sebastian could see a sigil of two dragons curling around a long sword, waving from a pearl-white beach that sat between two massive rocks on the ocean surface. "That is my family's sigil." His voice raised. "Castle Drake. House of the Dragon. How do Altanians have my banner?"

Valirus came out of his chambers for the first time since they sailed from Feldor Bay. He stepped over and looked at the island. "It is a form of welcoming. During any festival in Altania, the people decorate the paths with symbols and colors that represent the houses from which each visitor represents. I expect we will see one for Adurak as we enter the harbor."

"Yes, but where would they get the banner?" Sebastian said.

"I am unsure, but if I had to guess, it would be Cyrus," Valirus said. "If he believes Maxen is his only living family, he will turn to him for direction, and will have learned that his uncle does not conduct business for free, whether it be family or not."

Sebastian stepped away from the side and turned to his crew. "Everyone should get something to eat and some sleep. Tomorrow is going to be… different. I don't know what to expect from Altania. Many of you know better than I do, and I beg for your advice. But when we arrive, I suggest you keep your heads down and watch the tournament. I will speak with Maxen. Jace will join me—"

"As will I," Dani said. "My father will see me anyway. I can't hide from him."

Sebastian smiled. "Very well. Tonight, we rest. Tomorrow, we will dance with the devil and see who prevails." A flash of light across the sea caught his eye. "It must be a ship. Do you think they can see us?"

The others got quiet. Jace walked over to the rail. "Are they on fire?"

"If they are Altanian, then I don't pity them." Sebastian turned his back.

The light went away, and the others started off to bed. Sebastian stood in the dark and stared across the ocean as his gut kept telling him to look toward where the light once was. A pair of arms wrapped around his chest.

"Come to bed. I can't sleep without you," Dani said.

Sebastian held onto Dani. "Alright, my darling. I'm very tired."

"Then come to bed. Let me help you sleep." He kissed Sebastian's lips, grabbed his hand, and led the way to the captain's quarters.

Sunlight barged through the porthole, waking both Sebastian and Dani. Sebastian yanked the blanket over their heads and rolled over to kiss Dani's neck. "I don't want to get up yet."

"Then don't. Not yet." Dani wrapped his legs around Sebastian's waist. "Make love to me before we are forced to confront my father."

Sebastian pushed himself on top of Dani and kissed his neck. Footsteps echoed across the deck and a knock came on the door. "Not right now, Jace."

"You want to come see this, Your Majesty." Jace knocked again.

"Move out of the way." A voice came along with the sound of petite feet on the deck.

"Oh, no," Sebastian mumbled.

"Pretty boy, get your bottom up before I open this door and show the crew your naked backside."

Sebastian sighed and kissed Dani again. "I'm sorry," he whispered. He climbed out of bed. "Alright, Meecah. I will be out in a moment. Jace… thank you for ruining the perfect morning."

Dani was already dressed by the time Sebastian had found pants. His cheeks turned red, and he stared at the floor. "I'm used to having to dress quickly. Always had to be ready and waiting for the next man that would want me."

Sebastian sat on the bed. "I feel I know so little about you. Dani, I don't want you to fear telling me your stories." He cusped Dani's cheek. "Please, don't cry." Sebastian scooped him into his arms. "I will never let anything happen to you." He kissed Dani's cheek. "You are my everything and I love you so much." He turned Dani to face him. "Those days in the brothel are over. You are mine, and I will not let anyone take you from me, Dani. Do you understand?"

Dani choked and wiped his soaking wet face. He wrapped his arms around Sebastian's neck and cried into his shoulder. A flashing light peeked through the porthole, hitting Dani in the eye. "Are those sails in the distance?"

Sebastian swung around and gripped the window. There was a glint flashing against the morning sun, and a massive column of fabric could be seen in the shadows across the sea. "I'm not sure. It's too far away."

They finished dressing and hurried onto the deck. Sebastian stood at the wheel with Jace and Valirus. Dani waited on the rail where the silhouette of a massive ship came from beneath the sun's rays. "Turn west," Jace said, as his eyes stayed locked onto the oncoming vessel.

The water started changing from black to bright blue and then to clear. Sebastian left the wheel and walked to the bow where he could see fire flickering ahead.

"Ahh, there are the banners for Adurak," Valirus said. "And no, I don't know how they got those either." He smirked at Sebastian.

"You're a funny old man, aren't you?"

Adurak's banners were the same as NorthBrekka's. The Drake sigil, but the color was silver with black dragons instead of red. Sebastian caught a glimpse of a twinkle in the corner of his eye.

"That ship is not Altanian. Maxen's ships have white sails. Those are black, like your ship." Dani sat down on the rail.

"All ships from Erras have black flags." Sebastian stepped up to the rail, putting his hand on Dani's thigh. "It could be Cyrus. We might be sailing into a trap." Sebastian walked over to the wheel where Jace was steering.

"Orders, Your Majesty," Jace said.

"Men... and lady." Sebastian smiled at Meecah. "There is a ship approaching with black sails. We should be prepared for anything. If this is Cyrus, I fear we may be facing a fight. Turn the ship northwest. We are going to get closer. Ready the cannons." His voice was soft, yet it carried across the deck smoothly and gracefully.

The crew came alive, with men running in all directions. Jace turned the Hetta northwest and waited for new orders.

"If we go too far, we will miss the harbor into Altania," Dani said.

Jace gripped the wheel so tightly, his knuckles turned white. "If that ship is Cyrus, we will not be going to Altania."

"Do you think Cyrus is going to attack?" Dani said. "Would he kill all of us to get to Sebastian?"

Sebastian turned his head slightly as he listened to Dani. It didn't occur to him whether or not Cyrus would fire first. At that moment, his gut twisted, feeling like knives poking at his insides while his heart raced. He shook his head and looked at the ship again as it got close. The vessel was not as big as the Hetta but it was still large.

"Easy, men. Don't let the fog frighten you." Sebastian put his hand out before him, and a light breeze blew the clouds away from the deck.

As the mist lifted and the fog moved away, the nose of the other ship became clear. Sebastian's heart started racing. "That is my Father's ship. Do not fire unless I tell you to."

The Ophidias was the King of NorthBrekka's ship. It was built for Sebastian's great-grandfather and had stood through five wars.

The crew was silent, watching the approaching vessel closely. Jace eased the wheel toward the west again. The ship slowly drifted alongside the Hetta. Sebastian stood on the rail to get a better look. As the bow passed, he saw a blond-haired boy at the wheel.

"Don't fire!" A voice echoed from ship to ship. "Please, we already had an issue with fire and other things on deck." A head popped up from behind a cargo hold. "Fancy meeting you here, brother."

His heart jumped, and his face flushed. "Stand down, men," he shouted to his crew. "What are you doing here, Viktor?" He stopped and pointed. "Is that Kristoff steering?"

Kristoff hurried over to the rail. "Viktor kicked over a lantern last night and burned half of a sail. Hello, Sebastian." His cheeks turned bright red. He looked a lot like Sebastian, only now he was sixteen. Kristoff had Sebastian's face but blonde hair like most of his siblings.

"Nadya yelled at us," Viktor said. "She was worried about you when Tomas got your letter. We read about King Maxen."

Sebastian crossed his arms. "How did you know where to go?"

"Cyrus."

Sebastian squeezed the railing as his mind replayed Cyrus's face when he drove the dagger into his chest. "Tomas. How is he?"

"He doesn't walk so well, but he is the same Tomas otherwise," Viktor said. "I spent two years training with the Sinook. Dominic taught me himself. He misses you."

"That's impressive." Sebastian felt his cheeks burn. "I miss him too."

"Dominic? Who is Dominic?" Dani appeared seemingly out of nowhere.

Viktor and Kristoff both raised their eyebrows.

"A former lover, and close friend." Sebastian put his arm around Dani's waist.

"Tell us what is going on here? We didn't expect to see you or the Hetta," Viktor said.

Sebastian ordered both ships to anchor. The Hetta bobbled in the calm ocean, enough for him to sit on the railing and speak without shouting. He explained the tournament, while Dani told them about Maxen.

A voice came from Kristoff's ship. "We have two large ships strapped with enough firepower to take this king out."

"Jon?" Sebastian craned his neck.

Jon stepped to the edge and bowed. "I'm still living and breathing, Your Majesty."

CHAPTER 20
A Familiar Face Arrives in NorthBrekka

Tomas sat on the throne late one evening. Most had gone to bed, but he did not sleep much anymore. The pain in his leg stung worse when he rested, often keeping him awake until the early hours. He walked a bit better in the months since he sent Kristoff and Viktor away on the Ophidias in search of Sebastian.

Amara appeared at the door. Her long blue dress flowed behind her with each step. Tomas grinned and his eyes traveled from her face, down to her breasts, and her legs as the fabric lay thin against Amara's body. She spent much of her time helping Nadya with her newborn twins, but in the evenings, she would find herself alone in Tomas's company. "What is the matter with you tonight?" Amara smiled. "Is your leg bothering you?"

"Yes. It hurts. It always hurts." Tomas rubbed his knee. "It keeps me up at night. That and I am always cold."

"Your brother always complained about being hot." Amara laughed. "I miss him."

Tomas looked sharply at Amara. His stomach fluttered and his heart thumped in his chest. "It must be hard for you to let him go when you look at me."

Amara sat up straight. "What do you mean, let him go?"

"You are in love with Sebastian. Aren't you happy that he and Cyrus are no longer together?" Tomas said.

"No. I want him to be happy, Tomas. I tried to kiss him once. He let me, but he barely kissed me back. Honestly, it felt like I was kissing my brother. That is when I knew."

Tomas laughed. "So, when you kiss me, does it feel like you are kissing your brother?"

Amara's face turned red. "Of course not!" She tried to stand but grabbed Tomas's knee and squeezed.

"Ouch, Amara, easy." Tomas reached out to help her.

"I'm sorry, Tomas. Are you alright?" Amara put her hand on his cheek.

Tomas grabbed her hips and sat her on his lap. "Can I kiss you?"

Amara nodded. Tomas brushed his nose across her cheek as his lips lightly caressed her jawline. He gently pressed his mouth against hers. Amara trembled as her hand gently caressed his chest. She nestled her head against his neck, and each breath sent chills through Tomas's body. She kissed his ear. Tomas ran his hands down the back of her dress.

"I want you to be my wife," Tomas whispered. He unfastened the buttons as he spoke. "I haven't been able to keep my eyes off you since you came." He pulled her sleeves as he kissed her collarbone, making his way down her chest. Amara sat up, pulled her dress down, and put Tomas's hands on her breasts while she untied his pants.

"Is this how you propose to a lady?" Amara stood and let her dress fall.

Tomas squirmed on his throne as he pulled his shirt over his head and kicked off his boots and pants before pulling Amara on top of him. She gasped as Tomas pushed his hips against her pelvis. She dug her nails into his hair and kissed his ear and neck.

"Will you marry me?" Tomas stared Amara in the eyes as he made love to her.

"Yes." Amara kissed his lips. "I want you to get me pregnant," she whispered. "I want a lot of babies."

Tomas smiled and sat up with her on his lap. Amara arched her back and moaned loudly with every stroke of his body against hers. Tomas let out a few sharp breaths as he felt his eyes flicker. He rested her body against his, putting his head against her chest.

"I want to do that again. I just need to catch my breath," Tomas said.

"Maybe I should go run us a bath." Amara kissed him, then slowly stepped away to put her dress on.

"I will meet you there when it is ready." Tomas stood to dress. Amara reached over to help him. "No. I can do this by myself."

"You are stubborn. It must run in the family." Amara laughed as she slipped out of sight.

Tomas escaped through a backdoor that was locked at all times. He turned the key and went downstairs. With each step, a sharp pain jolted through his knee. When he reached the bottom, Tomas stopped and took a few deep breaths.

"Your Majesty, can I assist you?" The guard said.

"No. I am fine. Leave us," Tomas said.

"Alone?"

Tomas glared at the guard. "He can't do anything to me."

The guard hesitantly unlocked the cell, then walked up the steps and closed the door. Tomas jerked the handle, letting the door fly open. He saw his once handsome and strong older brother looking ill and helpless on the floor of his prison cell. Since Sebastian left, Tomas visited Barron once a week and watched his brother deteriorate each time.

Barron groaned. "Where is my wife?"

"You will never see Sara again," Tomas said. "What happened to you, brother? You could have been a great general, a knight, anything. Was all of this worth it?"

Barron stood and walked over to be face-to-face with Tomas. He looked at the cane, then back into Tomas's eyes. "I should have been king. Just because Sebastian is descended from Dragon doesn't give him the right to rule. Our father was soft on him and treated me like a bastard."

"Our father loved you, brother. He was a good man. He hid us to save the people from war. There is no forgiveness in these lands for he who inherits the dragon curse. But he also wanted to see our potential, even yours." Tomas moved closer to Barron. "You are hiding something from me, brother."

"My gifts are far worse than you know, Tomas. I discovered it just shortly after the incident with Sebastian at the lake. Father was panicking. Whispers began to ruminate across the north. Even King Roman sent letters about the sight of a young Prince Sebastian summoning lightning and saving the world from a freeze. He had me working day and night with the guard. One morning after training, Father scolded me for being slow with my sword. I was so tired..." Barron paused. Tomas stared at him with his head leaned to the side. "I got angry. I don't remember a lot, but I reached my hand in the air, and suddenly, it was pitch black. I got dizzy and scared, and when I fell, the light returned, and Father was looking at me horribly. He mumbled something like, "blackbird fly." Then, he told me Sebastian would be king and I, his servant." Barron put his hand on Tomas's shoulder.

"That's why you killed him." Tomas pushed Barron's hand away.

"No. That was our father's request." Barron stared at the ground. "He said he had to die for his son to rise."

Tomas began to cross through the door.

"Oh, Tomas. I think you forgot to lock my cell." Barron pointed to the open door.

"No, I did not." Tomas turned and walked up to Barron again. "I found documents buried in a chest under the floor in the cathedral. All of our father's secrets. Like it or not, you serve the prophecy, therefore you serve me."

Barron smiled. "So my smart and witty little brother finally figured it all out." He walked from the cell to the base of the stairs. "There are so many things our father never told us. Some things are monumental to your and Sebastian's survival. The history of our supposed allies is foretold in all our father's ramblings. What? Did you think I didn't already know?"

The season changed from winter to early spring, and snow melt from the mountains caused flooding across the castle grounds. It was quiet except for a few men walking along the wall. Wolves appeared from the overlook and slipped down the muddy hillside, with Dom right behind them. Inside the front room, the wide fireplace roared and crackled. Dom warmed his hands and patted them on the ground, telling the wolves to lie down. He jerked his head to the alpha and left the pack behind in search of Tomas.

As he entered the throne room, the alpha wolf began growling. On the throne sat the once-imprisoned Barron Drake.

"Where is Tomas?" Dom said.

"Where he should be; fucking his woman." Barron smiled. "Well, well. Dominic Alcala Sage, I can see why my brother likes you. You are a strong soldier."

"You're going to burn."

"Yes, yes, my impending death." Barron shifted his position. "You don't quite understand my position here, Dominic. I spent so much time knowing nothing about who I was until I met Sacha. When my father called me a Blackbird, I wondered what that meant. There is a hidden history of Blackbirds. Like the dragons, there are two Blackbirds. One controls light and dark while the other is of death and life. The Blackbirds of the ancients served Dragon. Therefore, my destiny is to ensure my brothers fulfill theirs."

"Where are the others? Your brothers and sisters. What did you do with them?" Dom said.

"My family is no longer your concern, Dominic," Barron said. "The Sinook worshiped the Blackbirds. You may bow to me, or you may leave. But if you choose to stay, I have a favor I need to ask."

Dom scowled. "I will not serve you. I serve Sebastian."

"And I am a ward in his absence. Fetch me Prince Cyrus." Barron waved Dom away.

Dom shook his head and backed away quickly. He ran out of the castle to the stables, took his horse, and headed into the mountains, riding for Torrdale, unsure as to why he was complying with Barron's order. Cut curiosity got the best of him, and he wanted to know why Cyrus was connected to Barron.

In Shadowmire, Dom picked up some of NorthBrekka's soldiers to escort him west. They rode through the night, passing into Torrdale from the northern border, along the coast. They rode down the sand as fast as the horses could handle until the castle on the edge of a rocky cliff came into sight. Soldiers met them at the gate to the village.

"I came urgently from NorthBrekka with news for Prince Cyrus. I must speak with him now," Dom said.

"There is no good news from NorthBrekka these days. That land is cursed," the soldier said.

"Let them in." A voice traveled across the courtyard. "Open the gate. Cursed perhaps, but they are still our ally."

The gate opened, letting Dom and his men inside the castle courtyard. "Cyrus, how are you?" You look well."

Cyrus's face turned red. "What news is so important that you came all this way yourself?"

"It's about Barron. I have a lot to tell you, and I need you to listen. Can we go inside?"

Cyrus nodded and led the way inside the Bolin Palace. They entered the large glass-walled room at the back of the castle. Cyrus sat, then stood quickly. "I haven't sat on this couch since I returned." He turned to face the large window that overlooked the western sea. "I keep having these images in my head." He pressed his hand to the glass. "I was really young. He was so beautiful that I couldn't stop staring." Cyrus walked over to the couch again. "Sebastian and I sat here holding hands, yet I hate him. I don't understand what is wrong with me."

"Let the Sinook help you, Cyrus. Please. My mother is a powerful enchantress. Maybe Lorna's powers aren't as strong as we believe. There is only one way to find out."

"Before I agree to this, tell me something." Cyrus straightened his back and fidgeted with his jacket buttons. "What if I don't love him anymore? Not the way I used to. I think letting him end my life on my terms is better."

"He won't do it."

"He has to. I am a weapon, and I have already done a lot of damage. There is nothing left for me out there." Cyrus turned his body toward the window. "No one will ever love me, Dom. Not like him, and anything less is unacceptable."

"Cyrus, that is not true—"

"What news do you have?" Cyrus tried to cover the tear running down his cheek.

Dom sat back, put his hand on Cyrus's back, and explained the story of the Blackbirds. "Barron is requesting your presence in NorthBrekka right away. I fear he would do something bad if you refuse. Servant of the gods maybe, but Barron Drake is still an evil man. There is no redemption for his kind. The Blackbirds are a source of dark magic that Dragon used to murder thousands of innocent people. I don't know what his plans are for you, but you are a prince and the head of the Bolin house in Erras. It is your duty."

"I cannot help you, Dom. I am sorry."

Dom leaned over and whispered in his ear, "He will always love you."

Cyrus jumped to his feet and strolled to the window. "Do you think your mother can help me?"

"The only other person who can help you is a curse breaker. Do you know anyone with that power?" Dom joined Cyrus by the glass.

Cyrus shook his head. "Why do you trust me after everything I have done to him?"

"Because I believe there is still good inside of you. Somewhere. I will take you to Icefall in the summer if you'd like, but for now, you must travel to NorthBrekka."

CHAPTER 21
A Joust Fit for a King

The Hetta led the way, passing two towering statues of sea serpents that stood on both sides of the port. Sebastian paced back and forth as Jace manned the wheel, watching the city get larger ahead. The beaches gave way to a tall stone wall that had ivy and moss growing near the bottom. Rooftops could be seen, but nothing took away from the sight of a massive castle that towered over the town.

Sebastian spotted a NorthBrekkian banner on the end of a pier. The people working on the docks started rushing toward them as the Hetta and the Ophidias neared the port. It suddenly grew darker and colder. Sebastian looked up to see the castle blocking the sun. He balled his fists, then felt an arm loop through his. Dani's sparkling blue eyes and smile melted his frustration until he felt calm.

"I will wait on the ship," Valirus said. "There is no welcome for me in Altania. It will only start a war." He made his way toward the lower deck. "But I am here if you start the war, which is more probable."

"That is a good idea either way." Sebastian smiled as he made his way to leave the ship.

The crew of the Hetta stepped onto the pier first. Sebastian and Dani were the last two off. The crew of the Ophidias set foot on the dock next.

"Holy hell, brother. Look at you!" Viktor threw his weight into Sebastian, knocking him to the ground. Then Kristoff piled on top.

Sebastian choked. "I love you both, but I can't breathe!" He shoved them away and wheezed while holding his chest. "What the hell happened to the two of you? You're both... grown." He climbed to his feet.

Samir grabbed Sebastian's shoulder. "That is what is important. Family. I can't wait to have a bundle of little ones."

Meecah stepped out from behind a trunk. "Do you want to raise children in these times?"

Sebastian turned to Meecah. "The world is going to change. Give that man his bundle of babies. Maybe one of them will turn out right." He winked.

Viktor grabbed Sebastian by the shoulders. "Cyrus came to our home, brother. He was freaking out. Tomas wouldn't tell me what happened, but Cyrus looked scared and sad."

"Did he hurt anyone?" Sebastian's voice got louder.

"No. He was acting oddly like he had a lot of regrets. Maybe over you, I don't know," Viktor said.

"Your Majesty," Jon said. "Cyrus is different. Not with the curse, but I think it may be... wearing off."

"That is impossible." Sebastian scrunched up his face. "He said it can never be broken."

"He has memories of you."

"I know," Sebastian said. "But I used my powers in those memories. That may be why he has them. It doesn't matter anyway. He tried to kill me."

"I don't know what possessed him to do that," Jon said. "Viktor is right. Cyrus is afraid of something."

"Either way, we cannot be concerned with Cyrus." Sebastian started toward the town. "We are here for a joust and will be in our enemy's company. This will not be easy."

"So, you are telling us there will be a lot of violence, fighting, and drinking." Viktor smiled. "And perhaps, women." He elbowed Kristoff and winked.

"Everything your heart desires," Dani said. "Just remember, anything here could be a trap. Even the people." He held Sebastian's hand and led the way. "We should go. My father will be so happy that his little boy came home. King Maxen. His name means, the god killer, by the way." Dani glared at Sebastian before leading the way.

Viktor pointed at Dani. "What is wrong with him?"

"He has a wicked past." Sebastian picked up his speed. "Now is not the time for stories, brother. Another time."

Kristoff crept up and stood close to Jace. "I've been cramped up on that ship for so long. It will be nice to see some action."

Jace smiled. "Well, they will be in for a surprise if they start anything. Or if he starts something." He nodded at Sebastian. "Kristoff, your brother is the most difficult person I have ever dealt with."

"Good to know he's keeping up with his spirits in these times." Kristoff nudged Jace with his elbow. "A man of mystery, that one."

"You both know I am standing next to you, don't you?" Sebastian smirked. They approached a bright row of banners along the road ahead. There were flags from many nations that Sebastian didn't know about. "Are all of these countries here today?"

"Doubtful," Dani said. "The flags represent all the countries that have come here since the first jousting tournament. Some still come. Many do not. My father is not easy to like."

Sebastian walked into a grand stadium with tents of all colors and sizes for merchants, competitors, armor makers, and blacksmiths, and finally, he saw where he was to be. The king's stage. Two thrones sat front and center, with two smaller chairs close by. On one throne sat a man.

"That's my father," Dani said.

Sebastian straightened his back and marched toward the stage. He stopped just before the first step and raised his head to meet the icy blue eyes of his enemy.

Maxen's head turned to Dani. He groaned and took a deep breath. "What is he doing here? He does not belong alongside a king. He belongs in the fog."

Sebastian stepped onto the stage. "The market is gone. Closed. I saw to that myself."

Maxen stood to face Sebastian nose-to-nose. "What gives you the right to change things in my land?"

Sebastian leaned his head back. "Those people are free men and women I have housed in Adurak. As for Dani. He is mine." Sebastian's chest burned and his throat grew scratchy. "If you think you will take him, you are wrong." A rumbling sound came from the distance and clouds formed over their heads.

"We are here for merriment and drink." Maxen raised one arm to the side, gesturing to the throne next to his. "Entertainment, young king. You learn more about your enemy when you are not in battle. I invite you to sit."

Sebastian noticed the seats filling up quickly. Women in their most delicate dresses. Men in expensive boots and new coats. Young ladies sat near the king's platform waving and giggling. Dani's head moved slightly to Sebastian before his gaze returned to the girls. Sebastian grinned and reached for his hand. "Dani. Come sit, my darling."

Maxen's head turned to Sebastian quickly. "My son, the whore, is your new lover. That's cute."

"Dani is no longer yours to sell." Sebastian felt his face burn. The sky became a dark gray until Dani kissed his cheek.

"Easy," Dani whispered.

Maxen laughed, then shouted, "Begin the tournament!"

Men sounded horns from a podium near the end of the seats. Voices traveled across the stadium as they waited for the first knight to arrive. Maxen lifted his hand in the air and snapped his fingers. Sebastian heard a popping sound and then a woman slipped into the seat by Maxen. Her long blue hair was braided back and laced with flowers. Her dress was a light shade of lilac that flowed gracefully across her legs. She pulled back her head scarf and batted her eyelashes. She had the same ocean-blue eyes as Dani.

"My lovely daughter, Petra," Maxen said. "She would have been a better choice for you, Your Majesty."

Sebastian saw Petra blush and grin before pulling her scarf around her ears.

"He is wonderful, Father," Petra whispered. "Can I have him?"

"You are married," Dani said a little too loud. "No, you can't have him because he is mine."

"Was married." Petra poked at Dani.

"That's enough," Sebastian said with a severe tone.

Horns blared and men on their decorated horses marched into the stadium. Sebastian sat up to see a little better. The first knight stopped before the kings, turned, and bowed.

"Sir Roki Dinora," Maxen said. "Some call him The Unbreakable."

The knight removed his helmet and winked at Petra while his tousled blond locks bounced with each movement of his head. His smile was confident and prideful. Sebastian stared until Dani squeezed his hand.

"You like him, don't you?" Dani said. "How could I blame you?"

"No." Sebastian brushed Dani's cheek. "He isn't my type at all. Too arrogant."

Maxen shifted in his seat and cleared his throat. Sebastian pretended not to notice as he looked at the next knight approaching. Maxen started speaking the man's name, but Sebastian focused on Viktor and Jon, who had joined the audience. Viktor nodded for his attention, then shook his head to the left. Sebastian saw Kristoff and Jace standing together by the entrance.

Maxen put his hand on Sebastian's shoulder. "Where is my dear eldest brother? I know he is with you."

Sebastian stared at Maxen's hand. "He would not step foot on Altanian soil."

"Coward," Maxen scoffed.

"He is trying to keep the peace." Sebastian was uninterested and annoyed.

Maxen cleared his throat. "Why did you come here?"

"You invited me," Sebastian said.

"No. To Midrel Istan. Why did you come here?" Maxen stared closely at his face. "You Drake's have always been a handsome breed. Well, some of you." He pointed in the direction of Viktor. "Your brothers have such sweet faces. But you, not so much. No, not kind at all. Scarred, hollow, pouty. The Dragon's Curse has truly taken hold."

"Father, stop," Dani said.

Maxen laughed and turned to watch the joust. With a rush, the knights lined their horses and thrashed through the sand in pursuit of the other. Their lances pointed sharply. Sebastian expected to see one knight fall, but Sir Roki jammed his lance through the helmet of his competitor. He leaped from his horse, unsheathed his sword, and sliced off the head of the knight.

Maxen nodded with a grin on his face. Sir Roki marched over and placed the head in the hands of a young girl who was crying. The girl fell back and screamed. Sebastian nodded at Viktor and Jon, then to the girl. Jon scooped her up in his arms and took her away quickly while Viktor picked up the head and threw it back toward Sir Roki.

"That's admirable," Maxen said.

"What are you trying to prove here, Maxen?" Sebastian's voice was louder than before. "That you are mean and that you don't care? Do you think that the image you just showed me will keep me awake at night?"

Dani squeezed his hand hard. "Quiet down, Sebastian."

Maxen burst into laughter. "Are you going to let him speak that way, Your Majesty?"

"Dani, why don't you cheer up?" Petra said. "You are so grumpy. It is exhausting."

"Where is your husband?" Dani snapped. "Shouldn't the emperor of Runeheim be here as well?"

"If he were alive, he would be." Petra rolled her eyes. "I couldn't stand being locked away in that fortress of a city any longer. Do you know how boring it is in Runeheim? No, you don't because you have never been there."

Sebastian tried not to react, so he let out a little laugh. He noticed Dani gawking at him with his mouth open. "Your family is insane. How did you come out so perfect?"

"It's interesting," Maxen said. "The two of you falling for each other. His Majesty has a taste for the Bolin bloodline, doesn't he, Dani?"

Sebastian turned his head toward Maxen. His eyes were opened wide, and his eyebrows furrowed.

Maxen smiled. "Oh, I see Dani didn't tell you. Our family name is Bolin."

Sebastian suddenly realized he didn't know Dani or Valirus's last name.

"Cyrus was your lover, correct?" Maxen tilted his head down and looked into Sebastian's eyes. "And now, you have taken Dani. Another Bolin in your bed. My brother, Valirus Bolin is your mentor." Maxen turned back toward the field. "If only you knew the truth behind the Drake/Bolin history. It's a shame your father was a weak man. Maybe you would be living up to your potential by now if he would have just told you the truth."

"History?" Sebastian mumbled. "Never mind. It doesn't matter what tales the past tells. My issue is you."

Dani grabbed his arm and squeezed.

"Has my son been telling you stories about me? Tell me, God of Fire… in training." Maxen paused with a grin on his lips. "Prophecies never lie. Why shouldn't I cut off your head right now?"

The knights took their positions. This time, they held no weapons. Sand sprayed into the air behind the hooves of sprinting horses. One of the knights gripped his saddle in one fist and jumped up into a crouching position. The crowd cheered as he dove at his opponent, knocking him to the ground. The knight rolled over and slammed into the stage at Maxen and Sebastian's feet, causing dirt to cover Petra's shoes. She grunted angrily.

Maxen stood and pressed his boot to the knight's face. "You dirtied the Empress's shoes." He looked at Sebastian. "Does this anger you?" He took a dagger from his boot.

Sebastian took a deep breath and stood, puffing his chest. He bared his teeth, grabbed Maxen by the collar, and jerked the knife away. "If I were him, I would have thrown dirt at her face." Sebastian flipped the blade in his hand and pointed it to Maxen's throat. He felt Dani grab his other arm.

Petra stood, smiled lustfully at Sebastian, and walked away.

"Dani, follow her," Sebastian said.

"Yes, come with me, little brother." Petra taunted. "Let's go have fun like we did when we were children." There was a loud pop, and she was gone.

"No." Dani shook his head. His eyes widened, and he backed away. "Sebastian, it is a trap. We have to find everyone!"

Maxen snapped his fingers.

Petra giggled as she reappeared, holding Jace by the collar. "This one is cute and strong. I like him." Maxen snapped his fingers, and she was gone.

"Jace! Where did she take him?" Sebastian said.

"Guards, contain this man now!" Maxen's growled and kept his eyes fixed on Sebastian's.

Guards rushed onto the platform. Sebastian pressed the blade, breaking Maxen's skin. "It would be a great pride to remove your head from your body."

Dani gripped Sebastian's hand and kissed his cheek. He leaned in and whispered in Sebastian's ear. "Let it go, just this once. Think about your brothers. About me."

Maxen smiled. "Yes, think about my whore of a son. I was honestly surprised when I realized how much money he made me. Those men ravished him, over and over."

"Father, stop!" Dani's voice cracked and a tear ran down his cheek.

Sebastian pulled the knife back and cupped Dani's cheek. "Don't listen to him. It doesn't matter anymore. I love you. I want you to marry me."

Maxen gripped Sebastian's throat, then threw him forward. Sebastian's head smacked onto the stage. Dani screamed as Maxen lifted him by his neck. Dani's face turned pale as he placed his hands on his father's face. Blood spat from Maxen's mouth as he gagged for air. He reached his hand in the air and snapped.

Sebastian saw Kristoff and Viktor running toward him, but Petra appeared, and a shriek of laughter filled the arena. She grabbed them both by the arms and disappeared.

Maxen snapped, and in a flash, Petra was standing by his side. She reached down and kissed Sebastian's lips.

"Don't touch him!" Dani screamed and let go of Maxen.

Maxen snarled at Dani. "Blackbird." He coughed blood and laughed heavily. "Petra, take Dani!"

Sebastian lunged for Dani, but Petra appeared by his side.

Dani pushed her away and reached for Sebastian. "Yes!" His voice was hoarse. "I will marry you." In a matter of a second, Dani disappeared. Sebastian landed in the dirt. He sat up too fast and felt his head spin.

Petra appeared, grabbing Sebastian by the arm. "Father, can I?"

"Take him far away." Maxen smiled. "We have everything we need. Let him rot."

His body felt like it was being crushed together. His stomach twisted and suddenly Sebastian tumbled across a hard stone floor and crashed into a wall. The room was as black as midnight and smelled of mildew. The sound of metal armor came from afar and a door flew open. A light beamed Sebastian in the face just as he saw the hilt of a sword strike him on the head.

CHAPTER 22
The Fortress of Runeheim

He woke up to the sun beating on his face. Sebastian sat up quickly, looked around, and realized he was in a soft bed surrounded by fresh-smelling red roses. His head felt as if it had been split open and the scent of the incense burned his nostrils. Sebastian pulled away the blanket. "Why does everyone insist on taking off my clothes?" He looked for his pants.

"Your clothes went into the fire, Your Majesty." A woman's soft voice came from the door.

He sat up and rubbed his eyes. "Where am I?"

"Arcadian Fortress. In Runeheim. I hope you slept well."

"Where is Dani?"

"What do you want with my baby brother?" The voice returned to a high-pitched whine. Petra marched over and stood before Sebastian's naked body. "You can have so much more. Imagine if you and I ruled together. Adurak and Runeheim as one united front."

Sebastian raised one eyebrow and laughed. "I have no interest in you whatsoever."

Petra put her hands on his chest. "You stink. I am going to bathe you. Follow me."

Sebastian stepped into the steaming water, closed his eyes, and laid back. Petra ran her fingers through his hair and washed his body.

"You are magnificent, Your Highness. You can trust me, you know," Petra whispered.

"Trust you." Sebastian sat up and tensed his muscles. "You won't tell me where Dani is, or my brothers, or Jace."

"Relax." Petra pulled him back. "Jace and your brothers are in Adurak. Safe and sound in your castle. I swear. As for Dani, he is resting. He had a bath and is asleep in a room down the hall."

"You don't sound like the Petra I met in Altania." Sebastian pushed her hand away and turned to face her. "What game are you playing?"

"I'm not playing anything." Petra stood and walked to the other side of the bath. "But if you insist on being stubborn, I will force your hand." She dropped her dress to the floor, revealing her soft porcelain body to Sebastian, then stepped into the water.

"Don't do this," Sebastian said. "I can hurt you."

"I can help him." Her voice was soft and low. "Cyrus. I know how to break his curse." Petra climbed onto his lap, ran her fingers down his stomach, and kissed his neck. "I can give you anything you want."

He grabbed Petra by the arms and jerked her back. "What do you want from me?"

"Be with me," she whispered. "Give me babies. You can have your Cyrus, but you will be mine."

Sebastian shook. "Go to Hell." He shoved Petra from him, climbed out of the bath, and reached for clothes that waited on the bench. "I am going to Dani." He heard a pop, then Petra appeared in front of him. He balled up his fists and growled. "Get out of my way."

Petra slapped him across the face. "You will never see Dani again. I lied. Dani is on my father's ship. Good luck escaping Runeheim, Your Majesty." She paused and looked him up and down. "You and I could have been so good together." She brushed his cheek, then Sebastian felt a pinch as Petra disappeared.

Sebastian stormed down the hall, throwing open doors. "Dani!" Sebastian's body turned hot within, and the hair on his arms stood. His eyes burned, and fire ignited from his fingertips. He crossed the fortress from top to bottom, screaming for Dani. Sebastian marched into the great hall and stood before a line of knights.

"Dani is no longer in Runeheim," one said. "We have been instructed to ensure you do not leave these grounds."

Sebastian took a deep breath. He slapped his hands together, then spread his arms apart, forming a fireball between his palms. "If you think you can stop me, you are wrong."

"Kill him," the knight shouted.

Sebastian sent fire crashing into the knight's helmet, throwing him into the wall. The others pointed their swords and stepped toward him. He threw his arms forward suddenly, sending a gust of wind so strong it threw the knights through the stained glass and into the courtyard. Men and women who worked on the grounds ran away screaming as stacks of wood and hay flew in every direction.

His body became hot, and his skin felt as if it were being seared over a fire. He felt angrier, his chest burned, and his eyes watered. Hatred washed over him like a dark cloud. It was hate for people, for love, for everything. It was hate he could not control. He crashed onto the floor. A surge of energy burst from his body causing the ground to shake.. Stone and glass fell around him. Chandeliers and candles smashed into the glossy floor. He let out a snarl and everything began to settle.

He looked up to see a stout, older knight standing over him. "So, it is all true. You really are Dragon."

Sebastian looked at him with his eyebrows raised. "I am much worse than Dragon." He tilted his head. "I am Chaos." Sebastian felt his entire body intensify. Lightning cracked from his hands. Thunder rumbled in the sky above. He stretched his finger out and faced them palms down as a ripple surged across the floor. The fortress rumbled again. The remaining pieces of stone fell from the walls, striking knights and guards. Sebastian threw his arms forward again, blasting away another wall.

Sebastian shouted, "I don't even have to touch anyone to kill them. Tell me where to find Dani and I will let everyone else live."

The knight stepped back, sheathed his sword, and kneeled. "You will never find him on your own. Dani is on a ship with Maxen on his way to Erras. Stop hurting my people, and I will personally escort you to Adurak."

Sebastian put his hands down and the storm settled. He stared at the knight in disbelief. "You work for the empress. I don't trust her. Why should I place my life in your hands?"

"We served the emperor." The knight paused. "Empress Petra turned him away from his people by forcing him to ally with her father. King Maxen poisoned his mind. He was a good man until his last breath."

"Who are you?" Sebastian said.

"My name is Treggar Harrow. I was born in Alta Prime. My father worked for the crown, but we came here when I was only twelve. I know the Bolin family well. Perhaps I may be of some assistance."

"If I am to trust you, then we must leave now. I have to get to my brothers, Jace, and then get to my ship." Sebastian started walking across the courtyard and through the market.

Treggar was quick to catch up. "Your Majesty, I have trained some of the fastest horses in the land. Please, allow me to take you to them."

"You still haven't explained why you are helping me," Sebastian said. "Don't say it is because I am who I am."

"You are the rightful King of Erras. When I found out you were here, I vowed to help you. I am sorry I could not help Dani. Petra hates her brother. Probably because he is more powerful than she is."

Sebastian thought about how Dani healed the knife wound in his chest from Cyrus. "He has never mentioned it before."

"I don't think he knows much about it. King Maxen sold him into slavery when Dani killed his mother." Treggar climbed into his saddle.

Sebastian twitched and tilted his head to the side. They rode toward the wall surrounding Runeheim. There were soldiers approaching from the market, and the click-clacks of hooves on the stone road grew louder and slower. Treggar mentioned the word "dragon," and the men immediately looked in Sebastian's direction. He held his head high and clenched his jaw. "Are you going to let us pass, or do I need to do to you what I did to your Empress's fortress?"

The soldiers looked past him. There was smoke billowing from broken walls and collapsed ceiling pieces. The city's people gathered, then a scream came from a woman who stood on a cart. "The Empress is gone. Destroy Runeheim. Destroy everything."

"This is not good." Sebastian smirked. He leaped down from his saddle and walked toward the growing crowd. He held up his hands.

Treggar stepped out in front. "We can trust him."

The crowd stared at Sebastian. No one spoke a word.

The woman stepped down from her cart. She was young and pretty with her black hair waving gently as she walked. "We have heard of a great king who ruled in Adurak, but speaking your name was forbidden. We are indebted to you, King Sebastian."

Sebastian smiled. "Prepare to depart. We have a long journey ahead. What is your name, madam?"

"Seville, Your Majesty. I was Empress Petra's maiden. I can help you learn everything you want to know about her."

Seville talked a lot. She took a horse and rode by Sebastian's side, spillingeverything she knew about Petra and Maxen. She explained that there was a hidden harbor with ships once used when Altania was allowed to have outposts in the east. Sebastian pictured sailing to Erras with an entire fleet of boats. He smiled and realized Seville was still talking.

On the last night of his journey east, Sebastian sat alone on a hill, staring at The Creed in the near distance. At that moment, he realized he truly admired the City of Thieves. A man sat next to him and reached for a stick to stir the nearly out fire.

"I brought some more wood, Your Majesty." Treggar stacked logs into the pit and stirred the embers.

"You don't need to do that." Sebastian reached his palm out. Fire whipped from his hand onto the wood, creating a bright orange blaze. "I always find it odd that everyone knows what I can do with my powers, yet they always want to build me a fire."

"Just being polite, my king," Treggar said.

"Please, sit." Sebastian offered a spot next to him on the log. "You said you knew the Bolins. So, you must have known King Roman. He was my Father's friend. Lorna, the queen, killed him," Sebastian said.

"None of the soldiers in Alta Prime trusted Lorna. People from Safareen are disturbing. I imagine Maxen will head there. It is his only ally."

"No, he will go for Torrdale. He will kill Cyrus, take the throne, and build a kingdom. He would never share the glory with the Safar." Sebastian stared ahead again. "Now that I must return to Erras, I find myself sad. I think that maybe Adurak is where I am meant to be."

"You will have to fight for NorthBrekka first. They are in grave danger if Maxen and the Safar plan to move against them. This journey home will not be a short visit. You are going to have to leave Adurak behind you."

Sebastian wanted to change the subject. He fidgeted with a stick andthen tossed it into the fire. "Dani told me Maxen killed his mother, or at least he thought it was Maxen, but you said Dani killed her."

Treggar lowered his head. "His mother passed away just after hugging Dani one night before bed. Maxen has hated him ever since."

"I don't care what he is. I love him. I must find him. I feel my duty is to protect him, but I have failed. If he dies—"

Treggar nodded and put his hand on Sebastian's shoulder. They didn't speak much more that night. Once the camp went to sleep, Sebastian lay by the dying fire and closed his eyes, listening to a light breeze roll through the grassy plains. The air smelled like berries, and owls sang their songs in nearby trees.

CHAPTER 23
A Dust Cloud on the Horizon

Jace stumbled and fell. The familiar scent of mountain air mixed with seawater filled the atmosphere. He sat up to see the empress staring back at him. Jace's mouth dropped open. She lifted his chin with her fingertips and smiled.

With a pop, Petra disappeared and Jace was alone in the dark. He heard screaming coming from the town market, the rustle of carts rolling down the road and doors slamming closed. Jace ran past the fountain and into the town in time to see torches disappear into The Creed. He heard footsteps come up behind him fast.

"Jace?"

"Kristoff?"

"Are you alright?" Jace hugged him. "Is Viktor here?"

"Yes. I am right here." Viktor joined them.

"Where are Sebastian and Dani?" Kristoff said. "Where are we?"

"Adurak. That is Sebastian's castle." Jace walked toward a firelight in the distance.

It was night in Adurak. The market was silent. The usual noise of bar fights and giggling whores was gone. Jace continued walking toward the castle.

"I don't understand," Kristoff said. "Where did everyone go?"

Jace walked to the forge where he saw a hint of fire from the castle. He hoped the blacksmith was inside working. Molten iron still sat in the pot and the fires were dimmed down to a deep red. He followed Kristoff inside The Golden Mace. Jace sat at the bar and stared at the bottles that lined the wall. Kristoff sat at the table next to the barkeep's coin box. He picked it up and shook it, hearing a light clang of money rattling around.

"Pour me a pint," Jace said.

"Sure." Kristoff hopped down and grabbed a glass from under the counter. "What do you think happened to everyone?"

Jace shrugged. "Petra. She did this."

"What did she do to my brother?"

"She took him somewhere." Jace took a gulp of warm ale. "She is a witch, and she has these powers that let her vanish and reappear in other places." He stiffened up and took a deep breath. "Sebastian could be anywhere."

"My brother is strong," Kristoff said. "He will get through this, but I wanted to ask. Are you doing alright, Jace?"

"I am as well as I can be. Has anyone told you that you look exactly like him?"

"So much that I am beginning to think it is my legacy." Kristoff paused, then laughed. "My last boyfriend told me he always had a thing for Seb. I know everyone finds the twins very beautiful, but I don't want people to only like me because of our resemblance."

"You like boys too, like Sebastian."

"Uhh, yes. I like both." Kristoff stared at his feet. "Girls scare the hell out of me, although I want children of my own, so maybe one day I will find one that isn't awful."

Jace burst out laughing. "I like both too, but I agree. Girls are horribly frightening."

The door flew open. "There you two are." Viktor looked exhausted. "I turned my back for a moment, and you were gone."

"Pull up a chair," Jace said. "If we are truly in hell, then we might as well get drunk."

The next morning, Jace awoke on the floor of the tavern. He sat up but quickly realized Kristoff was cuddled against him with his arm around his stomach. Kristoff was undressed. Jace stood and noticed his clothes were off as well. "Viktor?"

"He went back to the castle, remember?" Kristoff mumbled. "Last night when we were drinking... You kissed me... I kissed you... Viktor left."

"Did we?"

Kristoff smiled. "You were really drunk, weren't you?"

"I'm sorry." Jace's cheeks burned.

"Stop. Please do not insult me," Kristoff said. "It was great, by the way."

Jace started fumbling with his clothes. "We need to have a look around now that the sun is out." He stopped and stared at Kristoff. "I hope I don't upset you, but I think—"

"Last night was a mistake." Kristoff pulled on his pants. "You don't have to say so. I mean, we just sort of met, so I don't expect your hand in marriage or anything."

"I do like you," Jace said. "But I think I like someone else." He started fidgeting with his jacket buttons.

Kristoff grabbed his hand. "It's fine. I understand. You love Sebastian."

"What? No." Jace stepped back. "I mean, yes, but that's not who I was speaking about." He slipped on his boots and hurried to the door. "We should get moving."

The streets were empty. The carts filled with wares, weapons, and exotic foods were gone. The yawning drunks were missing from their usual stride to their homes in the early hours. Kristoff tiptoed alongside Jace, occasionally peeking over at him with a dreamy grin across his face.

In the castle, they found Viktor standing on the balcony that used to overlook a vast canyon. They walked along the stream, Kristoff stopping to look around every few seconds. The river that took its rightful place in the ravine was calm and flowing with ease.

"Viktor, good morning," Jace said.

Viktor began giggling. "Good morning, Jace. Kristoff." He nodded at his brother. "Look over there. It looks like smoke. What is that way, Jace?"

"Just empty plains. A few small villages and eventually, you will find the fortress city of Runeheim. But that smoke is not normal. Someone is coming." Jace ran to the armory with Viktor and Kristoff hot on his heels. They gathered swords, shields, and arrows before returning to the balcony.

"It could be my brother," Kristoff said.

"That isn't smoke," Jace said. "It is dirt. There are a lot of people on horses over that ridge."

The dust cloud filled the sky and fell into the river. "There are only three of us, but you are Drakes, and I have sworn my loyalty to your king, therefore, you. Whoever they are, I will fight to the death for you."

"As will I," Kristoff said.

Viktor gripped his sword. "I hope this is my brother."

The thump of horse hooves began to rift through the breeze. Jace turned his gaze to the north as a shadow cast across the way. The faint sight of a silhouette appeared to be a large number of men on horseback.

"Put the bow down, young Jace."

Jace, Viktor, and Kristoff jumped and swung around.

"Valirus!" Jace laughed. "How did you get here?"

Valirus held up his staff. "I am a sorcerer, you know." He let out a laugh. "When I discovered our king was in trouble, I took the Hetta and fled."

Viktor tilted his head "Wait, you left everyone behind?"

"Of course not. I told them to walk." Valirus patted him on the shoulder and walked to the riverside.

"Walk?" Jace said.

"No time to explain." Valirus pointed to the north. "We have company."

The ground began to shake in the distance. Jace stepped as close to the edge as he could, straining to see the army. Thunder cracked over The Creed, and a light rain began to fall. "Gentlemen, our king has come home."

"I can't see anything but dust." Kristoff squinted his eyes.

"No, they are coming in from the road to the north where a bridge will bring them here." Jace craned his neck down the river.

Jace turned and saw white sails poking their way between The Creed, where the river runs through the valley. The air became cold, sending a chill through his spine. The storm overhead began spitting rain as the river turned from calm to angry. The nose of a ship appeared around the last bend before the river curved into the valley.

Sebastian rode furiously across the plains, impatiently waiting for the sight of the bridge. He took deep, heavy breaths and a burning feeling filled his chest and stomach. The clouds swirled over Adurak. Sleet pelted Sebastian's face, stinging his eyes. He checked behind him and saw Maxen's ship turn the bend. Sebastian faced the sky. He threw his fist into the air and screamed. The sky popped and cracked, and a bolt of lightning struck the rocky embankment next to the ship, sending an avalanche of stone onto the vessel's broadside. "That will slow them down."

As they crested a hill, Sebastian saw the lush green fields of farmland meet the border of Adurak, turning from grass to rock. The large bridge that spanned across the river waited ahead. The swarm of soldiers from Runeheim, led by Sebastian, turned quickly and pressed forward across the roaring river. Sebastian saw ice forming on top of the water. He felt his body shake with pins and needles rushing down his limbs. His heart fluttered. Sebastian took an unsteady sniff of the air and twitched.

The riders passed through the gates of Adurak and climbed the lower mountains of The Creed until reaching the market streets. Sebastian halted and looked around. His horse moved slowly as Sebastian peeked into windows and down the streets. He looked up into the mountains, seeing the rain turning into a light mix of snow.

"Is this your doing, Your Majesty?" Treggar hurried to Sebastian's side.

"Why do you assume that?"

"Because it has never snowed in Adurak. Never." Treggar looked to the sky. "The stories say that it was you who brought the river to fill the lake. That will bring crops and fish to the inland. There will be mills which means men will have work."

"It was nothing." Sebastian turned his gaze ahead as the fountain came into view. "I said I would help the people have a chance at a future. I told them I would get rid of Maxen. I will fulfill my promise."

Sebastian urged his horse forward as they reached the marketplace's end. A scream and the echo of footsteps came from the castle. The soldiers rushed the palace. Sebastian saw the ship halted alongside the balcony and men storm down the gangway. "Maxen!" Sebastian shouted. "Come out and fight me." He leaped down from his horse and ran into the atrium. "Maxen!"

"Sebastian, help!"

He spun around to see three Altanian soldiers kicking Kristoff in his face and ribs. Sebastian plunged his sword into one man's back and kicked another in the stomach. Kristoff struck the third with a knife in the groin.

Sebastian watched the man squirm on the floor. He laughed. "I have to say I have never stabbed a man in his dick. I'm impressed, brother." He watched the Altanian men run through his castle. "Do you suppose they are looking for me?"

"It would be rude to keep them waiting," Kristoff said.

"Where are Jace and Viktor?"

"No idea. We all separated when the ship docked. Also, Valirus is here."

Sebastian stepped into the atrium again and shouted, "Maxen, come and face me, you coward. I am waiting for you."

"You intrigue me, King Sebastian of Adurak and NorthBrekka." Maxen came down onto the terrace. "You rule two kingdoms. No other king does that, but still, you know nothing of being a leader."

"Where is Dani?"

"I see you made friends in Runeheim." Maxen nodded to the soldiers behind him.

Sebastian heard the light taps of heeled shoes coming quickly across the deck. "Petra." He groaned and rolled his eyes.

"Did you just say my precious, beautiful people are following him?" Petra came face to face with Sebastian. "How dare you steal my people." She touched the tip of his nose.

"We aren't yours anymore, Empress." Treggar stood by Sebastian's side. "We serve the true King of Kings."

Petra looked at Maxen, then back at Sebastian. She stuttered, and her lip trembled. Maxen pulled her away. "Get out of here." He snapped. Petra nodded and disappeared.

The winds thrashed, causing waves from the river to slam into the canyon's sides, splashing into the castle. The air quickly turned to an icy chill. Sebastian could see his breath, and the water from the storm froze. The snowflakes fell like lumps of cotton.

Maxen looked over Sebastian's shoulder. A grin cracked across his mouth. "I was wondering when we would have a reunion, brother."

Valirus stood by Sebastian's side. "You would think after all we have seen and been through in our lives that you would know better than to anger the gods, brother."

Maxen grinned and turned his attention to Sebastian. "Chaos. Born of Dragon, God of Fire." Maxen turned to Valirus. "He doesn't scare me."

Fighting broke out on the deck of Maxen's ship. "Let go of me!"

Sebastian jerked his head toward the voice.

Altanian soldiers appeared at the gangway with their grip on the neck of a man screaming, "Sebastian!"

"Dani," Sebastian barely got his name out before he saw Maxen wave his hand. His feet seemed as if they were being ripped out from under him and felt the wind get knocked from his lungs when he slammed through the door that led to the kitchens.

Sebastian climbed to his feet and jerked his sword from his side and marched toward Maxen. He dragged the sword on the stone floor, then ran his palm across the blade, setting it ablaze. "Valirus, find Dani." He ducked to miss Maxen's sword.

Maxen's hand turned bright white and reached for Sebastian's head. Sebastian pushed it away and punched Maxen in the face, bloodying his nose. "Scrappy young lad, aren't you? Typical NorthBrekkian stock." He shoved Sebastian to the floor. "You are a demon, and I will make sure the people of Erras see you as the monster you were born to be. Your family, your people, all of Erras and Midrel Istan will bow to their new King of Kings when I stand on a mountain of victory with your severed head in my grip. Dragon!"

"Why do all you old men obsess over this cursed prophecy?" A voice came from the great hall, then an arm looped around Maxen's throat, throwing him to the ground. "You must kill me if you want to take my king's head."

"Jace!" Sebastian gasped.

"And Viktor," Viktor said as he appeared beside Jace. "Does everyone forget I exist?"

"Of course not," Sebastian said. "You are too tall to forget."

Viktor began laughing, and Sebastian jumped to his feet. He put his sword to Maxen's neck, then looked up to see Valirus walking inside with Dani.

Sebastian stumbled back and ran to embrace Dani tight against his chest. "My love."

"Don't let him take me," Dani said. His eyes were wide and his face pale. "He is trying to make me do horrible things, Sebastian. Help me."

"He will have to kill me if he wants to take you."

"Then so be it." Maxen threw Jace out of his way and sent Viktor flying into Valirus. "Get your pathetic, lazy little ass back on that ship, Dani, or I will slaughter your lover boy."

Sebastian saw his castle filling with the bodies of his men and women, as well as Altanians. His brothers and Jace went to help, but Valirus stood by Dani as Sebastian threw another punch at Maxen's mouth. He reached his hand to the sky. A bolt of lightning connected with his grasp, but Maxen waved his arm, once again throwing Sebastian to the ground.

Maxen laughed, pranced around, and clapped. "Weak, Your Majesty. You are still just a pathetic child."

Sebastian's gaze was drawn to the front of the castle. Coming down from The Creed with a loud rumble and rocks sliding from their feet were criminals, mercenaries, assassins, merchant traders, and innkeepers. The thieves had returned to the city they built to hide from the ridicule of the dangerous world that surrounded them. They were ready to fight. They stormed the palace, striking down Altanians with every swing of a blade. Sebastian's attention snapped back to Maxen, who was still flaunting.

"Did you not teach him to fight against a wizard's magic, brother? Tsk tsk. But you are getting quite old." Maxen opened his palm, and a ball of white light beamed. He reached for Sebastian's head.

"Father, no!" Dani threw himself over Sebastian, protecting him from Maxen. "Don't let him touch you when his hand is white. That is how he takes control of your mind."

"Shut up, Dani!" Maxen grasped a fistful of Dani's hair and threw him backward.

Sebastian stood and gritted his teeth and clenched his fists. The wind howled through the atrium, bringing stinging cold. The snow rushed inside. "Valirus, you always want me to make ice into a deadly weapon, right?"

"And yet you always refuse to do it, Your Majesty," Valirus smirked.

Sebastian threw his arms wide, and the stream lifted from the floor and formed into sharp icicles above him. He pointed one at Maxen's head.

Maxen drew his sword and whispered something Sebastian could not understand. The blade turned a bright white and sparked, and Maxen charged at Sebastian.

"No!" Dani threw his arm around Maxen's neck and knocked him to the ground. Dani's face turned pale, almost white, and the veins in his forehead popped while his eyes turned black. His mouth dropped, and an inhuman shriek came from his throat. Maxen lunged with his sword in hand. Dani ran into Sebastian's arms and pulled him tight.

Maxen kicked Dani, sending him to tumble into Sebastian. Fingers wrapped around Dani's throat and pulled. Sebastian wrapped his arms around Dani's waist. Maxen swung his sword around and held it to Dani's throat. The blade drew blood.

"Maxen, stop!" Sebastian grabbed the blade. Blood dripped from his fingers as the blade cut through his skin.

Dani's hands rested on Sebastian's chest. His stare turned icy and blank and his face became pale. He let out a shriek.

Sebastian's entire body locked into place. His arms fell tight by his side, and he was colder than he had ever felt.

Maxen snapped his fingers and with a pop, Petra appeared by his side. "Get me out of here, Daughter," Maxen snarled.

With another pop, Maxen was on his ship. Sebastian couldn't move. Valirus threw Dani to the ground. Jace, Viktor, and Kristoff ran over to help Sebastian.

"What did he do, Valirus?" Jace yelled.

"He almost killed our king." Valirus turned and stared at the ship, then back at Dani.

"I didn't mean to, Sebastian," Dani cried. "I swear I would never hurt you. I love you."

Sebastian was gasping to breathe. His voice was hoarse, and his body hurt all over. "Dani—"

There was another pop, and Petra grabbed Dani and took him away.

"Dani!" Sebastian's voice was high-pitched and cracked. It thundered so hard the river splashed onto the terrace.

There was a short silence before Treggar's voice echoed through the atrium. "Everyone take cover!"

Sebastian barely turned his head before he saw flicks of fire come from portholes in the ship. There was a blast and boom as cannons fired onto the castle. Pillars crashed around him but all he could see was Maxen holding Dani by his hair. The sails opened and the ship moved once again. A part of the ceiling collapsed mere feet from his head. Jace threw his body over Sebastian's and waited for the devastation to end.

Sebastian couldn't feel anything. Not Jace still laying against him, screaming his name. He couldn't hear and everything was a blur. He sat up and saw that the castle suffered minor damage. His people crawled out from their hiding places, yet the bodies of many still litter the floor. "We have to go after them," Jace said.

"Our king could die," Valirus snapped. "Dani has never been able to use his power, especially the killing part. He must have been so scared. Get Sebastian to his room. He needs medicine and rest. The curse of the Blackbird is still inside him. As for the rest of you, clean this place. Take the bodies to the field and burn them. We cannot travel until the king is well."

"We don't have time, Valirus." Sebastian's voice was shaky. His body ached and his throat felt like he swallowed fire.

"How do you suppose we catch him, my king?" Valirus said. "Maxen will be through the lake and down the river to the east before we can make it to the ship."

"Ships. There are ships." Sebastian paused to catch his breath. "Seville said—" His eyes flickered.

"Your Majesty, if you wish to lead an armada, I suggest you sleep and take your medicine as I ask. This journey will be harsh, and Maxen is ready for you."

"Fine, Valirus. I will rest. What happened to Dani?"

"You know as well as I that Dani would never hurt you, but his powers are surfacing." Valirus started to pace.

"What powers are you talking about?"

"Dani is very dangerous, Your Majesty. Chaotic, like you. He was so afraid of losing you that you were the unfortunate recipient. He didn't know what he did."

"I do not blame Dani," Sebastian said. "I lost him again, Valirus. I promised to protect him, and I have failed twice. Maybe I am not worthy of him." He took a deep breath and rubbed his eyes.

"Rest, Your Majesty." Valirus grabbed his shoulder and led him to the stairs. "I will send out men to search for food and find some herbs for tea. For now, get some sleep. I will send someone to watch over you."

Sebastian nodded and walked up to his bedroom. It was surprisingly quiet. He saw a faint sight of sails tucking between the mountains around Lastorum. He fell to his knees and put his head in his hands. "I will come for you, Dani."

CHAPTER 24
The Breath of a Dragon

A gust of bone-chilling wind whipped through Sebastian's bedroom. He lay awake but had yet to open his eyes. His body ached all over and he felt drunk. He took a deep breath and opened his eyes. The cold made Sebastian think he was in NorthBrekka, but the familiar smell of saltwater reminded him he was in Adurak.

He saw Jace fast asleep at the table. The fire was barely glowing. Sebastian smiled and shook his head. "Maybe I do need someone to keep the fires lit for me." He fetched wood from a basket and pushed his palm toward the fireplace, engulfing the logs in flames.

Sebastian quietly dressed and stepped to the balcony, seeing the snow falling hard over the river. He ran over to the table. "Jace, wake up. How long have I been out?"

"What? Good morning to you, too," Jace mumbled. "A few days, I think. It hasn't been easy. You were…I have never seen you like that before. I think everyone is afraid of you right now."

Sebastian pushed his hair back and stretched his back, groaning with every move.

"You are still not well."

"I am fine." Sebastian glanced at Jace before marching down the stairs. He found Kristoff and Viktor at the large table in the back of the dining hall with Valirus. Many of his people were at tables enjoying breakfast and talking loudly. When he stepped through the doors, the room fell silent. The people quickly fell to their knees and bowed. Sebastian felt someone run into him from behind.

"Sorry, Your Majesty. I didn't realize you stopped." Jace put his arms around Sebastian's shoulder. "Do you want me to bow?"

"Yes, Jace. I would like you to bow…"

Jace began to kneel.

"I am joking. May the gods bless me for having to deal with you." Sebastian rubbed his face. "What the hell did I do? Why is everyone staring at me and…" He tilted his head. "Shaking?"

"I will let Valirus explain it to you," Jace said.

Sebastian sat down. "As you were. Eat, relax while you can." There was a loud rumble of whispers across the room. He looked sharp at Valirus. "What did I do?"

"You died." Valirus had an unusually high-pitched tone. Sebastian stared at him with his mouth dropped open. "But then, you were alive again. That is all you should know."

"Excuse me?" Sebastian started.

"Tell him about the fire," Viktor said. "That was quite the show."

Valirus gave Viktor a stern glare. "You died, Your Majesty. Jace carried you away and suddenly you burst into flames. The screaming was horrifying. The lightning burned down buildings in the market, and then the blizzard came. Once the flames stopped, you lay there violently jerking and growling. Your skin looked like the dry lake did before the river came, cracked; only it was still burning with skin turning to ash. The people saw. They are calling you The Dragon King. But then, everything stopped, and you fell back asleep, completely unharmed. The snow, however, never stopped.”

“I don’t know what to say.” Sebastian closed his eyes. “Jace, are you alright? Did I burn you?” He reached for Jace.

“I am unscathed, My King.” Jace held Sebastian’s hand to his chest.

Later that afternoon, Sebastian left the castle to see the damage he had caused while dying. The courtyard was quiet, except for a few townsfolk bustling about. The market looked as if time had stopped. The usual hustle of merchants shouting prices for wares was missing. No children were playing in the street and no gamblers lined the bars with their cards in search of a hustle. Soldiers paroled the streets in groups of three.

Sebastian stopped them near the northern end of the town. “What happened here?”

A soldier stepped forward before the others. “We saw Petra and Maxen walk through our town, Your Majesty.” He wore a scowl and had an angry stare. “We may be the meanest bunch, but we are still small in numbers. We sent our people into The Creed and your militia stood strong. But as we had them surrounded, Petra used her gifts and disappeared with Maxen in tow.”

Sebastian entered the Fat Angry Cow and sat down at the bar. He looked up, noticing a painting of a large, angry-looking woman hanging over the mantel. A soldier sat down and stared at the painting as well. Sebastian glanced over at him.

“That is my mother,” the soldier said. “My father named the tavern after her.” He paused and turned to Sebastian. “She didn’t like that too much.”

Sebastian laughed and enjoyed his ale until he decided to continue wandering the town. People were moving quickly in and out of shops and homes. They took a sharp glance and bowed before moving along. A loud crashing noise came from a dark alley ahead. Sebastian walked toward it without fear. "Who is there?"

Another sound of metal smashing into the rocky pathway echoed towards him. Sebastian held a fireball in his palm as he wandered into the corridor. The tall buildings blocked the sunlight, leading into a small cul-de-sac with much older shops that sat against the mountain. The open walkway allowed for enough light so that Sebastian could see a short, fat man in the window of one shop. No others were around.

"I have my sword drawn. If you come any closer—"

"You would dare strike your king?" Sebastian walked faster to the storefront. "Who are you, and why are you here?"

The man kicked the door open and strutted outside with a large sack over his shoulder. "What's it to you?" He wore a smug expression, dirt under his nails and hair, and a heavy gait in his step. "I'm just trying to feed my family… Your Highness." The man chuckled and walked past Sebastian.

"Careful, sir." Sebastian grabbed the man by the collar of his shirt. "I asked you a question." He came within inches of the man's dirty face. "Who are you?" His jaw clenched tightly.

"Fenton Paark. There, are ya happy, Your Grace?"

"I am afraid we have not met. Where are you from?"

"You know exactly who I am. I am Dani's guardian." Fenton glared at Sebastian. "I know that bastard child has been staying with you. Folks from the fog market warned me about a rogue king in the south."

"So, it was you that whored him for money." Sebastian's nose tingled and eyes watered. "I should kill you for hurting him." He clenched his fists. "Dani is kind and good and you tortured him!"

Fenton threw his head back. "That evil, soulless disgrace to his royal name? A blackbird some called him. He was forced upon my family. Never wanted him, though, so I used him. So what?"

Sebastian felt a horrible burning pain fill his entire body at once. His head pounded, his heart raced, and his hands shook violently. Sebastian looked at Fenton. "Why did Maxen take Dani?" He saw his skin begin to glow.

Fenton stared at him nervously as he tried to break Sebastian's grip. "What are you?"

"Answer me!" An immense burst of wind shot from Sebastian's torso and rippled across the yard, breaking windows in shops and homes that surrounded him. His breath became raspy, with each exhale sending vibrations through Sebastian's chest. The sound of many feet rumbled down the alley.

"Sebastian, brother, what happened to you?" Viktor said.

Sebastian slung Fenton through the window. "Tell me what I ask!" The ground began to shake, and buildings broke and crashed down. He gritted his teeth, snarling as he crawled on top of Fenton and jammed his thumb into his eye. "I will make your death as painful or easy as you like if you tell me what I ask."

"Sebastian, no. Let him go," Jace said.

"Don't you dare stop me, Jace." Sebastian sat up and pointed. "Do not stand in my way of finding my Dani."

"Sebastian, you really have become—"

"Don't say it, Jace."

"Dragon. Look at yourself." Jace begged.

Sebastian yanked his hand away from Fenton's face and stood to look in the mirror. He didn't recognize himself. He was Sebastian, only his skin tinged with red burning lines, his eyes shined like rubies, and he had faint wisps of fire coming from all over his body. Cinders flicked away when he moved, threatening to burn everything in his path. Sebastian's chest expanded and he leaned his head back, feeling the rough and gargled air mix with the burn in his belly. He smiled as he approached his reflection. Smoke escaped his mouth as he laughed.

CHAPTER 25

Brothers Bonding

The dark room was lit by the summer afternoon sun shining down on the castle. Tomas slowly approached Barron. "Where is everyone?"

"They are safe. They remain in NorthBrekka. East Watch."

"What good was it to send everyone through the pass?" Tomas fell to his knees. "They will just follow Sebastian home if he—"

"Get up, brother." Barron grabbed his arm and pulled. "Stop being weak. You are a Dragon. Act like one." He walked over to face Amara. "You should send her to East Watch as well."

Tomas grabbed his arm. "You didn't answer my question."

"Because if Maxen reaches NorthBrekka before Sebastian, he will slaughter every last one of them." The room dimmed to where only a few candles remained lit.

Amara pulled Tomas aside. "You can't stay here alone with him, Tomas. He acts like he is on our side, but he isn't. Don't trust him."

"I don't," Tomas said. "But maybe he can help us for now. I have to stay. I need you to join my family at East Watch. Go and wait for my brother to come home. He will sneak into the East Bay Harbor, where no one else will sail. I need you to inform him about what happened before he arrives here. Amara, he needs you."

"And I will be there for my friend. I love you, Tomas."

Tomas watched from the garden as Amara mounted her horse and left with a legion of soldiers the following morning. He started breathing hard and felt cold, dizzy, and shaky. A cool sensation stung his eyes. Tomas's slipped and fell forward. His hands stretched toward the ground. He balled his fists, then spread his fingers apart. The pond froze and loud cracks echoed as the rocks broke apart. Tomas gasped and stumbled backward.

"Good job, you destroyed a 300-year-old pond. When it melts, it will be everywhere." Barron walked over and put his arm around Tomas.

"I can't control it." Tomas stumbled to his feet. "I don't know how."

"Sebastian will teach you, brother," Barron said. "When he learns his power, he will be unmatched by any in existence. He is almighty, and you... haven't done much."

"That is your fault," Tomas raised his voice. "You killed our parents. You tortured Sebastian and killed Will, Gentry, and—"

"Yes, I am well aware of what I have done."

Tomas started toward the castle. "Then why are you here, helping me? Sebastian is going to kill you when he sees you."

"If I am to die, I want to be remembered as the one who tried to right his wrongs. That is all."

Tomas stared at Barron, feeling like it was a trick, but the look in Barron's eyes told a different story. "I still don't believe you are doing this for us, but it seems as if I have no other choice but to trust you."

Barron walked to Tomas. "If the legends are true, there is another like me, and he is the only one who can kill you and Sebastian. If Maxen gets his hands on that power, he will be at our keep before the season changes. I don't want to watch the two of you rule the world, but it is either you or Maxen and trust me when I say that Maxen is the wrong choice to sit on the throne."

"Who is this man?"

"Cyrus's uncle." Barron led the way inside. "He was outcast from Erras by his brother, Valirus. When Valirus heard that Maxen was causing panic in Midrel Istan, he sailed immediately for Maxen's kingdom, leaving his children behind. Now, nineteen years later, Maxen returns for what he believes is rightfully his."

"The throne," Tomas said.

"And he will do whatever it takes to get the throne, so you better hope your brother gets his ass here before Maxen gets his hands on you. Did you know that the Bolins and the Drakes weren't always allies?"

Tomas tilted his head and stepped back. He took a deep breath and shook his head. "How do you know all of this?"

"I found journals. Letters, scrolls… Our father had a lot of secrets." Barron clenched his jaw. "It angered me at first. I burned everything except Father's journal. I lost control of my powers and lashed out against Sebastian all those years ago." He put his hand on Tomas's shoulder. "Imagine what the other one like me can do if he gets his hands on the two of you."

CHAPTER 26
A Last Glance at Adurak

Sebastian sat on the cliff's edge next to what was once a beautiful flowing waterfall and was now a stream that spilled gracefully into the river. The snow still continued to fall. Jace came in and out with food, sometimes to talk and sit with him. Jace fiddled with the buttons on his coat and turned his head away.

"I'm so tired, Jace."

"Rest, my king. You have to sleep sometime."

"No, I don't mean sleep," Sebastian said. "I meant I never wanted this gift. But now that it is more powerful than ever, I want more. What is happening to me, Jace?"

"Fulfilling the prophecy." Jace covered his face and laughed.

Footsteps could be heard coming up the stairs. "He just needs more training."

Sebastian squeezed his eyes closed and smirked. "Valirus. Thank you for understanding my pain." He straightened his back and turned his head.

"Come downstairs with me. You will want to see this." Valirus motioned for him to follow.

Sebastian walked into the throne room. His heart fluttered happily as he hurried across the room. "Jon, Meecah! You are alive. Samir, all of you." Sebastian hurried from person to person.

"What happened to him?" Meecah asked Jace. "Why is he acting all crazy?"

"He has transformed," Valirus said. "Your Majesty, please, sit and let me tell you everything that has happened." He cleared his throat. "When I discovered the lot of you were taken by Petra, I knew they weren't trying to kill you, only break you apart from your people and slow you down. They know they alone cannot kill you and your twin, so they took the only person who can and went after the weaker dragon first. I told the people to head east to pick up reinforcements on their way to Adurak. Meanwhile, I took the Hetta Horizon and sailed away from Maxen's cannon fire."

Sebastian looked around the room, seeing familiar faces from Feldor Bay, including the tall and broad Men of the Mountains, miners residing in the peaks south of the bay. Sebastian sat on the throne. "Fenton Paark called Dani a Blackbird, Valirus. I need to know everything before I risk my life to save him."

Valirus paced while twirling his thumbs. "Dani was young. His powers were coming to light, so to speak. When he would get enraged, he would kill bugs, sometimes dogs or cats. Not on purpose but he would just...touch them. No one noticed this but me. It was when he took his mother's life that Maxen sent him away for good. If Maxen knew what Dani was, he would have kept him and used him as a weapon."

Sebastian raised his eyebrows. "Will Dani attack his father?"

"No," Valirus said. He lowered his head. "Maxen made sure he could not."

Sebastian rubbed his face and made his way to the door. "We have a lot to do. Tomorrow, we ride." Sebastian paused and faced Valirus. "Where is my ship?"

"North, Your Majesty."

Sebastian shook his head and left the throne room, marched across the atrium, and strode out into the courtyard. He took a deep breath and sighed as his eyes moved across The Creed. He felt physically heavy and tired. As the thought of leaving Midrel Istan came over him, Sebastian's chest began to burn, and his head hurt. He slowly backed away and turned back to the castle and went inside to his bedroom.

Sebastian took one last look at his castle in The Creed early in the morning as the men and women of Midrel Istan marched through the market. He put his hand on the fountain and closed his eyes. "I will return one day. I promise."

The people tirelessly made their way through the archway and into the desert lands away from Adurak. Sebastian stopped to hear the wind howl as it echoed against the mountains. The cold gust of air and snow brushed his skin. Sebastian smiled and reached his hand to the sky, and a single lightning bolt kissed his outstretched fingers causing the snow to stop. The clouds parted and began to let the warm sun poke through. Sebastian caught up to his brothers, who waited at the bottom of the hill with his horse.

They rode through the night, passing Lastorum and continuing north, passing the swamp and coming into the dry lake that was not shrouded in fog nor dry, but instead, he could see how vast the lake was as well as the river that led to the northern Sea of Glass.

"A small cove is hidden along the river by a thicket of trees. The entry is enchanted. We need His Majesty to walk through it to break it. Only then will the ships be revealed," Seville said.

"The ghost ships," Valirus said. "That is how Maxen used to find people gifted in magic. The ones who had seen these ships were of magical origins. He killed them all, of course."

Sebastian urged forward, faster, heading east with haste. The smell of salt water filled the air around him as he began to climb a small hill. His horse galloped relentlessly against the wind from the open sea ahead.

Sebastian heard Valirus shout. "Your Majesty, stop!" Valirus's tone seemed desperate. Sebastian jerked back on the reins, and his horse yielded nearly to the edge of a sandy bank. He tiptoed to a place where the land had just stopped.

Seville and Valirus came to look over the steep decline of the sand that fell.

"That is a long way down, Seville. Are you sure this is the place?" Sebastian said. "I see no trees."

"This is impossible. The map shows it to be right here." Seville pulled a small piece of paper from her jacket. She read it over and over in a whisper only she could hear.

"Can I look at that?" Sebastian reached his hand out. Seville slowly passed it over. "This isn't a map. It is a letter." Sebastian read the letter. "The grotto can be anywhere along these shorelines. Which way do we need to go?"

"My Father wrote that letter to me years ago," Seville said. "He was gifted. One day my Father was fishing on the beach when he heard a noise. He followed it into a cove. When he returned home, he started dreaming about a man coming to Midrel Istan who would guide us to freedom. He told me to do whatever it took to find that man and help him. Soon, Maxen came for him. He left this behind for me. That man in his dreams is you. In Erras, they call you a monster, but here, we call you our guardian. Our king. We are at your mercy. I have carried this letter for ten years waiting for you. Before he died, he put a special message on the page which said that only our true king could reveal the map. I need you to burn this letter."

Sebastian stared at Seville in shock and horror. "If I burn it, it will be gone forever. Are you sure you want to lose something your father gave you all those years ago?"

"Please, Your Majesty. Burn the letter." Seville pushed the letter onto his chest.

Sebastian saw his brothers' faces looking back at him with raised eyebrows and gaped mouths. Jace put his hand on his arm and nodded. Sebastian lit a fireball in his fist and held the letter over it, letting the paper slowly char. Seville had tears running down her cheek. Viktor wrapped his arm around her and smiled. She blushed and smiled back, and they stared at one another's faces for a long, sweet moment. Sebastian smiled and looked back at the letter. He gasped as the letter turned blue, and Sebastian's flames sparked out of control. He jerked his hand back, dropping the note. It flopped on the ground making a wheezing sound before turning back into a regular piece of paper.

The letter was no longer filled with a father's last words to his daughter but instead revealed a detailed map of Midrel Istan with an orange-glowing 'x' where the ships were waiting. "We ride north," Sebastian said, walking to his horse and moving on without a word.

As the day turned to dusk, Sebastian came to a grassy field on the border of the desert. A lighthouse shone brightly over the calm ocean, and a firelight caught his eye. A farm came into view. Not a very good farm, but a small garden and a shack stood before the lighthouse. An older woman was picking turnips as the army approached. Sebastian towered over her.

"We have nothing, keep moving," she said.

"We are not here to take anything. Just a place for my people to rest, then we will be on our way." Sebastian held his hands up to show he was not there to cause trouble.

"You must be the Adurakian King. I apologize that we have not met. My husband disapproves of you. My name is Glendi Paark."

"You are married to Fenton," Sebastian said. "Dani used to live here."

"We never wanted Dani. King Maxen forced him on us." Glendi finished gathering turnips in a basket. "We had four children already we could barely feed, but when Maxen brought him to us, he gave us enough gold to last years. But Dani was a difficult child. We lived in fear of having him around our family. That is why we sent him away."

"You forced him to sell his body. You beat him, tortured him. Why? He was a child whose father threw him away. Now he is this, whatever he is—"

"Blackbird," Glendi said. "He is what they call a Blackbird. There are only two in the world. Just like there are two Dragons, there are two Blackbirds."

"I have heard this before. Who is the other?" Sebastian got close to Glendi, towering over her. The red glow returned to his skin.

"I don't know, but they say he has the power to destroy the sun. To make everything dark, cold, and deadly." Glendi shook her head and hurried toward the front door of the shack. "You are welcome to rest here but stay outside and away from our crops. Do you understand?"

"Yes, madam. Thank you, and good night. We won't stay long."

Glendi went inside and slammed the door. Sebastian grabbed Valirus by the bicep and dragged him away from the others.

"What is this about, Your Majesty?"

"Is Maxen going to use Dani to kill my people?" Sebastian started shaking.

Valirus put his hand on Sebastian's chest. "Dani would never. You see, where there is a good dragon and an evil dragon among you and Tomas, there is a good and bad among Dani and the other Blackbird. I believe Dani is the good one."

"Now Maxen is taking him to Tomas. I am already so far behind. He could already be there. Tomas could already be dead. There will be no rest until we are out to sea." Sebastian stood and shouted. "We move out, now!" He looked at the tattered little house, went to the door, and knocked. Sebastian reached into his pocket.

A pair of little boys opened the door and smiled. Sebastian smiled back and opened his mouth to speak, but a man appeared, slapped the children in the heads and shoved them away.

"What do you want?" Fenton scowled.

"I wanted to thank you for allowing my people to rest. I wanted to pay for your service." Sebastian handed Fenton a fist full of gold coins, then grabbed Fenton's collar. He felt the heat radiate from his body and saw his red flaring scaly skin in the reflection of Fenton's eyes. "If you ever hurt another child again, I will return to Midrel Istan to cut the throat from your neck and eat it in front of your family. Do we have an accord?"

Fenton jerked away. "Yes, of course, Your Majesty. Many thanks for your kind blessing on my house."

Sebastian stared at Fenton with a hint of laughter escaping his lips. He smiled, shook his head, and closed the door as he left to join his men. Sebastian led them north, following the map's guidance. He caught Seville looking over his shoulder as she steered her horse close. "Here, take it. It is yours." Sebastian handed the map to Seville. She smiled and returned to her conversation with Viktor.

"Idiot boy," Meecah came riding next to Sebastian with Samir at her side. "Do you have any idea where you are going?"

"As a matter of fact, I know exactly where I am going. I thought the two of you were staying in Midrel Istan."

"We cannot stand by like cowards," Samir said. "It is important that we play a role in saving our homeland and yours. We have a lifetime to settle down and start a family. But we have to give our children a future first."

"You are an amazing man, Samir," Sebastian said. "I am glad we had the pleasure of meeting."

"And what about me?" Meecah laughed. "I am your best friend, after all."

"I have never been happier to be best friends with someone who tried to kill me." Sebastian flashed a grin to Meecah. "I am eternally grateful for you to be in my life. I promise the two of you will never have to worry about anything ever again. You are family."

Samir and Meecah bowed graciously. Sebastian saw palm trees lining the beach ahead and the sand turned from yellow to a shimmering white. He stopped on the beach, jumped down from his horse, and walked until he saw a familiar stretch of land and the rubble of what was once a beautiful home he shared with Cyrus.

"Valirus." Sebastian waved for him to come over. "Do you think Cyrus can be saved?"

"He is my son. I will move mountains to help him. But why do you ask?"

"Even if Cyrus and I can never be together, I still want him to be happy. I want him to live a fulfilling life, even if it doesn't include me. I am alright with that now."

"This is where he tried to kill you, isn't it?" Valirus walked around in the broken debris.

"And where Dani saved my life."

"You really do love Dani, don't you?"

"More than anyone in the whole world." Sebastian took a deep breath. "I want him back, Valirus. I want my family, friends, and every damned person on this planet to live in peace and stop fighting and killing." His skin had orange and red lines forming on the skin as the burning returned to his breath and stomach. "I just want to live in a world where I am not being hunted."

Valirus turned his head quickly toward Sebastian. "You know what it takes to make that future real. It means ending the magic in the world. You would have to kill all of us. Dani is no exception."

Sebastian growled and reached toward a stack of stones that blocked his path. When he went to grab one, he felt a heavy sensation pulling at his fist. "Valirus, what is this?"

Valirus let out a few heavy fits of laughter. "My boy… this is incredible." He put his hands over his mouth. The others whispered behind his back. "There are not many gods on record that could manipulate the earth. It is truly unique."

Sebastian started twirling his fingers as the weight shifted to points on his hand where he felt the most pull. With each touch or movement, the rocks shifted. He smiled and laughed. "Am I supposed to know how to do this? I don't remember the earth gods."

"Your Majesty, you have literally moved mountains. But you have been right all along when you say you are not Dragon. Your name is Chaos. You are the god of all elements. You are a brand new power introduced to this world and it is extraordinary." Valirus's tone always confused Sebastian as it would change from serious to sarcastic within a quick phrase.

Sebastian let out a laugh. He began to rummage through the rubble some more, then a shimmer caught his eye. He turned to see the clouds and fog clear out at sea. The sun flashed off the metal rigging on the Hetta Horizon. "You did this, didn't you, Valirus?"

Valirus shrugged. "I had to hide it from Maxen. He would have blown it to bits like he did your brother's ship."

"What?" Kristoff said. "He destroyed my Father's ship?"

"Blasted it to hell. It is gone, boy," Valirus said. "But, I believe what we are looking for is just through those trees." Valirus pointed behind Sebastian.

"I've walked through these woods dozens of times—"

Valirus put his hand on Sebastian's shoulder. "You weren't transformed before. Go and have a look now."

"If I am going to walk through another curse, I might as well get it over with." He turned to the trees, straightened his back, and took a deep breath before walking into the veil of dark magic. A loud pop and a tingling hot sensation shot through his body. The trees shook and sank into the sea. Sebastian led his people into a deep grotto within the thick palm forest. Before them sat six ships. Their wood was old and weathered and their sails were tattered, but they bobbed carefully in the lagoon. "Well, the good news." He wrapped an arm around Kristoff's shoulder. "You have five ships to choose from. Have at it."

"Thank you, brother. Before we split up, I have to ask." Kristoff dug the toe of his boot into the sand. "Jace. Do you think he… likes me?"

"Wow." Sebastian giggled and backed away. "Umm, I don't really know. He's a good man though." He made his way down the dock where the Hetta was tethered.

"It's amazing they all fit in here," Viktor said.

"It's magic." Jace ran up next to Sebastian. "This is incredible. How did you break the enchantment?"

Sebastian shook his head. "I have no idea. Apparently, when I walk into spells, I break them. It's not as fun as it sounds."

"You are King Sebastian, the curse breaker." Jace laughed and patted him on the back.

"I don't need any more titles, Jace. Let's go home. Shall we?"

CHAPTER 27
The Ghosts

The Hetta Horizon cut through the Sea of Glass with a fury with Sebastian at the helm, guiding the wind through the many sails of the fleet. They neared the deepest part of the ocean where the rain and storms brewed dangerously overhead. The ship sailed for many days and nights with a crew of tired and weathered sailors working tirelessly to reach their destination.

As the sun rose and set and the crescent moon shined high in the starry sky, Sebastian sat with his chin on his knees, watching straight ahead. Kristoff took charge of a ship named Wind Ghost and had Viktor, Seville, Meccah, and Samir on board with a crew to maintain the sails. Jon took control of his own ship named Earth Ghost. Sebastian realized each was named after an element, leaving the fifth one to be named Death Ghost.

Valirus came to sit with him when the air turned cold, and the rain turned to snow. "We are close. Are you sure you wish to port in NorthBrekka? The ice is treacherous. It can damage the ships."

"It is the fastest way to get home. If Maxen is already there—"

"He isn't there." Valirus stood quickly, staring ahead. "Look, Your Majesty."

Sebastian leaned over the front of the Hetta and squinted his eyes. "Everyone to your battle stations!" He took a few steps back and raised his arms to the sky. The wind picked up, and with the snap of sails, the armada sped forward. "I do not know which ship Dani is on. Do not fire unless I give the word."

A haze and fog blanketed the water's surface. Rain mixed with snow made tiny shards of ice that pelted down on Sebastian's skin. There were three ships ahead, all sailing side by side. Sebastian stood at the tip of the Hetta's nose, glancing back and forth between all three of Altania's vessels before he spotted a familiar long blue mane of hair whipping in the wind. "Petra!" He gritted his teeth. "How do they not see us coming?"

"They know we are here," Valirus said. "Why are they ignoring us?"

"We have to get closer." Sebastian spun around, reached behind him, and made a waving motion with his arms. The Hetta creaked and moaned against the sudden force.

"Easy, Your Majesty. Do not get too close."

"No, I want them to hear me." Sebastian ran to the bow again. "Petra!" Sebastian shouted with every ounce of breath in his lungs. "Come get me."

Her head turned suddenly. She looked away, then, with a pop, she stood next to Sebastian. "My beautiful king has called for me." Petra smiled and brushed her fingers against Sebastian's cheek.

"Take me to your Father. Now!"

Petra giggled, then wrapped her arms around him. Sebastian felt the familiar burning pain of loathing and hatred fill his entire body. There was a pinching sensation before he was face to face with Maxen.

He stumbled and paused to catch his breath. "That is the most horrible feeling." He glared at Petra. He turned his attention to the man on the helm. "Maxen, release Dani to me now." Sebastian jerked free of Petra's grip. "Let go of me, woman."

"Then what? You can't get off my ship without my daughter's help, and she will not take you back to your little band of thieves unless I tell her to." Maxen seemed to enjoy the idea that he was right.

"Where is Dani?"

Maxen's head turned to a dark corner behind the stairway. Sebastian hurried over and saw black hair covering a face with sparkling-blue eyes peeking through the strands. He took the gag from Dani's mouth and held his cheek in his palm.

"My love—"

Sebastian held Dani in his arms and kissed his lips.

"That is all you get. Now, get off my ship. I have a country to rule." Maxen nodded at Petra and walked away.

"Petra, please, no!" He was too late. He felt her hand grasp his collar and then he stood on the Hetta once more, and Petra was gone.

Valirus reached forward. "Your Majesty—"

Sebastian felt his body ignite with rage. "I can save him." The sky cracked and boomed with lightning and thunder, and the sea began to swell and swirl. He signaled for Kristoff and Jon to take positions and be ready to fight. His fleet separated from the surrounding Altanian ships. Sebastian turned to his men as the Hetta inched toward the side of Maxen's ships. His men braced for cannon fire, but as the Hetta moved into a perfect position, the fog cleared, and Sebastian saw ships as large as his all waiting to intercept Maxen. "It's the Safar."

"Sebastian!" Dani ran to the side of his father's ship.

Sebastian jumped on the rail. "Jump, Dani. I will catch you!"

"Your Majesty!" A shout from Earth Ghost drew his attention straight ahead.

They were on a collision course with the Safarian lead ship. "Fire!" Sebastian screamed. The Hetta exploded in cannon fire and Maxen's ship jerked away, ducking between one ship from Safareen. The ghost ships came alive with the boom of guns and black powder. The Safar returned fire, damaging Fire Ghost with his Adurakian militia on board. Sebastian hopped onto the railing and reached the sky. A lightning bolt crashed into his waiting grasp, and the sea split.

A thunderous roar and unyielding waves came thrashing from every direction. Sebastian waved his arms in a circular motion and pushed toward the raging sea. The Hetta charged forward, leaning hard to one side, slipping into a whirlpool.

"Signal the other ships to pull back," Valirus shouted at Treggar. Treggar gestured for the rest of the armada to continue north and away from the Hetta. "Sebastian, get us out of this now! Maxen has escaped. We must flee."

The Hetta and the ship from Safareen were swirling across from one another. A thick fog and mist covered the ocean's surface. "When we crest this next turn, fire the cannons on my command."

"Your Majesty—"

"Do not question my authority, Valirus. I am still king!"

"Yes, but you have created a whirlpool." Valirus pulled his palms together. "If you don't get us out of here, you will have us all sunk to our death." Valirus spun around and rushed away.

Sebastian made his way to the wheel while keeping an eye on the captain of the Safarian ship. The Hetta climbed up a wave and crested over the edge of the cyclone. "Fire!"

Cannons shot at once. The Hetta lunged away and crested over the edge of the raging water. There was a boom and wooden shards exploded into the air. Sebastian gripped his hand on the rail and smiled as he watched the mangled ship descend deep into the abyss. He shook off a chill that ran down his spine as he turned the Hetta north. "What is wrong, Valirus?" The sorcerer slowly made his way onto the deck. "Were you scared? I wasn't scared." Sebastian grinned before letting out a laugh.

Valirus tried to be severe but broke at the sight of Sebastian laughing at himself. "I think it is time I stop doubting you, my king. Even if I think you are going to drown me."

Sebastian grinned and stared at the deck for a moment. "Once we are clear. I want everyone to get some sleep. We will arrive in East Bay by nightfall tomorrow. It is going to be very cold. I suggest getting a meal and a good rest before we climb the mountains."

Sebastian stayed at the wheel, watching his Ghost ships in the broken fog ahead. He waved his hands back and forth, bringing the wind to an otherwise still open sea. The water changed from deep blue to the obsidian black of The Midnight Sea. He stared at his hands. The soft red glow was gone, and the tinderbox of sparks were no longer dancing across his skin. He let out a little laugh and smiled knowing he had learned to catch lightning and move the earth. Sebastian shook his head and raised his arms again and reached out for the air to push the sails to their stretching point.

CHAPTER 28
Lords of the Land

Tomas stayed in bed late one morning. The cold air made his knee ache and Barron's badgering conversations made him depressed. "Tomas, shouldn't you be practicing? The enemy isn't going to go easy because you are untrained." Tomas mocked Barron's voice pulling his blanket over his head. "I hate my life." Finally, he climbed out of bed, dressed, and slowly went to the dining hall.

Tomas missed the chatter of his siblings, Amara's sweet smile, and the smell of freshly baked bread. Now, Castle Drake was cold and quiet.

Barron sat alone at the king's table, chewing on a piece of ham. "I have a thought, brother." He paused and waited for Tomas to get closer. "We need reinforcements. You in your infinite wisdom decided to let some of our best fighters go on a mission to find Sebastian, leaving NorthBrekka low on defenses."

"They didn't sail blindly." Tomas felt his heart skip a beat. "In Father's secret storage, I found maps. Loads of them, with places around the world we had never heard of, and Cyrus told us exactly which land mass to send them."

"Yes but what about this king who is out to destroy the Dragon bloodline? If he is as terrible as Cyrus said, then you sent our fighters into the wolf's den, unprepared and with little hope of survival. What if the king decides to seek revenge and sail here? Then what will you do, Tomas?"

Tomas sighed. "What are you saying?"

"I know people who can help."

"Absolutely not." Tomas limped to the table and sat before Barron. "The Kuhar are traitors."

"Yes, and they still think I am their king." Barron smiled. "Now that Sacha is dead, I am their one ruler. Their queen passed years ago."

"If Sebastian comes home to the Kuhar, he will—"

"Kill me, I know." Barron rolled his eyes. "Many of you don't seem to understand that I realize how much you want me dead. We have a fickle past."

"You are a traitor and a murderer. No Kuhar in NorthBrekka. None. I will not allow it." Tomas reached for a plate of eggs. "I am still king here, not you."

"You are wrong, dear brother. Sebastian is king. He will always be the king, and people like you and me are nothing more than lords of the land. Not the king." Barron passed Tomas a pitcher of wine. "I like my wine cold. Tomas, would you mind?"

Tomas placed his hand on the side of the jug and concentrated. "And a damn fine king he is." Ice escaped Tomas's fingertips, engulfing the pitcher. "You know he will lock you away when he returns, don't you?"

Barron straightened his back. "He needs me, whether or nothe thinks he does. You both do."

Tomas took a sip of Barron's wine. "It is better cold." He passed a goblet across the table. "I will make sure he knows you are trying to help us."

"Why do you trust me all of a sudden?" Barron asked.

"I don't." Tomas pounded his fist on the table. "But my instincts remind me that you are my blood. We need you, Barron. Please don't let us down."

Barron took a sip. "If these witches and sorcerers are allowed to take Erras, everyone, including the north and south, will be slaves to them. Once they kill Sebastian we stand no chance against King Maxen. No matter what I wish to believe, the world needs Sebastian."

"But everyone still believes he is the Dragon."

Barron looked away and took another drink. "Eat up. You have training."

"Wow. You are incorrigible." Tomas finished breakfast and left the hall with much difficulty. His knee shot blinding stabs of pain all the way to his head. Once the nausea subsided, Tomas continued his work.

The following day, he sat in the letter room, drafting a note for the crows to take to East Watch. One to Nadya and one to Amara with instructions to watch for Sebastian's ship and to inform him of what was happening in NorthBrekka. Mostly about Barron. As the crow carried the messages away, Tomas caught a glimpse of the long, braided hair of a Sinook warrior. "Dom." He smiled and stumbled down the stairs to greet them in the courtyard.

"Dom, good to see you, and…" Tomas turned his head to the side. "Cyrus? Why is he here?"

"Well, look at that." Dom pulled him in for a hug. "Tomas Drake does leave the interior of his castle. I'm proud of you." He glanced at Cyrus. "He is… well, actually, Barron asked me to fetch him."

Tomas shook his head while rolling his eyes. "You know what? I don't really have time to argue. Barron predicts Sebastian should be returning soon. I don't know how he has this information, but he seems to know a lot more than I do."

"Sebastian is going to kill him," Dom said.

"Oh, he knows." Tomas turned back toward the castle. "He keeps saying it."

Tomas led them inside and out of the cold. He sat with them in the library, quietly discussing what Barron had been doing. "He sent my family and the maidens and cooks to East Watch in case Maxen arrives here first. Also, I asked Amara to marry me." Tomas paused and smiled. "She said yes."

Dom clapped, then squeezed Tomas's shoulder.

"Congratulations, Tomas," Cyrus said. "You deserve to be happy."

"So, it appears that Barron is trying to protect his family from Maxen," Tomas continued. "I didn't know we had ties to Midrel Istan at all, but I do know that your family, Cyrus, are the ones coming to kill me." He walked over to Cyrus, feeling an icy tingle in his eyes. His hands got cold and turned white. "Are you on our side or theirs?"

Cyrus backed away. "Tomas, I would not have come alone if I meant to hurt you. I would have brought an army."

Tomas threw his hands in the air. "Where are the fighters from Torrdale? If you intend to help, shouldn't you provide militia?"

"Don't worry, they will be here. I gave the word to come the long way. That way, I could gain your trust first before they arrive." Cyrus patted Tomas on the back.

Tomas laughed. "So, you do still have some of your brains left. Good, because you will have to deal with Sebastian when he arrives. I am not getting in the middle of you two."

"Understood."

The door flew open. In came Barron looking confused, then smiling. "Gentlemen, welcome."

"How long until Sebastian arrives?" Tomas said.

Barron joined them at the table. "It is a matter of days. Word arrived yesterday that a fleet of ships was seen crossing from the southern Midnight Sea to the north. I should have another message letting me know when he passes into the realm of NorthBrekka."

Tomas stood. "Scouts. What scouts, Barron? I said no Kuhar."

"They are watching our seas. Initially, they were watching for a fleet from Midrel Istan. But instead, they sent word that they saw the Hetta Horizon, along with a fleet of gangly-looking ships filled to the brink with men." Barron paused and let out a laugh. "Our brother is bringing armies. Multiple ones. Whatever he has done while in Midrel Istan has been brilliant."

"He must have found the teacher," Cyrus said. "Barron, do you know who this teacher is?"

"Nothing, beyond that he is a sorcerer that was locked away in prison."

Cyrus sat down and stared at the wall with a blank expression. "What if the teacher is my father?"

CHAPTER 29
Back in The Break

The stars and moon drifted away as the sun passed over the horizon. The sea had a layer of broken ice and a trail cut through where ghost ships led the way. Sebastian closed his eyes and breathed in the cold, wintry air. "It is good to be home. We should be arriving in East Bay Harbor soon. Be wary of Kuhar ships. They will be looking for revenge."

Valirus turned to face Sebastian. "Revenge? What did you do?"

"Long story. Prepare to lower the sails. It is time for our journey on the sea to come to a close." Sebastian put his hand on Valirus's shoulder. "I appreciate everything you have done for me. I don't deserve it, but you have remained loyal to me, and if it weren't for you, I would still be blowing everything up."

"You destroyed Runeheim." Valirus held his arms in the air.

"Yes, but I knew what I was doing." Sebastian felt his nose burn. "Not that many people died. Not like before… nevermind, forget it."

Valirus nodded, smiled, and walked away, shouting to the crew to prepare to lower the sails.

In the break from the clouds, Sebastian saw a rocky cliffside come closer and closer. The ghost ships began to turn west with only one sail left standing. The Hetta followed suit and made its way to the port. The harbor was nicer than Sebastian remembered. It had two long piers where once broken pieces of wood and docks stuck out from the water. Sebastian and Valirus walked first down the pier to meet with the others.

Sebastian stopped and stood still once his feet touched the rocky ground. He closed his eyes and took a deep breath. The cold air and the smell of mountain snow filled his lungs. His body shook from the chill, and then warmed. He opened his eyes and saw his friends and family watching.

"Welcome home, brother," Kristoff said.

Viktor pointed to where he had watched his little brother die from an explosion meant to kill Sebastian and Will. "Don't worry, we had Gentry's body taken home finally. He is not on the beach anymore."

Sebastian walked over and kneeled, resting his palm against the sand. "I am happy he is resting among our kin. I'll be sure to visit him when we are home." He started the journey up the hillside.

The line of men gathered on the East Bay Pass as Sebastian stared at the icy peaks of The Break. "It is winter here. That pass is treacherous. Everyone must stick together and help, or you will not make it. Understand?"

A thunderous rumble echoed down the way.

"It looks like it is coming from East Watch," Viktor said.

Sebastian squinted, trying to see as far as he could until horses came into view. Sebastian's eyebrows raised and a grin crested across his cheek. "Nadya?" He ran forward.

"Sebastian!" Nadya leaped from her horse and ran into his arms. She held his face in her hands. "You're home and alive." She trembled as she tugged at his coat and hair. "Look at you. You are so grown up."

"I am home." Sebastian grabbed her hands and held them against his chest. "And very much alive. I missed you so much."

"We missed you too." Nadya gestured toward the others behind her, then ran into Jon's arms.

"Amara? Is that you?" Sebastian scooped her up in his arms. "Wow. You are as lovely as always."

Amara clung tight to Sebastian. "You have no idea how bad things have been here," she whispered. "Barron is no longer in the dungeons. He is gifted, Sebastian. He has powers, and Tomas lets him run about. He says he is doing it for you, but I don't know." She ran over to her horse and took something from the saddle.

Sebastian took a letter from her hand. "What is this?"

Amara shook her head. "Tomas sent this just yesterday."

He started reading as Amara, Nadya, and the others went off to meet the crews and greet their families. He read the letter word for word, touched the ink, and thought about Tomas. "It just says Maxen has not yet arrived at Castle Drake. I can handle Barron. He doesn't scare me anymore. If he does anything to hurt any of you, I will kill him." Sebastian started toward the road that led to the pass.

"We are coming with you," Nadya said.

"No, my love, the children." Jon stepped in front of Nadya.

Nadya's eyebrows furrowed. "Barron forced us to come here against our will." She crossed her arms. "I am not going to sit here while my family needs me."

"She is right," Sebastian said. "We saw Safarian ships and it was as if they were protecting Maxen. If he is working with King Lucian and the Safar, he will need time. Trust me when I say he is heading for Torrdale. There is no point for everyone to freeze out here on the water when they can be warm in the castle. Barron's precautions are nonsense." Sebastian paced and kicked at the snow.

"What does this man want with us?" Jon said.

Sebastian took a deep breath. "He believes he is to be king. The Bolin family has sat on the throne of the King of Kings for centuries. Maxen is a cruel bastard. I cannot allow him to rule." Sebastian smiled and drifted off. He felt his cheeks burn. "You all know how much I despise being the ruler of all, but I promise I will be a just king. With your loyalty, not only will Erras and Midrel Istan find harmony, but all the nations across the earth will live in peace."

"That is all you have ever wanted," Nadya replied. "Peace. Freedom. You found a way to get everything you wanted and sacrificed more. The people will follow you, Your Majesty."

Sebastian sighed. "Maxen took someone from me, and my first order of business is to get him back. I must have him back."

"Did you say, someone?" Nadya said.

"Yes, his name is Dani. He is small, with black hair and blue eyes. And he is my fiancé. I do not want him harmed." Sebastian turned to The Break and marched proudly.

"What is happening?" Amara said.

Nadya shook her head. "Did he say, fiancé?"

"Sebastian," Amara said as she and Nadya ran to catch up. "Fiancé?"

Jace burst out laughing. "It is a long story. Hi, I am Jace, Sebastian's advisor."

"Are you from Erras?" Nadya said.

"Yes, Oyster Cove. My father is the city master."

Nadya grabbed his arm. "Oh yes, I remember you now. My brother screamed at you to leave Castle Drake."

Jace laughed. "Yes... screaming at me to go away is his favorite thing to do."

"Not my favorite thing," Sebastian said. "But in all seriousness, your father is in danger if Maxen decides to sail to Blackport Bay. I can't save them both, Jace."

"My father is a heartless bastard. Let him fight his own battles," Jace answered.

Nadya approached with her head low and shoulders tense. "Sebastian, tell us everything we should know about you. It is a long walk home. We have time."

Sebastian stepped back to wrap his arm around her, taking her from Jon. "No need to fear me. I have changed, but I know who my family is and what they mean to me. The things you will see me do are not good, Nadya, but they are necessary."

"Good, because I want you to meet my children."

Sebastian stopped suddenly, turned, and faced a young boy and twins.

"Twins, Sebastian. These are my twins, Ivan and Marie. Marie is for Mary, who died a few years ago. And my oldest boy, Declan."

Sebastian smiled, looking down at the children.

Declan motioned for him to come closer. "Why are your eyes red?"

"Oh, that." Sebastian let out a little laugh. "They have been this way for years."

"Because you are the Dragon," Nadya said. "Sebastian, please, we have to know everything about you."

As they began the ascent into the slippery pass, Sebastian told stories of his journey through Midrel Istan. The night fell as they crested the highest point of the mountain. Sebastian demanded they continue to the caves for safety from the cold and the wolves.

Amara looped her arm around Sebastian's and buried her face in his shoulder. "My head is frozen, Sebastian. We can't keep going like this."

"Well, we can't stop here. Everyone would die from the cold, especially when we go into this part of the pass. It is windy." Sebastian looked back, seeing Jace walking close to Kristoff and Viktor while Nadya and Jon were on horseback. The children rode in a wagon with the handmaidens who pulled blankets tight around them. "We will stop for a moment and rest before descending. Get those children warm, Nadya. We will leave soon." Sebastian took a drink of his water. It was starting to freeze. Sebastian grasped the canteen, his hands began to glow orange, and the ice melted.

Amara stared at him. "What have you learned?"

"A lot," Sebastian said. He nodded toward Valirus. "That man has taught me things I never knew I could do. He is Cyrus's father."

Amara's eyes shot open wide. "Does Cyrus know? Wait, what are you going to do when you see him?"

"No, I don't think he knows," Sebastian said. "It is hard to say. I don't want to kill him, but I can't trust him either. Cyrus is low on my list of worries right now."

Amara nudged his arm. "You will have to tell me about Dani soon. I have great news to share with you, but I think I will leave that up to Tomas."

Sebastian smiled and pulled Amara in for a hug. He wanted to ask more, but it was time to depart. The accompaniment dragged through the slippery and frigid pass.

Valirus joined him at his side. "I don't know if you have noticed, but the high winds are threatening to loosen those snow caps. You could do what you are supposed to and take care of this, Your Majesty."

Sebastian heard the mumbling behind him stop. He turned to look at his people and noticed Jace raising his eyebrows and smiling. "We are almost to the cave..." Their stares were stiff and hopeful. "Fine, allow me." Sebastian walked forward and lifted his arms into the air. He felt his skin tingle and appear as if flint were sparking. He forced his hands together in a loud thunderous clap. The echo bounced across the canyon walls. The mountains lightly shook. "Valirus, if I do this, I could bring an avalanche on top of us." Sebastian held his palms out toward the angry snow.

"I thought you were Chaos, The Dragon King, and so on and so on... Are you saying you can't handle an avalanche?" Valirus stood with his hands on his hips.

Sebastian growled. "This is not the time for your lessons, old man."

Valirus straightened his back. "Are you arguing with me?"

The expressions on the face of his sister and the others were enough to make Sebastian's skin crawl. He clenched his jaw, took a deep breath, and released a heavy and raspy groan. He felt the fire burning in his throat. He held his hands out steadily and focused on the mountains that surrounded them.

Lightning flashed above as The Break began to move back and forth like a powerful dance. Sheets of hardened snow broke free of its peaks, threatening to bury everyone. Sebastian felt a sense of complete calm as if everyone had disappeared. There was no sound. It was just him and the snow. He rubbed his palms together, then flexed his hands and thrust them into the sky. The avalanche shot into the air and fell over the other side of the mountains. Sebastian stared at the bare mountains for a moment. "It would have been simpler if we had just kept walking." He rolled his eyes and spun around.

"Sebastian," Nadya gasped. "That was the most amazing thing I have ever seen."

"Well, that's the pretty version. Wait until you see the rest." Sebastian continued walking without looking back.

"Don't let him get to you, my dear Nadya," Valirus said. "He is like a child most of the time. But now, he thinks so highly of himself, he doesn't make time for anyone else."

"That isn't true," Sebastian said.

"Dani doesn't count," Jace said.

"I save everyone's lives and this is the thanks I get." He walked faster until he found the familiar opening of the place he had gone to hide from his family most days. "Thank the gods, we are at the caves. Everyone can be quiet and go to sleep." He quickly marched inside to find a place to build a fire.

The people ate and found places to rest. Sebastian leaned against a rock and looked out over the crowd. He felt his body grow cold, then hot. Sebastian buried his face in his knees and tried to picture what he would do when he saw Dani again, hoping he could stop him from killing everyone. "Valirus, can I ask you something?"

Valirus shuffled over slowly. "You look upset."

"Tell me more about these Blackbirds."

"Oh, your mind rests on Dani." Valirus nodded and got comfortable. "Blackbirds can do a lot, really. Dani can take life and give death, while the other—" Valirus's face hallowed. "The other is evil but necessary. One that can black out the sun and summon monsters from the underworld is a terrifying enemy." Valirus stared at Sebastian. "Dragon used the Blackbirds to win wars, and now you must do the same with yours."

"Wait," Nadya said. "Barron's gifts. He uses some kind of magic to darken the light."

"Barron is the other Blackbird." Sebastian laughed. "I mean, after I began to learn of them, I knew deep down that he was. I just needed the confirmation." He rubbed his face. "Now I can't kill him, which makes me angry, but maybe he can help me rescue Dani."

Jace sat down next to Sebastian. "If Dani is gifted with the life and death power, why doesn't he kill Maxen and Petra and get away?"

"He doesn't know how to use his power unless he is provoked. He had only used it to save my life when Cyrus ran a dagger into my chest…" Sebastian's hands shook. "And when he almost killed me in Adurak." He turned away from everyone and closed his eyes.

CHAPTER 30
The Castle in the Mountains

Early the next morning, Sebastian awoke to a dark cave filled with sleeping men and women. He crept outside and saw the encampment of his militia packing up their tents along the pass. He snuck away and headed for the overlook. The haze of dawn hinted in the sky. He was tired and sore but continued to find his familiar place on the mountain. The place he used to watch the castle light up as night fell, telling him it was time to go home. It was his favorite spot to get away but still be close. It was also where he and Cyrus had first made love.

The overlook came into sight as the pass came to an end. Sebastian squeezed his eyes closed and tilted his head to the sky. "I am home, Father. Sorry I was gone so long." His body suddenly felt like it was on fire. The hair on the back of his neck tickled as it stood. Sebastian felt uneasy. His excitement to see his castle was filled with worry. Slowly slipping toward the edge, his energy intensified.

Footsteps crunched in the snow. "There you are!"

Sebastian jumped. "Fuck, Viktor. Don't sneak up on me." He held onto his chest. "Are you trying to kill me?"

Viktor laughed. "Sorry. How are things at home?"

"How would I know?" Sebastian shook his head. "I was about to look when you scared the life out of me." He walked to the edge again, feeling anxious, then he stood up straight. "Is that?" He looked at Viktor and then over the castle once more. "What the hell has Barron done?" Sebastian marched onto the road.

Viktor peeked over the edge and then backed away fast. "Wait, brother. The others." He hurried back up the pass.

"Tell them to hurry up," Sebastian yelled. He watched over the courtyard again and mumbled, "What did you do, Tomas?"

Sebastian started his way down the path toward the castle grounds, hearing everyone rushing to catch up. He let out a soft laugh and turned to see Jace and his brothers coming fast.

"You just can't hold still for ten seconds, can you?" Viktor said.

Sebastian stopped at the closed gates of Castle Drake. The heads of two NorthBrekkian soldiers popped out from above. One gasped and darted to the crank.

"The king has returned! Clear the way." The young soldier's voice was high-pitched and cracked, making Sebastian scrunch up his face.

Sebastian winced, then let out a sigh. "How old is he, twelve?" He shook his head as Viktor shrugged.

The gates opened wide, but the courtyard was quiet. There was a light snow falling. The faces of the guards on duty, protecting his homeland, were not what he expected to come home to. Sebastian unsheathed his sword and motioned for his people to stop. "Jace, Viktor, Kristoff, you're with me. The rest stay back."

"Yeah, blowing up their island probably wasn't one of your best ideas," Jace said.

"You did what?" Kristoff said. "Are they here to attack us?"

"Why aren't they coming for me now?" Sebastian stopped and looked around. He marched up to a soldier, grabbed him by the throat, and held his sword to the man's neck. "Why are you here? Tell me!"

The door flew open. "Your Majesty."

Sebastian let go of the soldier and looked at the face of one of the most beautiful men he had ever seen. "Dom," he whispered as he sheathed his sword.

Dom embraced him with a warm hug. "I missed you."

"I missed you too." Sebastian held on a little longer. "I could have used you out there. It has been... hard."

"I know." Dom blushed and stroked Sebastian's face. "I was afraid when I saw Cyrus return without you. I told him to ensure you stayed there, but not to abandon you."

"Why did you want me to stay in Midrel Istan?"

Dom smirked. "For freedom...Come inside and talk to Barron. Trust me. It'll be alright."

Sebastian walked quickly alongside Dom. They entered the front room and Sebastian paused before the staircase. He looked around and smelled the familiar scent of his family home and felt the warmth of the burning fireplace embrace his aching body. "It's so quiet."

Dom shrugged. "Our people are spread across the villages and towns for their safety. Just in case Maxen arrived first."

Sebastian nodded and marched straight for the throne room. As he approached, he saw knights and soldiers of NorthBrekka line the aisle. Upon his entrance, the entire room erupted with a loud grunt and two pounds of a fist on the chest. They took a knee and bowed their heads as their king passed.

"Wow," Meecah said. "Now, this is the welcome home a king deserves."

"I was beginning to wonder if anyone remembered I still live here," Sebastian said.

The dark stone floor reflected the firelight from the candles in the chandeliers above. A warm glowcast across hanging red banners with black twin dragons and a sword stitched into the fabric. The first face he saw was Barron's. He held up his hand and the accompaniment stopped as Sebastian stepped carefully forward. He flared his nostrils and felt the burning and gurgling in his throat. His voice became soft but deep and hoarse. "You are one tricky bastard, brother." He grabbed Barron by the collar.

"Sebastian." Barron shoved him back and moved his head from top to bottom. "You have changed. Welcome home." His jaw clenched.

"Get out of my way, Barron." Tomas pushed his way between them. "Brother, it has been…" He froze at the sight of Sebastian. "It's been too long."

Sebastian glanced down at Tomas's cane and felt a sharp pain in his gut. "Well, I am home now." He hesitated, then wrapped his arms around Tomas. Whispers and gasps, and the word twins could be heard from those who had followed Sebastian from Midrel Istan. "You have no idea how hard I have fought to get here. To you."

"I know. I missed you too." Tomas sobbed on his shoulder.

"As for you." Sebastian let go of Tomas and got in Barron's face. "What in the gods' hell are you doing?"

Barron's eyes brightened. "Listen, brother, things have changed—"

"I know what you are." Sebastian got in his face. "You don't need to tell me your boring stories. Why are the Kuhar in my homeland?" He felt the burning pain build up in his chest. His voice cracked, and the fires in the throne room blazed.

Barron set his palms on Sebastian's shoulders. "They are fighting for me, for you. For us."

Sebastian backed away and shook his head, then looked at Tomas. "And you, Tomas. You approve of this?"

"Sebastian, you have been gone for a long time," Tomas said. "Things have changed. I will tell you everything over dinner. Meanwhile, introduce me to your friends. Also, why are your eyes not changing back?"

Sebastian took a deep breath. "They don't. They have been red for years."

A gasp came from several people in the hall.

"Cyrus, what are you doing here?" Jace said.

Sebastian swung around. His body intensified with the feeling of pins and needles from top to bottom. "What the hell are you doing in my home?" The fires suddenly dropped to a deep red glow, and thunder could be heard outside.

"It is my fault." Dom ran to stand by Cyrus. "I am helping him."

"He tried to kill me. He is not welcome here." Sebastian's fist burst into flames.

"Sebastian, please," Dom said.

Sebastian was pulled back by a hand that was gripped around his forearm.

"Calm down, idiot boy." Valirus's face was red. "Don't destroy your castle. Leave Cyrus alone. Let that be the only warning I will give you."

"Valirus—"

"He is my only living child," Valirus begged.

Cyrus shoved his way to the front of the crowd. "I was right. You are my father."

Valirus held Cyrus's face in his palms. "You were a lot smaller the last time I saw you."

"Why did you leave us?" Cyrus shook his head and backed away.

"Everyone should sit and rest. Let me explain everything you all should know and why we must win this war."

Soldiers from Khan Khar, NorthBrekka, and Midrel Istan filled the Great Hall.

Tomas grabbed Sebastian's hand and pulled him to the throne. "That is where you belong."

Sebastian didn't hesitate to sit. Tomas and Barron sat at the table beside him, along with Jace, Kristoff, and Viktor.

Valirus stepped before all. "When I was a boy, my parents split my brother and me apart, my mother taking Maxen to her homeland in Midrel Istan to raise him as an Altanian king. My father kept me in Torrdale to raise me to sit on the throne and rule in the west. Over time, we found wives, had children and kept little talks between us. One day, I received word from a Safarian spy that something unique was born in Altania." Valirus walked down the aisle. "You see, a darker version of witchcraft exists in the world. It had not been seen in a millennium, but there was one born in Erras that was kept a secret, buried within the halls of this castle. A few years later, Maxen's wife, Queen Pricilla, gave birth to another. They are called Blackbirds, and if they are not properly trained, they can do terrible things."

Sebastian's headshot to Barron, who met his gaze, smiled, then turned his attention back to Valirus.

"I left Torrdale in search of Altania," Valirus continued. "My wife, my queen, died before we made it there. She fell ill."

"You left to fight Maxen." Cyrus interrupted.

"To stop him." Valirus smiled. "He already had a daughter who was a deeply gifted witch. While she is mighty, he will use his son to kill anyone who stands in the way of the throne."

"Why doesn't his son kill him if he is this, Blackbird?" Cyrus looked confused.

"Because he doesn't know how to use his powers," Sebastian said. "His name is Dani. He is your cousin. And he and I will be married once I take him back from Maxen."

"Married?" Cyrus sat down quickly. "You are getting married to this Blackbird? Are you insane? He is a monster."

"So am I," Sebastian shouted. He was hurt and angry and stared at Cyrus for a moment. "All of you should get to know each other. I need time alone. To think." Sebastian stormed away, heading for a large staircase behind the throne room.

The war room was always cold and drafty. It was a large open room on the edge of the castle that hung over the woods. Dustings of snow danced across the large table that showed carvings of Erras, war strategies passed on from generations before, and the family crest. Sebastian put his hand on the table, replaying in his mind the memories of his father discussing routes, trades, and orders for troop movement. He removed a box from under the table and spread the pieces. He thought of where Maxen would have come to port and the roads, he could take to reach NorthBrekka. He heard a tapping sound coming from the hall.

"I thought you came in here to think," Tomas said as he limped on his cane.

"I am thinking." Sebastian watched Tomas. "Come over here. Let me show you some things, just in case."

"The lessons begin already." Tomas laughed.

Sebastian pointed to a spot on the map that represented The Midnight Sea. "We lost them just north of Alta Prime when they broke and turned west. Maxen would have arrived at the port in Oyster Cove one day before I arrived in East Bay. He will take the trade roads west. He should arrive in Sun Shadow in a few days. I will intercept and take Dani."

"Brother, you need to rest."

Sebastian took his brother's hand. "I don't have time to rest, Tomas." A soft red glow was met with a pale blue in their palms. The war room got colder as ice formed across the table. Clouds circled the sky above. Sebastian's mouth dropped open, then he pulled his hand back and stepped to the end of the balcony, his head turning from left to right as he towered over NorthBrekka. "I must strategize three armies, lock down this castle, and plan to infiltrate my enemy's camp to save the man I love. Meanwhile, I have to teach you how to use your power. If there is any time to sleep and eat, I will find it."

"You can't keep going on like this." Tomas reached for him. "You have been home a few minutes, and you are already biting everyone's heads off. Come lay down and sleep. Then we can go over everything on your mind at dinner."

Sebastian stared at the floor, clenched his jaw, and smiled. "Alright. Just promise me that you will stay by my side, Tomas. Don't ever leave me."

"We are together, forever."

Sebastian put his arm around Tomas to help him up the stairs once they left the war room. "I am sorry for what I did to you." He nodded at Tomas's leg. "I promise I will do everything I can to help you heal."

"It isn't your fault. It is our fault. I was involved in the collapse of the palace as much as you were." Tomas paused at the door to the king's chambers. "You really are different, you know? But I like it. It is the real you, not the show you used to put on to avoid being around us."

"Everyone says that." Sebastian rolled his eyes. "Once upon a time, I would have laughed and run away at the thought of having a drop of power because I was too selfish to want to do good for anyone else. Now I want to be the leader that people know will protect them, and that means sacrificing all those immature wants and desires I had. There is no peace for people like us, Tomas. We will never have that picturesque, content life of waking up to a castle full of babies and a lover to kiss us good morning. The people who love us must be strong enough to understand that they will sacrifice more. I think that is why I love Dani so much. He is more broken than I."

"This is probably a bad time to tell you that I am engaged," Tomas said. "She didn't tell you already, did she?"

Sebastian pushed open the door and went inside. He sat on the corner of the bed and smiled. "Amara didn't tell me anything. I am happy for you, brother. She is a fine woman."

"I knew she would tell you. Amara was in love with you. It took her a long time to get over you leaving." Tomas took off his coat, set his cane by the bed, and lay down. "I just hope I am good enough for her."

Sebastian scrunched his eyebrows together and looked at Tomas with his mouth dropped open. "Good enough? Seriously? You are a prince, a god, a Drake. And as weird as it sounds, a Dragon. You are good enough."

Tomas laughed and grabbed Sebastian's arm, pulling him to lie down. Sebastian wrapped his arm around Tomas's chest, buried his face into his shoulder, and closed his eyes.

When he awoke, the bedroom was dark except for the fire in the fireplace. Sebastian felt Tomas slip out of bed slowly, but he kept his eyes closed. He heard the gentle clasp of the door closing. He peeked to see who was there. "Is he alright?" He heard Amara whisper to Tomas. "Everyone has already eaten. Perhaps we should let him sleep."

Sebastian sat up too quickly. His head spun. "No, I need to talk with everyone."

"You need sleep." Amara pushed him down. "You're burning up. Are you ill?"

Sebastian felt hot and sweaty, but that was no longer unusual. "No, but I have work to do."

"In the morning. Everyone is tired. I will bring you something to eat, then you need to sleep. No arguing." Amara left the bed chambers in a hurry.

"She hasn't changed at all," Sebastian said.

CHAPTER 31
The Sight of Erras

Dani hung over the rail of the ship and threw up as the rough seas finally settled and the air became more humid. Maxen watched his every move as he returned to his dark corner under the stairs. He had Sebastian in his arms for a quick moment and felt happy, but when Petra took him away, the empty sadness had returned.

"Try harder, Dani." Petra sat down in front of him. "Everything would be easier for you if you tried."

"Leave me alone."

"Why are you so worthless?" Petra jumped to her feet and walked away, growling.

Worthless. Dani remembered Maxen always calling him that. He was used to being mistreated, which made being tormented by his sister so tolerable. Staying quiet and hidden was his only chance of surviving. He watched a bird fly over the ship, which meant land was near. He slipped from his spot and ran to the rail as a harbor appeared. "Erras," he whispered.

"Don't fall in now, Dani." Petra playfully pushed Dani, making him lose balance briefly. "You had better at least learn to create some kind of Blackbird powers, or Father will beat you bloody."

"Like you care if he beats me." Dani shoved her away.

The shoreline was stretched far. Dani saw mountains in one direction and palm trees in another. The cove where the harbor sat looked as if they were entering the mouth of a beast, but it soon came alive with ships, men, and a bustling town filled with shops and homes edging the water.

"That is Oyster Cove," Maxen said. "The people here are neutral between the north and the south. But my intent is not to stay." He yanked Dani from the railing by his arm. "You will not speak unless I tell you to."

"Why?" Dani straightened his back. "Are you afraid they will send word to Sebastian that I am here? You can't defeat him. Correction: you won't defeat him."

"No, but you can, and… you will." Maxen grinned wide and strutted away.

The crew began their departure from the long journey at sea and onto dry land. Petra was left in charge of keeping Dani from running away. Her shriek of a laugh carried into the town. Dani saw some workers stop and stare as she tied a rope around his neck and walked him like a mule.

Maxen walked into the center of a circle of armed knights. Dani stared at the ground that changed from a hollow wooden pier to solid stone and sand. He enjoyed seeing the blue ocean gently wash against the shore where children played in the shallow water. The rope made a sharp jerk from Petra at the other end. She held her hands up and growled at him.

He walked along the road behind his Father, only looking up to see townspeople staring and whispering. Maxen made no effort to address the people of Oyster Cove. No one spoke, not even Petra, who loved to make a scene everywhere she went. Suddenly, people leaped out of the way as an older gentleman burst through.

"Excuse me." He stomped toward Maxen but was met with the ends of swords pointing at his face. He held up his arms and stepped back. "You cannot just leave your ships there without paying." He was tall and slender with peppered hair mixed with blond.

Maxen called for his men to halt and then stepped from his protectors and over to the man. "You don't know who I am, so I will let that one go. My name is King Maxen Bolin of Altania. As I will soon rule as King of Kings, I declare your harbor mine. I will pay no fee, sir."

"And I am the City Master, Lord Astra. The Bolin king I served is dead. This country belongs to the Drakes now. I only serve them. You will pay your fee, or I will have my men turn your ships into reefs."

"How dare—" Maxen started.

"You are the City Master?" Dani walked past his father. "Is Jace your son?" He felt Maxen grab his arm.

"How do you know my son?" Lord Astra said.

"He is my friend. He is here, in Erras with King Sebastian."

"Dani, shut your mouth." Maxen grabbed a fistful of Dani's hair and shoved him back.

"My son is alive," Lord Astra said with a hint of happiness.

"Do what you want with my ships. I won't need them anymore." Maxen shoved his way past the City Master, dragging Dani by the rope around his neck. He stopped and turned back. "And just so you remember who your king is." Maxen pulled a staff from his side and pounded it into the ground. It burst bright as a force of wind exploded from the crystal. The people of Oyster Cove scurried away from the blast as their homes and shops were obliterated within moments.

Dani walked backward. "How could you, Father? They didn't deserve that."

"Shut up, boy. Turn around and walk, or I will drag you down the road."

They left Oyster Cove and took the road heading west. Six days passed before they stopped at a small village at the edge of a forest and the bay. As soldiers set up camp, Dani sat on the grassy hillside and stared across the forest and far into the distance sat mountains. He smiled, then he felt someone sit by his side.

"Father wants to see you," Petra said. Her voice was calmer than normal.

Dani stared at her with his eyebrows furrowed. "Why, so he can beat me?" He turned to his sister. "Why do you help him? You know how bad he is. He cursed you."

"Don't speak of that!" Petra snapped.

"It's true," Dani interrupted. "He cursed your powers. Remember when you were young, you used to be able to be invisible?" Dani smiled. "You used to sneak up on me and reappear to scare me. He changed you when he found out about me. He altered your powers and made you into a weapon, just as he will do with me." Dani snapped his fingers in her face. "I can't do what he wants. I love Sebastian." Tears streamed down his cheeks and dripped from his chin.

Petra pulled her knees into her chest and stared at the forest as Dani stood and walked toward the big tent in the back of the encampment. He slipped through the flap and was met with a hand around his throat.

Maxen slapped Dani hard across the face, causing his lip to bleed. "Stupid little child. What did I tell you about speaking to anyone? It is your fault what happened in Oyster Cove."

"My fault?"

"You will practice all night if that is what it takes." Maxen dragged him toward the opening. "You do not get a

scrap of food or a blink of rest until I see your powers work."
He threw Dani out into the cold and rain.

Hours passed and Dani sat on the muddy ground, shaking. Maxen tied him outside like a dog and set men to watch him. As the night was late, Maxen walked outside and lifted Dani to his feet by his neck. "Show me what you have learned." Maxen shoved one of the soldiers in front of him. "Kill him, my son."

Dani put his cold, shaking hand on the man's chest, clenched his jaw, and squeezed his eyes closed. He sighed and dropped his hand. "I don't know how to make it happen."

Maxen grabbed him by the rope. "Killing you would be too merciful." He turned to his soldiers. "Gentlemen, use him for whatever pleasures you desire. Beat him, strangle him, fuck him. I don't care." Maxen looked at the four men who stood in a circle around Dani and then walked away.

"No." Dani trembled. "Father, please. I will try harder."

"I know you will, but since you disappointed me this time, you will pay." Maxen went back inside his tent.

Metal gloves and boots scraped at Dani's skin. They struck him, ripped off his clothes, used him, and threw him into the mud when they finished. One soldier knelt and punched him in the jaw. "Stop, please." A soldier pushed his way on top of Dani, slapped his face, and yanked on the rope, choking him to where he could only inhale small gulps of air. Dani drifted off, closed his eyes, and emptied his mind so that he could not feel the hands clawing at his naked body. As the man thrust against his hips, he felt his entire body turn cold, and he no longer felt the man's weight against him.

Dani set his hand on the soldier's head and stared into his eyes. Blood splattered across his face and chest as the soldier gagged for a breath. Dani climbed to his feet and threw himself at another. He screamed as his hand clawed into the man's skin. A blanket was dropped next to him. Dani turned to see Maxen towering over him, smiling.

CHAPTER 32
And He Was Cured

Sebastian sat on the throne the following day holding his crown and watching the firelight glisten from the rubies. There was a tug at his knee as a small child climbed onto his lap. Sebastian watched Nadya's son reach for his face, touching his cheek and hair. He was a child who understood nothing of what was coming and what his future would bring. Sebastian put his arms around the boy, breathing in the feeling of pure innocence.

"Ivan? Oh, there you are." Nadya halted in the doorway. Her smile vanished as she stared at Sebastian. "I'm sorry, brother. Let me take him."

"Don't worry. Your son is fine. He just wanted to see the crown," Sebastian said. Ivan toyed with the jewels that rested against the black steel. "Everyone has been afraid to talk to me." Sebastian continued. "I'm not going to hurt any of you. Please know this."

"It has been years, brother." Nadya reached out to take Ivan. "Our people, our country all but collapsed and now we stand on the brink of war. The Safar will join Maxen and from what I know, that is a scary scenario no matter which way you spin it. Everyone is relying on you to make all the right decisions. One wrong move and—"

Sebastian laughed. "I know what it means, and we will not have an easy run. Many people will die, and I can do nothing about it. Make sure you and those babies get somewhere safe."

"You are the only person that can stop this, Sebastian."

"Wrong, Nadya." A voice came from the hall. "It isn't about him… for once."

"Cyrus." Sebastian's voice carried across the room.

Nadya took Ivan and left the throne room in a rush.

Cyrus slowly walked toward the throne with his hands held in front. "I know you don't trust me, but I am not here to attack you. Dom thinks he can help me with the curse, and I am willing to do anything—"

Sebastian pinched the bridge of his nose and took a deep breath. "You and I will never be together again. You do understand that, don't you?"

Cyrus's mouth dropped open and then closed. He took a few steps back. "I… I know. But maybe I want to be your friend and not your enemy."

"You tried to kill me." Sebastian stood and stepped forward. "This curse…" He froze in place and stared at his feet, then threw his head back and laughed. "Curse. I could have fixed this a long time ago." Sebastian looked Cyrus in the eyes. "Let me try something."

Cyrus opened his mouth, then closed it again and nodded. He tilted his head as he grabbed Sebastian's hand.

Sebastian rested his hand on Cyrus's shoulder. "This is how Dragon took the curses away from others." He squeezed his fist, cringed, and gritted his teeth. There were sharp, tingling pains shooting down his spine as if electricity was racing through his veins. Sebastian could see his hands turning red and scaly. He let out a scream as a loud cracking noise shot from his body, feeling like all his energy left him.

The force shook the castle's walls. Sebastian fell to his knees and struggled to catch his breath.

"What was that?" Jace shouted and ran over to Sebastian. "Your Majesty, what happened?" He looked at Cyrus. "What did you do?"

"I didn't do anything, I swear." Cyrus backed away with his hand on the hilt of his sword.

Sebastian was still and stared at Cyrus as his entire body tingled and hurt terribly. "The curse is broken. You are free, Cyrus." He curled over and coughed violently until blood splattered on the floor. His throat felt like it was filled with lava, and his chest was on fire. Sebastian let out a throaty growl and fire shot from his throat and blackened the stone floor under him. He fell back and pushed himself away from everyone until he reached his throne.

Valirus walked over to Cyrus, touched his face, and turned to speak to everyone. "Ever since Sebastian broke the curse guarding my prison, his transition has begun. Dragon was a curse breaker, and so are you, my king."

Cyrus stepped forward. "Are you saying that everything I was taught about you when I was cursed was true? Sebastian has become Dragon?"

"Yes," Valirus said.

"No." Sebastian interrupted. "I am not Dragon. I am his descendant. My name is Chaos."

"Yes, of course, Your Majesty." Valirus looked around the room, then back to Sebastian. "The change is already beginning. The red eyes, the ability to use your power the way you do, and now you breathe fire. If you keep this up, you will start to grow scales. Oh…I forget. You glow scales."

Sebastian cleared his throat and noticed every face in the room looking scared. "It doesn't mean what you are thinking." He shook his head and backed away through the rear door that exited the castle. The path led to a cliffside trail that overlooked the town and the lake.

"Would you slow down?" Cyrus came running to catch up. "I would think that after all these years of trying to help me, you would stick around after I am cured."

Sebastian shook his head. "It is not my priority. You are welcome, by the way."

"Did you know you could do that?" Cyrus paused. "And thank you."

"I realized it might work when I broke the curse in Mosisle Dur when Valirus started calling me the curse breaker. But no, I didn't know it would cure you."

"Sebastian, I remember everything. My memories are clear. You and me." Cyrus's hands were trembling. "I lo—"

"No, you don't. Don't even say it." Sebastian stopped. "I gave up on us a long time ago. I love Dani, and he will be my husband."

"I love you. I had to say it. Just one more time." Cyrus grabbed Sebastian by the chin and kissed him. Sebastian cupped his cheek in his palm and kissed him back, feeling that painful yet satisfying rush of love and lust surge through his body. He pushed Cyrus against the wall while Cyrus gripped a fistful of his hair. "I want you back," Cyrus whispered.

Sebastian kissed his neck, then backed away. He held his hand over his mouth. "I can't. I love him, Cyrus." The pain in his chest was almost crippling. He bit his fist.

"We were meant to be together, forever." Cyrus grabbed his arm. "That is what you said."

"Is everything alright?" Jace said. Tomas came into view through the castle door.

"Sebastian, please. We are not done," Cyrus said.

"We are fine, Jace. Cyrus, I said what I said. There is nothing more for us to say to each other." Sebastian signaled for Tomas to come with him. He turned away and closed his eyes, feeling the flutter in his chest. "It is time I teach you some things, brother."

Tomas tried hard to keep up with Sebastian as they made their way down a trail from the cliffside into the forest. "You must slow down if you expect me to keep up."

"Would you like me to carry you?" Sebastian turned and smirked.

Tomas's cheeks turned red. "You can carry me back up the mountain."

"Deal." Sebastian's head hung low. "I'm sorry to drag you all the way out here. I forget that you can't get around too well."

"Are you going to tell me what happened to you out there? Because now is a good time."

"If I must," Sebastian told his tales from the moment he left Erras, and about all that had transpired with Cyrus. "All those years I begged for him. I gave up my mission to be with him. I thought I could convince him. But when he left, it was like everything was crystal clear. I knew what I had to do and was positive that the only way I would accomplish my mission was to alleviate myself of the distraction." Sebastian helped Tomas over the stream that ran through the forest.

"You gave up what you wanted so much," Tomas said. "All you ever wanted in this world was him."

"I wanted to marry him." Sebastian held back a tear. "But he ran his blade through my chest instead, and at that moment, I was never happier. It was over, and the world would be safe knowing I was dead. The wars would end and things would return to normal. But when I saw Dani staring into my eyes, everything changed. The Dragon woke up."

They walked for what seemed like hours. Sebastian told stories of his journey to Mosisle Dur, Valirus's training, and how he was made King of Adurak. He closed his eyes and smiled while describing his castle and the City of Thieves within The Creed. They came to a narrow river that divided the southern part of the forest from NorthBrekka.

Tomas leaned on Sebastian. "I wish I could have seen that with you, brother."

"One day, I will take you there," Sebastian said. "Now, show me what you can do."

Tomas glanced at Sebastian, then the stream. He reached down, put his fingers into the water, and squeezed his eyes closed. The water froze and the ground around it began to frost. Tomas broke his hand free and stood.

"You don't have to touch it to make it do that." Sebastian stepped forward. "I will show you. But how about using the water as a weapon?" Sebastian shivered at the idea that he just sounded like Valirus.

"I don't know how to do that," Tomas said.

"Don't overthink this." Sebastian positioned himself next to Tomas. "You know the hand motions that Aspen taught you. The ones that make the water form into shapes. Now focus and use all your senses to turn the river into something sharp and pointy. Like this." Sebastian rubbed his hands one at a time, then lifted his arms. He pointed his first two fingers and they turned to frost. The water lifted from the river. Sebastian's hands turned cold and blue as the water turned into icicles in the air. "Take my hand, Tomas. You can do this."

The forest was dense and did not allow for much sun or snow to come through the leafy branches above. The forest floor became bone-chilling, and trees had ice forming on their trunks. Tomas took Sebastian's hand. He gasped for a few breaths and opened his eyes to reveal an electrifying blue. The wind began to howl, and a bolt of lightning crashed into a branch, bringing down half of a tree near where they stood.

"I said don't overthink this," Sebastian reminded. "Focus on what you feel, what you smell, what you taste, and what you hear." Sebastian grabbed Tomas's other hand. The fire in his chest and throat returned. "Wake up, Tomas!" He said. Tomas jumped and his eyes opened wide. "You have been resting too long. It is time to fight back. Come out of the shadows, Hydros. Where is my sea dragon? Show him to me!"

Tomas clenched his jaw and squeezed Sebastian's hand hard. "I don't understand what I'm supposed to do."

"Feel your powers forming inside you and on your skin. Feel the cold, tingling, and hot pricking needles in your arms and legs. Feel your chest burn like the dragon's breath." Sebastian reached for Tomas's cheek. "Feel everything that has ever made you very angry or incredibly happy and let it breathe from your skin." He leaned in to whisper, "Let it take you."

The ground shook, and the trees cracked and fought against the wind. Thunder boomed, sleet fell, and the icicles above shot down around them. Tomas screamed as his back arched and he lost his balance. His voice cracked and became hoarse as he growled. Ice formed from his fingertips and up his arms. An immense burst of wind brought the twins to their knees. They placed their foreheads together as the forces around them battled. There was a loud burst followed by silence.

Footsteps crunched through the broken limbs and leaves. "Well, the good news is, Maxen can't sneak up on us through the forest," Jace said.

"Did we do that on purpose?" Tomas stared at his hands and looked around.

"Yes," Sebastian said.

"You are both really magical and all," Jace said. "But if you are going to destroy entire topographies when you connect, at least do it on enemy land."

The trees were scorched black with ice hanging from dead limbs, and branches littered the ground. Sebastian smiled. "Trees will grow back. The good thing is that we didn't do this by mistake. We created a vortex of our power. Nothing can stop that."

"You are all mighty, Your Majesty." Valirus's voice was his usual hint of sarcasm when he was in a good mood. "But you still—"

"Have a lot to learn. I know," Sebastian said.

Across the forest, where some trees still stood whole and unharmed, was a movement. Too tall to be a deer and too small to be a horse. Sebastian's eye caught something shimmering in the sunlight. He crept through the wreckage toward the flash. The others followed at a close distance. Jace joined his side, with his sword drawn. "Shhhh," Sebastian said. The air filled with the sound of an eccentric cackle. "Petra," Sebastian whispered. He turned and faced the others. "Everyone, fall back. Except you, Jace. Follow me." A sweet-smelling rush of wind brushed his cheek as it transformed into the blue-haired empress.

"Hello, my love." Petra laughed then vanished with a loud snap.

"They are here," Sebastian said. "Get to the castle!" He ran forward where unharmed trees turned into a vast meadow and stared directly into the village of Sun Shadow. "Jace, get everyone back. When the night falls, I am going after Dani."

"Sebastian, no," Valirus said. "You have a kingdom to protect."

"This is my only chance to save Dani. I can't leave him there, Valirus."

"You can't go to their camp alone," Jace argued. "Petra knows you are here. She has already told Maxen by now."

Sebastian shrugged. "Good. That means they know what Tomas and I can do. Don't worry about me."

Jace walked past Sebastian. "Tell Tomas to prepare NorthBrekka for war. I refuse to leave my king's side."

Sebastian rolled his eyes and informed Tomas of his plan.

"Why are you always leaving me behind?" Tomas said. "Let me help."

"Tomas, you could—"

"Do not say that I will get hurt." Tomas's face turned red. "Let me keep watch, at least."

"Fine." Sebastian agreed and informed Viktor of the plan, not allowing any further demands to stay with him. He slipped away into the tall, thick grasslands south of the forest. All he could see were tufts of wheat growing higher than he stood until he suddenly stumbled upon a clearing. He knelt and watched over Sun Shadow. There were no fires flickering and no people standing watch. Sebastian felt a sinking feeling in his gut. "They are not here." He hurried down to the town's edge. "They have eluded us."

"Where have they gone?" Tomas said.

"Torrdale." Sebastian checked the ash in the firepit. "It's been days since they made camp here. Maxen is a Bolin. He is going to his family's homeland. We have to tell Valirus... and Cyrus."

CHAPTER 33
The Return of a Queen

Dani sat on a rock, fidgeting with the rope while waiting for Maxen to lead his army across the border of Torrdale. He shivered in his soaking wet clothes from sleeping on the hard ground as the rain fell throughout the night. He stared at the mountains ahead and then closed his eyes and thought about Adurak. His mind shifted to Sebastian. There was a pull on the rope and Petra cleared her throat. "I'm coming," Dani whispered.

"It's going to be cold." Petra stared ahead. "And you are dripping wet."

"There is nothing I can do." Dani stood next to her. "Come on before Father yells at me."

Petra reached into her bag and pulled out a small blanket. She wrapped it around Dani's shoulders. "Father wouldn't want you to freeze to death."

They arrived on the western coast just before sunset. Maxen grabbed Dani by the collar and pulled him to the top of a hill. Ahead was a beautiful sight that made Dani smile. Maxen pointed. "That is the Bolin Palace. This castle was built by our forefathers as a fortress to protect Erras from invaders from the western seas."

Dani said nothing. Though he wanted to see the castle and learn about his ancestry, he did not want to speak to his father. Petra rode up next to him, holding a dainty umbrella that barely kept her blue hair dry. She looked as if she wanted to scream as her knuckles turned white from squeezing the handle so tight in her fist.

"Shut your mouth, Dani." Petra pouted.

Dani burst out laughing. "I didn't say a word. Are you mad you are getting wet? You look angry."

"I said stop!"

Guards rode to the wall to meet them at the gate. Maxen released the rope and guided his horse forward. "My name is Maxen Bolin, King of Altania. This country is my birthright and I have come to claim it. Take me to Prince Cyrus."

Dani's grief turned to interest. He had never met Cyrus and had only seen him at the festival where he saved Sebastian's life. He wanted to know his cousin, even if he was a villain. He flashed a quick smile and returned to staring at the ground before Maxen noticed. The guards stepped away from the path, and the army urged forward.

As they passed through the castle doors, Dani noticed the intricate woodwork with crossed beams and griffins carved from stone along the corridor. Along the side, massive windows showed off the view of the ocean. The bear skin rugs on the floor and the large roaring fire in the fireplace entranced Dani. He kneeled before the fire and absorbed the warmth. His mouth twisted into a soothing smile.

"Hello?"

Dani jumped. He hoped to hear Cyrus, but the voice was a woman. "Hello?" Dani replied.

"Who are you talking to?" Maxen shouted.

"Don't yell at the boy." The woman's silky voice traveled through the room elegantly. "You must be Maxen. My late husband's uncle."

"Lorna." Maxen turned to her with an odd smile as he ran his fingers through his hair. "I have heard of you."

Dani shook with disgust.

"I hope it was all bad." Lorna touched Maxen's arm and then walked up to Dani. She held his chin in her palm. Her shiny blonde hair framed her face well, giving her a kind and graceful appearance. Her lips curved into a smile. "Why does he have a rope around his neck?"

"Because he is an ornery little shit, and I don't need him running away."

"Run where? He doesn't know where he is." Lorna scorned as she took a knife from her dress. She held the tip up to Dani's throat. "He is a prince. In Erras, we treat our royals respectfully. You will indulge in our ways if you plan to rule here." She made a fast slice causing the rope to fall at Dani's feet.

He smiled at her and hurried over to the windows. Rocks protruded from the water just off the rocky shore, with tiny spots of sand being lightly washed by incoming waves. Dani saw his reflection in the glass. He touched his hollow cheek and ran his fingers through his black hair. Dry blood crusted from his nose to his jaw, but his blue eyes shined despite the person staring back at him. A tear dropped on the floor by his feet.

"He's not coming for you," Petra whispered when she met Dani at the window. "He was in the forest by that little village, but it was several days past. He just missed us." She turned to walk away, then stopped. "Don't let Father see you cry."

Dani watched her hurry away to stand by Maxen. He wiped his face, crept his way back to his family, and listened to Maxen and Lorna chat.

"You do not have enough men to fight him." Lorna's voice trailed as he spoke.

"That is where you come in, my lady," Maxen said. "Are you not the crowned Princess of Safareen? Are the Safar not a fierce and noble tribe of bloodthirsty men?"

"What is in it for Safareen?" Lorna leaned forward and put her hand on Maxen's knee. "What is in it for me? Why should the Safar let you rule as King of Kings?"

"It is my duty as the leader of my family name to rule. A Bolin has sat on the throne for centuries. It will continue with me. As for your people, I promise them to rule over the southern lands of Erras. Have Alta Prime. It is useless to me. I will rule from Torrdale once I dismantle NorthBrekka at the source." Maxen smiled and put his hand on Lorna's. "As for you. You can be my queen."

Dani's head shot up. "She poisoned one of your nephews and cursed another. You can't possibly consider her as a wife?"

Maxen stood and walked over to Dani. "You are lucky to be alive. Do not push me."

Dani felt his entire body go cold and light. "You should be careful whom you threaten." His voice lowered. "You know what I am capable of."

Maxen's hand immediately wrapped around Dani's throat. "Your life hangs by a thread." Maxen let him go and turned to Lorna. "The curse you gave to Cyrus. Can you recreate it?"

"Of course. Why?" Lorna said.

"I want you to give it to my son. Make him hate Chaos so much that he is gnawing at the chance to rip apart that pretentious, ignorant man. I want Dani to destroy NorthBrekka."

Dani lost his footing and fell. He stared at Maxen shaking his head as he shuffled until he was against the wall and away from his father. He thought about running as fast as his legs could but remembered the guards outside the door would catch him. Then Maxen would beat him.

Lorna stared at Dani. "I do not have everything I would need to make the tea. I would have to travel home." She touched Maxen's cheek. "Leave the boy alone. If you want him to be the Blackbird, he has to sleep."

Maxen took a deep breath. "Dani. Go find a bath and some clean clothes. You can sleep in front of the fire."

Dani smiled and hurried away before Maxen could change his mind. He hoped they would leave him alone in the den so he could stare out of the windows all night while enjoying the massive fireplace.

CHAPTER 34
Love is Lost

Several days and nights passed. Sebastian sat on the throne with nothing but his thoughts to keep him company. The fires flickered as Sebastian moved his fingers in swirling movements. He grinned as the flames whipped and danced around. Behind him came the sound of someone clearing their throat.

"It's just me."

"Just you who has tried to kill me." Sebastian smirked.

"Can we talk, please?" Cyrus stood in front of Sebastian and kneeled. "Your Highness."

"Don't do this," Sebastian said. "I beg of you." He refused to look at Cyrus. He felt his face get hot and his throat tighten. But the sight of two men running to the throne changed his mind.

"Your Majesty, we bring word from Torrdale. Maxen has taken the castle and is engaged... to Princess Lorna."

Sebastian was speechless.

Cyrus moved toward the men. "When did this happen?"

"A few days ago, just after you left with the Sinook captain, Dominic," A soldier said.

"What is the point of a wedding between Maxen and Lorna?" Sebastian said.

Jace ran into the throne room, followed by Kristoff and the other Drakes.

"There's more, Your Majesty," the scout said. "Maxen has intercepted the army of Torrdale."

Cyrus squeezed his eyes shut.

Sebastian watched him close. "If he marries Lorna, he will have Torrdale and the Safar. Can we stop her, Cyrus?"

"She is a privileged princess who grew up with no laws," Cyrus said. "She doesn't love Maxen just as she never loved my brother. It was his power and position she craved. A crown. When Roman fell, she became desperate. She will help Maxen in the war so she can be queen again. Besides, no other man will have her after she murdered the King of Kings."

Sebastian smiled. "I'm going to bed. We will discuss more tomorrow."

The castle got quiet as the night crept into twilight. Sebastian's hands worked across the war room table as he pushed around pieces of wooden soldiers along the multiple routes out of NorthBrekka. "If I send Barron with a legion south of the lake, his army will reach the border into Torrdale in two nights. I can meet him at the wall, and we ride to the castle—"

"What happened to "I'm going to bed?""

Sebastian jumped. "I will sleep when I am dead, Tomas."

"That is what all the great leaders of the world say. They all die soon after." Tomas leaned against the table and set his cane across the battlefield Sebastian had created.

"It's because they were too tired." Sebastian grabbed the cane and looked it over. "Can you walk without this?" He slowly turned his head to Tomas.

"Not really. It hurts really bad when I try. My hip doesn't bear my weight anymore." Tomas rubbed his thigh.

Sebastian put his hand on Tomas's shoulder, then jerked him in for a hug. He held him for a long while, trying to stifle back tears. "You are not ready for battle, Tomas—"

"Don't you dare, Sebastian. You will not make me stay behind."

"Tomas, I cannot protect you if I am fighting Maxen!"

"We will be fighting him together, remember. Both of us."

Sebastian pushed his forehead against Tomas's. "I can't risk losing you."

"Then I suggest you teach me as much as possible before we depart." Tomas fidgeted with his cane. "It's not like you were going to sleep tonight anyway."

Sebastian caught Tomas grinning. He laughed and nodded. "You are right. Alright, let's go train."

In the courtyard, Tomas stretched his hand to the sky and the snowstorm steadied to a light flurry. Sebastian stood with his back against the wall of the archery field, admiring how easily his twin took control.

"You were always the smart one." Sebastian grinned. "It took me years to learn what you have progressed in a few days. Imagine how incredible you will be in a few months."

Tomas dropped his hands. "Don't go crying on me now, brother. Now what?"

"Now I want to see your raw, relentless power. Be fierce."

Tomas's eyes shined brighter than Sebastian had ever seen, unmasked by the rapidly increasing snow. Whirlwinds of sleet fell, pelting the twins' faces. Tomas reached up as if to grab the cyclone. He gripped his fists and moved his hands apart. The vortex turned into steady snow. The sleet stopped falling. Tomas dropped to the ground.

"Tomas!" Sebastian lunged forward.

"What happened?" Tomas shook hard and was freezing cold. His eyes rolled back in his head. "What is wrong with me?"

"Tomas?" Sebastian started to scream. "Guards! Someone, help me." He scooped Tomas into his arms and ran for the castle.

The doors swung open, and Valirus stood in the entry with guards waiting to take Tomas. "What did you do, boy?"

"Now is not the time to yell at me, old man." Sebastian shoved his way past Valirus.

Valirus grabbed his arm and yanked him back. "What did you say to him?" The sorcerer looked furious. "Your brother is transforming as you did before. What did you do to him?"

"This is what we wanted, right?"

In his bedroom, Tomas lay shivering and jerking violently. The walls froze and unfroze until a loud crack came from the door. The shattering of ice made Sebastian wince and he held Tomas in his arms. Nadya rushed in and sat on the bed next to Tomas. She put a warm towel on his forehead, then rested her hand on his chest and closed her eyes. "He will be alright." She let out a deep breath.

Amara slipped through the door and marched over. "What is going to happen to him, Sebastian?"

"He is transitioning, Amara. He will be fine."

"Fine? He is not fine!" Amara fired at Sebastian. "Look at him, Sebastian. He is dying. What did you do?"

Sebastian was getting angry. "I didn't do anything." He stood too fast, then sat back down and took her hand. "Do you not think I am worried too? But I made it through the changing fine."

"He is not you!" Amara ripped her hand away.

Sebastian grabbed Amara by her shoulders. "He is stronger than you think."

"That's enough!" Nadya pushed herself between them both. "You may be the king, but you are still my little brother, and I will slap you if you can't control yourself." She turned around. "Amara, Sebastian would never hurt Tomas. You know this. And now is not the time to make him angry."

"You're right, Nadya," Amara said. "I'm sorry, Seb. I'm just scared."

"I know." Sebastian closed his eyes. "Do you remember when we first met, and you took care of me and put up with me all that time I was ill?"

"How could I possibly forget how insulting and arrogant you were?"

Sebastian smiled. "I always knew you would be special to me for the rest of my life. When you told me you wanted us to be together, I honestly thought about it."

Amara's head turned to the side, and her mouth dropped. "You lie."

"No. I thought I would never get home and if I did, I imagined that no one wanted me there after discovering what I would become. I thought Barron would kill me, so I planned to stay with you." He reached for Amara's hand. "But it was you that changed my heart. You showed me the way and forced me to get off my ass and do something. If it wasn't for you, I would have hidden in that village for the rest of my life."

Amara squeezed his hand. Tears ran down her cheeks. "I have always loved you. I hoped for us to be together, but I knew you wouldn't be happy… not really." She sniffled. "Tomas has been here for me since the moment you left." She kissed Sebastian's cheek, sat by Tomas, and rubbed his head. "I beg you to get your ass out there… and you end Maxen's entire empire."

"You know that means killing Cyrus, right?" Nadya said.

Tomas started to toss and turn. The shivering slowed, but his breathing was raspy and heavy. Sebastian recognized it as it matched his own. "Seb—"

"I'm here, brother."

"Am I a monster now?" Tomas opened one eye and smiled.

Sebastian laughed. "Yes, you are a fucking monster, Tommy." He took a deep breath. "My brother, Hydros, are you ready to fight?"

"Maybe you should wait until he can sit up unattended," Nadya said.

"Fine. I'm going to bed." Sebastian stood up.

"That means go to sleep, brother. You need rest." Tomas grabbed his hand.

Sebastian nodded and left Tomas's room. He wandered down the old corridor where his other siblings slept. He closed his eyes and thought about when they used to run and throw toys in the hall. Gentry and Viktor played pranks on Mary and Sara while Nadya tried to get everyone rounded up for meals. He stopped at the room where he and Cyrus made love and put his hand on the door. To his surprise, it fell open, and he saw a beautiful face lying in the bed.

"Sebastian, come in!"

Sebastian stared at him for a moment then closed the door. He tore off his coat, dropped his belt with his knives and swords haltered, and crawled on top of Cyrus. "Kiss me," he whispered.

Cyrus met his lips. Sebastian held him tight and kissed his neck and mouth.

Sebastian ran his lips down Cyrus's chest and stomach. His mouth rested lightly against his hipbone as he untied Cyrus's pants. He felt fingers running through his hair, and a sharp pull as Cyrus demanded his lips meet his once more. Sebastian's hands clawed at the milky flesh of a man he had loved his entire life. He let out a moan and Cyrus's eye flickered as they made love. Their sweaty torsos made Sebastian grip his lover tighter and Cyrus gasped with every thrust.

Cyrus pushed his way on top and gave every ounce of energy he could muster into pleasuring Sebastian. He arched his back and breathed heavily while keeping his hands rested on Sebastian's chest. He clenched a thick piece of Sebastian's hair. Sebastian growled with intensity. Every movement of Cyrus's body against his sent him into ecstasy.

"I love you," Sebastian whispered into Cyrus's ear.

"I love you too."

The following day Sebastian woke to Cyrus sleeping on his chest. He let out a little laugh and clutched Cyrus's hair in his fist, pulling him in for a kiss.

Cyrus sat up. "What does this mean, Sebastian?"

Sebastian shook his head. "It means we fucked. Nothing more, Cyrus."

"You said you love me," Cyrus whispered.

"And I told you the truth." Sebastian kissed his cheek. "But you know how I feel about us."

Tears began running down Cyrus's face. "But… last night—" He stopped, stared into his eyes, and tucked Sebastian's hair behind his ear, causing Sebastian to let out a raspy gasp and flicker his eyes.

Sebastian kissed him again. "I'm sorry. I love Dani more than I love you."

Cyrus shoved him away and sat up fast. There was a knock at the door, followed by the sneering voice of someone Sebastian did not expect. The door swung open.

"Are you dressed yet? Oh, bloody hell, Sebastian. I thought I would never have to see the two of you naked together again, but here I stand, wrong again." Barron shook his head.

"Gather everyone in the war room. We have a lot to discuss." Sebastian climbed out of bed. "Oh, and Barron, don't forget that I am in charge here. Not you."

"I understand, brother." Barron smirked and bowed slightly. Sebastian turned his back to the door. Barron let out a loud sniffle. Sebastian glanced over his shoulder and narrowed his eyes until Barron hurried away.

In the war room, Sebastian waited at the table as the others joined. Tomas walked in without looking as if he was in terrible pain. Sebastian jumped to his feet. "Your cane… what happened to it?"

"I don't think I need it anymore," Tomas said. He still had a limp but could move easily. Sebastian's family and the leaders from Midrel Istan sat and waited.

Sebastian looked around the room. "This war is going to be one of the most important events of our lifetime. That sorcerer is planning his strategies with the Safar and Torrdale soldiers. He has incredible abilities and can take control of one's mind with a simple touch, and… he has my Dani." Sebastian shot a look at Cyrus. "Surely you have all been educated in what a Blackbird can do. As much as Barron is one, my Dani is the other, and he is the dangerous kind. If Maxen forces his abilities on his son, Dani can kill every single one of you with just a stroke of his fingers. I beg of you all, let me handle Dani. Only me."

Plans for infiltrating Torrdale were discussed. Cyrus explained different routes to take so that the militia would not travel through main trade roads. Sebastian sat back and listened; his mind rested elsewhere. The guilt overwhelmed him. He glanced up and saw Cyrus's chestnut hair shine under the candlelight. The fog and light snow cast a light mist on the war room. Sebastian stared at Cyrus's lips as he spoke. He followed Cyrus's eyes as they moved from person to person and his hands as they pointed to places on the map.

He stood and walked to the door. "Thank you, Cyrus." He walked from the war room quickly. He suddenly felt exhausted, and his legs shook as he rushed to his bedroom and slammed the door behind him. He sat on the floor and rested his back against the bed. Sebastian took shaky, shallow breaths, to steady himself just before a tear fell.

CHAPTER 35
The Way to the Mountains

Dani woke to the sounds of Maxen screaming at the maidens. He had slept on the couch in the room with the large windows. Outside, it was cloudy and drizzling, and the sea thrashed against the rocks, sending magnificent waves over the top of the cliffside. He snuck over to the glass and sat in a corner, hoping no one would notice him.

As the morning disappeared and afternoon peeked out from the clouds, Dani smelled the aroma of cakes baking and pork cooking. His stomach rumbled loudly and nauseatingly. Dani saw maidens running back and forth in the kitchen, dropping vegetables on the floor and spilling broth while mumbling about a ceremony. Dani snuck over to a table where fresh pies were cooling.

He felt a slap on the back of his hand when he reached for a peach cobbler. "That is too hot, Prince Dani. You will burn yourself and your father will have my head."

"My father doesn't care if I burn myself. He doesn't even feed me." Dani started to leave. "Please don't tell him I was in here."

"Wait, my dear," the maiden said. "Here. Don't tell anyone I gave you this." She handed him a roll and a large slice of ham. "You should eat that back here." She waved for him to follow.

Dani walked through a small door that led to the unguarded side of the castle outside. The rain had stopped, and the sun began to peek out. She placed her finger over her lips, pointed toward the east, and then slipped back inside. He quickly shoved the food in his mouth and crept around the wall, looking for soldiers. He saw men wandering back and forth around the courtyard and near the gate. Townspeople rushed in with their wares, and a group of ladies carried arms full of sheer white fabric and others with flowers, perfumes, and herbs. He rolled his eyes, slipped back by the kitchen door, and checked where the woman who gave him food had pointed. Dani pulled his hood over his head and began walking, not knowing what was ahead.

As he made it across the field, Dani turned back and saw he was not being followed. His heart skipped a beat and his body tingled. He darted toward the woods ahead. He hiked through hilly grasslands and pine forests, occasionally bumping into merchants who were late to the palace. One man with a wobbly wheeled cart jogged toward Dani. His breathing was gargled and heavy.

"Has he chosen a boot maker, young man?"

"Excuse me? Who?" Dani asked.

"King Maxen." The merchant bent over to catch his breath. "The Bolins have returned to Torrdale. Don't you know?"

"I have noticed." Dani hid his face. "I was not aware the king was looking for a bootmaker."

"Have you been lost, child? A royal wedding always calls for a bootmaker for the king's big day."

"I don't know anything." Dani kept walking.

"Wait," the man said. "You don't have any shoes on. It's much colder where you are headed."

Dani kept walking. He stopped late after the sun went down each day, sometimes finding tall grass to sleep in or boulders large enough to provide shelter. After long days of walking and the air cooling, one night, he stopped at an abandoned farm at the foot of low mountains. The farmhouse reminded him of being on the Paark farm in Midrel Istan. He laughed while he cuddled into a pile of old blankets and closed his eyes.

The morning was crisp, and an icy dew rested on the grassy field. Dani found small berries growing on sharp bushes that tamed his angry belly and allowed him to keep moving. The weather began to change when the sun tucked behind dark, gray clouds. Dani squeezed his thin coat around his ears when he saw snow begin to fall. As he topped a large hill, the magnificent sight of large, jagged mountains blanketed the way ahead. The hills had a thick jacket of snow. Dani halted suddenly, and the presence made his stomach flutter from excitement rather than hunger.

Across a large prairie, a short wall stood before a massive lake that majestically shined through the falling flurries. The storm let up, and the low clouds cleared, showing Dani the true picture of where the maiden in the kitchen pointed. The lake spread far, but above it, connected to the rest of the world by a few narrow, winding roads, sat a castle. Dani remembered Sebastian telling him stories of his homeland, the lake where he learned his power, and a palace on a ridgeline where he grew up. "It has to be."

Dani ran toward the wall, having to find a way to climb over without the danger of the loose rocks crumbling under his weight. He fell over the top and onto his face against the hard ground. His head spun a little but cleared once he realized how close he was free of Torrdale.

That evening, Dani sat on the edge of the beach, scooping up minnows from the shallow water and eating them. He lit a fire and laid his head against a small rock. He hoped he could find his way to the castle in the morning and would spend the next night in the arms of the man he loved. The sound of gentle waves splashing against the beach made him forget that it was winter, and his fire wasn't sufficient, so Dani closed his eyes before he was too cold to sleep.

Early morning came with a faint haze of daylight poking through the clouds. The snow was falling, and Dani's fire was ash under a thick frosted blanket. His bones ached and his neck was stiff. He stood with shaking knees and walked to the water to have a drink. The castle cast an eerie glow from fires lit around the grounds. The stonework of the walls glistened from hanging icicles. The sun crested over the distant horizon as the rays sparkled across the lake.

Dani paced, waiting for the light to shine on the path to the castle. He looked around him, seeing a way cutting into the woods and up into the jagged mountains, but he also saw the large step bridge across the lake that ascended the steep cliffs and stopped just before the castle grounds. He checked the shallows for more minnows, but they were gone. Dani pulled his coat tight and turned, stumbling and falling on his backside. "Who are you?" He shuffled away at the face of a strange man on horseback.

"Who are you?" The man repeated. "You are not NorthBrekkian or Torrdale. You don't look like anyone from Erras, which tells me that you belong to King Maxen."

"I am Dani." He stood and held his hands up to show he was unarmed. "I'm looking for King Sebastian." Dani pointed across the lake. "That is his castle, right?"

The man sheathed his sword and jumped down from his horse. "So, you are the man who has replaced me." He pulled his hood off his head. "We never officially met. I am Cyrus."

Dani backed away. "You are my cousin... I have heard a lot."

"The best route to the castle is that way." Cyrus pointed behind him. "You will come into a village called Shadowmire. Once you arrive, it is just a short walk to the castle."

Dani looked at the path and then back to Cyrus. "You're not going back?"

"Why would I do that?" Cyrus jumped on his horse. "The king doesn't want me in his country." Cyrus started to ride away.

"I'll never get to the castle without food and warmer clothes." Dani shivered. "I don't even have any boots."

Cyrus took a deep breath. "You made it this far—"

"Imagine if I die on the road and Sebastian finds out you could have saved me."

Cyrus laughed. He guided his horse over to Dani. "Get on." He reached his hand out.

"You're not going to leave me in the mountains to die, are you?" Dani turned his head. "I know about your enchantment."

Cyrus guided his horse toward the road. "My curse has been broken."

As they began ascending a steep pathway, Cyrus turned his head back. "This is called The Break. It was named by Dragon, the god of fire before. It was when Dragon and Litha divided Erras from The Far North, and the Sinook from the rest of the world. Shadowmire was once a meeting place for Sinook leaders and Dragon to unite in neutral territory. Now, it is a place for criminals and whores. Sebastian loves it there."

Dani didn't speak. He hurt his neck looking up and down and craning to see over Cyrus's shoulder. He wanted to ask a lot of questions but remained silent.

They soon arrived in Shadowmire. The usual business took hold, and no one tried to stop them as they passed. A heavy sweet scent filled the air. Dani's stomach started growling loud. He held his belly and remembered Cyrus saying it wasn't far from the castle. They descended a narrow road and Dani sat up where he could see ahead.

"Wow," he gasped.

"Tell me something," Cyrus said. "Has Maxen taken Torrdale?"

"Yes." Dani sat back. "I escaped your palace, thanks to the help of a maiden. My Father is marrying Princess Lorna so an alliance between Torrdale and Safareen can begin."

"That's disturbing." Cyrus shook his head. "Let's just get you to Sebastian, then I will take my leave."

They arrived at the gates that opened enough for his horse to slip through. Dani leaped down and stared in awe. His mouth fell open and a tear formed in the corner of his eye. He ran to the door.

"No, Dani, stop!" Cyrus said.

Dani looked back and then felt like he had slammed into a wall. He lay on the ground, quivering with pain.

"I don't know how things went for you in Midrel Istan, but in NorthBrekka, the guards will slaughter you for storming the castle like that." Cyrus walked toward him, laughing.

"I wasn't storming the castle. I was running to Sebastian." He pushed a guard away from him. Two pikes shot at Dani's throat.

"Easy, men. This one belongs to us." A voice came from the doorway. "Welcome home, Dani."

"Valirus?"

"My son, you returned. And you brought Dani. His Majesty will commend you for this," Valirus said.

"I didn't do it for him," Cyrus said. "Dani is my family. I have little of that left, so I couldn't have just let him get eaten by wolves or something." He walked inside.

"Is Sebastian alright?" Dani climbed to his feet.

"His Majesty is fine. Overwhelmed. That is all. He will be better when he sees you."

Valirus signaled for Dani to follow him inside. Dani stopped as soon as his feet crossed the threshold. The warmth filled his body.

"Dani, this is just the entry. You are freezing. Let's find someone to get you cleaned up." Valirus grabbed his arm and rushed away until he bumped into Meecah.

"The gods bless us. Dani!" Meecah hugged him. "Wow, you smell like something died."

"Where is Sebastian? I need to see him."

"He is in the woods with Tomas." A beautiful, blonde-haired woman, toting a child on her hip, came around the corner. "So, you are the infamous Dani. I am Nadya, Sebastian's sister." Nadya checked Dani over. "I will have to see if we have any of Gentry's clothes. They should fit you."

"Who is Gentry?" Dani said.

"One of my little brothers." Nadya took him upstairs and asked the maids to fill a bath. She sat him down, looking over his cuts and bruises. "You have the prettiest eyes I have ever seen." She smiled and continued poking at him.

A young lady knocked lightly on the door and informed them that the bath was ready. Dani walked in and started to undress. "I can bathe myself."

Nadya curtsied and backed out of the room. Once alone, Dani sunk into the steaming water. The tub sat next to a large window that viewed the mountains. Dani scrubbed his hair and face, then dipped below the surface. The hot water stung his sore nose, but he enjoyed the heat on his aching muscles. When the water became dirty and cool, Dani climbed out and wrapped himself in a robe that was much too big. There was a knock on the door.

Meecah and Nadya came in with their hands filled with clothes, boots, and scissors. Dani dressed quickly.

"Those are not for me, are they?" Dani pointed at the scissors.

"I just want to trim the mats away," Meecah said. "You are a mess, Dani."

"Did you expect my father to care for me, let alone feed me?"

"Oh, you are probably hungry," Nadya said. "Come eat and wait for the twins to return from practice."

Dani smiled at the word twins. He hurried to the hall and sat in front of a tray of different meats and tomatoes. There was a lot of chatter, but he was too hungry to look around. Once his stomach was full, he noticed Viktor and Kristoff sitting across from him, laughing.

"Good to see you again, Dani. Someone is going to be happy when he gets back." Kristoff grinned and bumped Viktor.

The sound of stomping came from the corridor, with loud laughter and celebratory cheering. Dani stood up as men began filing in. There were soldiers of different tribes andone entered with a wolf by his side. He was tall with long golden hair and walked right past Dani, smiling at him as he stopped by the table at the end of the room. Then he heard a familiar laugh. "Jace!"

"Dani?" Jace said. "Where the hell did you come from?"

Dani started to talk, but his eyes shot to the door, seeing the beautiful, dark-haired, red-eyed man he loved.

"Go to him." Jace nudged.

"Sebastian!" Dani took off in a sprint.

Dani was lifted into Sebastian's arms. His heart raced, and he could barely catch his breath. Sebastian clasped his face and kissed him when his feet touched the floor.

"My love," Sebastian whispered. "How?"

"Cyrus... he found me. I probably would have died out there if it weren't for him." Dani kissed him, then turned his attention to Sebastian's twin. "You must be Tomas." He touched Tomas's face, then turned back. "Sebastian. I have to tell you something." He slowly sat. "My father forced me to use my powers. I killed several of his men." Dani's stomach tightened and he was dizzy.

"Can we speak alone?" Sebastian asked.

They walked into a bedroom and Sebastian lit a fire. He laid Dani on the soft bed and climbed on top of him. "I will love you no matter who you are or what you have done." He kissed Dani's neck. "And I will make you my husband before we go to war." They made love until the wood in the fireplace was gray and hinted at the remains of a glow.

Dani woke up from a short nap. He rolled over to face Sebastian. "Did you mean that?" He put his hands on Sebastian's chest. "Are you sure that's what you want? Cyrus, he—"

"We get married tomorrow," Sebastian said. "Cyrus is no longer an option, Dani. You are the only man my heart desires." He planted his head back onto the pillow and pulled Dani against him and kissed his forehead. "I want to stay right here all day."

That evening, they joined the others in the hall for dinner. The conversations and rumbles of men and women moving about halted as Sebastian entered. Soldiers stepped from their tables to bend their knees to their king. Tomas and Jace waited at the head table for Sebastian to join them.

"Tomas," Sebastian said. "This is my fiancé, Dani."

"Wow. I have never seen identical twins before," Dani said. "You are both so—"

"Please, don't say pretty." Sebastian took a deep breath and closed his eyes.

Jace and Tomas burst into laughter, followed by Dani. Sebastian smiled and shook his head before reaching for some bread. He looked around the room as those from Erras and Midrel Istan met and enjoyed a meal. Meecah and Nadya quickly became friends. Valirus and Samir were in a debate about something Sebastian could not figure out, while Dom and Jon listened, offering their thoughts on occasion. The wolf came and sat next to Sebastian as he slipped pieces of chicken under the table.

"You have a pet wolf?" Dani said.

"It's Dom's wolf." Sebastian pointed. "She follows him everywhere, but she and I were friends first." He smiled and handed the wolf another chunk of meat.

Barron slowly approached the king's table. "May I sit and have a word with you, brother?"

Sebastian gestured to a chair.

"Are you going to introduce me to your friend?"

"Barron, I ask of you to stay away from Dani. That is my one threat to you." Sebastian squeezed Dani's hand. Dani set his head on Sebastian's shoulder.

Barron sat and locked eyes with his brother. "Maxen isn't ready for battle. Not yet. He has not mustered his men to the line. They are waiting for something."

"My father is waiting until after he weds Princess Lorna," Dani said. "Then he will have Altanians, Torrdale, and Safarian soldiers and they will all march here."

"The Safar." Sebastian chewed his food before continuing. "Ships from Safareen attacked us at sea, allowing Maxen and his fleet to escape with Dani. I went to battle and blasted a Safarian warship to the ocean floor. They will most definitely come after us."

"He made a whirlpool," Jace said.

"Jace—"

"What? I thought we moved past stubborn Sebastian and onto big and mighty Sebastian." Jace flapped his arms like wings or dragon wings, for that matter.

Sebastian felt his cheeks burn as he smiled, trying to stifle a laugh as the others around him giggled, and his sister began telling stories about him as a kid. Dani got up to sit by Nadya, saying he wanted to know everything about Sebastian. "Barron. How long do we logically have before we can expect Maxen to move?"

"You are asking for my advice? You really have grown up." Barron cleared his throat and looked away for a moment. "I just want to help. Then, whatever you need to do to make things right with me, I will allow."

"I'm going to ki—"

"Kill me. I know." Barron rolled his eyes and shook his head.

"As long as we are clear. But for now, yes. I want your advice." Sebastian stood and reached his hand out to Barron's. Barron met his stance and gripped his forearm. They nodded to one another as everyone watched.

Barron laughed. "Does this make us friends?"

"Not even by the slightest," Sebastian smirked, setting his hand on Barron's shoulder. "But we are brothers."

Barron nodded. "We have little time. A week, maybe."

"Barron, there is just one more thing I must know." Sebastian started to walk away, gesturing for him to follow.

"You want to know why I did what I did… It is a long story."

"Summarize, brother. I just need the important bits." Sebastian moved quickly toward the armory on the opposite side of the castle. The others followed. Kristoff and Viktor hung their heads close as Barron started to answer.

"Father always pushed me away. It was always, 'Barron, go and train with the men, go do this, go do that.' Meanwhile, he always had Tomas in tow. Everywhere he went, he had his precious Tomas. But you, Sebastian, were my worst nightmare. Father watched me train with knights. He watched me get beat down, injured, and even win, but in the end, he would say, 'you could learn from Sebastian. Sebastian has the mind of a king, be like him.' Barron shook his head and sped up. "It was awful living in my little brother's shadow. When Father told me you would be king, I got angry, and everything went dark. I heard him backing away from me, but I couldn't see anything. I don't know what I did, and when the light returned Father was holding a vial. He instructed me to put a drop in his and Emelia's glasses each night at supper. He told me the only way the world would survive was for him to fall. Forcing you to assume his place was enough to make your dragon come out.

Unfortunately, it was at the cost of our brotherhood. I hated you, Sebastian, but I didn't want to fight you."

Sebastian's skin tingled and his heart raced. "I live with these scars every day. I am not angry that you tortured me. I would have taken the punishment, so no other had to, but you betrayed us all for what? A promise of a throne? Did you think Sacha would remain loyal if I fell? He would have—"

"Killed me." Barron pinched the bridge of his nose. "I don't understand why none of you think I know this."

Sebastian let out a groan. "What must be done?"

"You, brother, have to be the one king. The only king. No more of this fighting between nations. One king will rule overall. You must become King of Kings. With Tomas, Dani, and I, along with your sorcerer, Maxen cannot defeat us. It is foretold, and I, for one, believe in prophecies."

"My prophecy said I would kill everyone and end the world," Sebastian said. "That is what everyone believes. I have the right to choose my destiny, and ending all life as we know it is not my plan for the future."

"This power I have made me see the truth. I hope you will tell me that you forgive me before you cut out my heart."

Sebastian sighed heavily, letting out a tired laugh as he patted Barron on the back and continued to the armory. "We are a seriously fucked up family."

Barron stopped. "Sebastian, I need to know where Sara and my son are?"

Sebastian shrugged. "Perhaps you should ask someone who has been here for the last few years."

"I thought they would have told you."

"I didn't ask." Sebastian could see the resentment in Barron's bloodshot eyes. Barron had been in the dungeon for five years and time was cruel. Although still handsome, his face was ghostly from the lack of sun and proper food. His usual pompous attitude was replaced by shame and regret. Sebastian didn't feel sorry for Barron, but he knew he needed him now that he was a Blackbird.

Nadya stepped between them. "Sara… may the gods protect her and that sweet child. She is in Torrdale. I sent her there years ago. She lives in a small village in the low hills south of the palace. I made sure she was comfortable and that Corbyn received the best care. But now, she is a Drake living in enemy territory. You have to save her, Sebastian."

Sebastian rubbed his face and pushed his way through the armory door, letting out a growl as he walked away from Barron and Nadya. He checked for weapons and gear, leather, arrows, and shields, finding his bow on a table. Sebastian ran his hand across the shaft.

A hand reached over and touched his. "You still have this?"

Sebastian smiled. "Of course I do. It is the best bow I have ever owned."

"You still have my ring too." Dom lifted Sebastian's hand in his. "The Oscura. It is a very powerful ring. It holds a spell that was cast by an ancient Sinook enchantress. She was a Blackbird. The Oscura was made for Dragon."

"What does it do?" Sebastian looked at the ring closely.

"I don't really know. But the jewel is cracked. The elders say it was struck by an evil hex, causing the stone to split. Maybe it does nothing at all. Either way, it belongs to you, Your Majesty. My mother gave it to me when she thought you and I would marry."

Sebastian saw Dani coming over quickly.

"Married?" Dani said. "You two were—"

"No," Dom said. "We are too much the same person. The legend says I was born for you, to be the one for you, but I don't think it means marriage. I believe we are just soulmates sharing a unique gift from the gods."

"I am lucky to have you," Sebastian said. "You are very important to me, and I believe it is time that is recognized, along with some others." Sebastian clapped his hands and spoke loudly, "My Father's army has suffered loss worse than most and we are now complete thanks to all of you. I wish to knight those who have been by my side all this time." Sebastian unsheathed his sword. "Jace, come here."

Jace hesitated. "Please don't cut my head off with that thing."

Sebastian laughed. "You have been loyal to me since the day we met. Even when I screamed at you, hit you, and forced you away, you still came back for me. You are the best person I know, and I want you more than my advisor. I want you to be a knight and captain."

"Thank you, Your Majesty." Jace sniffled and bowed his head.

"Meecah," Sebastian said. "I choose you to be a knight because I am afraid you will beat me up if I don't pick you."

"I've done it once and I would do it again, my king." Meecah knelt.

"You got beat up by a girl?" Nadya laughed.

"Yes… Moving on." Sebastian choked back laughter. "Jon, Viktor, Kristoff. We don't have all day. Get over here." He finished then turned to Dom. "I have something far more important in mind for you. We will discuss this later." Dom nodded and waited by Sebastian's side while he spoke again. "I find courage and honor in everyone in this room. Every last one of you is an intricate piece of this game we are about to play. Our enemy is not prepared for this, but neither are we. But we will strap on our weapons, tighten our boots, and march to meet them in a battle no matter how afraid, cold, hungry, or ready we are. In this room, we have some of the most powerful humans on this earth. Most of us are new to our power and that is all right." Sebastian walked around the room. "In NorthBrekka, our love for each other goes back decades. Our families are strong, and those we accepted into our home only make us better. Maxen is filled with anger and rage and with that comes failure. I know because I used to be exactly like him. I did not respect anyone around me and I hurt everyone I loved. But that is not who I am anymore. I want to take a page from my brother Barron's book when I say I am looking for redemption. No matter the cost, I will do what is right by everyone who has had to suffer for me."

"Good, because you used to be intolerable," Meecah said. She and Sebastian burst into laughter at the same time.

Sebastian set his hand on her shoulder. "You are the only one of your people here. Make them proud of what you have become."

"I will. I promise." Meecah wrapped her arms around Sebastian and squeezed. "And don't you worry. Not one of us is going to let our king die out there. You will live a full life with us protecting you."

"I sure hope so." Sebastian smiled. "Before I dismiss everyone, I must do one more thing." Sebastian grabbed Dani's hand. "Marry me. Right now."

He saw Cyrus's mouth drop, then close. He leaned against a wall and looked away.

"Samir," Sebastian said aloud. Samir walked over, and the room silenced. "I ask you to marry Dani and me. You are a city leader, so you have the power to do so, but you are also my friend, and I respect the ways of the people of Midrel Istan."

"Your home in Adurak will forever await your return, Your Majesty. Now, let's get the two of you married." Samir smiled and took both Sebastian and Dani's hands. "King Sebastian Drake and Prince Dani Bolin are united as one, in love and partnership. Through all darkness, they bring light. Their love was written before they were born, a destiny of two gifted forces from a legend of old. Lovers for eternity and bound by fate." Samir paused and turned to Dani. "You are no longer a slave to the king. You are the husband of the most powerful being on this earth. Be wise, Dani. Use your power and your position well." Samir turned to Sebastian. "As for you, King of Thieves and God of Fire. Remember why you fight and remember you are not alone. You are the husband of a Blackbird. He is your reason. Use your power and position well. Now, kiss and become one."

Sebastian felt his body burst with a cold, warm sensation as he kissed Dani's soft lips and heard the celebratory roar of his soldiers. He whispered in Dani's ear, "I have never been happier in my life."

Dani squeezed his arms around Sebastian. "I am still trying to process if this is real. Am I dreaming?"

Sebastian tucked Dani's hair behind his ear and grasped his chin with the tips of his fingers. "This is real, my darling."

Tomas hurried over and wrapped his arms around his twin.

Sebastian stepped back and shouted, "Wait, everyone! We are not through. Tomas, Amara."

Tomas laughed. "Wait, really?" He reached for Amara to take his hand. "Will you marry me now, Amara?"

"I was never a patient person." Amara hugged Tomas. "Oh, Tomas, I haven't had the chance to tell you. I'm pregnant."

Tomas's legs shook and he lost his balance, but then scooped Amara up in his arms. Sebastian clapped, hugged them both, and stood aside so Samir could perform their marriage.

That night, while the others celebrated, Sebastian and Dani slipped away to the war room and closed the door. The snowstorm had cleared, and the stars shone bright above. Dani stood in the moonlight. His blue eyes twinkled like diamonds. Sebastian admired everything he saw standing before him. A young, wounded soul. An exiled prince that had lived the life of a whore. He was hurt, bruised, and internally broken, yet he still smiled through his suffering and had cared for a man he didn't know would change his life.

Sebastian lightly passed his hand from Dani's cheek to his hip, pulling him in for a kiss. He felt Dani's heart begin to race. His face fell as he moved away and held Dani's hand. "Are you alright? You are shaking."

"I'm scared. I can't lose you. Not now." Dani started shifting back and forth. "What if you die because of me? I can't handle that."

"My sweet love, I am not going to die. Please don't be afraid. You and I will live a long, happy life together."

Dani choked back tears as he smiled and grabbed Sebastian's face, smashing their lips together. Sebastian picked Dani up and set him on the war table. He stepped back and threw his shirt off, seeing his new husband look him over and smile. His hands reached for Dani's belt. He kissed him again, then yanked the pants from his hips. Dani jumped off the table and fell to his knees, undoing Sebastian's pants as he worked his way to pleasuring the king. Sebastian gripped the wall and threw his head back, moaning and gasping while grasping a fistful of Dani's hair.

There was no one banging on the door or asking for Sebastian. It was just them, and that is all he wanted ever in his life—one perfect night of lovemaking with his husband. He questioned his choice of the war room, but it is where Sebastian felt safe in his own castle. He wanted Dani to feel what he felt. The power, the intensity, the cold air, and the love.

Sebastian set Dani on the table again and pushed his way between his legs, taking a haughty groan as he indulged in ravishing his lover. Dani wrapped his arms around Sebastian, pulled him down onto the table, and mounted his hips. He gasped with every movement of their bodies.

The night became still. A stark silence filled the halls. Sebastian handed Dani his clothes as he dressed. He couldn't resist touching his lover, running his fingers across his cheek, and kissing his neck.

"Should I continue getting dressed?" Dani laughed.

"You don't have to dress," Sebastian said. "But I want you in my bed now, so you can either walk through the castle naked or put on your pants."

Dani slipped his clothes on and followed Sebastian into the corridor, keeping his hand firmly placed in Sebastian's. "I am never letting you go again. Never. I'm afraid if I do, you will vanish, and I will be alone."

"I can get a rope and you can be tethered to me if you'd like." Sebastian laughed but quickly stopped when he saw Dani's face drop from smiling to trembling as tears filled his eyes. Sebastian held him to his chest. "My darling, did I say something? I didn't mean to hurt you."

Dani started shaking as he told Sebastian how Petra had tied a rope around his neck and dragged him across Erras. When they made it to the bedroom, Sebastian fell to his knees and laid his head on Dani's lap. Dani stroked his hair as his shaking retreated, and he felt calm again. They made love through the night until they fell into bed, fast asleep.

CHAPTER 36
The Red Headed Sister

A few wintry days had passed. The courtyard was reduced to a thick white blanket with footsteps quickly disappearing as the blizzard wreaked havoc on NorthBrekka. As dawn fell over Castle Drake, Sebastian snuck out of bed early in the dark, letting Dani sleep peacefully, and crept to the next room. He donned a thick leather coat over his linen and wool and strapped on his boots and gloves. He made his way to the war room as sunrise came upon the eastern horizon.

The storm cleared, leaving a light haze and a few clouds, and the sun's rays bounced off his face. Sebastian closed his eyes and breathed in and out the crisp, damp air. He heard the door creak open, but no one spoke, and Sebastian didn't open his eyes to look.

"Father would be so proud of you." Nadya's voice was soft and low.

Sebastian clenched his jaw, then nodded. "I haven't properly grieved for our father." He paused and looked out over the valley. "I hope you all understand my distancing myself from everyone. It's nothing personal. I just want to make sure this place is safe before I leave it behind."

"What about Dani? Is he truly safe here?"

Sebastian watched fires ignite in the town in the valley below. "When I officially met Dani, he was working in a brothel. Whether fate or dumb luck brought us together, he was meant to be mine. Now, I discover he is one of the two Blackbirds, and his powers are so violent that he can destroy large numbers of men with one outburst." Sebastian turned to Nadya. "Dani told me that it hurts. When he uses his power out of anger and it forces the evil inside him out. I cannot do that to him. I won't. He is safe with me and only me. If he gets captured, then this game will end with mass genocide. Over, Nadya. For all of us!"

"Would that be you or Dani at fault for said genocide?" Nadya's jaw was clenched, her eyes were wide, and she looked as if she wanted to slap his face with her fist tight at her side.

Sebastian smiled, letting out a grumbling laugh. "Are you angry with me?" He reached for her hand. "A Dragon is a curse over these lands. I do not belong here, and there will be darkness as long as I am. I have made a lot of enemies, and I will right everything I can so that all of you can live in peace. But when it is time, I will go." He noticed her fists loosen. "I belong in Midrel Istan. The people there think well of me. It's actually nice to be liked." Sebastian kicked his boot into the floor. "But only a little."

Nadya tried to hold back laughter, but she doubled over before pulling him in for a hug. "I love you so much." She held his face in her palms. "You have that choice. You are King of Kings. There is no denying it; you can rule wherever you wish. Your home will always be here, but I respect your choices, no matter what they are. Just promise me one thing."

Sebastian shrugged. "Anything."

"Take Tomas with you and Amara, of course."

"I already planned that. I haven't told him. Please let me," Sebastian said.

"Be careful out there." Nadya rested her head against his chest. "Bring our family home. Make sure Jon makes it home to his children. They need him." She trembled. "You come back, alive. Do not let me see them carrying your body on a wagon."

Sebastian held her tight. "I promise."

Sebastian found Dani in the hall at breakfast with his family and his legion, having their last feast before marching into Torrdale. Sebastian ate in silence, listening to the chatter around the room and seeing the children kissing their fathers goodbye. He watched Tomas place his hand on Amara's stomach. He glanced at Dani, then turned back to Tomas. Their eyes met. Sebastian envied Tomas for his grace and beauty and thought about what it would be like to have a child of his own. He shook his head and finished his meal and told Dani he was going to finish preparing to leave.

In the courtyard, he mounted his horse, Ossian, and reached for Dani's hand. As his people lined up, Sebastian couldn't help but watch Cyrus. He was still in love, and the look on Cyrus's face when he witnessed Sebastian marrying Dani replayed in his mind often. He felt arms wrap around his waist and a head resting on his shoulder. Sebastian smiled, and Cyrus turned away and fidgeted with his pack before turning his attention to Dom. Dom nodded at Sebastian and banged his fist on his chest twice. Sebastian returned the gesture, then kicked his horse and led his army on the path west.

As they arrived in Shadowmire, the shopkeepers, brothel girls, and innkeepers lined the road throwing roses in the path while bowing to their king. The pass weaved through The Break and offered little cover from the wind blowing in from The Far North. Sebastian caught Cyrus staring at Dani with his eyes narrowed. Dani tightened his arms and whispered in Sebastian's ear, "I love you."

Sebastian felt his body flutter. He held his hand and allowed his horse to guide them down the pass, into the hills, and to the end of Stormfire Lake. They let the horses eat and drink, and the army rest. Sebastian stood on the beach and looked at the sky.

"This is where I found Dani."

Sebastian jumped and turned. "For fucks sake, Cyrus. You know I hate when people sneak up on me."

"Sorry." Cyrus stood next to him and looked out across the lake. "He said he was drawn to the lake because he remembered your stories. Dani walked from Torrdale, in the winter storm, barefoot, with no food to get to you. He really does mean a lot to you, doesn't he?"

"He means everything. Cyrus, I—"

"You don't have to explain anything to me, Sebastian. It's alright. I'm letting you go, even if it kills me inside. I will always love you, but I do not belong in your world. It was never meant to be, and we both knew it from the beginning. We were blinded by lust, and I am so happy that you were my first love."

"Cyrus, I think you should give Jace a chance." Sebastian over his shoulder. "He has always cared about you."

"No, Sebastian. I don't want anyone. I always said it was you or no one and I keep my word."

Sebastian started to object, but Cyrus silenced his lips with his own. When he pulled away, he saw Dani sneaking over, hiding by a tree. "Dani."

"It's my fault," Cyrus said.

"Don't apologize." Dani joined Sebastian at his side and took his hand. "I understand the feelings you both have for each other. It's alright to love someone else if you don't use that love to hurt me."

"Dani, there is no one I will ever love more than you." Sebastian kissed Dani's cheek. "If I so much as make you frown, I have failed us, and we all know how much I hate failure."

"As I was saying," Cyrus said. "I am fine with this. And I think our time is over. It's time for me to find my place in this world." He hesitated, shook his head, and hurried away.

The soldiers cooked meat and let the fires burn out as they settled for sleep. Sebastian stood at the lake shore again when the morning sun poked up over the horizon. "This is where it began." He saw Jace come stand by his side. "Ten years ago, I stood at this spot after fighting with my father, and my life changed forever. No more hiding. Thank you, Jace, for everything. I truly treasure you over everyone here. I want you to know that."

"Everyone?"

Sebastian smiled wide, then laughed. The others began to wake and prepare to depart. He watched everyone close but realized he didn't see one person. "Where is Cyrus?"

"Haven't seen him," Jace said.

They walked over to where the others were packing tents. "Has anyone seen Cyrus," Sebastian asked.

"I believe he left." Tomas joined his side.

"Coward," Jon said.

"No. He is hurt." Sebastian stared at the ground for a moment. "It's better off this way. He was a distraction." He noticed Dani look at him quickly.

"We should go. We need to get to that village before sunset." Dani walked toward Ossian and waited.

They rode south to the gateway into the realm of Torrdale. Sebastian's army hastily passed the prairie lands where they were exposed entirely if Maxen had posted scouts. As the afternoon grew late, the grasslands turned into high hills. Over the tops of the highest summit lie a town alive with commerce. Lights from candles and firepits danced in the frigid wind, and shapes of people could be made out from a distance. Sebastian led his people down toward a river where the town was built. He instructed his soldiers to make a tent camp while he took his brothers, Jace, Jon, and Dani, into the village.

Barron walked on his side. "Thank you for doing this."

"I'm not doing it for you." Sebastian paused. "Nadya asked, and you and I both know when Nadya asks, she gets her way."

Barron laughed. "Either way. My wife and my son are in danger, and you set aside days of travel for them when you didn't have to." He watched the ground as he walked.

"You really feel ashamed of what you did, don't you?" Sebastian paid attention to Barron's body language.

"Can we not talk about this? I just want to hold my little boy again."

Sebastian nodded, letting a slight grin appear on his lips. "Let's split up. Jace and Dani with me."

Everyone branched out to different shops and inns in search of Sara. Sebastian went into a loud and bustling tavern with music and dancing. The energy and excitement lit a fire inside him as he had never felt. Women hurried over and offered ale and wine. Dani clung to Sebastian's arm until a young woman danced around to Sebastian and grabbed his arm, pulling him into the circle.

"Hello, I am Lydi. Who are you?"

Sebastian danced with Lydi but cocked his head. "You don't know who I am?"

"Should I?"

Sebastian smiled and continued to dance until they made their way back around. He passed her into Jace's arms before returning to Dani. "I think he likes her."

"But I thought Jace liked boys," Dani said.

"Well, his hand is on her ass, so I think he likes both." Sebastian raised his glass at Jace as they passed by again. He walked to the bar with Dani and asked the man behind the counter for another drink.

"Hey, I was here first." A voice came from a man standing next to Dani. He was rather large and sweat soaked through his shirt even in the cold air inside the tavern.

"I apologize. Allow me to buy you a drink, sir," Sebastian said.

"And who the hell are you, and why are you in our town?"

"Does no one here know who I am?" Sebastian smiled. "I like this place."

"We don't like strangers," the man said. "I can crush you."

"No, you won't be crushing him tonight or anytime soon." A voice came from the room behind the bar. "Don't mind him, Terrak." A woman appeared behind the bar with long red hair and green eyes. "He is the King of NorthBrekka."

The music was silent, and everyone stared. Jace kissed the girl he danced with, then slipped over to Sebastian quickly.

She stared at him for a long moment. "King Sebastian Drake. Welcome to Avant."

"Sara," Sebastian hopped over the bar and held Sara's cheek. "Do you realize you are in grave danger here?"

"King Maxen. Yes, I have been made aware." She pushed his hand away.

"Where is your son? The two of you must make your way to NorthBrekka for safety."

Sara slammed her hand on the bar. "Where is Barron?"

"He is here as well."

Sara looked around quickly. "I thought you would have killed him by now. Where is my husband?"

The doors to the tavern flew open, and a child's giggling filled the room. Sebastian turned to see Barron carrying a little boy in his arms.

"Barron!" Sara ran over and hugged him.

Sebastian spoke. "I have a legion of three armies ready to march on Maxen, and I do not wish to put any of you in harm's way. All of the people of Avant are welcome to take refuge in NorthBrekka until the war is over."

"How long will that take... Your Highness?" Terrak's voice was deep and loud.

"As long as it takes." Sebastian slammed his hand on the bar. "So, you can join me and fight for Erras and die in honor, or you can aid in escorting the lovely women, children, and elders to NorthBrekka. What say you, Terrak?"

Terrak narrowed his eyes. "Do you promise I will be honored if I fight for you and die?"

"I will bless you to Valhalla myself." Sebastian reached his hand out for Terrak to shake.

Terrak let out a toothy smile and laughed as he gripped Sebastian's arm.

"He has changed," Sara said to Barron.

"For the better." Barron sighed. "Trust him. Go home. Nadya awaits you and Corbyn with open arms. It will be good for my son to meet his cousins."

"Do you promise that we are safe there, Sebastian?" Sara said.

"I will not allow war to fall in NorthBrekka. I promise. No matter what I have to do, I will make sure my people will be safe for the rest of our days." Sebastian reached out to hug Sara. "I am sorry about the past. I should have been better to you."

The night commenced with food, dance, and celebration. Sebastian saw Sara and Barron kiss as Corbyn hid his eyes.

"So, she is your sister," Dani said. "But she is married to Barron, who is your brother." Dani shivered. "That's interesting."

"Sara is not a Drake by blood, but still odd, yes." Sebastian shook his head. "Let's get back to camp and rest. Where is Jace?"

"He snuck away with that girl." Dani giggled.

"Good. Let's leave the lovers to their evening escapades. Dance with me."

"What? Dance?" Dani's eyes grew large, and he curled back in his seat.

"It's alright. I have no idea what they are doing. Just run around in sequence and drink wine." Sebastian reached his hand out.

Dani smiled and jumped into the middle of the room where Torrdale men and women drunkenly strutted across the floor together. He spun around and laughed. Sebastian gently put his hand on Dani's waist and pulled him close. "I promise I won't let anything happen to you. I will protect you with my life."

"For once, let me protect you."

Sebastian stared long and hard at Dani, holding his face in his palm and kissing his lips. "I don't want you to have to use your powers. I know it hurts."

"I will do what I need to ensure we win and our people go home to their loved ones," Dani said.

"You said, our people. You are finally accepting who you are."

"I have always known, but my life has humbled me. I am Dani, the broken prince. I am a Blackbird and married to the most powerful man in the world. You and I together are unstoppable."

"Dani. I want to be alone with you. Right now." Sebastian wrapped his arms around Dani and picked him up. "I need you."

"I am yours. Always."

The night grew quiet. Sebastian made love to Dani more times than he had the strength for. His breaths became difficult as he moaned loud enough for anyone sleeping in the same Inn could hear.

The following day, Sebastian and Dani headed to the camp to join the men and women who awaited the last ride to Bolin Palace. He looked at the faces of Meecah and Samir, loyally standing by for their king's order while holding each other tight. Kristoff and Viktor exchanged weapons, Jace snuck to the camp from his night with the girl from the tavern, and

Sara and Corbyn kissed Barron as the company headed to NorthBrekka prepared to depart before the sun came.

Wagons made their way east with many of Avant's citizens. Sebastian sent men to protect them on their journey to the wall and sent crows with messages to Shadowmire and Nadya. As the tents were packed and fires stamped out, the legion moved north to Bolin Palace.

CHAPTER 37
Brothers Until the End

The green rolling hills gave way to flat prairies and abundant streams, with a hint of sea air whipping across the plains. Sebastian took a deep breath and smiled, thinking of Adurak. They stopped briefly to rest. He sat atop an old stone wall that separated the inner villages outside the castle from the rest of Torrdale. There was a faint glow from large fires along the beach.

"What's on your mind, Your Majesty?"

"Jon." Sebastian jumped, then gestured for Jon to sit. "I apologize if I have been distant. I am often overwhelmed and forget to make time for my family."

"That's fine, Your Grace. Nadya told me I had to sneak up on you to get your attention. I find it funny that a man of your stature is easily frightened."

Sebastian laughed. "I get lost in my own head, and my past haunts my dreams. The world is fucking scary, Jon. I won't sit here and say I am not afraid of anything. The truth is, I am terrified of what is about to happen."

"Are you ready?"

"To fight, yes. Everything else, no. If I don't make it—"
Jon squeezed Sebastian's shoulder. "Don't."

"If I don't make it, don't bury me in that castle."
Sebastian shook his head. "My home is a prison for me. It always has been and always will be. I love my home and family, and it breaks my heart to think so poorly of it, but everything bad that happened to me happened there. Tomas and I have to leave for peace to live."

"We can't lose you. My king, you are so important to us."

"In case I don't make it." He paused and held his hand up after noticing the shocked expression on Jon's face. "If I die, strap me to the deck of the Hetta, sail her out into the depths of the Midnight Sea, and blast her all to hell. I want to be close to home, but not in that castle. My legend must end there."

"Your legend will never die. Our world revolves around you."

"Well, it shouldn't. I will rule from Adurak. I want you, Jon, to take the role of lord of NorthBrekka. You and my sister will have reign. Your children will learn and grow in safety, and our family can continue to thrive, and if there is ever a need for my help, I will sail home as fast as I can conjure the wind."

Jon's jaw dropped. "I don't know what to say. It is my honor to keep watch over the north." Jon sat back and stared across the lands. "The prophecy said the Dragon would destroy and murder, but you just want to be left alone."

"Dragon's blood and power course through my veins, but I am not Dragon. I am Chaos, and I choose my fate." Sebastian stood and turned, seeing a crowd had been listening behind them, including his brothers, Jace and Dani. "Ever since I discovered my powers, I wanted to run away and hide. That is why I always disappeared into the caves. No one was coming in to find me." Sebastian closed his eyes and smiled. "It was so quiet."

"We get it," Viktor said. "You don't like people."

"Some of you are exceptions." Sebastian winked. "We all better sleep. Tomorrow, we move north to the castle."

Sebastian led Dani to his tent and made love to him. They held each other, Dani resting on Sebastian's chest. He was completely content. "I want this forever."

"You will. I will be with you, no matter what happens."

"Dani, my darling… if I die out there, promise me you will do what is right and rule in Adurak. Lead our people."

"I'm not losing you!" Dani sat up, and his face turned red. "Don't ever say that again." He started shaking.

"Dani, are you alright? My love." He held Dani in his arms and kissed his cheek. "I'm sorry."

"I will not let you die. I don't care what I have to do." Dani pulled away, and his face became hollow. His eyes narrowed, and he started shaking. "You will be mine for eternity."

"I'm sorry. I didn't mean anything by it—"

"You are mine." Dani's face turned white. He rested his hands on Sebastian's chest and got close to his face. "Forever."

"Dani…" Sebastian coughed until blood splattered on his hand. "Dani!" He fell over and struggled to catch his breath.

"Sebastian!" Dani stumbled backward and curled up against the wall. "Valirus!" He shouted so loud that his voice cracked. "Help, please."

Everything was blurry, his head hurt badly, and his muscles were tight. His chest burned, and he felt a fiery pain in his gut. Valirus burst into the tent and put his hands on Sebastian's head. He chanted a language Sebastian did not understand. A faint glow passed over his body, and Valirus stepped away. Sebastian wheezed, and he felt his eyes roll back in his head. His body felt frozen, and he fought for every breath.

"Move." Dani shoved Valirus out of his way and rested his palms against Sebastian's chest. A bright, white flash crossed Dani's eyes just before he closed them.

Sebastian's breathing cleared, his head stopped spinning, and he could see again. He grabbed Dani's chin and stared into his eyes. "I said I would never hurt you, and I failed."

"I lost control of my powers." Dani sat back. "The thought of you lying there, dead…"

"The two of you better get aligned, or else you will end up killing each other," Valirus said. He stood up and paced quickly, rambling, his face red and hints of light coming from his staff.

They went to sleep, and a restless night turned to dawn. Sebastian sat up and rubbed his face as Dani snored quietly next to him. He gently ran his fingers through Dani's hair and kissed his forehead before slipping out of bed and dressing. He saw a few men and women moving about. The sun had yet to break the horizon, but the hint glow of orange came from the east. The smell of meat searing over an open fire made his stomach rumble. Sebastian found Tomas's tent, where Kristoff and Viktor also slept.

He gently crawled into Tomas's bed and pulled the blanket over their heads. Tomas was still asleep. Sebastian curled his head into Tomas's chest and waited for him to wake.

"Seb?" Tomas felt around. "What are you doing?"

"We need to talk." Sebastian met Tomas eye to eye.

"Is this about you returning to Midrel Istan?"

"How did you…nevermind. I demand that you and Amara come back with me. I won't ask. Your child will live the best life you can imagine. You will love it there."

"Amara won't leave her family."

"This is dire," Sebastian said. "We cannot stay in NorthBrekka. Please, Tomas, come home to Adurak. It is where we belong. Amara will love it, and her family is invited."

"Seb, this is a huge change for us. Amara is pregnant. We have to think about our future as a family." Tomas kissed him on the nose. "I will be wherever you are, but please consider staying in NorthBrekka. It is your home." The blanket was pulled away.

"We can hear you," Viktor said. "Sebastian, wherever you go, we go."

"Some of you have to stay for Nadya." Sebastian grabbed Viktor's hand.

"She has her children, Jon, the Sinook. Dom will be there." Viktor turned to Kristoff.

"We are coming with you, brother. Until the end." Viktor sat on the bed.

"I am so proud of you both," Sebastian said as tears formed in his eyes. "I am forever grateful. Let's go to war, shall we?"

The men grunted loudly and prepared to march. Sebastian popped out of the tent and found Dani brushing Ossian's mane. He stomped on the ground and sent a fireball exploding into a broken wood pile. "Ladies. Gentlemen. My dear friends and family. You follow me blind into battle, unaware of why we are fighting. Maxen is a plague upon our lands. If we don't stop him here, he will march on NorthBrekka, and from there, the world. The north belongs to us. We have carved the history of this nation, and we will not let an outsider assert his power over our people. Fight with me and feel victory when their blood is spilled at our feet."

"It was such a moving speech," Jace said. "Until that last line. You just can't stop thinking about blood."

"Soon, he will be covered in it," Meecah said. "Always covered in blood."

Everyone laughed. Sebastian threw his head back, shaking it and rubbing his face. "Fine, no more speeches. Look out for one another. I want you to return to your kin when we ride home…" He threw his fist in the air. "Gentlemen and ladies… we ride."

The next afternoon brought them to a large clearing in the middle of a meadow. The high grass and forests to the east and west made for privacy as Sebastian planned their strategy. Two nights had passed until he decided he was ready to see for himself what lay ahead.

The following morning came and went. Sebastian snuck away while Dani and Jace were taking a nap. He checked over his shoulder to ensure he wasn't followed when he slipped into the cover of the tree line. Sebastian chuckled and started to run until someone appeared from behind a tree.

"Where are you going?"

Sebastian grabbed his chest. "Tomas! You scared the hell out of me."

"Answer the question," Tomas said.

"I need to see for myself."

"You could be caught. Turn around and go back to camp, now." Tomas pointed behind Sebastian and lightly pushed him backward.

Sebastian sighed and rolled his eyes. "No, Tomas. I have to know what is happening. It is my duty to protect you all. Stand aside, brother."

Tomas stood still and didn't speak. He shook his head.

"I can make your move. I am being fair because I don't want to hurt you, so please stand aside and let me do my job."

"Sebastian!" A scream came from the camp.

He swung around and ran into the clearing.

"Your Majesty!" Another voice shouted.

Tomas grabbed his shoulder. "Back to camp?"

"Back to camp. Come on!"

They ran as fast as they could. Sebastian felt his stomach and chest ignite with burning fury. His throat felt like he had swallowed fire. He looked at Tomas, who wore the expression he felt was on his own face. Tomas's eyes were shimmering blue, and I could see ice forming on his fingertips. "Be ready, brother."

As they topped a small hill and saw the camp, several Altanian soldiers stood in the open field before Sebastian's army. He and Tomas walked with caution, heading to stand before their people. Maxen's soldiers wore a stone, icy glare and stood still without a hint of movement. Sebastian drew his sword and pointed at the throat of a man.

"I know you can hear me. Show yourself."

The Altanians shuffled around, moving aside to reveal a covered wagon. He reached for the fabric and pulled back the cover. His eyes shot wide open, and Tomas shoved him aside to leap onto the wagon.

"Amara!" Tomas started to cut her binds and pulled the gag from her mouth.

Jon came running. "Nadya? My lady." He pulled Nadya into his arms. "Where are the children?"

"I don't know," Nadya gasped. "Men came to the castle the night after you had left. They raided the castle. I didn't even get to see my babies when they came for me."

Sebastian felt the intensity in his loins grow uncontrollably. He shouted, swung his sword, and cut the head off of a soldier. "Maxen!" He yelled. "I'm coming for you." He pointed to Amara and Nadya. "Get them to safety. We march to the palace and don't stop until Maxen's head is in my hands." Without looking anyone in the eyes, he shoved his way through his people and jumped onto his saddle. "Kill those men. No mercy." He reached for Dani's hand.

Jon unsheathed his sword and walked up to a soldier to whom Nadya pointed. "My wife said you hit her." He shoved the pointed end of his sword under the man's chin and through the top of his skull. Jon turned to Sebastian and gave a slight bow. "No mercy, Your Majesty."

Sebastian nodded and started to ride. "Follow me," he said to his people. Amara and Nadya rode in supply wagons at the back of the line.

Tomas hurried to ride alongside Sebastian. "My wife is pregnant, Sebastian. Send some men to take them home."

"Home is not safe. Nowhere is safe."

"What about Sara and my son?" Barron said. "They are with your soldiers."

"She is with my people from Midrel Istan. They won't take any shit from Maxen's men. Not anymore." Sebastian stared ahead. He tapped Ossian's ribs, sending the large, black steed into a full gallop across the grasslands.

They came upon a fast-flowing river. Sebastian looked over to Tomas. He reached his hand out. "The horses can't swim through those rapids."

Tomas took Sebastian's hand. They both reached their free hand forward, breathing deep and heavy with the fire from their bellies. The river began to thrash and divide. The army slowed as the twins' hands came together. One blue and the other red. Both faces fixed on the river until they pulled their arm in, pounded their chests once, and threw their fists back out. The river became still and frozen as the army passed over.

As the days had come and gone, Sebastian rode along the ridge next to the sea where the grounds changed from grasslands to open, flat lands with large boulders sticking up from the ground. As they rounded a bend, Sebastian's heart fluttered upon the sight. Dani tightened the grip around his waist. The majestic Bolin Palace sat gracefully aside from the ocean, but that was not what took Sebastian's breath.

He held his hand up to signal for his army to slow. There were rows among rows of men standing completely still in perfect lines with shields on their arms, bows in hand, or hands on their hilts. Sebastian halted his people and watched. "Why would a king hide behind his men?" He shouted. "Show yourself, Your Highness."

There was a light rustle from the back of the front line. Three Altanians pushed through with a heavily armored king in their wake. He stepped before his men. Sebastian couldn't make out his face as they were still too far. He waved for his army to slowly move forward. The horses walked, men marched, and Dani's hand was clasped on Sebastian's shoulder as his eyes were locked on his father.

"Dani, Jace, Meecah, Dom, and Tomas with me." Sebastian climbed down from his horse. "Everyone else, keep a wary eye but wait here." When he turned and started toward Maxen, he saw the long blue hair of a mad empress standing alongside her father. She blew Sebastian a kiss. He laughed and winked at Petra.

"That is disgusting," Dani said. "You and my sister flirting. I think I might throw up."

"Your sister becomes weak when I flirt with her," Sebastian said. "Then she makes bad choices. She is desperate for love, Dani."

"Yes, and she wants you!"

"My darling, she will never have me, but I think she could be useful if I can convince her to change sides."

"How are you going to do that?" Dani rolled his eyes and shook his head.

"Jace," Sebastian said. "I want Jace to seduce her and entrap her. Then she won't be disappearing with our people."

"Wait!" Jace grabbed Sebastian's arm, and everyone stopped. "You can't be serious. You want her on our side?"

"Stop whining, Jace. Someone with her power is handy." Sebastian started walking again.

They stood only a few yards apart from Maxen and the Altanian army. Sebastian halted, and the others spanned the line next to him, weapons in hand. He took two steps forward, and Maxen followed. "Your Highness, good afternoon." Sebastian refused to break eye contact.

"You're late. I expected you days ago."

"Sorry to disappoint you," Sebastian said. "We can do this easily, save everyone a lot of pain and loss, and you and I fight to the death. Whoever lives is the King of Kings. End of story."

Maxen started laughing. Sebastian raised his eyebrows, turned to Dani, and looked back and forth down the line.

"I don't think he liked that idea," Jace said.

Sebastian saw Jace nod at Petra. She blushed and rested her arm on Maxen's shoulder. Sebastian felt his chest burn and a flare built up in his throat. He stepped up to Maxen's face. "Did I say something funny?" His skin tingled as his hands began to glow. "I thought it was a fair offer." Sebastian's voice was hoarse. He smiled and moved back to his line.

Maxen whispered in Petra's ear, and she laughed, danced over, and kissed Sebastian's cheek. "You're going to like this." She spun away and disappeared.

Maxen glared at Dani. "How did my weak, pathetic, poor excuse for a son make it across Erras with no food and no warmth from the winter?"

"My choices were to stay alive and live with you or face death and try to find my way to NorthBrekka," Dani sneered. "If it wasn't for Cyrus—"

"Ahh, yes, Cyrus. My dear nephew." Maxen trailed off as a rustle came through the crowd.

Sebastian's mouth dropped open. He was met with the image of a brown, wavy haired boy he first saw when he was fifteen and afraid. His eyes watered, and his throat tightened as the man he loved undoubtedly stood alongside his sworn enemy.

"Cyrus," Sebastian gasped. "Why?"

Valirus rushed forward and pushed Sebastian aside. "My son, please don't do this."

"You don't even know me, Father!" Cyrus's face turned red. "You left me just like everyone else. Like you, Sebastian."

"I never left you. I did everything—" Sebastian started to shout but stopped and turned away.

"I told you," Cyrus said. "I was through with you. I never said I would stay. If these days are to be my last, I will be surrounded by my kin. The last of my name." Cyrus glared at Sebastian, then Valirus.

A thunderous boom echoed as the horses and soldiers of NorthBrekka, and Midrel Istan came to life in unison. Horses stamping, ready to gallop, while men and women on foot stomped and pounded their chests.

Petra reappeared. "Traitors! All of you." She noticed Seville, Treggar, and others of Runeheim.

"Fall back," Sebastian said to his front line. They turned and hurried across the meadow. Sebastian turned to Cyrus again. He felt a pain sting him in the gut, but he shook his head and backed toward Ossian. The Altanian soldiers stayed in place, moving only to don their weapons. Sebastian ran to his horse, pulled Dani onto his saddle, and rode fast after the enemy. Petra grabbed Maxen and Cyrus's arms, and they disappeared. The legion bolted full speed across the meadow, plowing into Maxen's cursed army.

Sebastian rode hard and fast, swinging his blade at every head he thrashed past. He felt a hand slip the dagger from his hip holster and saw Dani thrust it into the Altanian men's necks. The field was quickly filled with bodies. Sebastian checked for his brothers, halted suddenly, and hopped from his saddle. "Dani, get to the castle. Kristoff and Jace protect him."

"Sebastian!" Dani said, but Ossian kept his stride, and his knights sped past, each shouting for him and reaching for his hand.

"Your Majesty!" Jon leaped from his horse and stepped before Sebastian. "You are going to get yourself killed."

"Jon" Sebastian grabbed him by the collar. "Tomas is missing."

They looked back and forth. A man gripped a pike in his fist and screamed while running straight toward Sebastian.

"You take the left side, and I will take the right." Sebastian held his sword ready.

The man approached. Sebastian and Jon swung their swords, slicing the pike into pieces. They struck again, both running their blades through the man's chest. Jon grabbed Sebastian's arm. "We will find your brother together."

They ran into battle. Altanian blood splashed from severed throats, and guts spilled. The ground was soaked in red, and men and women of all kinds lay lifeless across the meadow. They checked bodies for familiar faces while making their way to the back of the line where wagons waited, along with Nadya and Amara.

"My lady." Jon rushed over and kissed Nadya.

"I'm not kissing you," Sebastian said to Amara.

"Gods, I sure hope not." She made a gagging expression. "Why are you two back here?"

"Tomas is missing. Have either of you seen him?"

Nadya started to panic. Amara held her stomach and breathed heavily.

"I'm sure he is alright, Amara," Sebastian said. "I will find him, I swear." He held her hand.

She moved his hand to her belly. Sebastian felt his heart pound faster. He opened his mouth and closed it again. She put her hand on his cheek. "Find him, Sebastian. Go!"

He burst into a sprint, back into battle. Jon joined his side, slicing down every Altanian who crossed him. They worked their way to the front of the line again, finding his people becoming more victorious by the moment. The number of Altanians falling was massive compared to his own. Soon, he could pass through the battlefield without swinging his sword or axe. He topped a hill that overlooked Bolin Palace. The sun shone high above while a chilly wind passed over the land.

Sebastian continued forward but noticed a glint of steel bouncing off the sunlight in the distance. He glanced over to Jon, then turned toward the light. As figures of people came clear, Sebastian slowed to a fast walk. "That is Maxen and Petra. You can see that blue hair from leagues away. What are they doing on the cliffside?"

"Waiting for you, Your Majesty."

They dashed off again. Soldiers lined the field near the edge of the land where the sea meets Torrdale. Sebastian gripped his axe and readied himself to strike.

"Let him pass." Maxen's voice echoed.

Soldiers moved aside. He saw Cyrus standing with his arms crossed, leaning against a signpost, and picking the dirt from under his nails. Petra delicately clapped and smiled as Sebastian got close. "I'm so happy you are still alive."

Sebastian shook his head. "What is this about, Maxen?"

"I want you to surrender, King Sebastian. Surrender the crown to me." Maxen brushed his beard.

"Sure, no problem." Sebastian mocked. "Now, seriously. Why am I here and not protecting my husband?"

Maxen laughed. "Husband. Dani is a horrid little beast. I don't need to kill you because soon enough, he will do that for me."

"Enough of your games!" Sebastian balled his fists. The sky filled with clouds, and lightning cracked, sending a roar of thunder to roll across the prairie. His fist ignited in flames as his chest burned, and his throat became hoarse.

"Easy, Dragon—"

"I am not Dragon!" Sebastian clapped his hands together, sending a ripple effect of thunder, and lightning flashed from his hands. "My name is Chaos, God of Fire, King of NorthBrekka, King of Thieves, and rightful heir to the throne of the King of Kings. I have taken your countrymen and the people of Erras. They follow me into battle, praying to the gods that I return with your head detached from your stone-cold body."

"You are incredibly dramatic… A Bolin has sat on the throne for centuries." Maxen smiled wide. "Daughter, can you help our friend make his decision?"

Petra pinched Sebastian's cheek before disappearing. Sebastian dropped his mouth open to speak, but before a word came, Petra reappeared and left him speechless. His entire body heated up, and the fury of his Dragon blood felt as if it were replaced by lava. His limbs seared, his bones ached, and fire escaped his mouth when he let out a snarl.

"Tomas!" Sebastian dove forward, but Maxen snapped his staff against the ground, and a gust of wind threw him back.

"You two are identical, aren't you? Identical twins are rare, and twin dragons... are a miracle. The both of you are the reason the entire damned world is in pure and untamed madness. Offing your heads is best for all." Maxen gripped Tomas's hair.

Sebastian locked eyes with Tomas. He tilted his head a little, and Tomas's eyes turned blue while frost formed on his fingers.

"They are doing that twin thing where they can talk to each other without speaking," Petra said.

Maxen yanked Tomas's head back and held a dagger to his throat. "Surrender, Your Majesty. If you refuse, I will cut your precious brother's head clean off, leaving the world with you. A curse on these lands. As long as Tomas is alive, you are stable enough, but without him, you are an inferno, and with Dani on your arm, you will become Chaos, God of Death."

Sebastian shook his head. "Maxen, take me instead. Spare my brother. I beg of you." Sebastian dropped his sword and fell to his knees.

Maxen leaned forward. "Do you know why this war is necessary, Your Majesty? The Bolins have ruled over human lands for thousands of years. My ancestors exiled Baze from Midrel Istan, then Dragon from Erras, and ruled over all as King of Kings. That throne is my birthright." Maxen gripped the blade and poked it into Tomas's skin.

Sebastian took a deep breath. It felt like the world screeched to a halt around him. The storm boomed powerfully overhead. The ground shook so hard that he saw Cyrus fall in the corner of his eye. Jon grabbed Sebastian by the back of his collar and yanked him to his feet, and shoved his sword in his hands. Jon screamed but Sebastian could not hear the words. His hand ignited with fire as it reached for Tomas. Tomas's arm was encased with ice as he stretched to meet his twin. As soon as their fingers touched, there was a loud explosion across the sea. The land jerked violently, pop and crack sounds filled the air, and the sea rose.

Blood splattered on Sebastian's face. He could taste it in his mouth and smell it in his nose. His eyes locked on the sapphire gaze of his twin. The storm brought massive waves that threatened to swallow them whole. Sebastian rocked back and forth until he closed his eyes and shook his head. When he looked up, Maxen stood, holding Tomas in his fist. The iron blade of Maxen's broadsword poked from the heart of Hydros, the God of Water. Tomas's body froze into a thick coat of ice, instantly thawed, limp, and fell into Sebastian's arms.

Maxen stared, still holding the hilt of the sword. "One down." He stepped back and turned to Petra. "Get me out of here." He raised his arm and snapped.

Sebastian twitched and let out a vile roar. "No!" He shot his hand forward and grabbed Petra's arm. The cliffside jarred, causing half to break off and crumble into the sea. His body ignited in lightning that rolled from his chest, down his arm, and struck Petra. She let out a horrid shriek and fell, gasping for air with every breath.

Maxen snapped his fingers. Petra was crippled over on her knees, with her head resting on the ground. There was blood running from her mouth and nose. Sebastian felt an arm loop around his waist and pull him back, then saw Jace pick up Petra and take her away. Maxen snapped his fingers again.

Sebastian laughed with a maniacal tone. "It's over, Maxen. Surrender to me." His voice was harsh and deep and he felt his head felt as if it was about to burst open.

"Arrrrrg!" Maxen snarled, gripped his staff, and struck Sebastian in the face. There was a bright flash of white light that filled the sky. Sebastian reached for Maxen's throat just as he tapped his staff on the ground twice. Lightning and magic exploded against one another. Sebastian felt his body jolt backward, slamming into Jon.

The ground quaked and cracked apart. Sebastian and Maxen were divided by a narrow gap that split the earth. Sebastian climbed to his feet and ran toward the other side as Maxen fled toward the castle. He felt a hand clasp his collar and pull him to the ground.

"Your Majesty, stop!" Jon said. "We can't lose you."

The cracked cliffside deteriorated. Sebastian realized if he had jumped, he would have fallen straight into the rocky water below. He crawled over to Tomas and held him in his arms.

CHAPTER 38
Dragon or Chaos

"Your Majesty, we have to go." Jon's voice echoed through Sebastian's head.

"Sebastian, I didn't know, I swear." Cyrus's voice trembled.

"You need to run away, Prince Cyrus," Jon snarled.

Sebastian glared at the sea. His fists were tightly grasped onto Tomas's coat, holding his twin tight. The blood coated his face and torso. He refused to look at Tomas. He couldn't bear seeing his lifeless face. Jon's arms wrapped around him, yet he still sat in his daze while brushing his fingers through Tomas's hair.

"Sebastian!" A voice carried from a distance.

He could hear horses coming fast.

"My love…" Dani choked. "Oh no." He fell to his knees next to Sebastian.

Jace knelt by his side, and the others took a knee.

It was silent for some time. Sebastian started to cry, unable to control his shaking as Dani tried to comfort him.

Valirus reached over to take Tomas. "Your Majesty, you must let him go now. You are still at war."

"Do not lecture me on war!" Sebastian's voice was so harsh that the skies ignited once more. "He is gone, Valirus. Maxen was right. Without Tomas, I am bound to my prophecy. The Dragon's Curse has taken hold of me. I want to destroy everything. I want everyone to die!"

Valirus yanked Dani away and wrapped his cape around Sebastian, shrouding him in darkness as Tomas was taken away. Valirus held him in the dark. "It is only you and me. Do you feel safe?"

"Yes."

"Good." Valirus took a deep breath. "You are the damned King of Kings, and you must overcome your pain and end Maxen before he moves violently on your lands. There will be time to grieve, but it is not this day. Honor Tomas by doing what is right by your people. On your feet, Your Majesty." Valirus yanked his cape away and stepped back.

Sebastian stood, still glaring at the sea, and turned to Dani. He pulled him in for a hug. "If I lose control, promise me that you will take my life."

Dani gasped, "My love, I can't."

"You must." Sebastian marched forward. He saw Tomas being led away in a wagon, knowing Amara would receive him soon. His heart broke in two. "Amara is pregnant with Tomas's child. Valirus, I want you to take a legion of men to protect Amara and my sister at all costs. No one else goes near them, or I will have your heads. Understand?"

Sebastian's attitude went from pain and crying to solemn and empty. He glared at Bolin palace and without another word, he moved ahead with his army of knights following. Dani held onto him the whole way as Ossian trotted along the grasslands. Sebastian felt odd. He felt like he should be hurting, sick, tired, and furious, but he felt nothing. Even Dani's voice seemed distant.

The saunter to the castle left enough time for Sebastian to consider his plan. Soldiers armed with iron and steel lunged toward Sebastian's people, yet his gaze stayed locked on the palace. The storm brewed and spun above, and waves grew larger while cyclones formed in the thrashing sea. Winds gust across the plains so powerfully that they blew soldiers to the ground. The rain turned icy and sharp, stinging their skin as they passed.

Explosions of green light brightened the sky across the grounds. The sounds of soldiers screaming put a smile on Sebastian's face. He hopped down from Ossian's back, helped Dani, and noticed the palace doors were left unguarded. He looked at his knights, then proceeded inside.

Bolin palace used to be bright, colorful, and lively. Sebastian remembered the sun beaming through the massive windows, bringing light to the front of the castle. But on this day, the beautiful palace by the sea was dark, still, and sad. There was no more love. Cyrus's usual uplifted strength and courage that brought a sense of cheer to these halls were gone, taken by Lorna and Maxen.

War spread across Torrdale. The sounds of violence and mayhem filled the lands, yet Sebastian continued his journey across the palace where King Maxen waited, with a crown on his head, seated on the throne of the King of Kings.

Sebastian stepped back. "That throne was in NorthBrekka. How is it here?"

"How are your beautiful sister and the pregnant peasant girl?" Maxen clasped his hands together. "My soldiers gave them to you as a gift and a warning. You left your castle unguarded. A good king never leaves a throne this great behind." Maxen rubbed his hand on the arm of the chair.

"No. A good king fights for his people and doesn't hide behind others." Sebastian scowled. "You took Tomas from me. I want you to know that I will not stop until I destroy every last piece of you. Every piece."

"Even Dani?" Maxen laughed. "He is still my son, my blood. Every piece includes my own child."

"Get off your ass and fight me," Sebastian said. "There is a slaughter happening outside. Yours and mine all dying for us. Why? I am standing right in front of you. We can end this."

Maxen climbed to his feet. His peppered gray beard was neatly combed, and his hair was still in place. It was clear he had not fought one person in this battle. Meanwhile, Sebastian was covered in the blood of so many Altanians that he could barely decipher it from Tomas's. He sheathed his sword, set it on the ground, unlatched his axe, and placed his bow and quiver on the floor. Maxen watched him with narrowed eyes and a hand stroking the hilt of his blade. "You're not very bright, are you?"

"I don't need iron to defeat you. I am a weapon." Sebastian took a few steps back to Dani. "Get everyone out of here."

"I won't leave—"

"You will do as I say, my darling." He turned and watched Cyrus enter the room.

Maxen stood over him. "Turning your back to the enemy. I don't know if that is brave or stupid."

The ground jerked like an earthquake shot through the castle. Sebastian's nostrils flared. "The connection was broken when you killed Tomas. I don't know what will happen, but the land is breaking beneath our feet. I can't stop it." Lightning flashed in his hands. "Fight me."

Maxen tossed his sword aside, grasped his staff, and sapped his fingers. He pounded the stick on the floor twice, with a bright light and a gust of wind. "I can do more than tamper with minds. Are you prepared to find out?"

The storm amplified as it flew in from the sea. Blinding rain slammed against the tall windows, and the wind howled through the fireplaces. The sky looked like daytime with the never-ending lightning. Sebastian swung his arms in a circle and pushed his palms forward, causing a strong gust of wind to throw Maxen to the floor. He grabbed his sword and took it to Dani. Sebastian glanced at Cyrus, his forehead wrinkled and eyes watered. "Please don't kill each other." He mumbled before returning to Maxen.

As Sebastian walked across the throne room, he spread his arms wide, and fireballs formed in his hands. He threw one hand forward, sending the fire to crash into Maxen, setting his coat on fire. The second one followed, but Maxen dodged it, and it set a Torrdale man ablaze. A loud click and a bright, white flash blinded Sebastian. He felt his head hurt terribly as blood poured down his face and he stood with difficulty. The room was spinning, but he could see Maxen's smiling face too close to his own before feeling another painful blow to the chest.

He tilted his head as he lay on his back, seeing Meecah taking out two soldiers with her small sword. Samir and Jon were in a fistfight, standing back-to-back with several men surrounding them. Kristoff and Viktor were in the most brilliant sword fight with a group of Torrdale men, and then there were Dani and Cyrus. Both were exhausted but continued swinging at each other. Dani was screaming, but Sebastian couldn't understand.

"My love, get up!" The sound echoed around the room and in Sebastian's ears. "Sebastian, get up!"

He kicked back and flipped onto his feet. Maxen chanted a spell, and Sebastian's fist collided with his mouth. A blast rippled dangerously around the castle. The windows shattered. Glass fell like melting ice from the bluffs of mountains, showering the room and sending men and women running away as the storm rushed inside. The rain pinned Sebastian's face like needles, stinging his eyes. He looked to the sea, seeing ships far out across the horizon as the lightning crashed around them.

"The Safar," he gasped. "Everyone, run for The Break. Dani, Cyrus, please. Retreat to NorthBrekka. Go!" Dani and Cyrus stopped fighting. Both doubled over panting.

"It's about time." A strong womanly voice trailed across the room. "I was worried about this hurricane you summoned slowing down my father's army." Lorna stroked Sebastian's cheek as she passed him and stood where the windows once lined the room. "You are still so handsome... I see Cyrus abandoned you even after you broke the spell, curse breaker." She laughed. "I knew it all along. I knew you would heal Cyrus someday, and I assumed the two of you would marry. After all, Cyrus loved you so much he tried to kill himself." Lorna looked at Cyrus and laughed.

"Kill himself?" Sebastian turned to Cyrus.

"Yes, he was depressed when he found his way to Alta Prime. The nightmares were frightful, and he thrashed night after night in his bed. Sasha was so good at caring for him, but Cyrus only yearned for one man. That is why I erased you from his mind. He is a Bolin. It is his destiny to fight against you. Your love was a mistake."

Sebastian fell to his knees.

Dani ran over and fell into his arms. "Don't listen to them."

"Sebastian, I swear, I never meant to hurt you." Cyrus backed away with his hands held in the air as if he was surrendering. "I have always loved you. I only came back here to try to save my family's home. Nothing more."

Maxen pounded his staff on the floor. A burst of light flew at Cyrus, throwing him to the ground. "You are an embarrassment. You are just like your father, weak."

Sebastian put his forehead against Dani's. "Get Cyrus out of here. Go find Valirus." He climbed to his feet and walked over to Lorna and Maxen. Flames burst from his limbs. "Enough games. I will fight both of you." Lightning and fire mixed with ice shot from Sebastian as Lorna and Maxen worked together to counter his attack. He threw them both on their backs, picked up his dagger, and walked to Maxen. "You can't defeat me. Surrender." He threw his hand forward, sending a lightning bolt, but Maxen used a soldier as a shield.

"I will never let a Dragon rule the lands." Maxen grasped Sebastian's arm. "Just look at what you are doing to Torrdale. Your powers will spread across the lands like a sickness, destroying all in its path. Without your twin, you are the apocalypse. Dragon, Chaos, whatever you call yourself. It has been foretold. Without Hydros, Chaos will end the world. It has already begun, Your Majesty." Maxen shoved him away.

The war had come to the edge of the land. The Safarian ships approached. Sebastian turned to his people again. "Go, get out of here!" He kicked Maxen in the face, grabbed Lorna by her hair, and dragged her to broken windows onto the rocky and sandy land below. His people were still fighting fearlessly against the Altanian army. Explosions of green catalysts of Barron's Kuhar army lit the sky around the palace. He saw his brothers fighting together. Barron as well. He searched for Dani but fell short and returned his attention to the ships coming in with the hurricane.

Winds cut through his wounds, stinging blow after stinging blow. He threw Lorna into the mud and moved to better see his people fighting. Maxen appeared at her side. His staff glowed bright, appearing as a beacon for the oncoming army loyal to Queen Lorna. Sebastian feared for his people down the shoreline as they were backed toward the edge.

Echoing shrieks filled the air. Sebastian saw people falling over the cliff. When he saw the Altanian men ram forward, pushing an entire line of men and women over the edge, Sebastian gave up on his mission to fight Maxen and ran to save his people. The destruction of Torrdale, the storms, and the lands giving way was Sebastian's fault. He knew losing Tomas would send him into a dangerous fury, but now his friends' lives were in grave danger because he could not control himself.

A stinging feeling hit him in the back, and he fell. His face crashed into a rock. Sebastian saw a bright flash, and everything else went blurry. He reached his hands out, and lightning shot from his fingertips. The only image he could see was Maxen being struck and falling over the cliff while Lorna fell to her knees. Her screams filled his head before everything went dark.

CHAPTER 39
The Perfect Death

Icy raindrops fell, the ground crunched with every step, and tree branches became weak from the weight of the snow. Sebastian turned over to keep the sleet from stinging his eyes. "What the hell is this?"

"You're finally awake. Thank the Gods."

"Nadya? Where are we? Where are Maxen and the Safar…" Sebastian sat up too fast. His head spun as he felt the gash on his brow.

"Easy, brother." Nadya pulled him back to rest against her. "We are near Stormfire Lake. The scouts haven't returned with news of Maxen. The storm is slowing them down, I'm sure."

"Where is Dani?"

"Here." A voice came from next to them. Riding high on the back of Ossian was the petite black-haired man Sebastian loved. "I left you alone for five seconds. You almost died!" Dani's face was red. He had tears running down his cheek.

"Everyone, stop!" Sebastian climbed out of the wagon. He helped Dani down and held him in his arms. "I'm sorry, my darling." He walked across the row of wagons, pulling back blankets to see the faces of the dead. His anger boiled to his bones as he recognized the people of Erras and Midrel Istan lying lifeless, knowing there were more left behind. He pulled back a sheet that caused his knees to weaken and his voice to crack. "Tomas."

Tomas's skin had a tinge of blue. Sebastian's hand shook as he reached to stroke his twin's hair. He made a horrible noise, laid his head on Tomas's stomach, and cried. He punched a hole in the wagon bed and screamed angrily, causing the storm to explode into a blizzard.

"Sebastian, stop!" A hand grabbed his arm and threw him off Tomas.

"Amara."

"Do not speak to me! I will never forgive you for this. Never." Amara walked away quickly. Nadya chased after her and begged her to calm down for the sake of the baby.

As the day pushed into the early evening, they made it to the lake. The snow continued to fall hard, and the lake was nearly frozen. Sebastian snuck away and hid behind a fat tree that grew on the shoreline. He could hear Jon, Dom, and Dani's voices shouting his name, but he remained hidden. Amara's words filled his head, making him shake uncontrollably.

"Why are you hiding back there?" A familiar woman's voice cut through him like glass. "You know your husband is in a full panic right now. Poor tired little thing he is." The sound of her laughter made Sebastian jump.

"Where is your father?"

"How should I know?" Her voice changed to sweet and smooth.

Sebastian met her face to face. "Petra." He shoved her against a tree and gripped her throat.

"Sebastian, no, let her go," Jace shouted. "She is your prisoner, as you asked." He approached with his hands up. "Sebastian, you have to calm down. I know you are hurt and angry, and you look extremely violent right now. You are scaring everyone."

"Everyone should get as far away from me as they can." His head turned as Dani joined the circle. "You should go too."

"Say whatever you want, my love." Dani folded his arms. "No one will leave your side. You are still our king, and we love you."

Petra blushed when Jace grabbed her arm. She became calm, almost bashful, a side Sebastian had never seen. He looked around at the massive army. All standing at the ready for his command. The anger consumed his heart, but his eyes stopped when he met Amara.

Sebastian stepped toward her. "I know you are angry. I know how bad it hurts."

"He was not a fighter," Amara said. "Tomas was a kind and gentle man. He didn't deserve this. He wouldn't have gone to war if it weren't for you."

"Tomas may have been kind, but he would have fought for his family just as I would. I did not force him to fight." Sebastian reached for Amara. "There is nothing I can say to ease your pain—"

"For the rest of my life." She pushed him away. "I have to look at your face, and I will be reminded that I lost everything again and again." She leaned forward and spoke softly, "He was perfect, Sebastian. Tomas was everything I had ever wanted, and now he is gone forever."

Sebastian's eyes filled with tears. "You wish it were me lying over in that wagon." His lip trembled. He unsheathed his sword, turned it around, and thrust the hilt into Amara's hand. "It should have been me. Take my life. The honor is yours."

Dani ran between them. "Are you insane? Stop this."

Sebastian pushed him aside, grabbed the end of the blade, and anchored it over his heart. "Let this relieve you from your grief."

Amara's hands shook. Her face was bright red beneath the dirt. She wrinkled her nose and pushed. The sword pierced Sebastian's skin, and blood ran down his chest. He saw the faces of his kin, friends, and soldiers watching with widened eyes. Some called out to him, but he held his hand up and returned his gaze to Amara.

She screamed, gripped the sword tight, and threw it to the ground. Sebastian expected her to yell in his face or hit him, but instead, she fell into his arms and sobbed. She didn't let go until the scouts returned.

A young boy almost tripped from running too fast. "Your Majesty. The Safar has arrived in Torrdale. Maxen lives. The sea broke his fall. The armies are in motion." He bowed and backed away.

"And we will meet them in battle again." He walked to Petra, grabbed her arm, and dragged her away. "If you betray me, I will personally take pleasure in killing you."

Petra slumped and let out a sigh. "What good am I to my father if I can't use my powers?"

"What are you talking about?"

"When your lightning struck me, I lost most of my powers. The ones my father gave me." She held her hands up and slowly began to vanish. Her voice had changed, her smile wasn't as evil, and her usual sneer was gone. She reappeared. "My father didn't want Dani when he thought he didn't have powers. But with me, he hexed my vanishing powers, only, I was under his control at all times. He has had his mind powers locked on me since I was a child. Now he won't want me anymore."

"It took me hitting you with lightning to realize that? I was going to apologize—" Sebastian shook his head.

"What are you going to do with me?" Petra grabbed his arm. "Lock me away in the dungeon for the rest of my life?"

"I would never punish the other prisoners so terribly." He smirked. "Maybe you can earn your freedom. Help me defeat your father."

Petra smiled and nodded. "I will do my best."

Sebastian turned and shouted, "Valirus!"

"He isn't here," Petra said. "Valirus went back… for Cyrus."

Sebastian turned to Dani.

"We got separated in battle. I tried to find them both," Dani said.

"My father is going to kill Cyrus." Petra walked over to Jace. "And if Valirus tries to fight him, he too will die."

Late that evening, Sebastian sat alone by the lake's edge. He told Dani he wanted to be left to his thoughts, so he wandered down the beach until he found a place out of sight from the camp. His heart ached for Tomas. The guilt surged through his veins like lightning and his anger worsened by the moment. He was angry with the others for guiding him back to Stormfire Lake instead of fighting to take Torrdale. He was furious with himself for allowing his emotions to show weakness to his enemy. "Tomas, I am sorry. You deserved better." Sebastian stared at the sky. "I should have ended this a long time ago." He let his tears flow freely. "You were good and smart, and because of me, your child has to grow up without a father. It should have been me."

He laid back on the wet ground and closed his eyes, thinking about all the times he and Tomas would play through the castle. He remembered them running too fast and breaking vases and tripping maidens, chasing cattle across the farmlands, and getting lost in the forest only to be scolded by the elders in the village. Then he remembered how frail Tomas had become after being locked away by Barron while he was away in Icefall training and the visions of the palace crushing Tomas's leg swam through his thoughts.

He jumped to his feet and stormed back to camp. "We march. Now!" Sebastian shouted. He tore off his coat and shirt, tossing away the ripped and burned fabric and armor. Sebastian turned to see Barron standing behind him. Barron bit his lip, looked at the ground, then met Sebastian's eyes. "Stop staring." Sebastian's voice was gruff. Every muscle ached. He walked to the lake, melted the ice, and washed the blood off his face and chest while admiring his reflection.

"Maxen could have ended you back in Torrdale," Barron said. "How much more are you going to punish yourself before you let us help you? We are loyal to you. I know I am the last person you want to hear that from, but it is the truth."

Sebastian washed his neck as he continued to stare at himself in the water. "How did you feel when you stood there and watched that Kuhar soldier beat me? What was in your mind?"

"Anger. Greed. Jealousy… Pain."

"You watched as my flesh was ripped apart. You listened as I screamed in pain." Sebastian stood, took his dagger, and held it to Barron's throat. "You stabbed me in the leg with this dagger. You murdered Fiona with this dagger. And this is the dagger Cyrus drove through my chest. This is the dagger I will—"

"Kill me with… I know."

"For now, I need you. I need all of you." Sebastian took a shirt and coat from a wagon. "You are right, Barron. I need help. So, let's go kill this bastard." He slipped the dagger back into his belt and held his arm for Barron to take. "To war, brother."

Barron gripped his forearm. "To war."

He sent the wagons with the dead and injured to NorthBrekka, along with Nadya and Amara. The rest departed into the snow and headed west. When they stopped for food, the storm started to ease. Sebastian felt calm and centered. He tried to keep the anger for Tomas in his heart but not his mind. "This is why Valirus always reminds me that I still need more training," Sebastian said to his closest knights. "I have destroyed Torrdale. I can't let that happen to NorthBrekka. We cannot allow war to follow us home. Castle Drake is the last stronghold in Erras for all free men. If Maxen and the Safar defeat us, he will enslave anyone who lives. When it comes time for him and me to fight, you all must leave me behind. No matter the outcome, you all must live on to tell the tales."

"Oh, here he goes," Meecah said. "That head wound must have damaged your brain." She stood next to Sebastian. "In case you haven't heard, over and over, we said that none of us are going to leave you to die. We won't even leave you to live, so stop telling us to run away."

Sebastian tried to suppress a smile, nodded, then walked away to have a look ahead. Dom joined his side, and they wondered where no other ears could hear.

"I fear I haven't given you the time and attention you deserve." He put his arm around Dom. "I feel disconnected from this world, but I am glad you stuck by my side all this time."

"I cannot imagine it any other way."

"Not at all?" Sebastian looked through the corner of his eyes.

"Well, if I could have you as my husband, I would." He winked. "But I always knew it would never be. I didn't leave my wife because I thought we would marry. I was destined for something different." Dom rustled in his coat pocket and pulled out a letter. "I received this a few days ago." He handed it to Sebastian.

Sebastian read the note aloud, then stopped. "You didn't tell me—"

"My father died," Dom said. "It happened just after the winter equinox. He passed away in his sleep."

"Dom, I wish you would have told me so I could pay proper respect."

"You will. His passing also means I assume his position in Icefall. Once winter passes, I will head home for good." Dom hung his head with a red face and teary eyes. "As much as I love my home, that is not the life for me."

"You don't have to stay in Icefall if I promote you." A grin grew on Sebastian's lips. "You can go back and forth just as you do now."

"What position allows for that?"

"High Priest of the North. You will have permission to roam on your own accord. In this position, you serve no one, Dom. Do you understand me? I want you to live as free as you deserve." Sebastian kissed Dom on the cheek. "And I will always love you, no matter what."

A tear ran down Dom's face. He hugged Sebastian tight. "I love you, too," he whispered.

They watched as far ahead as they could through the snow. Later in the afternoon, the army marched on. They crossed a vast field when the snow turned to rain and thunderstorms. It was the moment when everything became clear. Sebastian saw the armies of Torrdale, Altania, and Safareen spanning the coast as far as the eye could see. A bright, white light flashed ahead like a beacon.

"Maxen," Sebastian said. He paced before his militia. "No speeches." He shouted. "I say no words of wisdom. I am fortunate to be here with all of you, even when the enemy army surpasses our own by thousands. They want to take NorthBrekka, but they must get through us first!" Sebastian climbed onto Ossian's back and turned to his people. "One more time. We march."

The legion stomped and pounded their chests in the way of the Sinook. Warriors with their bows moved forward first until they reached target distance, knelt, and strung an arrow.

"Archers..." Sebastian raised his hand. Lightning danced overhead as rain poured down. "Fire!"

The release of bow strings caused a ripple of sound to drift across the plains. With each flash of lightning, the black wall of arrows illuminated the skies and disappeared within the cover of clouds. He watched Maxen's front line fall, then heard the shouts of men ready to fight back wail across the land.

"Archers, again!"

In unison, the Sinook warriors strung another arrow. A line of soldiers of NorthBrekka took their place behind the warriors and prepared their bows.

"Fire." Sebastian watched the arrows fly, then nudged Ossian and led his people back into Torrdale.

"This is probably a dumb question," Dani said. "But if we were going back to Torrdale to fight, why did we go all the way to NorthBrekka first."

Sebastian laughed. "I have no idea. I was unconscious." He felt his cheeks burn. "Something about that lake clears my mind. I guess that is why my brothers led us to Stormfire. We needed to regroup and to rest and I needed to recharge."

"Because that is where you discovered your powers," Dani said.

"Besides, I had to get my sister and Amara home safe."

"You know I will follow you into hell if you ask." Dani gripped Sebastian tight. "You and I are connected in more ways than love or marriage. If you die, I die by your side, but I want to live a long life, my king."

"You will, my darling."

Dani punched him in the shoulder.

"We will, my love." Sebastian grabbed his hand.

Armies from all over the earth met in battle. Swords, axes, arrows, pikes, fists, and magic all met in a clash of war on the fields of a once peaceful nation of the north. Sebastian left his sword sheathed and used the wind to throw groupings of men across the crowd, shouting for Maxen as he advanced closer to the palace.

Jace protected Petra, who insisted on fighting against an army that once trusted her lead. Viktor and Seville were on foot, fighting with their swords in one hand and holding onto one another with the other. Sebastian smiled at the blooming romance between his new friend and his brother. He scanned the field, and with a sharp pain in his heart, he saw Kristoff surrounded, with his sweaty face and blonde hair standing out over the mindless Altanian men.

Sebastian leaped from Ossian's back, and this time, Dani joined him. He passed the reins to Meecah, who was in dangerof being captured. She climbed onto the large black horse and rode away, knocking soldiers over as they went. Dani darted toward where Kristoff was in trouble. Sebastian watched his husband become stiff, quiet, and calm. His face became paler than usual, and his steps became more graceful as he found the crowd surrounding Kristoff.

Dani reached out and grabbed the arm of one soldier. The man shook violently. His legs twitched, and his back snapped. Dani remained unmoved by the dead man who fell at his feet. He touched the neck of another, who fell instantly to his death. A Torrdale soldier tackled him to the ground. Dani climbed onto the man's stomach and held his face in his hands. The soldier shrieked and jerked ashis face sunk in and turned white. He slowly slumped to a limp state and Dani stood. The remaining soldiers retreated.

Kristoff stood face-to-face with Dani. Sebastian ran in between them with his hands out. He grabbed Dani's shoulder, then fell to his knees. His body seared like he was being struck by a thousand bolts of lightning at once. He felt his heart pound and struggled to catch his breath.

All he could hear was the thumping of boots on the soil. Sounds of crashing iron rang in his ears, and the rain was cold and relentless on his skin.

"Sebastian?" The sweet and light voice of Dani overcame every sound.

"Stay away from him!"

Sebastian sat up quickly to see Kristoff pushing Dani away.

"You almost killed him," Kristoff shouted.

"No, brother. Stop!" Sebastian stumbled toward Dani.

Dani panted hard, tears pouring down his cheeks, and his face was soaked with sweat. He backed away as Sebastian walked toward him.

"Dani, come to me. I am alright, my darling. Please come to me." Sebastian reached for Dani's hand.

Dani backed away faster, shaking his head. "My father was right. I am going to kill you whether I want to or not. I can't stay with you, Sebastian." His eyes filled with tears. "I'm going to kill my father." He sprinted away, disappearing into the fight.

"Dani!" Sebastian ran after him but was stopped by Kristoff. He shoved his brother away. "We have to find him. He cannot face Maxen alone."

"I don't see why not." Viktor arrived with Seville.

"Dani can destroy Maxen," Seville said. "Let him use his anger."

"He can't," Sebastian said. "There is some kind of pact Maxen cast into a spell where Dani cannot use his powers to harm his father. I must be the one to end Maxen."

"Then we must follow him into battle." Kristoff put his hand on Sebastian's shoulder. "Besides, he saved my life. I owe him."

Barron, Jace, and Petra joined them. Sebastian jerked his head and continued toward the battle. "No mercy. For we, the house of the great Dragon, do not fear anyone. Maxen believes the Bolin bloodline is owed rule over this world, but a god sat on that throne long before any of his kin. It belongs to me. Follow me and we will end this now."

They took Dani's path into the mass of blood and guts that soiled the ground. Sebastian's attention was drawn to a white light where he saw Dani standing inches away from his father. Sebastian's body flexed as he pushed himself into a sprint. He felt lighter and more agile than before as the wind rushed in from behind.

Maxen took a few steps forward as Sebastian approached. His smile was almost deranged. "Well, well, here we are once more," Maxen said. "Are you going to run away again, Your Majesty?"

"I didn't run—"

"Don't lie!" Maxen said. "I would have thought a man who had endured being beaten, stabbed, cursed, tortured, and broken would be stronger than that."

"You murdered my brother!"

"I said I would end the line of the gods, but you, King Sebastian, are far too useful. I will gladly kill Dani, but not you." Maxen adjusted his stance. "I will keep you for myself. My pet dragon." Maxen burst into laughter. "I will break you until you are stripped of everything and everyone you love. You will be so empty that you will choose to do my bidding. Chaos destroys all."

Sebastian did not speak. He clenched his jaw and stared.

Dani fell into his arms. "I'm so sorry. I could have—"

"Don't, my love. You can't hurt me." Sebastian stepped in front of Dani. "Maxen, fight me now. Just you and me. They will not interfere. To the death." He reached his hand out to Maxen.

Maxen grasped his forearm. His forehead was wrinkled, and his eyes narrowed. "A fight to the death. You have an accord."

"Good." Sebastian jerked his arm back and backed away. He took his bow and quiver and passed them to Jace. "I don't need weapons to fight him. Dani, take my sword. It is important to me. My father gave it to me on my fifteenth birthday, just before I discovered my powers. If anything happens to me—"

"Don't talk like you are not going to survive this," Dani said. "I will end him before he hurts you."

"This is my fight. Do not interfere. I can't let it darken your mind. I love you, Dani. I have loved you since the moment you saved my life all those years ago." Sebastian held Dani's face in his palm. "You are my husband, and you are lord of the north. I need you to be strong now."

"Enough," Maxen yelled. "Romance is for the weak. Fight me!"

Sebastian spun around and slapped his hands together. He pulled them apart, forming fire between his palms. One hand flew forward, and a fireball smashed into Maxen.

"Is that all you have?" Maxen taunted. "Fireballs. A typical baby dragon. Spitting fire from his little paws."

Sebastian swirled his hands while flickering his fingers. The rain around them began to form and stretch.

"Make ice, Sebastian. Is that not what my brother would say? Ice, Your Majesty."

Sebastian dropped his hands. The rain slowed to the light mist. He paced before Maxen. "How do you know what Valirus said to me in Midrel Istan?"

"My brother is very powerful, but he has been trapped in a dungeon for years and has…well, gotten rusty. I not only can control minds, but I can also read one's mind if I wish, and when my dear brother returned to Torrdale to save his son, I was able to take a look into your training. I know every move you have been taught."

"Where are Valirus and Cyrus?"

"Oh, you still care for Cyrus? Pity." Maxen whipped his staff into the air and slammed it onto the hard ground causing a bright flash and a gust of wind so strong that it threw Sebastian and his followers to the ground.

Sebastian jumped to his feet. "I'm done with your mind games." His stomach burst with fiery pain. His throat burned like it never had before, and his arms ignited flames that whipped in the wind. He threw a punch that met Maxen hard in the mouth, causing him to fall over.

Sebastian reached into the air, and a lightning bolt met his grasp. "I am more than my power. I am more than my weapons. I don't need my crown or my throne to defeat you. I will win because I am a better man than you. You are the monster. Not me." He slammed the bolt into Maxen's chest. "You will suffer." Sebastian's voice became deeper and raspier than ever. He snarled, and flames flew from his mouth. Maxen gripped his throat, and Sebastian's entire body ignited. He balled his fist and raised it to strike again. Ice formed, shrouded by flames and lightning. The wind began to howl around them.

Sebastian saw the fighting men and women lose footing and get swept away. Maxen's soldiers ran to help him, but once they crossed into Sebastian's chaotic energy, they were thrown back. No one could reach them. It was just him and Maxen, and he was determined to destroy him once and for all. Sebastian's skin was red and seared in pain as he refused to relinquish the fire that blasted from within. Maxen's face was wrinkled and deep red as he struggled to push Sebastian away from him. Sebastian stared into his eyes, not blinking or looking away.

Smoke escaped his nostrils when he exhaled. He could see his reflection in Maxen's shield. His ruby eyes shined, and a tinge of red striping turned into a haze of red scales along his skin. He caught Maxen's shaking hand that reached for his staff. Sebastian buried his knee into Maxen's chest and got close enough for their foreheads to touch. "There is nothing that will save you now."

"No?" Maxen laughed. "Look up, Your Majesty."

Sebastian slowly lifted his head. He stared without speaking and with a hanging jaw. He sat up, still on Maxen's torso, and took a deep hefty breath that fluttered in his chest and stomach. His eyes met Maxen again. "What did you do?" The vortex dissipated. Sebastian saw Cyrus standing before all. His head hanging, with face ghostly pale, and his eyes bloodshot.

Maxen smiled. "Now, nephew!"

Sebastian felt a sharp blow to the chest. His back slammed onto the stone floor. In Cyrus's hand was Maxen's staff, glowing bright white. Cyrus's expression was blank, and his eyes met no one's face. Maxen took the staff and whispered something to Cyrus that Sebastian could not hear.

"We are here, Your Majesty." Meecah stood between him and Maxen. Jace joined her side while the others encircled him.

"What are you all doing? Get out of here." Sebastian pulled Meecah behind him.

"No, my love." Dani stepped forward. "My father has taken Cyrus's mind. He is gone, Sebastian."

Sebastian met Cyrus's stare. His eyes watered, then he looked at Maxen, and his throat tightened, and stomach burned. "Was this your plan?" He pushed his way around Dani and Jace. "Are you so cowardly that you would destroy your kin to keep from fighting me?"

"It was either him or Dani and if you remember correctly, I can't use my magic against my son. That means he can't kill me either." Maxen turned his attention to Dani. "No matter how hard he tries." He stepped closer to Sebastian. "Besides, I knew Cyrus would be the one to break your heart over and over. Just look at what you have done to Torrdale because of him."

Sebastian tilted his head. "What did you do with Valirus?"

Maxen began to back away, leaving Cyrus behind. "Like father, like son." He turned and walked away quickly.

"After him!" Sebastian said.

His legion lunged in pursuit of Maxen while Sebastian stayed behind. Dani and Barron stood by his side. He reached his hand out. "Cyrus..."

"He doesn't know who he is anymore, Seb," Dani said. "The only thing he knows is that he is to fight you."

"Cyrus," Sebastian said louder than before. "Please. Don't make me do this."

Cyrus tightened his grip around his sword and started forward. Sebastian's hand fumbled around the hilt of his blade, but with regret, he lifted it into a battle stance.

"Dani, Barron, back away." Sebastian hung his head. "The time has come."

"You don't have to do this," Dani said.

"There is no other way." Sebastian moved toward Cyrus. "He is gone. You said so yourself."

Cyrus's movements were precise and unbothered. His face remained emotionless and focused on Sebastian's every twist and turn. Sebastian's heart ached with every swing of his sword. Every sound of metal on metal, every spark from their blades, and every groan of strength he felt was a pain in his gut. Sebastian saw his friends and family run to fight the incoming soldiers. He turned his attention back and swung his blade again but was met with a boot to his stomach. He stared at the clearing skies while catching his breath on the cold ground.

Sebastian reached for his belt and wrapped his fingers around a handle, pulling it slowly as Cyrus screamed. He rolled onto his side and kicked Cyrus in the knee, hearing bones snap and pop. Cyrus fell to the ground with a thump, having no words other than screams of pain. Sebastian climbed over him and pointed to the ruby-encrusted dagger. Tears poured down his cheek. He pinned Cyrus's arms down.

There was a stinging feeling on his lips as he kissed Cyrus, then a sharp gasp sucked the air from his lungs. Cyrus's eyes went from manic to soft. His lips became pouty. He reached up and tucked Sebastian's hair behind his ear. Sebastian's eyes filled with tears. "Kill me," Cyrus said, as his body fell limp.

Sebastian felt his entire body cripple with painful emotional sickness, but still, he let his arm drop with the blade pointed at Cyrus. The light disappeared as he closed his eyes. The sounds of fighting abruptly stopped. Sebastian felt hot blood pouring into his hand as it rested against Cyrus's coat. He ran his fingers along the dagger's hilt toward the blade but couldn't feel metal.

Arms looped around him and dragged him across the ground. The battle had seemed to cease. Whispers, footsteps, screams, cries, and running were all he could hear, but none of it mattered. He could only feel Cyrus's blood on his hands. Sebastian opened his eyes to see Barron standing over him.

The battlefield was a mix of confused people and death. Sebastian looked all around for Cyrus, then his eyes shot open wide. "Where is Dani?"

He pushed Barron back and jumped to his feet. "Dani!" His voice rolled across the field with a booming roar. The storm moved away from the coastline, and stars began showing through clouds. The moon shined over him as Dani kneeled on Cyrus's side. "He's going to bring him back to life," Sebastian said.

Sebastian slowly walked up to Dani and put his hand on his back. He couldn't look at Cyrus. He refused. He saw the ruby dagger standing, pointed side down, and blood. The warmth of Dani's body against his was calming. Sebastian buried his face into his husband's back. Dani still had his hands against Cyrus.

"Open your eyes, my love," Dani whispered. "I can heal him if you wish, but he will never be the same. I can't make him the Cyrus you love."

Sebastian felt a vein stick out on his neck as he strained to hold back his cries. He sat up and opened his eyes and stared at Cyrus. A once beautiful, kind, and hopeful boy that fell in love with a cursed prince, was gone. Cyrus's story was over, and although Sebastian knew it, nothing could prepare him for the raw pain that pushed beyond fury into something that shut his entire body down.

It hurt to breathe. Sebastian moved Dani away, scooped Cyrus into his arms, and walked to the palace. He kissed his forehead and let his pain show through his tears and scowl. Sebastian carried Cyrus to the ceremonial chamber, laid his body on the stone, and rested his head on his stomach. The other faces in the room were a mix of sadness and anger. Sebastian's heart pounded, and his cries got louder. He screamed, gripping Cyrus's coat in his fist and straining to hold back his powers so he did no more harm to the man he loved.

Footsteps came down the hall, and Maxen and Lorna's faces became clear. Sebastian's tears stopped instantly. His head shot up, and his sorrow turned into the most chaotic, wretched mix of violence and murderous intent. Lightning cracked from his fingertips, and fire burst from his body. Sebastian ran to Maxen. Dani ran by his side. "Let me kill my father."

"No." Sebastian's voice was harsh. "He will suffer the pain I feel right now. It hurts more than anything I have ever felt, and he will feel everything, even if I have to cut him open and rip apart his organs with my bare hands. He took Tomas and Cyrus from me. I will not let him take you, Dani." His voice cracked. Then, he saw Lorna reach out and strike Dani, and everything was as if time had stopped. "You..." He lunged toward her, but Maxen stepped in his path. Dani took his knife and held his father by his throat. Sebastian grabbed Lorna and threw her against the wall. "I don't like hurting women, but you are no lady. You are a beast, and I take no issue with killing beasts."

"You have no idea what I am capable of, Your Majesty. I know all your secrets. All of them. I knew about Cyrus being madly in love with you before you even knew him. That stupid boy used to sneak into the woods to watch you across the border. He has been following you since you were both twelve years old. You were all he ever spoke about. Then he met you, and I felt his sweet, innocent heart ache with desire and fall deeply in love over the years. He wanted nothing more than to be your husband, King Sebastian. My job was to hurt you in every way I could muster. I hurt Cyrus, Sasha, your father, your stepmother..."

There was a sudden jerk, and bloodshot from Lorna's throat. Sebastian saw Barron appear behind her, holding a sword in his grasp.

"And you hurt me," Barron said. He shoved Lorna forward and let her body slide free of his blade. Barron stared at her as she took her last breath.

Sebastian turned and marched over to Maxen. "The war is over. The throne is mine." His hand sparked with lightning as Sebastian moved closer to Maxen's head.

"The war will never be over." Maxen jumped to his feet and punched Sebastian in the face.

They locked in a fistfight. Dani scurried out of the way as the others guarded the entrance against soldiers. Sebastian found his axe and swung at Maxen, slicing a gash across his face as he ducked out of the way. Sebastian screamed and the castle shook. The ground cracked and the windows that overlooked the stables shattered. He stopped and stared at Cyrus for a moment before he felt a painful blow to his stomach.

"Distracted again, I see," Maxen said.

Sebastian let out a deep gasp. "I said I would alleviate myself from distractions. Therefore, Cyrus had to die." He clenched his jaw. "Now it is your turn." He tucked his hands into his chest and then threw them out. Maxen slammed against the wall. Sebastian picked up his axe once again. "Stand still and I will make this quick."

"Valirus." Maxen's voice was low but echoed through the room.

Sebastian spun around.

Valirus looked pale. He slowly walked forward with his staff in hand. It began to glow, and he raised it and pointed toward Sebastian.

"Kill him," Maxen said.

Valirus stared into Sebastian's eyes. His staff lit brighter than usual. He let out a growl and then slammed his staff into the floor. A bright light filled the room, then Maxen screamed.

The wall was blown out from the castle and Maxen stumbled from the pile of rubble and ran away.

"He only thought I was rusty," Valirus smirked. "Go, Your Majesty. After him!"

Sebastian followed but landed outside in time to see him retreat on horseback. He mounted a muscular white stallion and bounded off behind him. "Maxen!"

Maxen looked back, kicking his horse in the ribs, and pushing his steed to gallop with all its might. Sebastian cracked lightning in his hand and slapped his horse on the hip. He felt a jerk. The wind cut at his face and stung his eyes. Maxen was a blur, but Sebastian pushed his stallion to run faster. With every thrust, he gained momentum, getting closer to catching Maxen. He was inches from the tail of the horse in front of him.

Sebastian lit a fireball in his palm and threw it at Maxen's head. It crashed against his collar and Maxen screamed and fell forward, almost falling from his horse. He threw another, but it missed and exploded into a tree. Sebastian reached his hand in the air. Lightning came crashing down around them, then a bolt connected with his hand. His skin glowed red and a hint of scales formed across his arms and chest. He dropped his jaw and screamed as the lightning violently flashed in his fist. "You took my brother from me. You die, tonight!"

The forest floor shook, and the wind blew from every direction. The horses stumbled and fell, throwing their riders to the ground. Sebastian snarled, clapped his hands together, pulled them gently apart, and pinched his index fingers to his thumbs. The clouds swirled into a cyclone that lowered above Maxen. Lightning crashed, thunder growled, and rain turned into stinging, icy needles.

He stood and screamed to the sky, then there was a searing pain in Sebastian's ribs. He looked down to see a blade dripping with blood. A hand gripped his shoulder and spoke into his ear. "My name is King Lucian, ruler of Safareen." He twisted the sword. "The reign of the Dragon ends, now." Lucian yanked his blade out of Sebastian's side.

Sebastian shrieked in pain and felt his warm blood pouring from his wound. With a shaking hand, he unsheathed his sword and pointed it at Lucian.

King Lucian laughed and grabbed a fistful of Sebastian's hair.

"Unhand the King of Kings." An angry, deep voice came from behind them. The woods went completely dark except for shadows that moved in the flashes of lightning. A figure stood between him, and Lucian as Maxen retreated down the path.

Sebastian gasped for air as blood pooled around him in the cold, damp grass. His head spun and his eyes closed.

CHAPTER 40
The Darkness that Saved Him

Dani sat at Sebastian's bedside and tended to the bloody gash on his forehead. He waited for Nadya to arrive with a needle and thread before taking a walk around Castle Drake. As the day moved on into afternoon, he wandered down to the burial chamber where Tomas lay after he was washed and awaited burial. Dani leaned on the table and stared at Tomas's innocent face looking angelic under the flicker of candlelight.

"I wish I could have got to know you." Dani set his hand on Tomas's chest. "Sebastian spoke of you like you would be the one to save the world. But you were fragile and your brother blames himself. He fears the idea of losing everyone. First you, then Cyrus." A tear ran down Dani's cheek. He clutched Tomas's hand and sniffled. "Seeing you like this." He choked and clutched his chest. Dani ran his sleeve across his eyes then rested both hands on Tomas's body. "Your face is the same as his," Dani whispered. "And seeing you lying here, lifeless, rips my heart from my chest. I only see him, dead, because of me…"

Dani squeezed his eyes shut and buried his face in Tomas's chest. "I'm sorry, Tomas. Sorry for what my father did." He felt his body get icy cold, then warm and his stomach fluttered as he shivered and stepped away. Dani walked to the door but noticed a shadow flick on the wall before him. He swung around and gawked at Tomas for a moment with his mouth dropped open. Yet Tomas lay still on the table. Dani reached for the door handle, glanced at Tomas one last time, then zipped through the doorway and made his way back to Sebastian.

A warm ray of sunlight woke Sebastian from his dream about dragons, only this time, the dream was different. Cyrus no longer fell from a cliff. In fact, Cyrus was no longer in his dream. Instead, the world was on fire. There was no one. Just Sebastian and a golden dragon flying above the overlook. He stood and walked to the edge and stepped over. The dragon caught him, and he vanished. He snapped awake and sat up.

The bedroom was empty. He realized he was in Castle Drake. Sebastian dressed and walked to the window. The sky was blue, and the warm sun beamed down on the courtyard. Merchants gathered around the castle grounds, selling vegetables, silks, and more. He felt his stomach rumble angrily. Sebastian put on his boots and pulled his shirt over his head. He stopped and ran his fingers across his ribs, feeling only a scar.

He hurried down to the kitchens. Cooks and maidens hopped out of his way. He grabbed bread and a thick chunk of lamb and ate them on the cutting block. The servants stared but did not speak. Sebastian swallowed large bits at a time, then gulped down a goblet of wine, before leaving the kitchen with a rush.

He had many thoughts in his head but dared not to speak. He didn't want anyone to talk to him as he strolled to the mausoleum. He leaned his back against the stone of his father's tomb and drank a flagon of ale. The newly carved rock stood out where he saw the name "Tomas Ivan Drake" scribed on the plaque. There was a space beside it where his body was meant to lie one day.

Still resting against his father's burial place, Sebastian finally spoke. "I failed, Father. Again. Tomas and I were supposed to be together. I guess we never know how long forever lasts. Cyrus and I once said we would be together forever; now he is gone too. Forever must only mean for them. I will never say it to anyone ever again. Then maybe people we love will stop dying." He buried his head in his knees. "This is all my fault. I'm sorry. All of you."

"Death is just the beginning of their journey." A voice echoed from the stairway. "War brought their death, not you, Your Majesty."

"Valirus?"

The gray-haired old man stepped into sight, smiling at Sebastian from across the tombs.

"How did I get here? What happened in Torrdale?"

"Barron," Valirus said. "He saved us all."

Sebastian tilted his head to the side.

Valirus stepped forward but stopped and set his hand on a tomb. Sebastian leaned against the wall where his twin lay, then moved over to Valirus. His heart skipped a beat when he read the plaque. "Cyrus Vaseris Bolin."

"Vaseris was my father's name," Valirus said. "It was Nadya's idea to bury him here."

"What happened in Torrdale?"

"I think Barron should tell you," Valirus said. "Everyone is waiting for you to take the throne."

Sebastian went back to his bedroom and dressed in his finest attire. Valirus helped him with his coat and his sword. He brushed the soot off Sebastian's boots, then took something from a wood box on the bed. Sebastian stared at his reflection as an onyx and ruby crown was placed on his head. They walked out together, down the hall, and to the throne room's doors. Before the guards opened the door, Sebastian stared at the floor and breathed deeply and steadily. "I'm ready."

The large oak doors swung wide. The massive crowd stood, then bowed as their king entered the room. Dani stood from his throne and bowed. Sebastian walked to the front, turned, and sat. His people rested in their chairs and looked to him for guidance.

"Barron," Dani said. "Tell our king what he has missed." Dani's tone was serious and powerful. Sebastian squeezed his hand and grinned. Dani blushed and gripped his hand tight.

Barron stood before all. "That night in Torrdale, when you chased Maxen from the palace, I followed you. Lucien cut through the woods and found you before me. I took the light and demons attacked. You ignited like nothing I had ever seen. The fire..." His voice drifted off. "You have been asleep since. All of spring has passed, brother."

"It's summer?" Sebastian gasped. He looked at Dani, who had tears running down his porcelain skin. "My darling—"

"Don't apologize." Dani grabbed both of his hands.

The room fell into talks among one another. Sebastian held Dani while watching his friends and family talk among the villagers and merchants. His mind kept creeping back to the image of him jamming Barron's dagger into Cyrus's chest and the feel of blood running everywhere, and how it felt when Cyrus's heart stopped beating. There was a deep nauseating feeling in his stomach. Sebastian kissed Dani's cheek and focused on his husband's beautiful face which was smiling back at him.

"I know you are hurt," Dani whispered. He held Sebastian's cheek and kissed his lips. "I love you so much. I am never going to leave you. I promise."

Sebastian hoped Dani wouldn't say the word forever. "Dani, I feel like there is still so much I don't know about your powers."

"You want to know about my mother." Dani shook his head. "I was just a boy. My father never told me what I was capable of, but he pushed me hard every day. One day, he beat me with a cane." Dani brushed his hair to the side, revealing a scar that ran from behind his ear and down the back of his neck. "He hit me so hard, I fainted. When I came to, my mother was holding me in her arms. We were in my bedroom. Maxen stormed in and slapped my mother across the face, slicing open her eye. I panicked, and every thought I had became blurry, and I felt cold. I reached up to hold my mother's face and stop the bleeding. She let out the most horrid sound before she collapsed. Afterwards, My father locked me away in the dungeons for months without food or water. I ate rats to survive."

"Dani…" His throat tightened. For the remainder of the evening, he listened to stories and told some of his own, and not once did he let go of Dani's hand.

The next morning, Sebastian woke to Dani resting gently on his chest. He felt his heart flutter as his fingers brushed the scar on Dani's neck. "I have never been so happy."

Dani shifted a little, and a smile streamed across his face. "Good morning, my love."

"I would give up everything to wake up with you in my arms every day."

Dani sat up and kissed his lips. "You changed my whole life and have made me feel love. You will wake up to me, for—"

"Do not say forever!" Sebastian realized he had shouted too loud. Dani jumped back. "I'm sorry, my darling." He explained why he was afraid of the word forever.

"You are paranoid!" Dani laughed. "I'm sorry, but a word did not bring deathly fate to Tomas or Cyrus. They are dead because of Lorna and Maxen. Now Lorna is dead, and we only have to find Maxen and take his life."

Sebastian sat up. "Where is Maxen?"

"No one knows. He has been missing since you fought in the woods."

Sebastian fell back into Dani's arms and made love to him for the remainder of the morning. He wanted to lie in bed with his lover all day, but something bothered him that forced Sebastian out of bed as the afternoon sun shined bright above. Sebastian dressed, ate, and went to wander the castle. He went to the library and flipped through a few pages when a snooty voice came from right next to him.

"Those are called books, you know?"

Sebastian grinned. "Sara. I see you made it here alright."

"You mean after Maxen kidnapped Nadya and Amara? You're not doing a very good job at protecting the family." Sara held up her hands and backed up a few steps. Her face turned pale. "I'm sorry, Sebastian. Tomas... I—"

"You're right. I'm glad you and Corbyn are home safe." Sebastian nodded. "Trust me. Things are going to get better."

"Corbyn means everything to me. As long as he is safe, I will ask for nothing more."

"You have nothing to worry about, Sara. I'm a changed man. Forgive me for the things I did when I was a boy."

"Forgive me for trying to steal your boyfriend. To be honest, I only did it to make Barron jealous." She smirked.

"It's still weird."

"I know." Sara shrugged. "But I love him."

"Good. Live your life. Be happy. All three of you."

"I thought you were going to kill him?"

Sebastian stared at the floor. He quickly shook his head. "Perhaps I will reconsider."

Sara dropped the book she was reading and looped her arms around Sebastian's neck. She kissed his cheek, picked up her book, and left the library.

Later, Sebastian took off to the stables to saddle Ossian. He noticed a blacksmith working on shoeing the army's horses.

"Afternoon, Your Highness."

Sebastian waved. "Hello. Who are you?"

"Mikhail. I was hired to care for your stables and make weapons for NorthBrekka." He bowed to the king.

Mikhail was young, stocky, blond-haired, and reminded him of Will.

"How old are you?"

"Twenty, My King."

"Where are your parents?"

"Umm, I was separated from my parents when I was a boy. Then I found myself in Alta Prime years before you destroyed it."

"You don't have to explain anymore. I am glad to have you." Sebastian nodded his head and continued to Ossian.

Mikhail took the saddle and reins from Sebastian and prepared Ossian for a ride. "Your Majesty, this is my job. I understand you wish to do everything on your own, but please allow me to prove myself. It would be what Will wanted."

Sebastian shook his head. "Will?"

"He was my cousin."

Sebastian smiled and allowed Mikhail to continue his work. He rode off to the east, wanting nothing more than to go to Shadowmire, play cards, drink, and maybe pick a fistfight. He looked over his shoulder to ensure he wasn't followed if Mikhail alerted the guard to his departure.

At the Inn, he sat at the usually busy card table. Only Grimmel, the innkeeper from Shadowmire whom Sebastian used to play cards with, joined him. "Fancy a game, Your Majesty?"

"Please. I need a distraction. Where is everyone?"

"Searching for that king from Midrel Istan. Are you alright, My King? I understand you lost that young prince you used to run with."

"Cyrus. Yes. My Cyrus. The love of my life." Sebastian paused. "I killed him." His eyes blinked quickly. "I killed him," he whispered. "I will never get over this."

"And what of this young prince you have brought to power?" Grimmel passed cards to Sebastian.

"You mean Dani." He looked at his hand and set two down on the table. Sebastian smiled and sat up straighter. "Dani is perfect. He makes me happy."

"Like Prince Cyrus used to," Grimmel said.

"Stop it, Grimmel." A woman popped out from behind a door carrying two bowls of stew. "This is the king and you are making him feel bad." She set the soup before Sebastian and patted his shoulder. "I am so sorry for your loss. But if you love your new husband, lean to him to help you heal, and please, bring him to meet us."

Sebastian ate the soup way too fast. "This is delicious." He dropped a fist filled with coins on the table. Grimmel's smile vanished, and he started to throw away his cards. "No, don't do that." Sebastian flipped his hand over to reveal the most terrible cards Grimmel had ever seen.

"Your Majesty..."

"Take it. You need the coin more than I do. You won, fair and square." Sebastian winked. "I guess I lost my touch."

Grimmel laughed. "I guess you have. Why are you here all by yourself, Your Majesty?"

"I just need to clear my head." Sebastian stood and walked around the Inn.

Grimmel went to the bar and poured another ale. "You can't let this pain be your legacy. You are Chaos, God of Fire. I always thought you were a snobby little brat, but I knew one day you would rise. And now, you have. I need you to know that you are loved." Grimmel handed him a pint. "My son was just like you. He got sick when he was only a boy. Your sister, Nadya, even tried to heal him. The royal court suggested we send him north for help, so we allowed it. He looked a lot like you. That is why I gave you a hard time all those years. He was a good boy, but he never returned from the north. The healers there said he got up and ran off in the middle of the night. It has been years. The pain of losing a loved one always haunts you. But I believe Mikhail is here in spirit. It is like I can almost feel his presence."

Sebastian grabbed Grimmel's arm. "Mikhail?" He set his ale down and led him toward the door. "You must come with me now."

He dragged Grimmel down the pass, as his wife rode on Ossian's back. The day was getting late as they approached the stable. Sebastian shouted for the blacksmith.

Mikhail came out with a smile. "Yes, Your Majesty?"

"Grimmel, I believe this is your missing son." Sebastian released his arm and walked away. He heard Grimmel's wife gasp. She hugged her son, and they cried in the courtyard as Sebastian slipped through the servants' entrance to the kitchen. He smiled as he shifted through the swarm of cooks, and through the door to the dining hall.

"Where have you been?" A voice coming from around the corner made Sebastian jump.

He squeezed his eyes closed. "Dani."

"How dare you run off and not say a word." Dani breathed hard.

Sebastian reached for Dani's arm. "My darling, I swear I never meant to frighten you."

Dani pulled him in for a hug. "I will destroy the world to find you. Please don't force me to. I was so afraid."

"Never fear my absence." Sebastian embraced him even more tightly. "I will always come back. I just needed to do something good. The way Tomas would have."

"I will do anything to help you." Dani hugged him. "We all will, my love."

"First, we must find Maxen. We have to end this, no matter what. I have lost too much. I killed too many and said goodbye to the ones I love." Sebastian squeezed his eyes shut.

CHAPTER 41
The Order of Thieves

Sebastian woke early one morning and quickly scribbled a note while Dani slept.

Dani,

Today is my birthday, and I can't celebrate with everyone just yet. I hope you understand that I need to be alone for a while. Without Tomas...I promise to return later today. Forgive my rudeness. I love you.

-Sebastian

He left the castle and took the path down the cliffside that led toward the eastern side of Stormfire Lake. Sebastian watched the town come to life as he rested on the shoreline in the sun that shined brightly above. The summer solstice had arrived, yet all he wanted was to hide from the festivities in The Far North and NorthBrekka. Singing echoed from the courtyard of Castle Drake. His people came to celebrate. Colorful silks, flowers, banners, and the most delectable smelling foods were seen around the nearby town. Sebastian rubbed his face, realizing he was tired and didn't feel well.

He dipped his fingers into the water and froze the lake along the beach. "I should have been better, Tomas. I just stood there and did nothing. I could have stopped him." Tears filled his eyes, his face fell into his palms, and he cried with his whole body. "I should have never left. I'm so selfish." The sun began to fall as the afternoon began.

Footsteps thumped from the trail behind him. "You shouldn't be out here crying on your birthday."

Sebastian barely turned his head, catching a glimpse of Barron before returning to freezing the water. "I want to be alone."

"I don't care." Barron sat down.

They sat without speaking for some time. Sebastian stopped playing with the water and held his stomach.

"Hungry?" Barron said.

Sebastian's stomach growled. "I don't want to return to the castle... but yes."

"Catch a fish."

"I hate fish." Sebastian scowled. "They taste like... fish."

Barron burst out laughing. "People always said Sebastian is strong, handsome, and brave, but no one ever said Sebastian is smart."

"And everyone says Barron is an ass, and well...they are absolutely correct." Sebastian laughed harder.

Barron sighed. "I know it means nothing, but... happy birthday, brother."

"Thanks." Sebastian sat up straight and faced Barron. "I've been angry for so long that I forgot how to enjoy these things. I don't want all the attention. It makes me feel uncomfortable and nauseated."

"You're shy," Barron said. "You are allowed to be. But don't let the anger keep you from enjoying what is important now. Think about how much Nadya has been running around the castle making sure every tiny thing is perfect. She is disgustingly excited for you to see what she has done. Then, there are the townspeople who just want to eat and drink and take a glimpse of the always . And there is Dani, who is shrieking at people with that annoying voice right now."

"I used to make fun of his sister for having the annoying voice, but now that you mention it, Dani sounds just like her, only a few octaves lower." Sebastian doubled over in laughter. "The gods blessed me with Dani."

"You are the gods," Barron said. "The only god left."

Sebastian shrugged. "Let's hope it stays that way. Let the curse die."

"For what it's worth when you asked me how I felt when I had you whipped." Barron stopped speaking for a moment and picked up a stone and threw it into the lake. "It was the worst moment in my life. Standing there watching the captain striking you over and over while I had to hold my composure was horrifying. I threw up half the night after that."

"So did I." Sebastian's eyes shot to Barron and then back to the water.

Barron stood and held out his hand for Sebastian to take. "Come on. Go and pretend to have fun. Smile, show appreciation, then go to bed early."

"Fine."

Sebastian walked two steps behind Barron the whole way, dragging his feet on the road to the castle.

"Shouldn't the king be leading the way?" Barron asked.

Sebastian giggled. "I'm using you as a shield."

"Hilarious." Barron shook his head.

They arrived on the castle grounds. Sebastian was met with townspeople cheering and dancing around him. Barron glanced at him, then slipped away to where Sebastian saw red hair waving in the breeze. People bowed as he passed. He stopped before a group from Midrel Istan led by Seville. They performed a dance popular in their nation. Seville tried to teach Viktor the moves, but he always took a step too big or turned the wrong way. Sebastian laughed and interlocked his fingers, holding them against his chin. He admired the lengths others were willing to go to for his special day.

Once the dancing stopped, they turned and bowed to Sebastian and Viktor kissed Seville.

"Happy birthday, Seb." Viktor smiled.

"I'm happy for you, Viktor." Sebastian left the courtyard and went to sneak into the castle through the servants' entry.

The back kitchen was always a little less busy than the front as they were responsible for making bread and cakes. Sebastian could slip through and sneak to his bedroom undetected like he had been doing so since he was first allowed to roam NorthBrekka alone. He was greeted by bakers who offered him biscuits and pastries and smiled cheerfully as he spoke to them. "If anyone asks, I was never here." He turned through the door and smashed into his sister.

"You're not as sneaky as you think," Nadya said.

Sebastian gasped and rolled his eyes. "The decorations look lovely."

"You haven't even seen them!" Nadya grabbed him by the collar. "No running away."

"I was coming in. I'm trying, Nadya." He pointed to his cheek. "See, I'm smiling and everything."

She shoved him toward his father's office. "You need to change. Everyone is dressed in their best. I picked out something for you to wear."

Sebastian looked her up and down. "You look lovely, by the way."

"And you are a mess. Let me help." Nadya yanked his hair down and began untangling the knots.

"I can dress myself." Sebastian dropped the pile of clothes on the floor in defeat.

"I've seen you naked. Just get that dirty shirt off." She yanked back on the collar.

Sebastian slipped the shirt over his head, revealing his back to Nadya. She gently touched his scars, while he changed into clean pants and boots. He caught a glimpse of a tear trickling down her cheek. "Don't do that."

Nadya pulled her hand away and stared at his reflection.

"Don't feel bad for me." Sebastian paused. "The past is done. If we don't change and grow, we will always be fighting for the present. There is no future in that. Not for anyone."

Nadya let out a whimper. "You sound more like Father every day."

Sebastian turned toward the window. "I will not rule as he did. Everything is going to change. I'm going to ensure that anyone who wishes ill upon us will know that we are to be feared. Others will flock to these lands. They will build, bring in their trade and wares, and it will push our little kingdom into the future."

"I thought you wanted to live in Midrel Istan."

"I didn't say I had to be here for NorthBrekka to be the future of all the lands." He slipped on his coat, brushed back his hair into a knot, then Nadya placed the crown upon his head. They walked to the hall where a few others began to gather.

The decorations were of red and gold silks and tapestries of dragons. Lanterns burned bright, hanging from pillars. The tables were covered in incredible flower centerpieces, trays of cookies, and pitchers of wine. He took a cup and held it up to Nadya. "This is perfect. Thank you. All of you." He sipped his wine. A glint of light flashed in his eyes as someone walked through the doors.

"Don't be nervous." Amara's voice filled the room. She was dressed in a beautiful purple gown with gold bracelets and a thin gold band around her head. "Come on. He is waiting." She appeared, dragging someone behind her.

Dani stumbled through the doorway, and his eyes instantly fell on Sebastian. His wavy, black hair that usually covered his face was neatly combed to reveal his sky-blue eyes. The black linen of his clothes was accented by light embroidery on the collar and cuffs. But the silver, diamond-encrusted crown rested on Dani's head like it was made for him.

Sebastian cupped Dani's cheek in his palm, kissed his forehead, and then held him against his chest. "I am the luckiest man in the world."

Dani blushed and kissed Sebastian's lips. "Happy birthday," he whispered. "Are you alright? I know this is hard for you."

Sebastian nodded. "This is all so wonderful."

"Well, I hope this doesn't spoil it." Dani pointed behind Sebastian.

A girl with too-familiar blue hair walked into the room.

"I know you are hating your life right now," Jace said. "So, I hope you're not angry about this."

"No. It's all great." He noticed Jace and Petra holding hands. "All of it." He stepped up to Petra and looked her up and down. "I'm glad that annoying shriek disappeared with your powers."

"Quiet down or I will bring it back," Petra smirked.

Sebastian sat down and listened to everyone make speeches, drink until drunk, sing, eat, dance, cheer, cry, and celebrate. He would occasionally ask Dani to dance, but he mostly watched the room until it was time for him to retreat to speak to Tomas.

The tombs were dimly lit with torches. Sebastian found a space and crawled inside. He rested against where Tomas's body was encased within the stone. "Happy birthday, Tomas." He curled into a fetal position and cried for a long while. It was quiet and peaceful. The only sounds were his own sniffling. Sebastian didn't want to leave.

He snapped awake to the sound of footsteps. It was dark since the torches had gone out, but a person lit them again and walked through the corridor. Sebastian stuck his head out, then saw Kristoff stumbling onto his backside.

"Sebastian! What the hell?"

"I think I fell asleep." Sebastian crawled out of the space.

Kristoff pointed. "In there? Where you go when you are dead?"

"Just talking to Tomas."

"I-umm." Kristoff shifted his weight. "Need to talk to you, but I came down here to talk to father, so I guess you both can listen." His hands shook.

"You're leaving." Sebastian joined Kristoff's side.

"Yes. How did you know?"

Sebastian closed his eyes and smiled. "You are just like me. I can see the desperate cry for freedom on any face. You don't need to explain anything."

Kristoff sighed. "Can I take my new ship?"

"How else are you going to run away? You're not taking my ship." Sebastian grinned. "I saw what happened to the Ophidias."

Kristoff sighed. "I want to see the world... discover new lands, and maybe find a woman who will love me along the way."

"I have a feeling you will get everything you want." Sebastian put his arms around his brother. "I wish I would have been there for you more, but I will always be here if you need me. I love you, Kristoff."

Kristoff hugged Sebastian. "Thank you, brother. I love you."

Sebastian smiled. "Remember to visit Adurak too."

"So, that's your plan... to end the wars and head back to Midrel Istan."

Sebastian nodded. "I believe that is my path."

"Good." Kristoff grinned. "Because you don't seem very happy here. You should be free too."

The summer brought upon the wedding of Viktor and Seville. Dom and the Sinook traveled across Erras in search of Maxen and his men. Kristoff departed on his next journey, and scouts were sent to Safareen. Sebastian continued his training with Valirus, becoming stronger than before. Dani took on learning to rule with Nadya and Barron coaching him every step. Amara spent the remainder of the summer in Northpost to rest before returning to Castle Drake. Jace and Petra's relationship flourished. Jace even made amends with his father and helped with the rebuilding of Oyster Cove.

Sebastian took Dani to Sedda to celebrate Dom's birthday. No word of Maxen came from the north or the south. By the time the following spring came, Sebastian had led NorthBrekka into becoming the capital of Erras.

One morning, Sebastian left Castle Drake early, stealing a cake on his way to the stables. He mounted Ossian and rode into the Eastbay Pass. Up high in The Break, Sebastian stopped at his favorite place to hide from everything. The mouth of the cave invited him in with the warm sun beaming into the open cavern. He went inside and found the crawlspace that led down further into the mountain. He stopped when he felt water on the floor.

Sebastian disrobed, lit a fire in his palm, and slowly swam into the underground lake. The water was icy but soothing on his tired body. He floated on the surface until the cold made his bones feel stiff. He made a small fire and ate some dried fruit, enjoying the sound of silence.

He knew the time had passed into mid-afternoon as he began to climb up, but a strange sound stopped him in his tracks. He crouched to the floor and slipped behind a boulder. Clink! Clink! Then there was a splash and another. Sebastian checked to see if there was any light coming from the noise. He quietly stepped into the tunnel that led to the room above.

"You cannot expect me to swim." A snarling voice echoed. "A bunch of worthless morons you all are."

Sebastian felt a deep, burning pain in the pit of his stomach. His throat tightened, his heart raced, and his arms and legs shook. After a deep breath, he stepped from the safety of cover. He lit a fire in his palm. "Maxen!"

The soldiers stopped swimming. Then, he saw Maxen swim from the cavernous dark waters until he found his footing. Maxen marched from the lake, dripping wet, with his lips twitched into a snarl. Sebastian pulled his axe from his belt and let out a growl. His body flashed with lightning and fire, with a glow of dragon scales covering his skin.

Maxen let out a cocky laugh. "Dragon."

"Chaos." Sebastian snapped.

The men lunged for one another. Sebastian's axe blocked Maxen's sword, and the sound of iron rang through the cavern. Maxen swung, his fist smashing into Sebastian's lip, throwing him back into the wall. He slung a fireball that crashed into Maxen's armor, then kicked him in the stomach. Sebastian jumped, landing with his knee buried in Maxen's chest. He gripped Maxen's throat and let out a roar so loud the cave began to shake violently.

The kings thrashed to their feet, both gaining their weapons in hand. Sebastian's body ignited in flames. He cracked lightning in his fingertips, and brought his hands together to interlock his fingers. He looked up at Maxen, grinned, and threw his arms open wide. He brought his hands together in a thunderous clap that shook the earth. Sebastian thrust his hands forward. A strong, booming gust threw Maxen backward into the crowd of soldiers that were emerging from the water.

Maxen and his men went under, and Sebastian retreated. He clawed his way up the path, digging his fingers into the mud. He had to reach the upper level and Ossian before Maxen breached the surface. The echoes of men's boots on the hollow floors below sounded through the cave. Sebastian's arms were sore and tired, but he pulled his way to the top. He stopped at the upper cavern, took a deep breath, and with a furrowed brow, he reached his hand out.

The cave shook and groaned, causing rocks to fall from the ceiling. The collapse blocked Maxen and his men from reaching the top. He bounded down the pass for Castle Drake. As Ossian tore across the road toward the castle grounds, Sebastian shouted, "Close the gates!" He passed through in time for the soldiers to initiate the locks.

He stormed through the castle, calling for everyone to meet in the throne room. The hall was packed with nervous looking men and women. Sebastian wasted no time. He marched to the front and turned. "Maxen has breached NorthBrekka."

Scouts returned to Castle Drake as the warm summer ended and no news of Maxen came from The Far North or Erras. Sebastian stood in the courtyard. His body ignited, singing fire embers peeling away and floating behind him. His hands held both fire and lightning. A thunderstorm swirled overhead, with rain falling heavy across The Break. The foundation beneath his feet shook, and his army mustered on castle grounds.

Valirus stood before all. "Ladies, gentlemen, soldiers of Midrel Istan and Erras. That is what the gods strived for. To unite all nations. One world, under one king." He turned to face Sebastian. "Some call him Dragon while others call him Sebastian Drake. Before you stands the last of the gods. He is Chaos and he represents everything surrounding us. He is the movement of the earth as our footsteps stamp the ground. He is the air that wafts as we pass through. Chaos is the water we drink and the fire we use to keep warm. He is in all of us. Chaos is life. Chaos is king. Our one true king. God of Fire. The one we follow until the bitter end." Valirus took his place among the people.

Sebastian cleared his throat. "From this moment on, my most trusted will train under the most powerful warriors I know. The Sinook. And from this moment forth, you will be known as my order. The Order of Thieves."

Sebastian closed his eyes and took a deep breath, listening to his people. But it was the chill in the wind that caught his attention. Barron and Dani joined his side. Soldiers gathered behind the Order of Thieves. Men and women from all over the world. Of all nations and races, the people united, blanketing NorthBrekka. Sebastian let out a little laugh and took Dani's hand. He climbed onto Ossian's back and led the way onto the pass.

Dani sat upon his own horse but rode by Sebastian's side. "Where are we going now?"

Sebastian turned his head to The Break. "To the heathen lands of The Far North. "We still have a lot to learn." Sebastian glanced at Valirus, grinned, then urged Ossian into the high mountains. "Keep up everyone. We have a long road ahead before we are ready for war again."

The order followed their king across the pass, through Shadowmire, and to where the road splits. One road headed south toward the lake and Torrdale, while the other led into the frigid tundra where the oldest and deepest secrets of Erras were kept hidden from the rest of the world.

"When I trained with the Sinook, there was a poem the warriors would say before bed each night." Sebastian sighed and took a deep breath. "In the darkness, we cry. Where no other can see. In the shadows, we lie, until our hearts become lost. On the coldest of nights, we rest our heads beneath the shelter of a painted moon and starlit sky."

To be continued...

www.ingramcontent.com/pod-product-compliance
Lightning Source LLC
Chambersburg PA
CBHW072041190726
48294CB00005B/1358